After You Left

ALSO BY CAROL MASON

The Secrets of Married Women
Send Me A Lover
The Love Market

After You Left

Carol
MASON

LAKE UNION
PUBLISHING

This is a work of fiction. Names, characters, organizations, places, events, and incidents are either products of the author's imagination or are used fictitiously.

Published by Lake Union Publishing, Seattle

www.apub.com

Amazon, the Amazon logo, and Lake Union Publishing are trademarks of Amazon.com, Inc., or its affiliates.

ISBN-13: 9781503942363
ISBN-10: 1503942368

Cover design by Debbie Clement

Printed in the United States of America

For my husband, Tony. Ever my champion.

ONE

Alice

2013

The alarm goes off, and, for a moment or two, in my semi-awake state, I think I am still in Hawaii. I slide a hand across the mattress and make contact with his mid-back. I can hear his mammoth breathing, never quite a fully-fledged snore. With the gentle clawing of my fingers on his bare skin, he rolls over now. He looks across at me, sleepily, and we smile.

But the rainbow-coloured bubble of my happiness doesn't hold. Instead of Justin's warm, waking body, I am patting cold sheets. Then comes the blunt, quick scutter of disbelief. I am endlessly astonished how I can be hit so unexpectedly by something I already know.

I've made a terrible mistake. I can't go on, for everyone's sake. I'm sorry.

Events of four days ago have cruelly lain in wait on this side of my consciousness, keen to be relived – as if I haven't played them over enough already. But each time I do, it's neither more, nor less, real.

I woke up in Kauai, like I've just woken up now. Justin wasn't there. I imagined he'd gone for a swim, like he'd done the previous three mornings. I got up, drew back the white voile curtain to let the sun in.

I stood there in its path, gazing out across a blazing turquoise ocean to where the black army of early morning surfers was riding the waves.

I couldn't see him. Of course, I wasn't even remotely perturbed. I just liked spotting his head. *My husband.* The noble-shaped skull and thick, dark hair. His arms windmilling as he cut a course at right angles to the tide. It's my favourite thing to do: watch him when he's unaware, imagining I'm looking at a stranger.

I let the curtain fall away, and went to the minibar to take out the cream. I was just about to insert a coffee pod into the Nespresso machine when I saw the tented piece of paper beside the two cups and saucers. On the front, *Alice*, in his writing.

I remember the hesitant reach of my hand. The words on the page that didn't make sense. Then the open wardrobe door. Half a dozen or so empty coat hangers. The bare luggage rack where his suitcase had previously sat open.

The Hawaiian cop was a blank-eyed bulldozer of a woman. Her hair was shaved off, leaving only a clump of spiky fringe like a goatee at the wrong end of the face. I wanted to describe her to Justin when he came back, and tell him how intimidating she was, but then I had to fathom it all over again: Justin wasn't coming back. The hotel manager had been the one to call the police; he was nice enough to let us use his office. I'd been wandering around, disorientated, in my bathrobe, telling people that my husband had disappeared. A couple of hotel staff had helped me search the beach. They were very kind, but I could tell right away that the policewoman wasn't going to be.

Leaning forward, she dropped her enormous breasts on top of the desk. 'Sweet cheeks, this is not a suicide note, if that's what you're thinking. Someone who is about to kill himself doesn't disappear in the middle of his honeymoon with a laptop and a suitcase full of his clothes.'

I hadn't said a thing about suicide. The word landed and revolved in my head.

I can't go on . . . ? She was giving me that look that said, *I'm only tolerating you because you're English, blonde and possibly a lunatic.*

Then she read the note out loud again, as if I could have possibly forgotten it. She clapped it down in front of us, looked at me quite gravely and said, 'Honey, you've been dumped.'

The rest is a blur of packing, trying to think straight enough to change flights, a disorientating six-hour wait in Los Angeles, the numb journey home. Then back here, to nothing . . .

I'm supposed to get up now, to go into work. The sun comes in our bare, floor-to-ceiling windows. I lie there, aware of its warmth on my arm and of how dog-tired I am; I cannot move. On the radio a man is talking about his efforts to rid his lawn of moles: 'So you know what I did? I went into my garage, I fired up a road flare, and I smoked the effer out.' Justin and I would have found this funny. The cavernous echo of his absence almost takes my breath away.

In the shower, I can't adjust the hot and cold, and realise I should have done this before I got in. I stand there, alternately scalding and freezing myself, wiggling the tap but failing to get to grips with something I've done automatically so many times before. One thing I am aware of is feeling like a half-sized version of myself. I am sunk in right below my ribs. I am never this un-fleshy. I think it's because, for some reason, every time I even think about eating, the memory of greasy pizza at LAX is there, warning me off. The urge to throw up before the last of it was down. The single-minded trek to the toilets. Barely making it there. Heaving before I reached the bowl, a cascade of puke. People stopping to have a look. A cleaner standing with a long mop, unfazed: it's all just part of the job.

Justin left me. Vanished into thin air.

It was like I was vomiting him up along with the pizza.

I stare at the bottles of hair product lined up in rows on the shower shelf. Which one is the shampoo? I'm suddenly incapable of reading a label. There's a buzzing of panic in my head. How did I ever imagine I could go into work? See people? Act normal? Talk about the honeymoon? Tell lies? Act a lie? Because no one can know. When Justin comes home, I want everything to return to normal – after I've half killed him, of course. By saying nothing, there will be no embarrassment around anyone who knows us, no public legacy of his having once, momentarily, lost his mind. The goose-bumps come out on my arms. The chill of dread down my spine. How am I going to do it?

Then again, realistically, what are they going to ask?

How was the honeymoon?

Wonderful.

That's about all anyone wants to know of someone else's holiday, isn't it?

I squirt hair product into the palm of my hand. All the other questions rush at me now, as I tip my head back and let it hang there. How had I not seen this coming? Had he been different lately? Distracted? Unusually stressed? Had he seemed tired? Unwell? Less enthusiastic about life in general? When he had said his vows, had he looked for one minute like someone who was feeling strong-armed into getting married? Someone who was having second thoughts?

No.

Or had I been too caught up in how happy I was to notice how unhappy he was?

There is a flurry of doubts and questions – endless questions – but they just float there like dots unable to join before my eyes; I can't grasp on to them or make them add up to an answer. I slide down the wall, squat there, staring at the drain. The water pelts off my knees, which quickly hurt from hyperextension. Shampoo has run into my eyes and they're stinging. I shove the heels of my hands into the sockets. *Pull yourself together.* The echo of my mother's tough love. Then some shitty sentiment about *men!* Always, *men!* who let you down. Ever since my dad upped and left us, my mother was always male-bashing. That was the day she became the bitterest person I've known.

Out of the shower, I try to towel dry my hair, but my arms are like two dead weights. I stare at my mobile phone on the night table. I've never actually registered the acute and terrorising silence of an un-ringing phone before. How many times have I dialled his number? How many texts have I sent? How many emails from which I've received no read receipt? I stare at the phone as though it's going to suddenly leap and attack me, but I check it again, in case it rang and I didn't hear it.

In the kitchen, I set about making a cup of tea, but it feels like a gargantuan undertaking. Bag in cup. Water in kettle. Something reeks in the bin, but what do I care about smells? I stand there, unblinking, in a trance, while the kettle hustles to life, its blue light in my peripheral vision. Then I give up, and walk back into the bedroom. The phone is still sitting where I left it. I dial her number.

'Louisa . . . Hi. It's Alice.' The race of my heart. Justin would never fail to account for his whereabouts to his secretary. I used to joke that if we were on a sinking lifeboat he'd hurl me to the sharks before one of his clients. It wasn't true, of course. But it still always made him smile that viral smile that stretched unrestrained and infectious across his face. 'Why do you have such a low opinion of yourself?' he'd ask. And it was a good question.

'Is Justin there by any chance?' I try to sound confident. *No one can know.*

But I can hear the tremor in my voice: the insecurity, the uncertainty; the dread of him coming on the line, the dread of him not. The exact same feeling I would get every time I tried to ask my mother questions about my past. That urge to know. The entitlement. The anger at finding yourself in the position of having to ask. That conflicting impulse of bursting to get everything off your chest, and clamming up and shutting down all at the same time.

There's an ominous pause, then Justin's secretary, in her perpetually astonished North East accent says, 'Alice! Ah, hiya! Er, no. Justin's not here. I wouldn't have thought you'd have expected him to be.'

She knows! Then I think, *No, she can't know.*

'He's probably on his way in,' I stumble. 'It's odd, but I can't get him to answer his mobile.'

It's not odd. Louisa would know that Justin never took phone calls while driving. Justin was scrupulous about many things that generally might not make it on to your average thirty-eight-year-old male's moral radar. He always gave up his seat to women on trains, and they didn't have to be old or pregnant. He'd never jump a queue, even if the person ahead of him were unaware. He once told me that he had never consciously told a lie.

'Is everything all right, Alice?' Louisa sounds genuinely concerned.

'Of course. Everything's fine.' I stare at the single blue shirt-sleeve dangling over the top of the laundry bin, unable to fathom how barren the sight of a piece of his clothing can make me feel. 'Will you tell him to ring me as soon as he gets in?'

'Well, yes! I would. But that's the thing . . . I thought you knew. Justin's going to be working from home for a while. I mean, that's what he said when he rang in this morning.'

The earth shifts. 'He rang in?' I expected he'd be in contact, so why is this the worst thing I could possibly hear? Almost as bad as if I'd heard he died?

'He did, yeah. About an hour ago.'

My head swims with this new knowledge. Justin can ring his secretary but not his wife.

The desire to fall down, even though I'm already sitting. 'Oh . . . that's right. Sorry. I forgot. He did tell me. I think I was probably only half listening, as usual.' Then I wonder, why isn't she asking how the honeymoon was? Because he told her? 'I'm at work right now . . .' Does she know I'm lying, and that we're therefore having a very ridiculous conversation indeed? 'I'll ring him at home.'

When I click off, I sit here in the wake of that conversation, listening to the strangely hypnotic, funnelling sound of my pulse in my ears. Then I realise I have to get dressed.

Justin's going to be working from home.

I walk over to the wardrobe, but instead of pulling out a skirt, I can only see the many shirts, trousers, jackets and suits that are lined up in perfect almost-colour-coordinated order, plus an equally orderly row of his shoes. All his stuff that he will be needing at some point. He's going to need his stuff.

So he'll definitely have to be back.

I emerge from the Metro station into the grey morning. I always get off one stop early so I can walk the rest of the way to the gallery. This is what I used to love before I had a husband who left me after only five days – these twenty minutes alone, walking to and from work; they were like peaceful bookends that held each day together. But today they're just brackets around a blank. I cross the road and barely note the car horn, the person who hangs out of the window and shouts, 'Watch where you're going! For fuck's sake!' My shoes clack on the cobblestones of Grey Street. I hear them as though they're louder than they really are, and bury myself in their rhythm. The rest of rush hour is conducting itself around me with the 'Mute' button on. A workman in a parked white van says, 'Nice legs.' Normally, I would smile. Who is immune to a compliment? But the note is suddenly there again, stopping my legs and my heart. *I've made a terrible mistake. I can't go on, for everyone's sake. I'm sorry.*

Cars slide by me, and people mill around me, and I am stuck here, in the middle of the street, in a different band of time. I have read it and read it until the words have blurred, like writing over writing. But I haven't seen this before. It doesn't say for my sake or your sake, or both of our sakes.

Clearly, there is someone else's sake to be considered.

TWO

'Realism is a tricky word. The artist sets up a narrative, but we have to bring our own story to it.'

The young journalist scribbles away. Whenever I give interviews, I always worry I'm going to encounter someone who knows more than I do, though that's rarely the case. Usually, they're like this one: young, impressible and slightly out of their depth, sent to cover a major exhibition, the first of its kind in the region's history, when, really, they just need words on a page by 2 p.m.

'This exhibition features two iconic, mid-twentieth-century American artists. Andrew Wyeth, who is famous for capturing the land and the people around him, and revealing the unspoken emotion of simple people and things. And Edward Hopper, who possessed an outstanding ability to identify the monumental drama of people engaged in doing nothing apparently extraordinary, or even noteworthy.'

He pauses, nods, scribbles. In the absence of a question, I press on.

'Looking at Wyeth's work, we find a bittersweet familiarity with things that have gone before. You are often left with the feeling that over time we have lost something; that sense of the past being slightly more perfect than the present.' For a moment, my words give me pause. He looks at me, attentive, waiting. 'That's what makes *Mood and Memory* such a fascinating exhibition. Because we can integrate so well with the enigmatic isolation and contemplation expressed in the paintings.'

Has he got it? We've been at this twenty minutes and I'm not sure what's penetrated. If only I could write his article for him. Justin says I'm a bit of a control freak.

I've always thought that there's something about the pace at which art inspires the world around it to move, a devotional calm, that puts you so wholly in the moment. When you look at an awe-inspiring painting, you literally forget about everything else; you subconsciously free up space in your mind so there exists a pleasurable nothingness. I studied art more by accident than design. I needed to get a degree. I'd had no passion for any particular subject. This course had sounded fractionally less dull than most of the others. I applied, and was surprised to find I was accepted. A few other random events took me from there to here. And I'm lucky because I think I was made for this job. The slow procession of visitors through the gallery and the quiet thrum of their observations reach me like a cross between yoga and hypnotherapy. I love fancying myself living in the world the artist has created on his or her canvas. There's something so compelling about Hopper's uneventful subject matter, Wyeth's hauntingly beautiful portrayal of life and the people of Maine. Something unattainable that simmers beneath the mantle of their simple lives. It pulls me in, toys with me, and refuses to let me go.

'Which of his paintings speaks to you the most?' the journalist asks now, out of the blue. My phone *choo-choo*s – a text.

The pulse in my neck flicks like the wings of a trapped bird. The phone is too far away on the desk for me to see it. I try to strain, but no.

'Wyeth's *Christina's World*,' I say. 'His starkly atmospheric painting of a disabled girl wearing a pink dress. Christina is on her hands and knees in a field, almost crawling toward a house far away in the distance.' I slide the brochure across the desk, with the image on the front cover.

The phone *choo-choo*s again, pulling my eyes. 'There are really only three elements to it – the land, the girl, the farmhouse. Yet there's some profound hankering or tragedy that lives in her, that we need to know about her. That *I* need to know about her. It's that sense of wanting to learn about someone else in order to illuminate something in oneself.'

He smiles. But I recognise the slightly vacuous expression of the daunted. He makes no more notes. The interview comes to a close bang on the thirty minutes I had allotted for it.

The second he's out of the door, I lunge at my phone.

But it's only my service provider sending me my bill, and telling me I've earned one hundred more free texts next month.

Rain lashes the window of Leonardo's Trattoria. I sit opposite my friend Sally at a small table that overlooks the Theatre Royal. Three or four white-haired Italian waiters efficiently work the room, slapping down giant pizzas or bowls of pasta and full glasses of house wine – the popular lunchtime special. I've always wondered why the Italians choose Newcastle to open their restaurants. Surely there are warmer parts of England that might remind them more of home? A young and voluptuous Newcastle girl is waiting on our table, looking frenzied.

Despite being determined to not utter a word of any of this, the minute I see my friend's face, it is impossible.

I don't think Sally moves, or breathes, even. Then her lips part. I am aware of astonished green eyes staring back at me among a mass of freckles, and of myself being oddly fascinated by her reaction.

'You are not being serious,' she says, when she can speak. 'My God! The bastard! Alice!' She covers her nose and mouth with her hands and gasps into them.

I catch the slight tremor of my head, and realise my hand is tightly gripping the end of the flimsy cotton tablecloth by my leg.

Bastard. It's what my single friends would call the host of dysfunctional boyfriends they've all encountered. It seems absurd applying it to Justin – like a case of mistaken identity.

Sally is still looking stunned as the waitress returns, and we order the same thing we always do, without needing to look at the menu. The girl goes away, then returns and sets down some fresh focaccia and oil, her slender arm sneaking in between our faces, as though her female antenna has picked up on the seriousness of our conversation.

'Why would he do that? Have you any idea?' Sally asks, once the waitress has left us again.

I can't believe that I can talk about it, yet feel so removed from it. It's as though it's happening to a mutual, absent, third friend, whom I like, but whose happiness and well-being I'm not inextricably invested in. For want of a better reaction, I just shrug.

'You literally have no idea?'

'No,' I say. 'None.' I stare at her lovely hair that falls to just above her shoulders – not quite brown and not quite auburn – at the freckles on her chest and the gold locket that sits centrally in the V of her blouse, unable to bring her into proper focus. Then I have to look away to try to right my eyes. I gaze across the room, suddenly aware of things I don't believe I've noticed before: a revolving display cabinet containing slices of tired cheesecake, chocolate cake and a plate of slightly more promising tiramisu; and a pleasingly large and colourful print of the Amalfi Coast, that makes me think distantly of my honeymoon, or perhaps more of a sense of everything being truly idyllic.

'How are you feeling?' she asks. Her question pulls me back from wherever the print has transported me. 'What are you thinking? Have you any idea what you're going to do?'

'I don't know.' I frown, unsure which question to answer first. 'I mean, what can I do? I suppose I'm doing all I can. I'm just putting one foot in front of the other, trying to keep my sanity, and get through my day.'

The words *everyone's sake* come back, filling my head and my vision.

No. Justin doesn't have someone else. It was a turn of phrase. How many times have I said it myself? I feel fractionally better now I've formed that conclusion.

'I've tried ringing him, texting, emailing. I know he got on his flight because the airline confirmed it.' The police had checked. 'His car's gone, so I know he must have come back to the flat at some point, but he hasn't picked up any of his clothes – not that I can tell, anyway. I've rung every hotel in the area. Even the ones he used to stay in when he travelled for work . . .' I shrug again.

'But there must be something else you can do! There has to be! You can't just . . . just sit and wait and be entirely at his mercy.' She is shaking her head, mouth gaping in amazement again.

I know she means well, but it puts me on the defensive. In fact, I feel a little breathless with it. Sally is nothing if not direct. I've always appreciated that. She's the one person whose opinion can make me second-guess my own. But I don't want to be told what to do. 'Is there? Like what? I can't exactly put him on the regional news. He's not missing. He managed to ring his secretary and say he was going to be working from home!' It sounds ridiculous, but it's real. 'Clearly, if he needs to be away from me so badly that he'd abandon me halfway across the world, what's the point of even trying to find him? He mustn't want that. Maybe when he wants to talk to me, he'll talk to me. In his own time.'

I glance out of the window, at the rain coming down; the abject colourlessness of this city on a dark day has never got to me before. The waitress sets down my plate of pasta and makes some excuse to Sally about the wood-burning oven being backed up.

'You seem so . . . calm or something. So rational,' Sally says, after a moment or two. 'I'm surprised you're not angrier, I must admit.' Her eyes roam over my face, my hair, my upper body.

Sally is normally the person who tries to understand me even when she doesn't understand me. That's all I want – her to feel for me and to constructively commiserate, not to tell me how to feel. I stare at the bread basket and contemplate this assessment she's just made. 'I don't know what to say. I wouldn't say I'm calm – more numb. I suppose I'm worried more than anything else. We don't know what's wrong with him, do we? What his reasons are . . . And it must be something. It's just too out of character for him.'

She is watching me with an element of incredulity. 'Admittedly, though,' I add, 'I was more worried about his welfare earlier, before I learnt he'd rung his secretary. So we know he isn't dead. He wasn't rendered mute. He's had his act together enough to prioritise his job . . .'

She dips a rectangle of focaccia in a small bowl of rosemary olive oil, and brings it quickly to her mouth before it drips. 'But why do his reasons matter?' She frowns. 'I mean, what could he possibly say that would make what he did okay?'

I suddenly have a profound sense of my own inadequacy. She's right. Why *aren't* I more furious? Why am I being so charitable? 'I don't know,' I tell her. We sit there in silence, just looking at one another, neither of us knowing where to take the topic next.

Sally is my closest friend. I've known her since I moved here from Uni in Manchester. We met at the Baltic Centre for Contemporary Art, at a function she'd organised – she's an event planner. The one downside of moving to a new area was that I was lacking a proper friend, and then there was this woman around my own age who was so straight-up and funny and fresh. We'd both shown up in the same peacock-blue and emerald-green dress – an immediate conversation starter. We'd even joked that she'd bought it for eighty-nine pounds and I had only paid fifty. The rapport was instant. There is nothing I haven't shared with her over the years. Nothing she hasn't been able to relate to. No boyfriend horror story that she couldn't take on board as if it were her own, even though we have led very different lives when it comes to relationships.

Sally married John, who was her first boyfriend, and has seventeen-year-old twin girls. I have had one long post-Uni involvement that ended when I was twenty-eight because he suddenly decided he wanted to go and live in Australia – and not with me. Then there was Colin, who didn't want marriage and children. Between Colin and Justin there were a few ill-advised flings, just to prove to myself that I could do casual without always being on the lookout for *The One*. Or, perhaps because I was hoping that if I stopped trying too hard, what I wanted would waltz along, loosely affirming the laws of attraction. Somehow, they had all just felt like stepping-stones on the path to Justin.

'It's just such a monstrous thing to do,' Sally says now, looking at my food. 'I just don't know what kind of person would abandon his wife on their honeymoon, halfway across the world!' It comes out a little loud. The couple at the next table look across. Suddenly, it's as though the eyes of a thousand people are on me, instead of just two.

'I don't know,' I say again. I realise I've said that too many times already.

The smell of grated cheese hits me. I stare at the sickly-looking, sloppy white pasta. It appears to be wobbling. But then I realise it's not the food moving, it's me. I'm trembling with the force of reality rewriting itself. The quiet panic. The distant urge to throw up again.

'Are you okay?' she asks. 'You look awful.'

'I don't want to judge him, Sally. Not yet. Not until I know more.' I can't look her in the eyes. I can feel her watching me and thinking that I'm either very fair or quite pathetic – neither of which means much to me right at this minute.

'There was a phone call while we were away,' I say, after a while. He hadn't been himself. The delayed responses, the distant stares off to the side of my head when I was talking. He always had multiple things going on in his mind. Sometimes, you had to fight for your spot there, but when you fully got his attention, it was worth it. At the time, I felt like saying, *We're on honeymoon! Can't you just leave work back in bloody*

Newcastle? But it's only now that I'm bringing it up that it blazes with significance.

'We were sitting on our balcony, drinking wine. When he answered the phone, he quickly left the room – just sort of shot up out of his chair.'

Justin always went somewhere private to take calls. I found it a bit insulting. But he never normally went with this alacrity. 'When he came back, he seemed in a strange mood. Dark somehow. Very changed.'

I can see him sitting in profile, motionless and unblinking, a moment or two after I'd asked him if he thought I should open another bottle of wine, and he hadn't seemed to have heard.

'Who do you think it was?' Sally appears spellbound. 'Did he not say? Didn't you ask?'

'He said it was something about a file at work. But it would have only been 4 a.m. in the UK. Who would be ringing him from work at that hour?'

The waitress sets Sally's pizza down and offers another apology, mumbling something about a free dessert. Sally, who normally has the appetite of two construction workers, doesn't even register the arrival of her food.

'What if he's in some sort of trouble?' I say. 'You know how stressful his job can be. He once said that if he committed professional negligence, he would move to Buenos Aires and never come back.' All these conversations that were a bit strange at the time. I'd assumed he was joking, of course. But he certainly appeared to have his plan thought through! 'Or maybe he's got money problems. I know he's highly leveraged. The apartment building he owns, and then his interest in the firm . . . Maybe he's made some terrible mistake at work.' It was too exaggerated to be possible – besides, Justin wasn't that careless. And yet the possibilities were more palatable than the idea that he had someone else.

'Then why couldn't he just tell you? Why would money problems mean he has to walk out on you in the middle of your honeymoon?'

I feel the distant rumble of panic. 'I don't know. I honestly have no idea . . . Say he was having second thoughts about us, Sal, why wouldn't he have just told me before he married me?' I take a steadying sip of my wine. 'I've had a million break-ups. I'd have coped. How could he have married me knowing he was making a mistake?' It's a question more to myself than to Sally. 'He must have known he didn't want to do it – we'd only walked down the aisle a few days before! It's not even like him to do something as reckless as this. He doesn't make stupid decisions. He always thinks of the consequences and contingencies. He's too aware of the fallout. Too sensible . . .'

'It's completely mystifying.' Sally shakes her head, and finally picks up her cutlery. 'I wish I could speculate but you can't, can you? It's just such an insane thing to have happened.' She bisects her pizza, as though she's aggrieved by it.

'I wonder if he's ill.'

The fork freezes halfway to her mouth. 'Ill?'

'You know his dad died suddenly in his early forties with a heart thing. His twenty-year-old nephew is waiting for some big procedure. There's a lot of ill health among the men in his family. Remember? I told you. That's why he was always so paranoid about staying fit. I always sensed he was convinced he was never going to see old age.'

Justin is always jogging, pumping iron, checking his BMI, weighing himself. His fixation with zero trans fats, low salt and omega 3 fatty acids is an ongoing joke between us. But it's not feeling very funny now.

'He's not ill, Alice. His note said he can't do this any more. Those aren't the words of a man who's just heard he's dying.'

I nab the waitress as she passes. 'I don't want this. Sorry.' Suddenly, I need it all gone. The food. The smell. Sally. Perhaps it's just me, but I'm finding her disappointingly unsympathetic, which is not like her. I want to run out of that door and keep going, to run until all this falls off me, until I don't have to carry it any more. Whose husband walks out on them on their honeymoon? Whose?

'Me neither,' Sally says to the waitress. 'Take this away, too. All that bread filled me up.'

As the girl removes the plates, I have to fix on a spot of oil on the tablecloth to try to steady my thoughts and suppress the meltdown that I sense coming. Breathe!

Then Sally says, 'You know, have you considered that maybe you never knew him? Maybe you just thought you did.'

'Knew him?' I'm not sure I'm hearing straight. 'Of course I knew him.'

'But you did only meet him a year ago. You have to admit, it was fast. I mean, I could tell he's a bit like that. When he wants something, he wants something. It's his personality. But you've never been that way. You're far more level-headed than the person you became after meeting him.'

It's so odd hearing someone describe you, who knows you so well. Especially when they pinpoint a change in you that you don't entirely disagree with. It was a little true. I had allowed myself to suspend my cynicism about men when I met Justin. 'But we didn't need to wait longer. Look where waiting got me with Colin! Justin and I knew we wanted a life together. And, frankly, I'm a bit sorry you'd think I'm so whimsical or easily influenced.' My heart is pounding from the effort it takes me to say this to her. I recognise we are on the brink of having words, which feels insane. Not at all what I was expecting from this.

I should have kept quiet.

The restaurant has gone from warm to instantaneously suffocating. The pungent smell of garlic and charred salami makes my stomach lurch, and I burp up the taste of sick. I'm gripping the edge of the leather seat. When I release my hand, it's dripping with sweat.

'I didn't mean it that way, Al. I really didn't! Sorry!' Her eyes are full of concern for me. Sally and I never have confrontations

– disagreements, yes; but that's different. 'I just didn't know what the rush was, that's all. Wanting a family is one thing . . .'

'I didn't marry Justin just to pop out his baby! I could have had one on my own if that was what I'd wanted. There are ways.' Ways I would never have taken up, of course. 'I didn't wait because there was nothing more I could have learnt about him that was ever going to change my feelings for him, that's why.'

It's there in her face. *No. Maybe there wasn't then. But you can bet there is now.*

We eat the free tiramisu in silence. The words *everyone's sake* are back, but now they're underlined with doubt in red ink. I feel the profound shift of things. The inescapability. The unlikeliness of us ever going back to the way it was – or to earlier perceptions, even – no matter what happens next.

We pay up and leave. As I'm slipping on my coat and we step outside, I say, 'He's gone. And yet I still think he's going to come back.'

There. The truth. So quiet, I am not even sure I've said it. Sally looks terribly moved for a moment, then puts her arms around me and gives me a long, tight hug. I am stiff as a board. It strikes me that I'm unable to cry.

We begin walking, and I slide up my big red umbrella. When we get to the Monument Metro Station, we stop, and she gazes at me with eyes full of sympathy. Then she says, 'You know, it might not count for much, but John never cared for him.'

I watch her lips with the hint of pinkish neutral gloss, and frown. 'What do you mean?' Our umbrellas are touching. My red one is casting a warm glow over us. Yet the dampness suddenly gives me a shiver – the kind that locks your spine, and won't dissipate.

'I just think he finds him a little . . . unknowable.'

Unknowable. The word rebounds. I try to think, *What does this even mean, and why are you telling me this?* 'And you agree with that?' I ask.

'Oh, Alice, my God . . .' She glances around her, avoiding looking at me. People part around us. They disappear into the subway immediately behind, and an odd, draining sensation comes over me, as though part of me is detaching and disappearing into the ground, too.

'I don't know what to think,' she says. 'Not at this moment. But he's a Scorpio, isn't he? You know what they're like? They're driven, successful, have great sway over people, but rarely display their true feelings, and are filled with inherent contradiction.'

'I better get off,' I tell her. Sally is self-employed, so time might not be much of a concern to her, but I am already fifteen minutes over my lunch break.

'Call me if you hear anything,' she shouts after me.

I nod. I trot away. I don't look in her eyes and give her the usual, genial goodbye gaze. I sense her staring at my back, for a beat or two.

Scorpio! It's so stupid. Sally always puts such great stock in superstition and that sort of thing; that's one way we're very different. But I play over that brief description. Admittedly, some of it does sound like Justin.

THREE

When I see the name in my email inbox, I almost forget who it is; that's how far removed I now feel from anything to do with my wedding. Aimee – the photographer – is sending me a link to the photographs. I'm supposed to go through them and tell her which ones I want and in what format. I stare at the link, but can't bring myself to open it. Not here. Instead, I pick up a folder containing applications to our summer internship programme; my assistant said she'd flagged up the best ones, but she wanted my quick input. I get halfway down the first one, then have to put my head in my hands.

This is hopeless, so I wander into the gallery instead.

Art can play havoc with my mood. Landscapes suit me best. My mind and airwaves seem to open up in their presence. I am revitalised to face new challenges. Portraits bother me most. I am never fully at ease with them. Something to do with the fixed nature of light, shadow and perspective that gives the eyes their uncanny ability to follow you. I understand it from a technical standpoint, but the illusion of reciprocity bothers me on a more vital level. Here are real human beings trapped forever on canvas, on the wings of time. They have no say in the way they are being scrutinised. You can very often tell they're displeased.

And I feel so bad for them. I can never hold their eyes for too long. Perhaps because I sense they see things about me, too, that I wish to keep private. It's an unnerving two-way street.

Today, though, as my feet echo on the wooden floor, I am entering a hallowed place of melancholy silence, a temple of human solitude that's both eerily familiar and pleasantly disquieting. I look first at Hopper's *Morning Sun*, on loan from the Columbus Museum of Art, in Ohio. A woman sitting alone on a bed in an austere, cell-like room, with sunlight streaming in from an open window that overlooks an uninspiring building. She is dwelling in her solitude, and the morning. But you don't know if she's happy or sad, if she has lost something, or someone, or if she has found an enviable contentment away from the drill of everyday life. *Nighthawks*, all the way from the Art Institute of Chicago. Three unspeaking strangers who are drawn to an American diner in the middle of the night, perhaps self-medicating their inability to face going home to nobody. *Office in a Small City*: the ordinariness of a man as he sits alone, daydreaming out of a window in a tall building.

I can't help but think about the concept of loneliness, of having no one – how tangible melancholy is. If the artist were to paint me, I'd be a young woman standing alone in a room full of paintings about lonely people. A faceless figure captured from behind; her loss, palpable. Perhaps someone would speculate she is entirely on her own for the very first time – without a mother, a stepfather, a blood father; without a husband. They might sense all she has is questions, endless questions, and never any answers. And they would be right.

I'm so flooded with the naked reality of this, that at first I don't notice that someone else is here.

She's standing in front of *Christina's World*. A slim, well-dressed little thing, perhaps in her early seventies, with the effortless carriage of a ballerina. She's so passive and subdued that she could be a painting herself.

'It's beautiful, isn't it?' I cross the room and stand beside her, leaving a respectful distance between us, and I look at the painting.

At first, she doesn't seem to hear. Then she says, 'Yes. It's haunting. Christina is haunting.' She glances at me now, and she has the loveliest green and almond-shaped eyes. I notice that she studies me for a beat or two longer than usually happens with strangers.

'So you know the piece?' If you polled most people in England, they probably would have never heard of Andrew Wyeth, let alone *Christina's World*.

'Of course. Wyeth's most famous work. Bought in 1948 by the Museum of Modern Art for $1,800. One of the greatest bargains in the history of American art.' She gives me a coy, self-satisfied look that says, *See, it's not just you who knows her stuff.* Her hair is a halo of platinum, a perfectly cut bob that frames her spectacularly pretty, heart-shaped face.

'How very right you are.' I look back at the painting. 'Wyeth was fascinated by this house and the girl who lived in it. He had a summer home in the area – in Cushing, Maine – and he became very close to the family. You know Christina was paralysed? He used to watch her. Wyeth said that each window is an eye or a piece of the soul, and a different part of Christina's life.'

'It was Christina's lifelong home. That's why she's looking up at it with such reverence and longing. She's enraptured by her memories.'

We stand there, together, not saying anything, just observing the enigmatic Christina. For some reason, the easiness between us makes me think of my mother, by contrast – how lacking in harmony we were when we were together, how stilted the conversations. It was always there between us. The distance. Her disappointments. Things she should say, but was never going to say. Sometimes, it's hard to believe she's been gone for four years, and other times it feels like she's still here, loosely in my sphere, still as much a mystery to me as any of the women in these paintings.

'I'm under the spell of her,' this lady says. 'Aren't you?' She's a good five inches shorter than me, and cute in a way that makes me imagine her having been the lead singer in a 1960s all-girl group. Yet despite the apparent soft centre, there's a certain fortitude and forbearance about her. The combination is slightly infatuating.

'Yes,' I say. 'Actually, Christina is more real to me than anyone I've encountered in art. I just feel like I want to ask her about her life. I want to know what it is that she's so nostalgic for, because there's something. I can feel it.'

It's an oddly intimate confession between strangers. Most visitors to the gallery ask very predictable questions or make superficial observations; they never actually connect with you on a level beyond the obvious, so she is refreshing. 'I forget who it was that said everyone you meet loves something, longs for something and has lost something. Maybe that's why she's so easy to relate to. Because we see ourselves in her.'

Suddenly, Justin's absence hits me with belting force. It's like the way you hear bad news – that swoop to your senses, the felling that comes right before you've had a chance to disbelieve it. Good God. Panic rises from my feet and disperses to every cell of my being. I don't want to see myself in Christina – alone and somewhat thrown down in the middle of nowhere, staring at memories of a past happiness I can't find my way back to.

This woman is observing me as though she has the gift of reading my thoughts. 'Have you looked at all the other works? The Hoppers? Wyeth's *Helga*?' I ask, quickly glancing down the room so she won't see the horror or despair or whatever the hell it is that must register on my face.

'No,' she says. 'I'm only interested in Christina.' She turns her eyes back to the painting. Somehow, with the calmness of her demeanour, and her quiet focus, my terror subsides. I gaze at the girl in the pale pink dress. 'You know, someone who once wrote about Wyeth's work said you notice the flint first. You have to get close to feel the fire.'

She says nothing. But I know she feels the fire. We are strangers, but I know.

'I often wonder if she was in love with Wyeth.' I find myself dreaming again, slightly. 'How they spent their days . . . I can imagine it would be quite easy to fall for someone who was so fascinated by you that they were prepared to immortalise you in art history.'

'Or, maybe, like many of us, she was in love with a time. A time when she was loved.'

Her words – or perhaps it's the way she looks at me, with a certain explicit tenderness and longing – give me a small aftershock.

What about the time when I was loved?

'I think I should probably leave you and Christina alone now, and get back to work,' I tell her, almost unable to get the words out.

'It has been lovely speaking with you,' she says. 'I do hope we repeat this. I intend to come back.' Before I can say, *You too*, her gaze has already returned to Christina. I look at her for a moment, at the angelic line of her face in profile, but she doesn't seem to register me any longer.

As I walk away, I happen to notice she's wearing the kind of excruciatingly pointed kitten heels that even I gave up on years ago.

I can't help but smile.

FOUR

The flat is eerily quiet. I don't think I've ever noticed how silence is a sound of its own. Walking in is surreal. Normally, just the very expectation of him coming home soon would lend a fullness to the air. I stand there stock still, barely in the kitchen, and for a moment his absence draws air from my body again.

I can't even tell myself he's away, in London, on business; he'll be back Friday. Because it doesn't even feel like that scenario either. The numerals on the oven's clock flash at me. The fridge suddenly ticks to life. And yet there is that same cavernous emptiness both inside and all around me.

Absently, I pull off my jacket, and kick my shoes on to the small rug by the door. I walk into the bedroom, unzipping my skirt, letting it drop on the floor – things I would never do with tidy Justin around. His shirt-sleeve is still dangling out of the laundry bin like it was this morning. It seems to take up more space than a sleeve has a right to. If he was home, he would correct that; Justin can't handle sloppiness. He would pair up my shoes in the cupboard, remove the hair from my brush in the bathroom. 'How will you ever live with a slob?' I once asked him. He said, 'Oh, I'm quite enjoying learning every day.' His dry-cleaning is still hanging in see-through bags behind the bedroom door: two of his best suits that he'll need for work at some point. Doesn't he want his things? If he is staying in a hotel – one I've overlooked – is he sending out his laundry? Washing his underwear in the sink? Justin would hate that. He needs order. He'll want his things. If he's managed to come from the airport and pick up his car, why has he left his clothes if he really is leaving me? So does this mean he isn't really leaving me?

My mobile rings. I realise I'm fixating on his stuff because it's the only thing that's bound to bring him back at some point. It's not lost on me that his stuff might mean more to him than I do.

It's Sally. I stare at her name and freeze. That comment still stings. Dry, ambitionless John, who has done the same admin job at the Civic Centre since he left school. John, who only ever talks about house prices, and who rarely has an opinion on anything, but suddenly he has opinions about Justin. The thought of talking to Sally fills me with a terrible dread. I have never dreaded my friend before. It's the strangest feeling to have.

I listen as she leaves a message, her softly lilting North East accent filling the room. 'Hiya, Alice. Look, just wanted you to know that I've been thinking about our lunch today and, well, there's some things I wish I'd said differently. I think I was just shocked, so things came out wrong. Of course, it's not like I have any right to be, compared to you. I hope you're not cross. I regret saying John never trusted him. It was tactless, or something.'

I am riveted to her words. *John never trusted . . .* That isn't quite what she said before.

'Anyway, give me a ring whenever you want to talk. If you still want to talk to me, that is. I'm here for you. You know. Always. Okay? Let me know as soon as you get any news.'

When she rings off, the hollowness returns. I go back into the kitchen to find something to do, to force away the small stampede of panic that starts up in me again. I stare into the fridge, but it's still empty as I forgot to get any groceries on my way home from work. I haven't even got any bloody milk. On the counter there's a neatly stacked pile of takeaway menus, but the thought of going through them, having to make a decision – curry over Chinese, over pizza – is more than I can be bothered with. I walk back into the sitting room, typing as I go. I'm not cross. X. Because I'm not – not really. My text whooshes off into the ether.

I perch on the arm of the sofa. I catch sight of our answering machine. The little red light is flashing. Very few people call us on our home line any more. I get up and press play. Justin's mother's voice fills the silence. 'Hi!' I hear her say. She sounds tentative. The line crackles, then goes dead. Brie usually rings Justin on his mobile if she only wants to talk to him.

We have never been close. Not through my lack of trying. I was never close to my mother, so I quite liked the idea of having a good relationship with Justin's. She has never shown much interest in me, though. Sally once said there are those mothers who welcome their son's choices with open arms (in Sally's case), and others who only have eyes for their boys. Justin's relationship with his mother has frankly always been a bit mystifying to me. The midweek dinners, every Wednesday. Brie phoning her son whenever she has man problems, sometimes at 2 a.m. When the three of us were together and Brie was telling us a story, it was only Justin she would look at. Though I do feel sorry for her. She was only the age I am now when Justin's dad died. Justin said he had a profound sense of wanting to protect her, even though he was just a little boy. He took it upon himself to try to fill the gap his dad had left. I remember him saying he could stand his own unhappiness but not his mother's. It was all a little intimidating for a future daughter-in-law. I felt a little cowed by her, by their closeness. So no, I'd be no more inclined to ring her in a crisis than break my own kneecaps with a hammer. But if anyone will know what's going on with Justin, it will be Brie.

The second message is her, too. 'Sorry,' she says. 'I think my other phone died. Anyway, just ringing to see how the honeymoon was. You'll be well and truly back to reality now. Hope your flight home wasn't too tiring. You'll be at work today. Anyway, hope you are both doing fine. Call me when you're settled again.'

She doesn't know.

My stomach turns, though I'm not sure it's from hunger. I go and lie on the bed, and try to will the feeling of a meltdown away. I must nod off, because suddenly I am jumping at the ping of my email. It's dark when I open my eyes, and the lights from the Tyne river twinkle through our huge, uncovered windows. I peer at the clock. Three a.m.

Justin is a shitty sleeper. I can imagine him emailing in the middle of the night when he's at his lowest ebb. It's going to be him, and he's going to say, *Look, I'm sorry! I don't know what came over me! Can I come home? Can we pretend this never happened?*

But it isn't Justin. It's an old pal from Uni who works in Athens. Her idea of keeping in touch is copying me in on unfunny jokes, chain invitations to recipe swaps and YouTube videos of spaniels who polish glass doors and empty the rubbish.

I am fully awake now, though. Before I can talk myself out of doing it, I find the last text message he sent me and begin typing.

Talk to me. This is not fair. There's nothing you can tell me that's going to hurt me more than I already am.

But I'm not so sure it's true.

I stare out of the window, aware of the long darkness, and the slightly jagged rise and fall of my breathing. A moment or two later, Justin is typing a reply.

FIVE

Evelyn

December 18, 1983

The newspapers were full of the story. Six people dead. Seventy-five injured. Mark was seated at the opposite end of the polished walnut dining table, with only his large hands visible around the expanse of the *Sunday Times*.

'The bloody IRA rang the Samaritans thirty-seven minutes before the blast! They warned them they were going to do it! So no one seems to know what took the police so long! Murderers! Daring to bomb Harrods on a Saturday right before Christmas! When will this reign of terror end?'

He hadn't really noticed her this morning. Hadn't noticed the change in her. Hadn't looked twice and detected anything that might hint at the turmoil inside her, the unstoppable thrashing of contradictory impulses in her head. Mark never noticed. That was why it was so easy to hide things from him.

I'm sorry, I don't know how to tell you this. I have had a change of . . .

Plan? Heart? Mind?

'I thought we might go out to dinner tonight.' He was looking at her from around his newspaper, as though fondly enticing her back from another land.

She still hadn't touched any of her breakfast. She heard his voice distantly. She was aware of an out-of-body sensation. Whoever was sitting there in the Queen Anne chair was just a shell, and she, the contents of the shell, was across the room, off-camera – an onlooker seeing herself as a stranger would see her: an attractive, properly composed wife eating breakfast in a room with a high ceiling, where the air was scented with fresh coffee and kippers.

'What do you think?'

But Evelyn wasn't following the question. Evelyn was gone. She was back home on a tidal island battered by north-easterly winds. A young girl. A loner who could waste entire mornings stamping over grassy dunes that banked a gunmetal-grey sea, humming popular melodies, dreaming of a fanciful stranger who would take up residence at Lindisfarne Castle; who would peer out of his window and see her playing aeroplanes across the pastureland, arms outstretched, the thin sleeves of her dress flapping like birds' wings. A stranger who would think to himself, *Now there is this castle's next queen.*

'Evelyn? Are you even listening to me?' The affectionate despair.

But Evelyn was being propelled by the air. She was levitating with possibilities, gliding like the puffins, blackbirds and terns that made their home on the island's north shore, where she would wander and dream. She was dreaming again now. Seeing it for how it could all be again. And yet there was the harsh grounding, the pulling down to earth with strong hands, the indomitable forces of her reality.

I don't know how to tell you this. I have had second thoughts.

She stared at the polished silver place setting laid out by their housekeeper, Tessie – the morning pomp of their breakfast table – aware that the tears were ready to come, and she chanted in silent pleas, *Don't let me cry. I must not cry. Mark must never know.*

'Evelyn?' he said, a fraction impatient. 'I'm asking you if you'd like to dine out tonight.'

She looked at him, somewhat blankly, then shook her head. 'I don't want to think about dinner, Mark. We're just having breakfast.'

'What's the matter with you?' he asked, bewildered.

The matter? The matter was she couldn't properly draw a breath. The anxiety, the dilemma, had twisted her; her windpipe was wrung dry. She met his eyes, searched his face, but it wasn't his face she was seeing. She would never look at him and see him again, which was so unspeakably sad. There was only one face she would ever see.

He returned to his newspaper with a sigh. 'I just imagined we might go out and celebrate the fact that I'm still alive, that's all. But, then again, perhaps you wish I wasn't still alive. I can never tell with you.'

Last night was there so freshly – the choice she had made. She could still undo it. She could just tell him right here and right now. Instead, she said, 'Don't make light of it, Mark. You were there, shopping along with all those other terrified people. It could have very easily been you. Sometimes, you don't realise how lucky you are. You sail through life . . . You shouldn't take it for granted.'

He was looking at her with a mix of adoration and frustration. 'Yes, Evelyn, my darling. You're right. I was there. It could have been me. But it wasn't me, was it?'

'We'll see,' she said, a beat or two later. 'About dinner.'

'For heaven's sake. What's to see?' He was looking at her as though she always managed to be two people: the one he knew inside out, and loved, and this other who was a work in progress that he never bargained for.

If she didn't leave the room, she would cry, and then she would have to tell him. Mark might be a little blind, but he wasn't stupid. She'd had the dream again. And, as was always the case when it happened, she was beside herself for days after. It relentlessly haunted her. Only this time she was beside herself for new reasons altogether.

'Can you take this away?' Mark said to Tessie, who had come in the room to refresh the coffee. Then he added, 'Please,' because Mark was consummately polite.

'Just your plate, sir?' Tessie hovered, flummoxed by this break in their routine.

'Everything.' He swept a hand. 'Mrs Westland is apparently on a hunger strike.'

Despite his claim, all those years ago, that he was attracted to her because she was the opposite of the girls from his 'world', she was sure that Mark had never managed to forget that he no longer lived at Blenheim Palace. That's what she liked to call his family pile, just to put into perspective how privileged he was, just to remind him, when she felt he needed reminding, that most people didn't come from this. She certainly hadn't come from this. This wasn't how normal people lived.

Tears were building. The weight of her secret was almost stifling her. How had she got here? She could only take quarter-breaths, tiny hypoventilations. Of course, if he saw her crying, he'd probably think she was just being melodramatic again.

I'm sorry I couldn't do it . . .

How would she ever land on the right way to say it? She might be a writer, but she would never find words.

'I'm not feeling too hungry. I think I might go back to bed.' Her voice quivered at the end. She left the table somewhat abruptly. Tessie momentarily took her attention from the bacon platter, and Mark looked like he was about to say something – perhaps, *Bloody hell, what's wrong with you?* – but changed his mind.

She walked into their bedroom, aware of the unsteadiness of her legs. Her actions yesterday had undone everything, and she was wrong about one thing: she couldn't undo it again. She had allowed her will to be weak. But she had committed to her path, and now she had no choice but to stay with it, for all their sakes.

Her head thumped, and there was a small spasm under her right eye. The defeat registered itself with the weight of a physical one; she literally couldn't emerge from under it, so there was no point in trying. She lay down on top of the eiderdown. She stared at the hairline crack in the ceiling, telling herself she had to get a grip, if for no other reason than to stop herself bursting. That's how she felt. As though she was going to blow up. It was probably a couple of minutes before her heart rate returned to normal. She closed her eyes, and tried to go back to the dream; she just wanted to see him again, even if this was the only way.

It could have been one of several memories, really, but it was always this same one. Not of the first time she had set eyes on him in 1963, or the last, a few months ago. But the second.

1968.

Newcastle's Mayfair Ballroom.

The Long John Baldry concert.

Four years after she had married Mark.

They had gone back up North to see her parents; usually she made the trip alone, but on those rare occasions that Mark came with her, she would take him somewhere she thought might impress him – to show off the North East in its best light. This time, she'd been determined to prove to him that Newcastle's high-life was every bit as vibrant as London's. She had such treasured memories of nights out at the Mayfair when she was eighteen years old, perhaps nineteen. She loved Long John Baldry. So it couldn't have been more perfect that he turned out to be playing there.

She had never expected to see Eddy there.

In this dream she'd just woken from, she had time-travelled so impeccably to 1968. Every molecule of detail – she could see, smell, taste and feel everything that she'd seen, smelt, tasted and felt then, with crystal precision – even details she hadn't consciously been aware of at the time. The blue cloud of cigarette smoke that drifted just above the coiffed heads of dancers moving with the slow tide of Baldry's 'Let the Heartaches Begin'. The citrusy tang of the rum and pineapple she'd spilled on the breast of her red halter dress. Mark's mohair jacket grazing her bare arm. The way he would inch closer to ensure his arm kept contact with hers while he stood there, transported by Baldry's hot-blooded ballad of regret. Every time she moved fractionally, he moved fractionally. She found herself shifting slightly to see if he would follow, and follow he did. Never had she been more aware of an arm, and of the pleasingly maudlin lyrics, and how easily they could quash her if she thought too much about them. And Baldry, all six-feet-seven of him, dressed immaculately in his dark suit and ruffle-front shirt complete with oversized black bow tie, standing almost reverently still in a hazy spotlight as he sang about his grief at the love he once cast away. His molasses voice and the gentle mime-like gestures of his left hand, combined with the steady entrancement of the slow-dancing couples, reflected a void in Evelyn, one which, until that very moment, she hadn't even known existed.

She stood there, racked by overwhelming despair at this sudden new insight into herself. Then somewhere into the second repetition of the chorus, she was aware of a gaze. A gaze so hot on her, it reached from across the room.

She had to blink and look again. But, yes. It was him.

Eddy.

She would never be able to say if he was with someone, or alone, what he wore, if he'd recently had his hair cut, or what he was drinking. Because all she knew, and all she would ever remember, was the way he was looking at her – his unending, unflinching, rebuking gaze – combined with the mesmerising undertow of Baldry's gravelly, tear-jerking voice. Neither one could have singularly dismantled her like the force of the combination. It was a moment set apart from all others. She would come back to it years later, either dreaming or awake, and somehow she had known she would, right as it was happening.

Never did Eddy's eyes leave hers for even one second, nor Mark's sleeve stop touching her arm – not until Baldry's last lyric, and the audience's clapping. Then Mark shattered the spell by looking at her and smiling before breaking into applause himself. It was as though someone had suddenly turned up the volume and life was too loud. She gazed at her husband's profile for a second or two after his attention had returned to the singer. Then, when her eyes were pulled back to Eddy, there was only the startling hollow of his absence.

She didn't hear Mark leave for work. When she woke, it sounded like the rain had stopped, and the sun was trying to break through. Time felt as though it had shifted, and yet she was exactly the same. It hadn't gone away. She had hoped she could have slept herself into an alternate reality. But she was still very much in this one.

The shock of finding him gone in the dream, before she'd had a chance to do anything, still lingered. She lay there for a while, trying to bridge the present with 1968. It must have been ages, because the rain started up again. Then she got up and walked across to the window. Tessie was fussing around in the next room. The place still smelt of breakfast. It always did, until dinner. The pavements of High Street Kensington below were slick, and people were shaking off their wet umbrellas as they backed up into shops and ducked into taxis. She wanted their life. She wanted anyone's life but her own right now.

She went into her bathroom and splashed her face twenty times with cold water, mechanically counting each clap of her hands on her cheeks. Numbly, she stared at the sight of her freshened-up self in the mirror: a forty-year-old woman with a small face, pink-cheeked, eyelids slightly puffy. Back in the bedroom, she sat down at the writing bureau and reached for the pad of champagne-coloured Basildon Bond. The pen was like a foreign object between her fingers. She didn't know how long she must have sat there, entirely debilitated by the task. Tessie had left, because the house had become eerily absent of sound – save for her heartbeat, which was overly loud in her ears, and the dull scratching of the pen on the paper as she wrote his name.

Eddy.

Tears plunked on to the page. The letter *E* had come out all jagged, and now it was smudged, too. She chose a fresh sheet, wiped her tears and tried to start again.

Eddy,
I've made a terrible mistake. I can't do it, for everyone's sake. I am so sorry.

There would have to be more. But this was enough to begin with.

SIX

Alice

Discovered something before wedding. Still trying to process. Need space.

I read his text once. Twice. Three times. The thought that he is still there . . . I scramble to type quickly before he goes again. Pick up the phone!

I am riveted to the small screen, unable to breathe. After about thirty seconds, up come the three little dots that indicate Justin is typing.

I wait, but nothing follows. The dots disappear.

Pick up the damned phone! I type, kneeling on the bed in a shaft of moonlight.

The dots appear immediately. But then just as quickly they go again.

My fingers hit all the wrong keys, and I have to keep backspacing and telling myself to calm down.

What's going on? RU ill? Tell me! Please!

No, comes the instant reply. I'm fine.

Then what? My legs suddenly have a mind of their own. I am propelled off the bed into the middle of the floor, then I don't know where to go. As I stand there, I realise I am juddering with nerves.

No more dots.

I don't know why he's doing this! Why? But if he's there, responding at this hour of the morning, he's open to having it prised out of him, or he wouldn't have replied in the first place.

Where are you? I write again. Tell me!

I wait for a moment, then when nothing comes, I dial his number. It rings and rings and he doesn't pick up. The water glass is on my bedside table. I pick it up and hurl it at the wall. The shock of it smashing is like fireworks. I'm convinced the entire building has heard it.

Then I see the three little dots again.

Whatever he's writing is long. The dots seem to be there forever. I continue to stand in the same spot, half petrified. He's telling me . . . I'm going to know . . . I want to look and can't bear to look at the same time.

But then up pops, Will. Soon. Promise.

My heart sinks before almost stopping. Three words? That can't be it. I gawp at the screen, aware of an urgency, a grasping need to know, to wrestle an explanation out of him. I wait for him to write more. But there is nothing.

After the possibility of him still being there subsides, I put the phone back on the bedside table, and go to the toilet, taking care not to step on the broken glass. It's only when I come back into the bedroom that I remember the wedding photos.

Discovered something before wedding . . . The words perform a combative tango in my head.

I run and get my computer and pour myself a new glass of water. I have to log in with a password that Aimee gave me. Moments later, I am staring at a collage of dozens of small photographs, endless images of my own happy day – a tiny, cropped hint of a wedding dress, the front of a tuxedo, pale pink peonies, laughing faces, a flute of twinkling champagne, the sea, the stunning sea . . .

We married at a small Catholic church on Holy Island. Justin always claimed he wasn't religious because he said no God would have robbed a little boy of his father, but religion was an undeniable part of him. He still attended church at Christmas and Easter, and whenever he needed some time to step away from all the noise and just think. I accepted that about him, though to me, church meant very little. I had never gone as a child. I had no idea if my mother and father had married in a church because I never saw any wedding pictures of them; after he left, she destroyed everything with his face on it.

When I moved up here from Manchester, I was enchanted by the idea of an island that was cut off from the mainland twice a day by the tide. It was so magically different from Stockport, where I had grown up. I went over there on one of my first weekends, crossing early on a summer's morning right as the three-mile causeway had just opened up to cars. There was something hauntingly evocative about the small land mass, with its green pastureland dotted with goats and sheep, its mudflats with upturned fishing boats and the tiny streets of honey-coloured houses with their terracotta roofs. I remember sitting all alone on a bench listening to the ghostly music of a light wind wrapping around the Cheviot Hills and the occasional bleat of sheep – and nothing else; no other sound. Lindisfarne Castle sat perched on a craggy outcrop, like something built from sand by children. A structure that, impossibly, you'd imagine could be washed away by a high tide, or trampled by somebody's rambunctious dog, and yet it had survived stalwartly from the sixteenth century. I had read about its history, its many owners, one of whom was the founder of *Country Life* magazine. From up there on the castle walls, you could see out to the Farne Islands, while the wind whipped your hair and you inhaled salty air blown in from a steel-grey sea. If you were a writer or an artist, you could find no finer inspiration than here. If Wyeth had been British, he would have wound up on Holy Island, and found his Christina among the local girls, who were probably all just as captivating and inaccessible.

When I discovered that the castle could be booked for weddings, granted, it lost some of its mystique. Now it was just another national treasure that got pimped out to random brides with a big enough budget. Nevertheless, I wanted to be one of them. But Justin had wanted a Catholic church, so that's what we did.

I click on the first photograph of myself. It's bizarre; I can't relate one iota to that person in the white dress. It's like finally meeting the twin you never knew you had, and knowing you should be able to forge a connection, but you just can't. I am not interested in whether my hair held up, or if my make-up was too heavy, or how my dress looked from behind. All I see is a woman I can't identify with, on the arm of a man who must have been wondering what the hell he'd done.

'I want a big wedding,' he'd said. 'I'm only going to be married once.'

'What if I die early?' I'd asked him.

'Makes no difference. I only ever want one wife.'

It was so very Justin – not really the way anyone else thought. But he'd won me over with it; I was going to be that wife.

I come across one of him in close-up, cropped just below his deep cream buttonhole, semi-profile. His unfairly thick eyelashes. The unblemished, olive skin. Those eyes that are neither properly blue nor properly green – windows to the soul. But it strikes me that they're the eyes of the man I can't have truly known, who I lost so indistinctly. Was any of it real? A mute hysteria builds in the back of my throat. The need for answers is suddenly greater than my ability to handle them – perhaps I will just disappear into never knowing. Perhaps it'll be easier. I take another drink of my water and click through the photos, hurrying past ones he isn't in. Latching on to the ones of his face – staring at them until my eyes hurt – searching for any possible subtext in his expressions, in his body language, in the way he was holding a wine glass or scratching his cheek, looking for a moment of truth, something that will leap out and make me say, *There it is! Justin, in the throes of realising he's made a mistake!* A forced smile that would belie some inner maelstrom of regret and despair. But there is nothing.

In every photo, he looks exactly as you would expect him to look.

Except for one.

When I see it, my stomach gives a small lift and fall. I enlarge it to its fullest size – not that this really helps, given it happens to be the only photograph in which you can't see Justin's face. He is with Rick, his best man.

Looking at it now, I realise exactly when it must have been taken. We had just been standing for photos alongside the upturned former fishing boats, once part of one of the largest herring fleets to sail off the east coast of England.

'You were right, it's so beautiful here,' he had said. His voice had a woeful quality to it. His hand was both light and firm in the small of my back; I can almost still feel it. We were officially husband and wife. I had always wanted to be married. Friends were happy to live together. To me, that felt like keeping a door open – one of you clearly must be reluctant to make the ultimate commitment. I'd longed to meet a man who wanted that door firmly closed. That, to me, was the very definition of romance. Perhaps it was because I had never agreed with my mother not wanting to marry my stepfather, despite him asking regularly, despite his profound disappointment every time she said no. Because my real father had been a lying, philandering bastard, she vowed she would never tie herself to another man again. I'd thought that was so petulant and selfish – if he was good enough to live with for a lifetime, he was good enough to marry.

'Maybe we'll buy a place here,' Justin had said. There was a quality to his voice that I couldn't quite pinpoint: wistfulness? Or was it sadness? Why would he be sad? 'Once I pay off some of my debts, we can get a weekend place. Somewhere our children will enjoy – when we have them.' He smiled at that. 'Maybe we'll get a boat, even.' The photographer asked him to try not to talk. I chuckled. Justin always had to be planning, thinking ahead, putting every moment to good use.

Out of the blue, it started to rain. I remember us running back inside. The clutch of his hand round mine. 'I'm happy,' I remember telling him. 'Me too,' he said. 'More than you might ever know.' He stopped briefly, and looked at me solemnly for a moment. I thought he was just intensely moved. I remember Sally running up behind us, off the beach. 'My God, this is quicksand!' She laughed. Previously, she'd been a little peeved with me. I hadn't used her to plan our wedding. I had wanted to keep it casual and without fuss. But all was well between us now.

She'd thought we'd been wrong to marry in spring. 'You don't want rain on your wedding day!' she'd said. 'You know what that means!' I hadn't. 'Post-wedding tears that will be cried,' she went on to tell me. Sally had a superstition for everything. I didn't believe it, but, nonetheless, I'd experienced a sudden vision of myself crying in my wedding dress, and I'd had to push it away and vow not to listen to any more negative stuff, because clearly I wasn't immune to it.

But look – it had rained – and Sally had been wrong. And all I remember is that the air was spiked with the scent of the sea, and the rain clung to my face and hair, and I was the happiest I had ever known I could be.

Inside, the staff brought around champagne and Lindisfarne mead, and tiny crab sandwiches, an island speciality. I mingled with the forty or so guests, as a man strummed 'Greensleeves' on a Spanish guitar. 'Where's Justin?' I whispered to Sally.

Her pretty green eyes glistened with tipsiness. 'I think he took a phone call. I saw him walking toward the library.'

I slipped away, and followed the small corridor that led to the room with the tall windows, with its comfy seats and bookshelves, but when I went in there, the only sign of life was a fly that kept hitting the window in its frenzied attempt to get out. When I returned to the main room, Sally was holding two champagne flutes. 'Here. Best you get your fair share, as you're paying for it.' We had joked earlier about how some of Justin's friends were knocking it back. She passed me a glass. 'Did you find him?'

'No.' We chatted, but I was on a mission. Where could he have gone for all this time?

Well, this is where he'd gone.

In this one last photograph, Justin is standing outside with Rick, his friend from his Oxford days, who had come up from Gloucester with his wife, Dawn. They're on the small stone balcony that overlooks the sea. It's raining heavily, but clearly they are not minding that. Rick's eyes are fixed on Justin, and his face is serious. I can only see the back of Justin's head, but I can't take my eyes from it. What were they talking about? I can almost feel secrets in the air, as though I am right there, back in the moment, watching them from the very vantage point where Aimee must have been standing.

I remember them coming back in, drenched, and Rick saying something about them having gone for a walk.

But, clearly, they hadn't gone for any walk. They had been immersed in conversation on a balcony. And whatever they had been talking about was private enough for Rick to feel he couldn't quite be honest about it.

SEVEN

My assistant, Victoria, pops her head around my door. 'You've got visitors from Sunrise Care Home.'

It takes me a moment, then, 'Oh! Right!' The old folk. The phone call with the woman, right before our wedding. *Some neurologists believe that looking at visual art can awaken the memories of those suffering from dementia.* The woman's polite, well-pitched voice. The pent-up, tremoring quality in it, like an interviewee who was trying not to show how desperate they were to land the job.

We thought we might be able to help our elderly friends who wander lost in their minds. We hoped Andrew Wyeth and Edward Hopper might be able to help them find a way back.

It had sounded almost rehearsed. Yet it touched me. Her intensity had.

I step into the foyer and come face to face with the elderly lady who was in the gallery the other day. She is with a man probably around my age. He's stocky and not particularly tall, with a pelt of unruly hair and kind brown eyes.

The woman is already extending a hand. 'I'm sorry, I should have introduced myself on Monday. I'm Evelyn Westland, and this is Michael Morretti—'

'Evelyn's chauffeur,' he says. He rumples his hair, languidly, like he's just woken up from a long nap, then offers me his hand.

Evelyn tut-tuts. 'He's not my chauffeur! Michael is a nurse at Sunrise Villas. But he did drive us all here today, so I suppose he has a point.' She sends him a teasing, almost flirtatious little smile.

A nurse? I wouldn't have thought. He looks more like a tough guy not given to complex self-expression: a B-list actor in a mob movie, perhaps.

'We've got them in a van outside.' He flicks his head toward the door. He's standing, somewhat rigidly, with his hands crossed in front of his crotch. 'We wanted to check with you before we brought them in. To make sure you're ready for us. If you can ever be ready for us.'

I can't help but smile. I remember telling the woman to bring them on a Wednesday afternoon – the day when the gallery is least busy. 'How many of them are there?' I ask. I forget what she's told me before.

'Only three,' Evelyn says. 'Ronnie, Martin and Eddy.'

She is impeccably dressed in wide-legged cream trousers, and a cream, three-quarter-sleeved cashmere jumper. 'Go on!' she gives Michael a not-so-subtle nudge.

'Yes, ma'am!' he salutes her, then glances at me and there's a twinkle in his eye. 'I bet you can guess who wears the trousers in this relationship,' he says. Then, 'I better go get them before they break out and ransack Eldon Square.'

In the room that houses the paintings, Ronnie and Martin appear agitated, even a touch afraid, giving me doubts that this initiative is going to be a success. Somehow, though, Michael manages to coax them into sitting on the bench in front of Hopper's *Morning Sun*, and they settle down a little, thankfully.

The tall, slim and no doubt once handsome man – Eddy – is different. He doesn't appear to be bothered by being here at all. In fact, he seems lost in a world of his own. Evelyn catches me looking at him.

'You know, Saul Bellow said that everybody needs their memories. They keep the wolf of insignificance from the door.'

'That's beautiful!' I say. 'Or tragic. I'm not sure which.'

'It's both.' Because she isn't very tall, she has to look up at me when she speaks. With her appealing intensity and sweet little face, it's like being won over by a tiny pocket angel. 'When you think about it, all we really have is our ability to place ourselves in the context of meaningful things – the family we were born into, the people we have loved. Those things are our emotional compass. If we don't have that, we have nothing.' She stares at the backs of the three men sitting on the bench, lined up like soldiers waiting for a train to war.

Suddenly, I am filled with thoughts of Justin. Of life without him. Of the end of my life without him.

'What do you think of when you look at this painting of a woman sitting on a bed in the sunshine, Ronnie?' Michael says. He has a nice voice. It's calm, and somehow brings me back to the present.

'I think of a woman on a bed in the sunshine,' Ronnie parrots him.

'Would you say she looks happy?' Michael ruffles his hair again – clearly a habit. I imagine it'd be either endearing or slightly irritating if you got to know him. 'How do you think she feels, sitting alone in this empty room?'

'Have you tried guessing how a woman feels? If you have, good luck.'

Michael chuckles, and glances at me. We smile. 'Ronnie, I do believe you've got a point there,' he says.

Suddenly, Ronnie is looking at me, too. He's eggshell bald, with rounded, almost black eyes that are soulful and make me think of a seal. 'What about the naked one?' he asks me.

For a second or two, I'm puzzled. 'Ah!' He means the girl on the stool by the window, turning her face toward the shade. 'That's Andrew Wyeth's *Helga*. Someone he painted for fourteen years without his wife or the model's husband knowing. It caused quite a scandal in the art world when so many sketches and drawings of her eventually came to light.'

'He's not emotionally attached to her.' Martin suddenly joins in. 'If he was, he wouldn't let everyone see her with no clothes.' For an elderly man, his voice has a remarkable ability to project itself.

'Oh, come on!' Evelyn shoots me a look that says, *What kind of old curmudgeon is he?* 'She likes him seeing her naked. It empowers her.'

Michael and I smile again.

'They seem very sensible,' I whisper to him as Evelyn trots off to the other end of the gallery. 'Is this what normally happens? I suppose when she told me they had Alzheimer's, I wasn't sure what to expect.'

'Well, there really isn't any normal.' His kind brown eyes meet mine. 'We do a lot of creative therapy at Sunrise, in particular music and art therapy. Sometimes we paint, or we show them the work of famous artists. Paintings can help them remember things – usually things stored in their long-term memory. They'll tell us stories, presumably about past events in their lives. They tend to remember a point rather than a period of time. They can be quite chatty and find words that they normally can't access. It's fascinating to hear what it can draw out of them.' A look of pride comes over his face, which seems so sweet. 'Their families, loved ones, they often can't believe the transformation . . .'

Listening to him talking, it suddenly dawns on me what's so puzzling about him. He has a tender, compassionate side that doesn't fit with his tough-guy exterior. In fact, he's a bit of an intriguing contradiction altogether.

'Alzheimer's has phases. Language is very often one of the first things to go, but creativity is lost much later. So the therapies allow them to express feelings they can't express any other way. They get to bypass their limitations and go to their strengths. It's amazing how well they can respond to the scale, colour and vibrancy of a painting. They process it in a way that's real and in the moment.'

He looks at me the whole time while he talks. It's a long, languishing gaze that's calming to me, rather like his voice. He clearly loves his job. 'I've got lots of fascinating articles on it. I'll email you them, if you'd like.'

'Sure,' I say, though, actually, I'm not at all sure I'm going to have huge use for them. 'What about this man?' I point to the handsome one, who is wearing a shirt the colour of ripe tomatoes. He has a fine head of silver-grey hair and a rosy-toned complexion. I think he might be a little younger than the other two.

'Eddy.' Michael smiles. 'Eddy's a grand fellow. We think his dementia was caused by something that happened to his head a long time ago. It's actually a very sad story . . .'

'I don't think I can hear a sad story right now,' I tell him. He gives me a curious look, and I realise I may have pre-empted him; that's probably all he'd been going to say. Anyway, it would feel disrespectful talking about them as though they're not there. I watch Eddy, though. He sits in a world of his own, where he seems happy to be left. There's something masculine and capable about him, an echo of the man he must have been, which makes me want to know about him. He has a marvellously straight back and big, broad shoulders. He almost looks familiar, like an actor in those black-and-white films my mother used to watch. The ones in which the heroes and heroines got to perform those climactic, closed-mouth kisses at the end, to the swell of hammy music; I was addicted to them. 'I bet he was quite gorgeous in his day.'

'Evelyn seems to think he still is.'

The way Michael looks at her could only be described as slightly in awe and doting. 'Who is she to these men?'

'Oh, Evelyn is Eddy's shadow. She never leaves his side. She sits with him in the sun room, reads to him and walks with him in the gardens – he likes to ride the drive-on mower with the gardener. I think Eddy and Evelyn have some history; I'm not sure what. But you can see it in the way you will catch her looking at him. One thing's for certain, she won't give up on him. She's fixed on him having some sort of breakthrough.'

'Breakthrough?'

'She wants him to remember. Something. Her? Himself? Something between them that happened? I don't know what. She's a bit of a dark horse.' He looks back at me. 'Because it happens from time to time, you know. The tiny miracles. The kernels of hope.'

He isn't much taller than me. Perhaps five-feet-nine. He has a broad upper body – one of those body types that's either muscular or out of shape; in the unflattering sweater he's wearing, you can't tell. I wonder what he gets out of all this.

'So they were never married?'

'Not that I'm aware of,' he says.

'I can see how they'd make a good couple. His ruggedness and her femininity.'

'He reminds me of a cowboy. Clint Eastwood meets Burt Reynolds.' He brings his warm, heavy-lidded eyes back to mine. 'Evelyn used to live on Holy Island, but she moved closer to Sunrise so she can be near him.'

When he says *Holy Island*, all I can hear is the distant whisper of my wedding day, ready to pull me back if I let it.

'She bought a swank apartment,' he goes on. 'Well, swank by my standards, anyway. She doesn't drive any more, so this way she can walk every day to see him. She's a fixture in there, and she's always bright and cheerful. I find her fascinating. I think beautiful Evelyn once knew a much grander life.'

'Beautiful Evelyn!' I beam a smile. 'You sound a little in love with her.'

He chuckles. 'Everyone's a little in love with Evelyn. You should have seen pictures of her when she was young.'

I glance at the pair of them again – Evelyn, standing in front of Christina, and Eddy sitting on the bench. There is something about his face – the even, balanced features, the noble shape of his head and his fine, long neck – something that keeps me wanting to look at him, I don't know why. Perhaps it's what Michael just said. Good-looking older folk make you want to follow the moving image of them, starting far back in time . . . 'Do you think they were lovers?' I ask.

'Possibly. But, in a way, I think it might go deeper than that.'

'Does he have any other family?'

He shakes his head. 'No. Nor does she, I believe.'

All I can think is she sold her house to move near to Sunrise. She's here, in the gallery, because she wants him to remember something. Whatever it is, it must matter dearly to her. And, once again, I'm pulled back to Justin being gone. Who will be around to care if the end of my life has quality? It's safe to say it probably won't be him.

'Are you all right?' I hear Michael's voice. He is studying me. 'You seem . . .'

'I'm fine.'

'Come!' Evelyn waves us over.

Suddenly, we are staring at the painting of a girl in a pale pink dress, almost crawling toward a house in the distance, in the middle of nowhere. 'So who was Christina?' Michael asks with sedate curiosity.

'The girl in the painting, dumbo,' Ronnie growls. 'Isn't it obvious? The painting is about the girl.'

'I think it's really a painting about a house,' Martin says. 'It reminds me of *The Wizard of Oz*. The house looks like it just landed in the picture, after the tornado, with Dorothy, in her dream.'

'That's a great image, Martin.' Michael pats his shoulder.

'Christina was paralysed,' I tell them. 'She had a problem with muscle deterioration. You can see how frail her arms are.' I draw with a finger around Christina's elbow joint. 'She was a lonely figure, whom others might have felt sorry for, but he obviously saw something heroic in her.'

'She was paralysed?' Martin looks bemused. 'Well, in that case, if she was ready to crawl all that way up to the house, she must have really wanted to go back there.'

'I love how they put such a positive spin on things,' Michael whispers to me.

'Christina lived there all her life,' I add. 'Her nostalgia for her home practically seeps out of the canvas. It's like a kind of scenery all of its own.'

'I love that!' Evelyn looks at me suddenly. She is examining me as though I've said something massively enlightening. 'A kind of scenery . . .' She smiles. 'Well, one thing is true of life. You never forget your home and where you came from. I can attest to that.' She lowers her eyes and seems sad for a moment.

'There's something about it. It's haunting,' Michael says. 'You feel like she's been away and she longs to go back.'

'It's the way she's looking up at the house.' Martin pretends to look through the camera lens he's making with his hand. 'The house is on high, and she's looking up at it. It means a lot to her.'

I'm amazed how surprisingly tender and astute their observations are, and how moved we all are by the enigmatic Christina and her attachment to her house.

'Christina has lost something that she still wants,' Evelyn says, gravely. 'It's a terrible, terrible curse. And unfortunately, like a lot of us, she hasn't learnt the art of letting go.'

I think of the concept of letting go, the idea of me having to let go of Justin. Or the thought of him having already let go of me . . . It calls to mind an image of a person freefalling through time and space, without a parachute.

'I think she's really sad.' Ronnie wipes his brow in distress. 'There are a lot of burdens on her.'

'Wyeth said he found in people the fugitive quality of life and the inevitable eventual tragedy,' I tell them, with quiet reverence. 'Someone who wrote about him said that when you look at his work you have to listen to the eloquence of things unsaid.'

We all fall silent, paying respect to Christina, listening for the eloquence.

'She looks like she's seeing something that doesn't exist.' The voice comes from behind. We all seem to have forgotten about Eddy.

He comes and stands right behind us. He's the tallest among us, but so thin for his build. Yet his voice is strong and sure of itself.

'She's seeing her memories,' he says. 'A lot of things happened in that house. Things that mean a lot to her.' He taps his temple.

Evelyn gasps quietly, and a hand flies to her mouth. We all seem to notice. Michael looks at me as though to say Eddy has just put the sun back in Evelyn's sky. I find myself curiously spellbound.

'He's right!' The whites of her eyes have turned watery and red. 'Christina did something a long time ago, something that had terrible consequences.' She looks right at me; I am held fast by her intensity. 'She has lived her entire life wanting to put it right.'

I want to say, *What? What did she do?* But, of course, it would be entirely inappropriate. I can't help thinking that Evelyn isn't talking about Christina; she's talking about herself.

I glance at Michael, and give him a slightly shrinking smile.

EIGHT

Evelyn

Holy Island. June, 1983

At first, all she saw was the back of his head. He was on the other side of the vast laurel tree that divided two sections of the garden. His white van was parked right outside her mother's gate. It was the first thing she had noticed when she rounded the corner hugging a plastic bag of groceries like a baby because its handle had snapped; she'd just had to pick a week's supply of tins and vegetables from the middle of the road.

He always came on Tuesdays, her mother had told her. The naturalness of his name on her mother's lips during their long-distance phone calls had rubbed off on her; she felt like she knew him herself. But she wasn't feeling sociable. She was no longer used to the introspective lens of small-town Northern England. There was something buffering about the anonymity of London, the steady revolutions of her social life there, her ability to pick and choose whom she talked to, and when.

He clearly didn't hear her when she opened the gate. Only when her fashionable platform shoes announced her arrival did he look up.

When she saw his face, her ability to react, even to breathe, was somehow put on hold. He was standing fifty feet away, wearing a red shirt, in the process of cutting back a clematis. The stray grey tabby cat her mother had been feeding lay washing itself on the lawn, methodically pulling down its left ear with its left paw. She was aware of the film-camera precision of her eyes, her keenness to observe every last detail of this extraordinary surprise.

He swiped the back of his hand across his cheek. A smile started, then stopped itself. 'Evelyn,' he said, sounding as taken aback as she felt. She thought he swayed slightly, with the force of the surprise.

'Eddy.' His name came out as a croak. In all her mother's mentioning of Eddy, Evelyn had never once connected him to *Eddy*. She placed a hand on her heart as the unlikely reality of it sunk in. 'Good heavens!'

For a moment, all he could do was stare at her face. Then his gaze dropped down her from head to toe. In the glare of his scrutiny, she felt too done-up in her burgundy velvet pedal-pushers and black studded boots from a rookie designer called Jimmy Choo, which she had purchased from a Saturday market in Liverpool Street. Eddy's rake was planted in the soil next to him, and there was a lawnmower beside a heap of newly cut grass. Despite her still being suspended in a state of shock, Evelyn's eye for peripheral detail was sharper than ever.

He hadn't changed. Not that she'd have imagined he would in the fifteen years since she'd last seen him at the Long John Baldry concert at the Mayfair Ballroom.

'You look good,' he said, clearly both charmed and reduced by the sight of her. 'Better than good, actually.' He laughed a little, out of his depth, and she now knew that he really was as shocked as her.

She was inwardly flustered at the compliment. He was still truly handsome; in fact, he redefined the adjective. He was tall and fit and tanned. So unlike Mark, who was average height, lean-limbed and pale, as if he had been constructed out of cigarettes. Eddy still had a full head of black hair, and his eyes were the colour of sapphires. But he'd always possessed some other appeal that couldn't be attributed to looks alone. It was something she felt in the core of her, rather than something she saw. She couldn't really have described it then, all those years ago, and she couldn't now.

'You look much the same too, Eddy. I'm just . . . !' She laughed, nervously. 'I'm not sure how this . . . I thought you worked for the shipyards, but here you are, in my mother's garden . . . A gardener?' None of this made any sense. In all their conversations, her mother had never let on. Evelyn truly couldn't fathom it.

She had a feeling she'd been toyed with. It was like her mother to derive some pleasure from imagining the two of them might meet again one day – through her. Somewhere, up there, Evelyn was sure she was looking down and relishing this.

He was unflappable. 'I did work for the shipyards. I was laid off. Made some changes.'

It's a shame it's not summer. Then you'd have met Eddy. Her mother's words when she had come back in the winter to nurse her through cancer. It was said in a nudge-nudge-wink-wink way. Still Evelyn hadn't connected it. If she'd had a penny for all the Eddys she'd known, she'd have filled a jar.

They were stuck in an awkward moment where neither seemed to know what else to say.

She found herself laughing again, slightly. Not because this was funny. Purely because she was still astonished. 'Look, I need to put this down.' She had just remembered the bag was nearly falling apart. She struggled to the door, forgetting where her key was. All her memories of how they met – that day, at a wedding she wasn't even meant to attend – were rushing at her, and she felt the need to still them because they were so overwhelming.

'Can I help?' he asked.

She shook her head, and felt in her pocket, balancing the decrepit bag of groceries on one arm. She could sense his gaze on her bottom, which brought back the memory of when they had danced, his fingers pressing the small of her back. Those fingers she could still feel hours after he'd removed them.

'I'm very sorry about your mother,' he said, as she missed the lock with the key. She didn't go through life feeling fluttery when men looked at her. In fact, the sensation was entirely foreign to her. 'Mrs Coates was a good woman. We used to have our chats, you know.'

She nodded, quickly. She couldn't talk about her mother. The grief was too fresh. And she certainly didn't want to talk about their chats. She was still smarting that she had cooked this up. Her mother had never thought that Mark was right for her. She said he was too measured and mature. Besides, her mother had no respect for office types. Real men worked with their hands, like Evelyn's father. It didn't seem to matter that virtually everything Evelyn had was thanks to Mark being exactly the type that her mother disparaged. It was an argument Evelyn had had many times with her, but one she could never win.

By the time she had got the door open, Eddy had walked down from the top of the garden and was standing close behind her.

'If you want to know, I'm as surprised to see you, as you are me,' he said.

She turned around and met his eyes again. Those eyes she'd had such a hard time forgetting. Thankfully, they weren't tinged with the same terrible reproach as they had been fifteen years ago in the Mayfair Ballroom, when she'd last seen him. But then again, she knew he'd married. Her mother had seen it in the local newspaper, and had made a point of telling her.

'Oh, I'm not so sure about that!' she chided. 'Given you were obviously in some sort of cahoots with my mother.' She pushed open the door and stepped inside.

'I wasn't in cahoots with anyone.' He sounded mildly affronted. 'She needed a gardener, so I've been helping out.'

Evelyn couldn't meet his eyes.

'I never expected you to walk in the garden gate, Evelyn, if that's what you're thinking. I can promise you. Not in a million years.'

She had placed the groceries on the table, and turned to look at him. He wiped soil from his cheek, with his knuckle. She glimpsed his wedding ring. 'I never expected to see you again, to be honest. I avoided your mother's funeral. I thought it best, even though I would have liked to have been there. I hope you understand.'

Alluding to the past this way implied it had mattered. She nodded. It was June. The funeral had been a week before Christmas. This was Evelyn's second trip back North in seven months. 'Of course,' she said. He hadn't wanted to see her at the funeral. After all these years, what she'd done must have still bothered him somehow.

'I had better let you get on.' She looked over to where his rake was standing in the soil.

His eyes remained on her for a second or two. 'I still can't believe I'm looking at you,' he said. Then he gave her a somewhat sad smile, and turned to go back to his task.

'We will not speak of him again,' Evelyn had told her mother, after she'd asked Evelyn if she wanted her to send her Eddy's wedding cutting from the newspaper. 'Why would I want to see his wedding photograph?' She had been aghast. And they hadn't spoken of him again. Was this why her mother had conveniently neglected to tell her that Eddy was now her gardener? Because she was honouring Evelyn's wishes?

When she closed the door, she realised she was trembling. In fact, she had to sit down for a moment.

Being in the home she grew up in always brought out Evelyn's melancholic side. But never more so than now. Sometimes, she was so crippled by her nostalgia. She often wondered if it was because she'd never had children. Perhaps having other childhoods to focus on would have detracted her from thinking so much about her own.

The house was nothing special to anyone but Evelyn. It was a simple stone cottage with a red-tiled roof and a navy front door, in a quaint landscape of rolling fields, sheep, low tides and tea rooms. There was a lawn at the front, and opposite, a flower garden. In the summer, it was ablaze with colour and her mother always smelt of the plums she'd pick and stew from the tree that grew out back.

The Farne Islands lay off in the distance like sleeping hump-backed whales. And when the wind gusted, it played a song that drifted across the Cheviot Hills like a choir of ghosts. 'What's that strange noise?' tourists would ask, and Evelyn's best friend, Lorna, would make up all kinds of horror stories while Evelyn struggled to keep a straight face. Droves of tourists came to Holy Island in the summer: day-trippers to the Castle and the Priory who would leave before high tide, and others who were more intrigued by the island's geography than its history, the concept of living somewhere that was stranded from the mainland twice a day. Every summer, someone would foolishly ignore tide tables, and Evelyn would chuckle to see the stranded cars nearly submerged in the sea. That is until she reached her late teens, and the isolation of the place felt more like fodder for dark novels, the kind written by virgin sisters from Yorkshire who suffered early deaths. Looking back, it was probably just a growing phase, but at the time, leaving had become her reason for being.

In the kitchen, she got up from the chair and dipped the blinds so he couldn't see in. Eddy. In her garden. She still couldn't put the two ideas together. Her mother had schemed this. Hadn't she? Or had it just happened the random way that the improbable often does?

The house hadn't been updated much over the years. The kitchen still sported the same Formica countertops and tatty linoleum flooring. There had been the odd addition of a washing machine and a monster fridge whose arrival in the family had caused a stir. The fridge had been replaced by a smaller, more efficient version, like the TV. But even the radio looked like some leftover antiquity that a certain type of person would be drawn to at a garage sale.

She turned it on now, jumped from Spandau Ballet's 'True', to Rod Stewart's 'Baby Jane', and then finally left it on Elton John's 'I Guess That's Why They Call It the Blues'. Eddy looked up briefly toward the house when that song came on, and she wondered if he could hear it. She peeked through a slat of blind again, noting the dust on it. She was saddened to see the neglect that had fallen on the place now there was no one here to take care of it, just a friend of her mother who popped in once a week to keep a general eye on things, but she couldn't be expected to dust.

Eddy was a quick worker. She could imagine him appealing more and more to her mother's concept of the ideal man as he sweated it out there. After she had seen him again at the Mayfair, the force of the coincidence had possessed a kind of finality to it. *I won't ever see him again*, she had thought. *Improbabilities don't happen twice.*

She let the blind fall away from her finger. Even with the radio on for company, the house was eerily empty. Every room held a host of memories. She could recall the oddest details, the threads and weaves and tones that made up the tapestry of her childhood: the scratch on the word *yearning* on her father's record of Mario Lanza singing 'Be My Love'; the squeak of the floorboard by her bedroom door and how she'd tiptoe around it when she snuck home an hour past her curfew; the fading of the yellow flowers around the border of their oval dinner plates. Once or twice, she had been certain she'd heard her mother calling her name. She'd come close to replying, then caught herself in the agonising realisation that she was gone. She had convinced herself that coming back here after her death would be impossible to bear. And yet being back somehow helped her get in touch with herself. It always had.

She left the window, and put the things in the fridge that she was going to prepare for dinner. Local crab. New potatoes. A peach melba, because she could never get them this good in London. She was conscious of going about her tasks indoors as he went about his outside: the odd symbiotic domesticity of them. A thought sailed through her: *If I had never left, this could have been my life.*

At one point, she looked in the mirror. The fine bones of her face, the green eyes accentuated by mascara – the only make-up she ever wore – dramatically curling up her lashes at the outer edges. Her heavy, dark eyebrows that gave her face *stature*, as an old boyfriend had once told her. She'd loathed them ever since. And there was something else – there was a slight flush to her cheeks. She looked alive again.

At exactly 4 p.m., he knocked on the door. 'I think I'm all done for today.' His eyes travelled over her face, over the top of her hair, as though the sight of her pleased him all over again. Years ago, when she had danced with him, she'd thought it would be futile trying to fall out of love with those eyes.

'So you'll be back in two weeks?' she asked. His eyes were telling her that he still thought she was beautiful, and she felt herself blushing with the heat of them.

'Yes. Of course. I imagine you're going to be selling.'

She nodded. 'That's why I'm here. To spruce the place up.' He had lurked in her mind on her wedding day. Not with repining and weeping, just with the irrevocability of closing a door that hadn't even been properly open. She'd thought something similar when her mother had said he'd married. *What will be, will be. Perhaps. But one thing's for certain: we won't be.*

'When are you heading back to your castle?' he asked.

'I don't live in a castle.'

He continued to affectionately take stock of her. 'I thought you married an earl.'

She tutted. He had always been a little fresh with her. 'I didn't marry an earl.' Where was her wit when she needed it? To leave here was a mark of having bettered oneself, as though Northern England were somehow universally acknowledged by its inhabitants to be inferior to the rest of the country. It was a perception that the leaver could never live down, so there was no point in taking offence at it. 'Do you think you could keep coming until I find new owners? Or should I get someone else?' His presence was somehow reducing her to size, and she wasn't familiar with feeling this small.

He frowned. 'Why would you get someone else?'

'No reason. Only if you want me to.' She looked an inch or two past his head. He'd know she was being a little sparky with him.

When she met his eyes again he seemed a little disappointed in her. 'Right,' he said. 'I suppose I'll see you again in two weeks.'

With that, he gave a curt nod and then was gone.

NINE

London. 1963

'You have a delivery,' Matthew, the cheeky young concierge, told her when she arrived on shift on the front desk at Claridge's at 3 p.m.

On her twentieth birthday, Evelyn's gran had pushed a tidy sum of her savings into Evelyn's hand and said, 'You can live your life or you can waste your life.' She had squeezed her fingers tightly closed around Evelyn's, like a clam. 'Don't waste your life.'

Her gran had always known her well. She had sensed a restlessness in Evelyn that didn't seem present in other girls Evelyn's age. Evelyn was world-weary of where she lived, given that she'd been visiting Newcastle bars since she was fifteen years old, and had tried on for size a variety of menial jobs that other girls seemed so satisfied with – hairdresser in training, hostess in a prim hotel restaurant, perfume demo girl in the region's number one department store – jobs that she could never make fit. She should have gone to college, but grammar school had eluded her by a painfully narrow margin. She'd had some vague idea she'd quite like to write books, but whenever she'd voiced it, her family had scoffed at her, so she had learnt quite quickly to keep that sort of silly idea to herself.

As Matthew passed her the splendid bouquet of red and white roses, the knuckle of his index finger deliberately grazed her breast. To think she'd had a bit of a crush on him when she'd first arrived. She didn't know what to do or say, so she pretended it had never happened. She clutched the flowers that burst with fragrance, anxious to open the small white card.

'It's from Mark Westland,' Matthew informed her, petulantly, as though she should know the name. 'Seems you've got yourself an admirer.'

'What? Wish he'd sent them to you instead?' she quipped. She was dying to ask him who Mark Westland was, but she wouldn't give him the satisfaction. Walking into reception, she tore at the card, sensing the breathless weight of having been noticed by someone possibly important; the possible grand, great romance of it all. Since moving to London, into the flat-share of five girls that had been already set up before she'd even left the North, by the sister-in-law of a friend of a friend, her life hadn't quite lived up to the hype she'd expected. It had so far been a lot of work for very little pay. Perhaps things were about to turn around.

Please have dinner with me this Saturday. Annabel's. 7 p.m.

Yours, Mark Westland.

'*Yours, Mark Westland*?' Matthew put on a girly voice. He was craning to read over her shoulder.

'Go away.' She flapped him off. 'It's none of your business. You child!'

Matthew gave a mocking laugh, deliberately sweeping his eyes over her breasts again, as he stupidly blushed the colour of a beetroot. She suddenly despised him – all men. What right did they have to try to intimidate women and get away with it? Well, she despised all of them except, perhaps, for Mr Westland.

It was enough to be sent flowers. Let alone to be going to a posh new private members' club. She didn't realise it at the time, but for the however-many hours that Mr Westland's invitation was in her head, Eddy wasn't.

It was a shame that she had a train ticket to go back up North that weekend. She wouldn't be going now. She only hoped Mr Westland wasn't fat.

Or old.

Or had a wart on his cheek.

Holy Island. 1983

When she heard the knock shortly after dinner, she somehow knew it would be Eddy. She opened the door, and he was standing there, smiling.

'Forgot my rake.' He leant against the doorframe with his left shoulder. 'Does that sound like a pathetic excuse to come back and talk to you?'

'Extremely.' She tried to sound like this sort of thing happened every day. She must have looked as red as someone being held over a fire.

He had changed into a long-sleeved, green jersey T-shirt that emphasised his muscular upper body. He was as fit as someone half his age. His black cap almost blended in with his dark hair, except for the few grey curls at his temples. She wondered what excuse he'd given his wife.

'Did you really just come back here to see me?' she asked, guilelessly.

'Yes. From the minute I left here, it was all I could think about.'

They held eyes. Something in the way he was trying to lean casually against the doorframe told her that he wasn't doing this quite as effortlessly as he would have liked. The tendon in his neck kept flexing.

'You've brought a lot of memories back for me, Evelyn. I've been reliving them all afternoon.'

'Don't you have anything better to do?'

He laughed, perhaps recalling how they had joshed all those years ago. 'Apparently not!' His eyes were full of warmth for her – the warmth that speaks of a disarming narrowing of the distance between the past and now. 'Actually, the older I'm getting, the more I tend to think about days gone by.'

'You're a bit too young to be doing the "in the olden days" thing, aren't you?'

'You're right. Sad, isn't it?'

She wasn't sure if he was teasing. He would be in his mid-forties now. He was five years older than she was. Turning forty had been a wrench for Evelyn. Her thirties had blitzed by, and perhaps for the first time she had truly taken stock of her life. *I'll probably never bear children. We'll probably never adopt. I'm sure we'll stay together forever if we've made it this far. It's unlikely I'll ever fall in love again.* The last one had been a rogue thought, and she had wondered why it had even entered her head.

'Anita and Billy were only married for three years, you know. I knew it wouldn't last,' he said.

Eddy had been Billy's best man. Anita was friends with Evelyn's friend Elizabeth. 'I wasn't even supposed to be there!' Evelyn found herself thinking back. It was as fresh as yesterday. 'If Elizabeth's boyfriend hadn't run off with someone else, I wouldn't have been dragged along in his place, and you and I would never have met.' The past was hurtling back to her, details slightly softened by that one incandescent memory of how bowled over by him she had been.

'Why did you do it?' he asked.

'Go to the wedding?' She knew he didn't mean that.

'Stand me up.'

'Eddy . . .' It was so unsettling to find herself having to explain the unexplainable all these years later. She had often grappled with it: with *why*. 'I don't quite know how to say this,' she said, honestly. 'When I met you – that night – I was leaving for London exactly one week later. Through the very generous referral of a total stranger, I had a flat set up, and I'd paid a deposit on the rent. I had a job! When you asked me out, I should have just told you that, but in the moment, everything was so magical I couldn't have it end on that note. You had made such an impression on me. I didn't want to say goodbye.'

She was surprised to find herself becoming ruffled, slightly short of breath. She had time-travelled back to twenty years ago. She could recall the tug of her dilemma as though she was in the grip of it right now. 'But then leading up to it . . . I just thought, there's no point. It was the craziest idea for us to see one another again. I needed so badly to leave. Back then, and I know it sounds dramatic, I wanted to be so much more than there was opportunity for – even though, to be honest, I didn't know what the hell that something was. So I just thought, why on earth would I risk going out with someone who . . .'

'Might make you want to stay?'

'Please don't look at me like that.' She shielded her eyes, briefly. She just remembered thinking, *What if I fall in love with him? I can't fall in love with him because I'm leaving. I'm twenty years old and my future can't be here, for the simple reason that I've already decided it won't be!* How many times had she looked back over the years and been completely unable to identify with the girl who had thought that way?

'I went back to your house a second time, you know. I knew that business of you having to work late was a lie. Your mother told me you'd moved to London. I'm sure she could tell by my reaction that you weren't just a passing fancy for me. I think your mother was quite intuitive.'

Evelyn hadn't known this. Her secretive mother had never said.

'I'm not proud I stood you up, Eddy. I've never done that once I've made a promise. It was a horrid thing to do.'

'So I was just the unlucky one, eh?'

He might have been faking hurt feelings, but perhaps that was wishful thinking; Evelyn saw genuine regret in his eyes, and she was a little dumbfounded by it. 'It was twenty years ago, Eddy.'

'I was devastated when I knocked on your door and you weren't there. I was surprised I could be so bothered about it, actually. And it was more than just a pride thing. It was because I'd expected better of you – of the situation. I thought meeting me had left you feeling the same way it had left me. I remember dancing with you and thinking, *Right at this moment, looking at this girl, this could be what holding* The One *feels like*. That's how big of an impression you made on me, Evelyn.'

'You'd probably just drunk too much.'

He looked neither disappointed nor surprised that she was making light of it, just reflective. 'Anita said you were always a bit uppity and high on yourself.'

Evelyn's jaw dropped. 'What? How dare she? She didn't even know me! I'd never even met her until her wedding day!'

His serious face burst into a smile.

'You're teasing me!'

'I am.'

'Good heavens, you haven't changed one iota!' He was exactly the same Eddy.

'Yup, I bet you left for your nice life in London, and you never even gave me a second thought!'

She extended him one of her withering blinks. 'Actually, when I left, I had no idea what sort of life I was leaving for. I just wanted to get away from here at the time; that was all I'd ever wanted for some insane reason – to not have a life like my mother's, and like that of every other woman I saw. Though right now, I've no idea what was exactly wrong with it. But can we please stop trying to make me feel bad? It's becoming tiring.'

'I was only getting started.' Again, that smile.

'And if you must know, I didn't leave without a backward glance. I had some serious misgivings. I think I had a very strong sense that, in order to go off and pursue what I thought I wanted, I was walking away from something . . .' She couldn't find the right word. Something monumental. Someone who perhaps only came your way once. 'I suppose right when I thought I'd been everywhere, seen everything and done everything in my home town, you came along and you were different to the rest. And strange as it was, I never really knew you, yet I felt the loss of you as I was leaving. And I went on feeling it for a long time after I left.'

She remembered sitting on the train thinking, *Why am I not exhilarated about what's ahead? Why am I thinking of what might have been? Why is it that I want to pluck him up and take him out of the North East? Why is it that I can't?* And, finally: *Why am I so damned messed up?*

'But you obviously found what you were looking for, because you never came back.'

She wondered if he were referencing Mark now, if he were remembering him from that one time at the Mayfair.

She pulled her tangerine cotton cardigan tighter across her chest. He seemed to notice her every move. His eyes kept casting over her hair. She had taken it out of its ponytail earlier, and it hung freely around her shoulders. She wondered if he was faithful, if he was still attracted to his wife, what kind of husband he'd have made.

'So you're really going to sell this place?' he asked, and she was relieved he'd changed the topic.

'I don't think I have much choice.'

'You don't sound too enthusiastic.' His eyes circled her face like a hummingbird around a petunia.

'I don't know. I've always loved Holy Island. It's such a part of me. Of course, I didn't know that until I left. I sometimes think my heart will break to see the home where I grew up go.'

She remembered those trips back here in the early days of her marriage, when she had an inkling that she wasn't as happy as a new bride ought to have been. Being here made London and Mark feel like another life. And it always saddened her that she missed neither in the way that she believed she should have. She and Mark had met six months after she had arrived in London. She had always imagined she'd have had a few more dalliances first. And yet Mark had qualities she could never have hoped to find in one person. While she was living alongside him, she could never make sense of her discontent, especially given that she had a privileged life, one that would have been unattainable for most girls of her background, and it was in Evelyn's nature to be grateful. Plus, she loved him. Yet as soon as she came home, she saw it straightforwardly. She had gone to London not really knowing where life would take her. But somehow she had arrived too quickly, and found out too soon.

'Don't grieve for a house, Evelyn. It's just a structure. The really important stuff is locked away in here.' He tapped his temples. 'You carry this with you always . . . If you're happy with your life, it's best to let your past stay in the past and just treasure it from a healthy distance.'

Her brows pulled together. 'This is making me sad.'

'Don't be sad. You have great memories, and nothing can take them away. And you're lucky, you know. That's more than many people have.'

She was touched by his words. Meeting his eyes, she registered the unsteady pencil line around the possibility of his having been The One, if only she had stayed. 'Perhaps we would have hated one another if we had gone on that date,' she said.

'We wouldn't have. But that's in the past now.'

She looked around at the garden, and the sudden weight of inexplicable regret dragged down the corners of her mouth. 'Lindisfarne is the most magical place on earth. I'm torn between bursting to tell everyone about it and desperately wanting to keep it secret.' Tears came to her eyes. 'Sometimes, I wish the tide would close us off permanently from the rest of the world and I'd be captive here, even though as a young woman that used to be one of my worst nightmares!'

'You'd eventually wither and die, or start swimming and drown. Then your children would be bereft.'

'I don't have children.'

'The earl, then.'

They looked at one another again. The casual way he made reference to Mark made her remember something. He was someone else's husband. She was someone else's wife.

'You probably need to get off home now,' she said.

'You mean you want me to get off home now.'

'Maybe.'

He studied her for a moment, then started walking to the garden gate, seeming to naturally assume she would follow, and she did.

It didn't feel like it was just today that they had met again, that today they had talked for the first time in twenty years. There was an ease between them, an ease that you wouldn't have thought could be there, but it was. 'My dad grew those in his greenhouse.' She pointed to three or four mounds of frothy pink-and-white bell-head fuchsia by the gate. 'When he died, Mam planted them here, not really expecting they'd take off, but they did. I think my dad must have been giving her green thumbs from heaven.'

He bent down beside one of the bushes of red and purple ones, and carefully held a flower head, and the memory of his hands came back to her with a rush. 'These are called Lady's Eardrops because of the shape. But some say they resemble a ballerina. See, the stamen look like the legs of a dancer, while the petals are the dancer's tutu.' He inadvertently glanced over her legs, and it sent a small charge through her. She remembered how desperately she'd wanted to sleep with him, but she was a nice girl and it had felt like the wrong way to behave.

'You're right.' She gazed at the small and vibrant flower in his upturned palm. 'It really does look like a ballerina.' She pulled her eyes away from his hand.

At the gate, he hesitated. 'So, Countess of Lindisfarne, if you're planning on doing this place up, I could help. I'm quite handy.'

'I'm just going to paint it. Nothing huge.'

'I'm great with a paintbrush.'

'I can't ask you to do that.'

'You didn't. I volunteered. I could even start tomorrow, if we want.'

We want? She almost laughed. 'Don't you have other gardens to do?'

'It's going to rain.'

'Is it?' She looked up, doubtfully, at a bright blue sky.

'I'm going to pray for it.'

She did laugh now. His boldness was still there, and it was refreshing. She experienced a flash of herself as that twenty-year-old woman again. That's what was missing from her marriage: Mark no longer wooed her. He no longer thought he had to, or that it mattered. He would probably have never guessed that she even missed it.

Turn him down, she was thinking. *Or no good will come of this.* But she had reached a precipice and was catching herself in the act of jumping off into thin air. She would either soar and fly, or crash and burn. But either way, the movement was exhilarating. 'Well, I could certainly use the help . . .'

He studied her for a moment as though he might back out, then said, 'Tomorrow then?'

Pressuring her like this made her slightly delirious. She could almost feel her mother looking on, with bated breath, saying, *See! Second chances . . .* 'Tomorrow,' she said.

He reached to shake her hand. It was an oddly formal gesture. She registered the strong clasp of his fingers around hers. And, as she looked into his eyes, she suddenly possessed a discomfiting perspective on herself. Her life felt like a grand mansion built without any proper foundations. It could crumble with the right little earthquake.

TEN

Alice

Our relationship started like a runaway train, with no brakes and no one driving.

There was nothing particularly original about it. We met in one of Newcastle's busy, uber-trendy cocktail bars. I was with Sally, who rarely got a night out because she worked unsociable hours and was a parent.

'Two o'clock.' Sally nudged me as we clung to our wine glasses. We had just been lamenting the coincidence of how, over dinner two hours previously, we'd witnessed my ex – Colin, who couldn't commit – proposing, on his knees, complete with diamond and spellbound onlookers. Colin, who actually shed tears when he told me how much he loved me but how fervently against the idea of marriage he was. Fortunately, the girl had looked mortified.

My eyes moved to two o'clock. There was a dark-haired guy in a suit trying to order a drink. He was thrusting a hand into the air in that assertive way only a very tall person can pull off, and which comes across to everyone else as slightly obnoxious. I could only see him from the side. A fine head of hair. Nice build. A thatch of white shirt-cuff protruding from his jacket's sleeve.

Spotting him somehow dampened sound. I suddenly seemed to bloom like a flower. As though someone had just given me the right combination of sun, wind, warmth and water. As I studied him, time slowed to footpace. And then, almost as if he felt the pull of my eyes, he turned around. And even though the room was crowded, and there were so many other faces he could have looked at, it was mine he homed right in on. I gave a small, involuntary smile. He responded likewise, looking charmed. We were held there, like wind-hovering birds, until I was the first to look away.

I don't really know when my faith in men went out of the window. Perhaps I'd never had much, so I'd managed to attract ones whose shitty behaviour wouldn't fail to disappoint. I may have learnt this from my mother who, despite having Alan as a wonderful partner for so many years, lumped all men in with my true father, whose heinous crimes were too numerous to identify. It's not as though I ever had the sort of unrealistic expectations my single friends always harboured. If he was intelligent, kind, somewhat fun, with a good sense of humour, if he had one feature that pleased my eye every time I looked at his face – that could be enough to fall in love with. But still, it had never really happened.

'He's handsome,' I said to Sally. But the weight of another possible new start was just too much. 'I can't do it again, though. It's over for me, Sally. I can't handle being let down any more. I can't put my mind or my body through one more traumatic break-up.' The image of Colin proposing had wounded me more than I was ever going to let on. Maybe he hadn't loved me enough to want to marry me, because I wasn't worthy of being loved. 'I honestly think I'm destined to be alone. In fact, I'm looking forward to it. Alone doesn't mean lonely. I'm going to chant that every day, in my celibate, Buddhist monk's temple.'

'Here he comes,' Sally said.

'Who?'

'Him.'

'No!'

'Yes.'

'Oh God.' I clapped both hands over my face. 'Alone doesn't mean I'm lonely!'

Sally chuckled. 'You are so full of shit!'

'Please, please, make him go away! Let him meet someone else on the way over here. Please.'

'Ah! Shoot! He's gone. Girlfriend! False alarm.'

I swung around, gutted, to look for the girlfriend. And when I did, there was Justin right behind me, grinning madly. He was even more attractive up close. Not boringly handsome. Rather beast-like and full of character, with kindness twinkling in those remarkable blue-green eyes. I gave Sally a glance that said, *Why can I never stick to my guns?*

'Listen,' he said. 'I don't do this chatting up in bars business very well, so fortunately you're going to be spared my grisly attempt at hitting on you. Thing is, I don't have a lot of time – I have to go back to work – but I wondered if you might go out to dinner with me?' He was shouting over the music. His eyes searched my face, and were brimming with expectancy. 'I was thinking some place with good old-fashioned seats to sit on, where we can talk like civilised adults instead of having to shout at one another.'

He was asking me out to dinner before he'd even asked my name. And he didn't act like he thought that was in any way weird. 'Are you serious?' I said.

He held my eyes, steadfastly. 'Why would I be anything less?' The whiteness of his shirt against the darkness of his skin under these lights was bedazzling. *No,* I thought. *He is bedazzling!*

'You want me to go out to dinner with you – a perfect stranger? What makes you think that would be a good idea?'

There was a hint of a cheeky smile now. 'I never said I was perfect. In fact, far from it.'

I had to laugh.

He leant in slightly; I could feel the warmth of his breath on my ear, though it didn't seem like a *move*. He didn't seem like a player in the slightest. 'I've just seen you across a crowded room . . . Your face has pretty much just taken my breath away. But sadly, I have to leave. And I don't want to walk out thinking I won't see you again.'

'But you just ordered drinks?'

'For friends.' He nodded to a group of men. 'They don't have anti-social jobs like I do.'

He was waiting for my answer. Despite the madness of it, I said, 'Okay.'

A slight note of triumph and pleasure lit up his face. He suggested the place, date, time. Then he repeated it, uncertainly, and I thought, *No, he's definitely not a player*. More like slightly nerdy. The guy who peaked late.

His top button was undone, and his red tie had been yanked halfway down his chest. 'You're not going to stand me up, are you?' He cocked me a sideways, playful glance but I could tell he was actually quite serious.

'No . . . That's generally not what I do.'

'Promise?' He placed a hand on his heart. 'Because my fragile self-esteem will never be able to handle it, if you do.'

I laughed. 'I don't believe that for one minute!'

'It's true. But, more to the point, I'll have to sit there on my own and wonder, *What if . . . ?*'

He looked at me as though all the *What Ifs* were flickering there, waiting to be known. As though he were silently saying, *Be as excited as I am about it.*

I couldn't quite believe he'd said such a lovely thing. I stared at him and noticed the tiny scar above his top lip. 'I'll be there,' I said.

A slightly roguish smile spread across his face this time, sending deep lines fanning around his eyes. Maybe he wasn't such a nerd after all. Hmm. We would see . . .

'Tuesday, then?' he said.

'Tuesday,' I repeated.

I'd reckoned it was 50–50 that he would show up. But, then again, that was generally about as positive as I got when it came to dates. He studied me long and hard from across the table. The hostess had considered the floor plan, then seated us in a conspicuously romantic corner, leaving us with a slightly envious and knowing smile.

He had the most amazingly healthy eyes: blue-green with ultra-clear whites. Stunning eyes.

'What would you like to drink?' he asked, right off the bat. 'Do you normally like a cocktail first, or do you want to go straight to wine? And a bottle, or by glass?' He reached for the wine list. The way he fumbled with it made me think perhaps he had been honest when he said he didn't do the chatting up thing/dating thing very well. Plus, he wore a well-ironed, checked shirt with a button-down collar, and his hair looked slightly over-combed. The nerd had resurfaced. I must have been looking at him oddly, because he suddenly looked up, studied my face, and smiled, then said a suspicious, 'What?' I grinned. He did too now, fully.

'Nothing!' I sat back in the chair, crossed my arms and studied him, as if I were a doctor and he my patient.

He laughed a little, nervously, which amused me, too.

'I think we would be insane to skip cocktails and proceed to wine,' I said.

'My thoughts exactly.' He looked relieved to put down the wine list.

We ordered two Hendrick's martinis. 'Do you normally ask women out on dates before you've even said hello to them?' Our eyes did a little dance over the rims.

'Never,' he said. 'I've actually never done that before. But, as they say, life's short, isn't it? Once you want to make something happen, you've got to just go for it. Or it never does. Or someone else will . . .' The waitress set down a little antipasti plate of cheeses and ham. He reached for a toothpick, and I noted his nice square fingernails and strong hands.

I liked his reply. The *someone else will* part. It felt significant.

'Besides, as I said, you're a very attractive woman. And I sensed you're intelligent right away because there's, you know, a brightness in your eyes. They're very expressive eyes, actually . . .' He held them now, as though they had the power to stop all thought. 'Plus, you were dressed nicely: classy, like you're an individual rather than a sheep. And your friend looked normal, which is always a good sign. And you weren't overly intoxicated. Women these days are nearly always pissed, I find.'

'That's it, then? I'm attractive and I don't seem to be wasted?'

'You're mocking me now.' He tut-tutted, and passed me the bread basket. 'I was trying to pay you a compliment.'

I watched him lightly butter his bread, and found myself inwardly smiling. 'You paid several.'

'Anyway,' he said. 'To go back to what you asked me . . . To be honest, I can't really say I date all that much. What with the fact that I'm married to my work . . .' He held up his hands in surrender. 'As I said, I've actually never done anything as crazy as this before, and I honestly never expected you'd say yes. But you did. So that was a lucky strike.'

I found myself being so awake to him, so in tune. He was different. Nice different. I felt oddly at ease with him and trusting of him, which was a novel feeling for me. 'So you'll be doing it all the time now? I'll have started a trend?' I wasn't sure how I was going to manage to eat; there were tiny birds' wings in my stomach.

'I hope not. That would spoil the coolness of this. Wouldn't it?'

He ordered us wine once we'd perused the menu, and I liked that he asked if I wanted to choose it, or if he should. Over dinner, our conversation was surprisingly unstoppable: a crash course in what we did for a living, where we had grown up, our friends. We talked about music, TV, royalty, anorexic actresses, his recent trip to Machu Picchu, my desire to go on an African safari if it weren't for the fact that I was terrified of having to get all those vaccinations. I told him how my job had brought me to Newcastle from Stockport. Justin said he'd grown up in a council house in Durham, then had gone to read Law at Oxford, but he had left after the first year to travel the world. 'I just hated the routine and demands of Uni. I realised I'd gone there before I was really ready.'

'So you walked out of Oxford?' Was he mad?

'Well, yes. But I went back.' After a doubting look, he said, 'I was always going to go back, Alice.'

The way he casually said my name felt unexpectedly familiar and flattering. He grew on me in leaps and bounds, just with that one tiny little thing.

All was going swimmingly until he asked my age. 'Why are you asking me that?' I replied, then joked about how you never ask a lady her age.

He looked slightly wrong-footed for a moment. 'I don't know why I asked,' he said. 'I didn't realise it was such a bad question.'

I hated that I'd been touchy. 'It's not. I'm thirty-four.'

'Well,' he said, appearing genuinely surprised. 'I'd have guessed no more than late twenties . . . And you want to have kids, I assume?'

The waitress was fussing around us, and I was certain she heard that, so I held back until she left. 'Yes. I think I do. What about you?'

'Of course. I think my life will be in danger of becoming a bit self-centred if I don't. Not that it would be necessarily any bad thing to just have to please yourself until the end of your days. But I think a child would add a lot. I'd like to have something of myself passed on . . . The good parts, anyway. I think I have a lot to teach a child. I mean, I like to believe that.'

He was disarmingly frank. I wondered if he was disappointed that I was a little bit older, then I berated myself for my insecure thinking.

Over dessert and Armagnac, I learnt that his father had died when Justin was only eleven. He was a doctor. 'My mother was lost without him, and seemed to remarry at breakneck speed. Charlie, my stepfather, was a bastard. He wanted my mother, of course, but I was in the way. He always seemed to have it in for me. Never cheered for my successes. Always seeming to be looking for me to fail . . .' He went off, seeing distant memories in close-up. I wondered if he always talked so intimately to people he didn't really know. 'He was a belittling, criticising prick, to be honest.' He must have recognised that he was turning the conversation dark. He launched a smile. 'Other than that, he was fabulous.'

'That must have been rough, losing your dad so young.'

'For a boy of that age, it's probably the most defining thing that can happen to him. I never quite got over it.'

His words, his face, when he spoke of his father, touched me.

'I had a great stepdad,' I told him. 'I was lucky, I suppose. I was only about seven when he came into my life. He was a decade older than my mum. He'd really wanted a family, my mother said, but it hadn't happened for him. So he took to me wholeheartedly. I couldn't have asked for more.'

Justin listened intently. 'What about your real father?'

'Oh . . . I don't know all that much.' This topic hadn't come up in a long time. 'He wasn't a good person. He left us when I was little. I don't think my mother ever forgave him.'

'But she had a happy life with your stepfather? Was she in love with him?'

I thought about this. 'Hmm . . . How do I know if she was or she wasn't? I think she loved him in a quiet way – if that makes sense. I think she'd loved my real father in a more heartbreaking way. At least, I'm guessing.'

'Did you never want to ask him to find out?'

I frowned. 'My real father?'

'Yes. Didn't you want to know more about him?'

It took me a moment to reply. 'Gosh, I don't know! There was a time when, yes, I was curious. When I was younger. But my mother couldn't bear him mentioned . . . He had a lot of women. You know . . . affairs. I think he was a bit of a drinker, too . . . Besides, once you get a bit older, you see things more objectively. He abandoned us when I was little. He never once tried to see me. So I don't know why I would miss someone like that, or why I would want to try to find him.'

I didn't say how angry I'd been at my mother for keeping so much back. How the questions had been undercut the moment I had brought them up. How, eventually, it was easier to just stop asking them.

Justin was scrutinising me. He was clearly thoroughly engaged by the topic. I just wanted it to end. 'But don't you want to know what his reasons were? Aren't you curious to know if you've got half-siblings out there? You might have a whole other family. And you know, blood is blood.'

'Is it?' There had been a time when I'd wondered if I might have had a half-sister or brother. I was once mistaken for someone else in town, when I was about fourteen. The person said, 'I think you must have a twin!' It had sparked thoughts. But I was a child. My mother would never have tolerated that conversation.

'But his reasons . . .' Justin prompted. 'Weren't you curious?'

'I'm not sure reasons really matter, do they?' I was tired of this, and turning defensive. 'He did what he did. That's fine. It was his choice. We all make choices . . . But Alan was the one who was there for me. He wasn't my blood father, but it never made a difference to me. I mean, how can I be expected to care about somebody who didn't care about me? You reap what you sow in this life.'

'I believe that,' he said. 'But, personally, I'd have wanted to know all the facts first.'

The air seemed to go out of our balloon. How quickly just one topic and a difference of opinion could dispel all optimism. This was all heavier than any first-date conversation I'd ever known. Justin had delved into territory that had never been touched by all my past boyfriends put together. I wasn't sure that he was aware, though. He just went on studying me, contemplating me, his chin resting on his upturned hand.

'I feel like you're judging me,' I found myself saying. 'Like you've come here with an agenda, and I'm not measuring up.' As the words came out, I regretted them. It was the wine. I was feeling loose and brave. He had hit a nerve, and now I wanted to punish him for it.

His pupils flickered with mild amusement. 'Agenda? Like what? Tell me.'

'I don't know. You're a bit personal and a bit intense.' Stupidly, I felt like crying. I tried to stare across the room, at the door, willing the feeling to go away. If I cried, he was going to think I was mental.

'Justin,' he addressed himself after a good pause. 'Is Alice a bit pissed off with you for some reason?'

It was playfully done. It made me smile. He had chosen to make light of it. I was never more grateful. 'I'm not pissed off with you, Justin. I just don't know what to make of you. What you want.'

What he wanted? It sounded so tart and un-charming. Good Lord – why did we have to get on to the topic of babies and families? I was convinced I'd never set eyes on him again.

But suddenly, I caught something in his eyes. It was a look of quietly burgeoning adoration. 'Well, Alice, I, on the other hand, know exactly what to make of you . . .'

He was imploring me to smile, to save this. 'Let me guess,' I said. '*Alice, you're a cynical, un-trusting, nearly over-the-hill woman who bears little sentimentality for family, and if it weren't for that, you'd be perfect?*'

He laughed now. 'Close-ish. But no. What I was going to say was, you're a lovely, multi-layered girl. Well . . . woman. You're interesting to talk to. In fact, I've had a better time with you tonight than I can remember having with anybody in quite a long time . . . You're real and you're honest, and you're a good person, I can tell . . . And, well, to be truthful, I wasn't really expecting this . . .' He shook his head as though rendered speechless. 'I'm impressed, Alice. I'm very pleased we met. And if I say much more, it'll probably spoil things . . .'

I was completely taken aback – by his sincerity, by the look on his face, by everything. He'd stopped me from having a meltdown. I was suddenly fonder of him and felt more affinity for him than anyone should have a right to, considering we were strangers until a couple of hours ago.

'Justin MacFarlane . . .' He addressed himself again, which made me grin because it was a strange quirk of his, and it had only been a few hours, but I was already getting an idea of his quirks. 'You don't meet girls like this one every day. So the pressure is on to ensure you don't say something to put her off you – like grill her about her family and put her on the spot.'

'Multi-layered, you said?' It just came back to me. 'Like I'm a German pastry.'

His face lit up. 'It's another compliment. I'm clearly crap at giving them.'

Our eyes did a little dance again. I wondered what it would be like to kiss him. If he would want a debate on that topic first, too! Or if he would say, *Justin MacFarlane, do you think this is the right time to kiss her?* As I looked at his face, I pictured it. That electric rush when his face would move in and my eyes would involuntarily close. And then I would feel his lips, the slightly fuller bottom one, and the top one with the small vertical scar that lined up with his right eye tooth. I wondered how he got it, and if I would be able to feel it with my tongue.

He was watching me, full of suspense. I didn't know what to say; didn't know how to not disappoint him. Perhaps because I always tried to make such a good impression with men, I decided that, this time, I'd just be myself, and see what happened. 'Justin, I'm going to be honest. I'm caught in this strange place of wanting more of you, yet feeling like I've had enough. You're not like anyone I've ever met. And I don't know if this is a good thing or a not-so-good thing. Or maybe it's just a new thing.'

He went on watching me. His expression didn't change. 'Well,' he said, after a while. 'Why don't we leave it at, *It's just a new thing*? I think that sounds more promising.'

When he walked me home, he pressed a lengthy, gentle kiss on my cheek. At this point, I had zero idea if I would ever see him again. Perhaps he was just being gracious. It might well just go down as the weirdest 'first and only' date in history. Yet even though the thought of inviting him in for a passionate tumble was appealing, it felt like the fastest way to ruin possibility.

'How did you get that scar?' I pointed to his top lip.

He suddenly looked besieged by me, as though he'd bestowed much greater significance on the question than I had intended. He touched his lip. 'I fell on some glass when I was a little boy.'

'Aw! I suppose your dad must have made you all better, though?'

'He did, actually.' He looked wistful suddenly. 'I remember him telling me it was okay to cry, because I had a thing about not crying back then, apparently. And that was all it took. As soon as he said that, I bawled my eyes out, because deep down it hurt like hell.' He smiled deeply into my eyes. Words petered away, and we were held there in the suspenseful, wondrous liveliness of our chemistry, of what would happen next.

After a moment or two, he said, 'Alice, I feel like I should be coming on to you in a seriously big way . . . I'm running a bit fast and loose with you.'

'But you're just not that into me?'

'No, I am definitely that into you. But my instincts are telling me to slow down or I'll spoil it.' He kissed my cheek again, fractionally closer to my lips this time, then when I opened my mouth to speak – to tell him those had been my thoughts exactly – he popped a kiss there. It was neither brief nor prolonged. But I would think about it so many times after, relive the loose and lovely choreography of it.

'So even though I might kick myself later,' he said, 'I think I'm just going to follow my instincts.'

He tucked a strand of hair behind my ear, and I was aware of everything, every last detail, as all this played out – a heightening of my senses. 'Goodnight, Alice,' he said. 'And if you can stand having me do it, I'll ring you some time tomorrow when I'm at work and we'll formulate our next plan of attack.'

'Don't say it if you don't mean it.' I was only half teasing.

'I never say anything I don't mean,' he said.

ELEVEN

His face takes up half of my computer monitor. His mugshot from the 'Partners' page of his law firm's website. His eyes are locked into mine. I can't stop staring at them. The real Justin is nothing like this photo, which has an imperturbable, even slightly slick, quality to it – something about his smile. I told him to change the picture. Of course, he completely disagreed, and said he had bigger things than that to worry about.

The gallery was quiet today. I click off the Internet and delete my history – evidence of my pathological time-wasting. I have visited this page too often today. I am addicted to his face. Because it's after 5 p.m., I'm able to wander guilt-free into the Hopper/Wyeth room to visit my solitary soulmates.

I am scarcely in there ten minutes when I hear my name. When I swing around, Evelyn is walking toward me, all smiles.

'Maybe I need to find you a job here!' I greet her with a kiss, which feels surprisingly natural to me.

'I take the bus into town three times a week. I volunteer at the charity shop on Monday afternoons. There's only so much looking in shops that a person can do. So I'm taking the opportunity to come and see Christina while she's still here.' She sits on the bench beside me, opposite Christina.

'How are the fellows?' I ask. She's impeccably dressed in a lemon, knee-length coat – the kind a young Newcastle reveller with an evolved sense of style would wear, rather than the Queen.

'No worse, I suppose.' She sounds defeated, and I am already able to recognise that this is a little unusual for Evelyn.

'How's Eddy? Do you think he remembers his visit here and how he spoke about Christina and her house?'

She shrugs her tiny, square shoulders. 'I'd like to think it means progress. Or, at the very least, that he takes something comforting away from it. Something that lives in him longer than we might believe.'

'You want it to be more than just a moment.'

Sometimes, the way she looks at me, I think I've said the wrong thing.

'You shouldn't minimise moments, Alice. Our whole life is made up of them. It shouldn't always be the big, dramatic events that make you sit up and take notice. The value of your life is in all the unexceptional details.' She looks at the painting of Christina staring longingly at her home. 'Christina knows that.'

I find it fascinating how she talks about Christina as though she were real. But then again, Christina had lived. She had been an ordinary person whose conflict – perhaps prosaic at that – just happened to be captured here in oil paint for eternity.

'The object of her heartbreak,' Evelyn says.

I stare at the one clump of mascara that's gluing up some of her eyelashes. 'You mean Christina's house? I've never imagined a house could break someone's heart. It's usually a man, isn't it?'

I am back in the heat of Evelyn's scrutiny again. I wonder if she always looks at people too deeply and for too long.

Then she glances down at my wedding ring hand, at the simple platinum band. 'I hope you have a good man in your life. I hope you got it right the first time. Because we all want that, don't we? Time advances, we have opportunities for better education, better jobs, a greater say in national politics, yet the love of the right man is still the thing we want more than anything else, even though we're supposed to be more self-sufficient than that.' Her eyes move swiftly back to the painting, as though she had never made that brief foray into personal territory.

'And if I haven't got it right the first time?' The image of Justin's smile on that website blazes in my mind again.

'You'll survive,' she says. 'We all do. Though it often doesn't feel like a very nice way to be living. We only realise that surviving is an achievement once we're old. When we're young, we feel we were meant for more obvious triumphs.'

'Did you get it right the first time, Evelyn?' I wonder why it is that I find myself so curious about her.

For a moment, I'm sure she's not going to answer. She dips into her bag and pulls out a white cotton handkerchief with pink embroidered edges, then just holds it, tightly, in her slightly trembling left hand. 'That's such a very difficult question. To say I didn't would be desperately unfair to someone I loved. And in a way, it wouldn't even be true.' She meets my eyes, steadily. 'There are so many different aspects to love that render it all so very complicated. And sometimes you are just simply . . . torn.'

I think about this. The words *for everyone's sake* come back to me. I stare at her miraculously unblemished little white hand holding the pretty handkerchief.

'You know what I discovered a very long time ago?' Evelyn's eyes have shifted to Christina again.

I am aware of how surprisingly keen I am to hear what Evelyn has discovered.

'If you want to be in love, you have to accept that you run the risk of having your heart broken in such a way that it's almost impossible to mend. Some of us can live quite happily without that wretched experience. But some of us can't. We have to put ourselves through it to feel we're alive. We thrive in the extremes of unparalleled joy and abject misery. What we can't much tolerate is the middle ground.'

Evelyn looks distantly across the room, in unfinished thought. 'I suppose what I'm saying to you is you have to take your love story, and you have to take how it ends, too. It's called life.'

I know she isn't talking about me, per se, but she might as well be. 'Did you have a love story that ended, Evelyn?' I'm fairly certain she was talking about Eddy.

Evelyn doesn't answer. I feel bad. Perhaps I shouldn't have tried to force intimacy.

'I don't know,' she says, at last. 'I have a story, and it's definitely about love. But in some ways it hasn't ended yet.'

'Interesting,' I say.

She looks in her bag for something, and pulls out a small Polaroid. She hands it to me.

'Good heavens! I haven't seen one of these in years!' I can't help but smile at the black-and-white image with its thick white border. 'What is it?' I ask. The picture quality is poor.

'Christina's house.'

I wonder if Evelyn is just one of those people who enjoys being mysterious. But for a moment I believe it might be Christina's farmhouse, that Evelyn has some strange connection to the painting, or to Wyeth. Perhaps she's going to say she'd been Wyeth's lover, or Christina's cousin, or that she had lived there, in Cushing, Maine, not far from the weather-beaten farmhouse in the middle of nowhere. In my longing to believe something, I might be inclined to believe anything.

But it isn't Christina's house, though there's a similarity in the atmosphere and content of the two images. It's a picture of a small stone cottage with a blue front door. In the background, at the top of the attractive garden, a slightly built girl with long, dark hair stands casually and unsmilingly, with her hands behind her back.

'Is that you, Evelyn?' Like Christina, the girl has a woeful aura about her. 'It is you, isn't it?' I'm so touched and flattered she would show me this! I can't help but think, *Ah, maybe one day I'll be like Evelyn – alone and desperate for someone to tell a hand-me-down story to.* 'Is it where you lived, Evelyn, before you moved away? Where you grew up?'

'How did you know I moved away?' Her cat-like green eyes widen in amazement.

'Just the way you look. The way you speak. Everything about you says you don't really belong here.'

'But I do! I very much belong here! I always did. Even when I left here, I was pulled back. Just like Christina. The way she's staring at that house – I can fully relate to that feeling, because that has been me my entire life!'

She looks so zealous. I hope I haven't upset her.

'Do you ever feel highly nostalgic for your upbringing, for things gone?' she asks. 'Nostalgic to the point where you can barely recover from the ache?'

I realise I'm not required to answer.

'*Nostos. Algia.* Means *homecoming. Pain* and *suffering.* Some doctors believe nostalgia is a neurological disease. Did you know that? You see, we long to go back, but we can't because the past didn't actually exist. It's only a composite of what we remember, and, of course, it's always the "feel-good" memories we hang on to. We filter out the negative ones.' She nods briefly to the painting. 'That's what Christina is doing.'

'Where was your picture taken, Evelyn?' I ask her.

'Holy Island, where I grew up. Back then, I'd decided living on a tidal island was the singular most depressing thing on earth. So I moved to the part of the country that Northerners love to hate.' She smiles. 'I was a journalist for a publication in London. Do you know a magazine called *Cosmopolitan*?'

I place a hand on my chest. 'Good heavens! You wrote for *Cosmo*?'

'Yes. When it first launched in the UK. In 1972.'

'That must have been so exciting, and glamorous! Impressive back then, too.'

'I wrote a book as well. A novel.'

'You wrote a novel? Seriously? Was it published? What was it about?' This woman is an endless revelation.

'Of course it was published!' Evelyn seems surprised by my surprise. 'It was about, well, let's just say, moral dilemmas and the difficult choices we make for love. Maybe you will read it one day, if I ever find the one remaining copy.'

I'm flattered she implies our acquaintanceship may have longevity. 'You're an intriguing lady, Evelyn. I'd absolutely love to read your book.' I briefly touch her hand. 'Do you ever think that sometimes you have to meet people for a reason?'

Evelyn seems beguiled by me again. 'I do. Everything happens for a reason. It's not a cliché, I can promise.'

I smile. 'I like that idea.'

'But that doesn't make it any less painful. Not when you make the wrong choices in your personal life.'

She's on the brink of saying more. I'm dying to say, *What choices that were so wrong?* But I'm not sure I dare go there. Am I finding myself caring about an elderly woman's troubled love story as a distraction? Or is it to gain some kind of corresponding clarity about my own?

I give her back the photograph. 'It's beautiful, Evelyn. I'm very happy you showed it to me.'

'This is where it all started,' she says. She stares at the photograph the way you might study something that's slightly mystifying to you. When she looks up, her lovely green eyes are flooded with tears.

'Where what started, Evelyn?'

I scrutinise her pale face, but she is gone now, gazing off into the distance, like someone searching for that childhood best friend she never forgot. I'm not even sure she's heard me.

Then, after a moment or two, she says, 'Where I met him.'

'Who?' I ask, already feeling I know the answer.

'Eddy,' she says. 'Though I'd met him long before then. I suppose what I'm saying is this garden is where something began that would change the course of our lives, and I don't know that either of us was quite prepared for it.'

She glances at me now. 'I'll tell you, if you'd like.'

'I would love that.'

She looks at her watch. 'But you are probably due to go home now.'

I think of that lonely flat and another long night of my own company ahead. 'No,' I tell her. 'I have nothing to rush home for. Would you like to go get a cup of tea?'

She smiles. 'That's a wonderful idea.'

TWELVE

Evelyn

Holy Island. 1983

He came to her shortly after nine every morning. The weather had answered his prayers; it had poured down virtually every day.

She had chosen sage-green paint for the kitchen, and a rich cream for the rest of the main floor. He would do the detail, then she would apply the roller in long strokes. He gave her lessons in the proper way to do it. Once, his hand rested briefly on her upper back while they assessed her progress, and she registered that it was the first time he'd touched her in twenty years.

They talked a lot about their childhoods, their not especially happy school days, his dreams of playing professional football that ended when his dad lost his job in the pit closures. 'My dreams didn't matter when you couldn't pay the rent. I went into the shipyards as an apprentice, but then, of course, that was another one of the North East's industries that came to a sad end. So I decided to try gardening.' He ended it there. 'Tell me about your life in London,' he said. 'I'd like to try to picture you . . .'

She told him about where they lived, about their country home, the gardens, her writing job, dance classes, friends and their gossipy lunches. She told him how she skied mainly because Mark had insisted she learn, and she went sailing, even though she found nothing enjoyable about being bossed around on a boat. He laughed. 'I can't imagine anybody bossing you around, Evelyn. You're a force to be reckoned with.'

One day, when the sun broke out, she made them a lunch of local speciality crab sandwiches and a beer. They ate in the garden, and talked about dreams again. Nat King Cole sang 'Unforgettable' on the radio. Eddy told her about how he was going after a large contract for the civic green space.

'I thought you were happy with your job the way it is? Don't you employ four men and look after the hospital grounds and a local park?'

'Yes. But my wife wants a better house and more clothes, plus I'd like to give my daughter a better life. I'd hate her to ever have to give up her dreams to support us, like I had to do. I could never let that happen.'

'How old is she?'

'Five.'

'What's her name?'

'April.' He smiled, proud. 'She hates April. No one she knows is called April, you see. She likes to copy things she knows. I keep trying to tell her it's always best to be different, but she's too young to understand. She'll get it one day, I suppose.'

The heads of the fuchsia had been weighted down from all the rain; the flowers had been drooping like exhausted ballerinas. But now hosts of them were glissading and pirouetting in the breeze that blew across the Cheviots, a living painting of pink and white, and purple and red – shoulders low, heads high, in floating arabesques.

'I was telling my wife that I'm working for Mrs Coates' daughter, the one who ran off to London.' He glanced at her boldly. 'Of course, I didn't mention that she was the girl who once stood me up and left me a wilted, withered, broken-hearted, bitter, distrusting mess.'

She tutted at his exaggeration. 'What did your wife say?'

'She asked if you were pretty.'

If only there was a way to stop a rampant blush when you felt it coming. 'What did you tell her?' The stray cat her mother used to feed, who was kept alive now by a kind pool of neighbours, meandered around Evelyn's bare leg. Eddy watched.

'I told her you were. And lovely on the inside, too.' He met her eyes in a way that made her burn.

She blinked. 'You told her that?'

His face burst into a smile. 'No! But I did tell her you were pretty. Because it's just the truth, isn't it? It's the first thing anybody would say about you.'

She held his gaze until the bold intention of his stare made her look away.

By the end of the week, they had done most of the rooms except her bedroom and the bathroom. It wouldn't be long before she would be returning to London. When he came to her the following morning, he said, 'I can't work today. I have to run to Warkworth to deliver some garden plans for a builder. I'm meeting my friend Stanley there at eleven o'clock. He's a plasterer, and I'm trying to set him up with some work. I wondered if you wanted to come for the ride.'

He was wearing a new dark-red shirt. She couldn't look at him for fear of giving away how happy she was to be asked. 'Oh, well . . . How long would we be gone?'

She glanced up and thought she saw a tell-tale flicker of optimism in his eyes. 'Maybe an hour or so to run the errand, then I thought we could drive back slowly and stop somewhere for lunch.'

She couldn't fully breathe. He was oppressively bearing down on her with his obvious hope that she would say yes. 'I'm not sure. I've got so much to do around here . . .' She shook her head in feigned exasperation at all the imaginary tasks that were keeping her from accepting his invitation.

'I think you should forget what you have to do and come with me. To compensate for standing me up all those years ago.'

'All right,' she said. 'You've made me a proposition I can't refuse.' She turned and went back into the house so abruptly the door almost slammed shut in his face. She caught him looking at her through the blinds. He gave her one of his telling, red-blooded smiles.

She sat in his van while he talked to the men. On the radio, Heaven 17 was singing 'Temptation'. She cranked it up, and pretended she wasn't watching him. But it was a huge act. She couldn't *not* watch him. She couldn't stop marvelling at the quirk of fate that had brought them together again. Once or twice, one of the men – Stanley, she imagined – looked past Eddy's head into the vehicle, perhaps wondering who she was, this woman sitting in Eddy's van. She wondered what Eddy would say. The illicit tangle of it thrilled her.

When he climbed back into the vehicle, he threw it into reverse. 'Right then. I'm all yours now . . . My friend wanted to meet you, by the way.' He shot her a glance. 'He's quite fascinated by our story.'

'Do we really have a story?'

He met her eyes again, briefly. 'I quite think we do, Evelyn.'

They drove slowly through the pretty village, past the galleries, boutiques, chocolate shops, bread shops and tea rooms, following carefully behind two young female riders on horseback. Evelyn admired their deportment. When she told him she hadn't driven the coastal route in years, he immediately diverted course. Soon, theirs was the only vehicle on the road, and the sun shone, and Culture Club sang 'Church of the Poison Mind'. She hummed along to it. His fingers tapped the steering wheel, and she stole glances at him.

From time to time, he whistled along, and caught her looking at him and smiled. She was so comfortable with him, she almost forgot that she had spent most of her adult life with another man, that she even had another life.

A person often meets his destiny on the road he took avoiding it. Who had said that? She couldn't stop looking at his hands wrapped around the steering wheel.

He parked the van parallel to the sand dunes, and Evelyn got out, stretched and raised her face to the sun. He had stocked a small box with beer and pieces of cooked chicken. In a separate bag was a stick of fresh bread. 'You knew I would come!'

He grabbed the box and a blanket. 'Hoped.'

They found a spot across the dunes, overlooking the vast, deserted yellow sand beach with Bamburgh Castle behind them. He shook out the blanket, and they cracked open two beers.

'How did you really end up as my mother's gardener?' she asked him. 'I mean, be honest. It's not as though you need the work.'

He lay on his back and stared at the sky. 'There's no big mystery. I've done some projects on Holy Island. I'd bump into her occasionally, and we would chat. Once, when your dad hurt his back, I helped secure their fence after a bad storm took it down . . . Then another time I brought her some peaches . . . She needed help after your dad died. I offered because it really costs me nothing to help people out a little bit.'

He helped secure the fence? Brought her peaches! Her mother hadn't breathed a word of this, and Evelyn didn't know whether she was touched by it or infuriated. 'Did you ever talk about me when you had these cosy little chats of yours?'

'They weren't cosy. But no. Never.'

'Never?' she laughed, slightly. 'Why do I find that hard to believe?'

'I asked if you were well. That's all. She didn't add any more and, well, I didn't stick my nose in beyond that.'

She couldn't believe they'd had some sort of acquaintanceship, if that was the right word. She'd honestly just thought the first and last time her mother had set eyes on him had been that day he had come to take her on the date. 'She liked you,' she said, more in bewilderment than anything else. 'She was really fond of you.' *Eddy this . . . Eddy that . . .* His name, and how often it had come up, echoed with such significance now. How oblivious she'd been.

'Maybe she felt sorry because I was the idiot she had to look in the eye that night and make up a story for. Or maybe she was used to covering for you when it came to boys. Maybe there were loads of teenagers whose hearts Evelyn had broken running all over Holy Island.'

Evelyn remembered being in such a nervous tangle that day. Why had she agreed to go out with him so close to her leaving? Then, once she'd decided it had been the maddest idea in the world, there was no means of contacting him to tell him not to come. She had instructed her mother to say she'd had to work late. Her mother had tussled with her: she wasn't Evelyn's lackey, and it was no way to behave. But in the end, Evelyn had won by going into hiding in her bedroom, leaving her mother with no choice. She had heard the knock on the door, and stood there, in the middle of her room, bone-still and barely breathing, while she listened to his voice. The brevity of the conversation. The clicking of a door closed. With the idea of him leaving, and her never seeing him again, all her misgivings rushed at her; they beat in her, madly, along with her heart. But still she just stood there, paralysed by something she couldn't even explain to herself. When she was certain he wouldn't be looking back, she crossed to the window and peeked from behind the curtains. Seeing him from behind as he walked to his car – his noble head, and confident, manly walk – brought a fresh reminder of all she was letting go. But he was gone now: she felt a tiny note of relief in that. She let the curtain fall away from her finger.

'It wasn't like that,' she said, drawn back to the present, feeling desperately sad. 'There really weren't other boys. The young men, they were always such fast movers. They didn't really have any way about them, any style . . .' She curled up her nose, recognising it was something she'd thought back then, but she wasn't so sure it had been true. 'The ones that liked you just seemed to want to marry you and get you pregnant so you would live a life just like their mother's.' It had been an unkind assumption, and yet here she was still parroting it. She wondered why her mind had been so made up that way, why she'd needed to put down everything about where she'd come from, especially since she'd spent half her life pining to have it all back. 'I wanted something more romantic than that. I just wanted more from my life than I felt they were offering.'

'I remember standing at the altar, in my tuxedo, and feeling completely out of my comfort zone.'

It took her a moment to realise he was reminiscing about how they had met.

'Billy was fidgeting. I remember the tiny church and the white lilies. I remember looking around at all these girls, all these ordinary faces, and then I saw yours.' He was looking into the distance, lost in the memory. She was fascinated by his expression. 'You were wearing a black dress and a leopard-print pillbox hat, and your shoulder-length hair was flipped up, a bit like Jackie Kennedy, only prettier.' He smiled a little. His voice had taken on a tender quality. 'You had this fabulous dancer's posture, and an incredible little heart-shaped face. I thought I'd never seen anybody more beautiful, and I couldn't take my eyes off you, no matter how hard I tried. I almost forgot what I was doing there.' He laughed, clearly amused by his younger self. 'All I could think was how much I wanted it to be over so I could find a way to talk to you.'

'I remember thinking, *How can the bride be standing there knowing she was about to marry Billy and not be wishing it was you!*

'Really? You were thinking that?' He looked at her, sceptically.

'Really. I was. What made you such a romantic, Eddy? The coal miner's son from Newcastle?'

He shrugged. 'I don't know. I was just twenty-five and smitten. You became my reason for why I was even at that wedding. The minute I saw you, I had my purpose.'

'Better not tell your poor old groom that!'

'He'd probably not care, anyway, given he's on to his second wife.'

'I remember you serenading me with The Ronettes' "Be My Baby", when you were supposed to be singing it to the newlyweds!' She hid her face in her hands. 'Oh dear! I wanted the ground to swallow me up!'

He threw back his head, and she recognised his hearty laugh from twenty years ago. Recognised it at the core of her, as though the *then* and *now* were one.

'You were completely drunk. It was terrible.'

'Not true! I mean, I was terrible, but I wasn't drunk. I was driving, remember? And I was enjoying watching you squirm.'

'Okay, I stand corrected. But you did really embarrass me. I just thought, *Oh my God, he's way too extrovert for me! If he were my husband, I'd be so in the shadow of his humongous personality that I'd never get air!*' His bravery and his charisma and the way he'd belted the song out to her, with his surprisingly good voice, had made him massively fanciable, and she would never, ever, forget what it was like to be under the spell of attraction like that.

'You were picturing me as your husband?'

'Well, no. I was just assessing you from all potential angles.'

'I think me singing that song to you instead of to them – about adoring each other until eternity – probably explains why they were divorced three years later.'

She chortled.

In her mind's eye, she could see them dancing. The memory had been crisp for so long, then had distilled into these few fine-spun details that she would come back to in her quiet, questioning moments: the press of his fingers on her lower back; his grip on her right hand as his thumb gently stroked her clammy palm; his breath in intermittent draughts on the crown of her head.

He propped himself on his elbows. 'Do you ever think, *If only . . .* ?'

'I try not to.'

'I thought *If only . . .* for a long time, and then I saw you with your husband at the Mayfair.'

She met his eyes again. 'Let's not talk about that night. It upsets me . . .' She could hardly bear the reminder of how stupid she had been. 'Tell me something nice. What would our date have been like? Tell me that instead.'

He lay back on the sand. 'I was going to take you to Lindisfarne Castle, to the private walled garden, for a picnic. You know, so you could pretend for a moment that you were the princess I saw you as being.' He cast her a sideways glance. 'My uncle was the caretaker, so I knew the owner was away. You'd have loved the view of the castle and the sea from the garden. It's unique.'

'You were going to break into private property, for me?'

'It wasn't really breaking in. It's a garden.' He smiled. 'I wanted it to be something we'd remember. Because that's how certain I felt that we'd have a future.'

She ignored that, feeling herself buckle at the beautiful idea of it. 'Well, it's the best first date I've never been on.'

They looked at one another. All the possibilities of what might have been hung there between their gazes, in glorious torment. Eventually, she forced herself to break it. 'What's Laura like?'

He shrugged, and seemed to think. 'Laura's a good person. She's a good mother. We get along well, I suppose, as friends.'

'So you're happy?' The beer had made her brave.

'There was a time, yeah. I suppose we must have been to get married, mustn't we? But we change, don't we?'

She was lying on her side, propping up her head with a hand, and absorbing his face like an artist who would later paint him from memory. He kept glancing at her thigh, where her dress had ridden up slightly. 'I knew her before I met you. I started seeing her again shortly after I lost you.'

'You didn't lose me. We didn't even go on a date.'

'Oh, I felt I did.' He held her eyes for a moment, poignantly. 'With everything in me, I felt I had lost you, Evelyn. I married her the year I saw you again at the Mayfair Ballroom – just a few months before, actually. She really wanted to be married, and I could tell my father was thinking I wasn't going to get it together, because I always got the impression he was disappointed in me. I think this was my way of showing him my stripes.' He snickered, sadly. 'Plus, I thought a lot about her, obviously.'

He caught her expression, and pulled a resigned smile. 'There was a time when I'd have done anything to make Laura happy. But then you realise that all your trying really doesn't change anything between you. You've become a certain way. There's no romance, no passion . . . The man, you know – he's the hunter. He likes to hunt . . .' He faltered, as though embarrassed by his rambling. 'Even with his wife . . . Some of that needs to be kept alive. Sometimes, I think she doesn't even register I'm a member of the opposite sex. I try to tell myself, well, we're good friends. But it still doesn't feel like it's enough.' He looked at her frankly, and she could see all the disappointment backed up in his eyes. 'The mad thing is, I've had to reach my mid-forties before I've really known who I am, before I've had the guts to be my own person.'

She loved him saying all this, loved his candour, loved his priceless sapphires. She could gaze at them for ever.

'Have you ever had an affair?'

He looked genuinely surprised. 'An affair? No, of course not. It has never occurred to me.'

'But you must get women after you.'

'But I'm not after them.' He dismissed the subject. 'There were a few baby issues that put a strain on us. Miscarriages. The women in Laura's family had difficulty carrying girls. We gave up trying for a while. Then out of the blue, Laura gave birth to a girl. I'm sure if we hadn't had April, we'd not have stuck it. We make it work for her. And she's all the more special because we thought we were never going to have her.' He glanced at her quickly. 'But we're not really setting her a good example by staying in a loveless marriage, are we?' He shrugged, as though life had burst one too many of his bubbles.

She could feel the frustration emanating off him. She sat up and stared at the sea as he was doing. It twinkled for them. Or so it felt. Everything about the day felt sparkling to her. They were revealing tiny chips of their innermost disappointments to each other. She loved it.

'What about you, Evelyn? How happy are you? If it's okay for me to ask.' His eyes seemed to demand her honesty.

No one had asked her this before. It definitely wasn't a question that would have crossed Mark's lips, even if it had ever crossed his mind. 'Mark's a good man. I love him dearly. But I suppose, if I were to be honest, there's something missing, even though I feel traitorous in saying that. Some days, you can forget about it and focus on all that's good about your life. But it catches up with you once in a while.' She shrugged, abashed by her confession. 'But maybe that happens in every marriage.'

'I don't know. I'd like to think that some people are just right for each other and they stay that way, and it never occurs to them that they could be happier with anyone else.'

Would that have been us? she wondered.

'I'm trying to remember the beginning. It's so hard to recall how we thought and felt so far back. I'm not sure if I ever felt right with Mark, or if I just really wanted to. In some ways, I think your memory is a combination of your reality and your dreams.' Sometimes, events ascribed to her past were like reflections on water; they might have existed, or she could have imagined them.

He seemed subdued, perhaps by her bringing Mark into the picture.

'What's your biggest fear in life, Evelyn?'

'Oh!' she blanched. 'I don't know. Perhaps never knowing the answers to all these questions I keep torturing myself with!'

He interlaced his fingers behind his head, and her eyes followed the one pronounced blue vein that ran down his inner arm. 'Mine is looking back at my life and thinking how one wrong choice ended up defining everything that happened to me.'

'Urgh!' She shuddered. 'Let's not think about wrong choices.'

London. 1963

She arrived at Annabel's in an emerald-green, ankle-length dress from Harrods. The price tag still dangled on a string down her back; she'd return it the next day. She recognised him as soon as she saw him, of course. She'd seen him many times around the hotel: seen him, without really seeing him.

He leant a little closer to hear her over the music. 'I had to really work up the courage to ask you out. In the end, I could only do it with flowers. I don't find these things easy, I'm afraid . . .'

She believed him. He was a little clean-cut for her tastes, but he was modest and unassuming, and she liked him instantly. He had warm, honey-brown eyes, a quiet charm and a confidence that would work well on women who would have normally been out of his reach. He smoked Cohiba cigars, and she remembered thinking he was probably the only man who could hold his pinkie-finger in the air and still look masculine. She would always remember how he looked at her that first time, as though she was the springboard for a sudden shift in his priorities. It all felt very signed and sealed, very fast, and in the dark crevices of her mind she was thinking that if only she had felt more infatuated, it would have been storybook.

On their second date, he took her to Hyde Park for a picnic. 'There are people starving all over the world, and we're feasting on all this!' She had never tasted expensive champagne, let alone eaten caviar or oysters. 'There are things in that hamper that I'm not even sure are edible. I think we're eating hamper bunting!'

'You don't have to eat it, if you don't want to.' He playfully tried to snatch a small lamb chop from her hand. She laughed. They sat by the Serpentine in the dappled shade of a tree, only her bare feet spot-lit in a random patch of sunshine. People passed by and looked at them. She felt like Eliza Doolittle at the races. He kept watching her wiggle her toes. Once in a while, he would meet her eyes. He was studying her, as though he was trying to work out how not to lose her.

One month after their first date, he slipped her best cerise cashmere cardigan from her shoulders. Underneath, she wore a simple cream shift dress that she'd teamed with pearls. She remembered his gentle kisses down the back of her neck, and thinking that she'd never been so tenderly picked over by anyone. He was patient with her when she told him that she didn't have vast experience. In being trained by him, she somehow became his.

He took her everywhere. A whirlwind of 'in' bars and members-only restaurants. She rubbed shoulders with shipping magnates and European royalty. They had front-row seats to witness Beatlemania before the Queen and Princess Margaret at the Prince of Wales Theatre. He took her shopping on the King's Road, where she bought one of the first-ever Mary Quant miniskirts. 'Why do you never wear that stunning dress you wore on our first date?' he once asked.

She told him how she'd had to return it.

He took hold of her hand. 'I promise you, Evelyn, if you stick with me you'll never have to return clothes again.'

Part of her loved this idea; the other part was the one she was frustrated with.

For Christmas, he bought her a car: a newly launched Rover P6. In the new year, he suggested she leave her job at Claridge's.

And then Mark Westland had his bride on his arm. Evelyn's head was still spinning when she entered the small Gloucestershire church, the day that Elizabeth Taylor first married Richard Burton. 'I love you, Mrs Westland,' he said.

'I love you, too,' she replied. And she meant it. But serenely, without fireworks.

Mark had introduced her to his parents just one month before the wedding. It was then that she understood how rich he was. He had kept it from her because he so desperately wanted to be perceived as ordinary. He was the youngest of four children, and she later learnt that he barely got on with his siblings. Only in time did she understand how he could occasionally be stubborn, and that this could cause rifts among his family that he did little to rectify.

Her parents came to the wedding. There was a marked divide down the centre of their photographs, especially the ones of the happy couple flanked by both sets of parents. She thought she'd never seen her mother look so pretty, and yet so weathered and out of her depth. Her father's rugged fisherman's complexion beside the insipid fairness of Mark's father said it all without words.

'You should have got married in your own church,' her mother reprimanded her. 'That's what brides do. They marry in their own home town.' Her mother was right. Evelyn regretted that all her life.

'You'd better get home before the tide strands you here,' she said to Eddy, as his van turned down her street. It was a little like déjà vu. It had almost happened this way before.

He parked at her front door, and there was a moment when they both just sat there.

Conflicting thoughts sailed through her head. *You only get one life. Do unto others as you'd be done by. No regrets.* She placed her hand on the door handle, but couldn't move it. She knew he was experiencing a similar dilemma. A strange and unsettling traction existed between them; she needed to break it, but was powerless.

'Evelyn,' he said, very quietly.

At what point had she already crossed a line? When she had held his eyes in the Mayfair Ballroom, in the presence of her unsuspecting husband? When she'd allowed him to help paint the house?

Don't do it, she thought. *Don't make a good life complicated. Be honourable to Mark because that's who you are. A decent person.*

She was palpably aware of her heartbeat, of his leg just inches away from hers, his left hand on the wheel, the way he kept clenching and unclenching his fingers.

'Evelyn,' he said again, this time more assertively. 'I need to hold you again. I can't know you went back to London and I didn't get to do that.'

She could hear her pulse: a loud whishing in her ears, so distracting that she wasn't sure if he had said it or if she had imagined it. She opened her mouth to reply.

Yes was poised to come out.

But then she saw Mark's kind face, and her life, and their home, and his trust.

'No,' she said, and then, 'I'm sorry! I can't do this!'

She dove out. As her foot met the pavement, she stumbled and twisted her ankle slightly. She hobbled quickly for the refuge of her house, registering the tingling pain and the embarrassing melodrama. Her rejection of him weighed on her like an albatross around her neck. She could feel his gaze attaching itself to her, could feel the enormity of his regret. When she quickly glanced back, he was still sitting there. His hands were clutching his head as though he was having some sort of brain burst.

I mustn't look, she thought. *I can't bear it.*

THIRTEEN

He didn't come the next day, or the next. She made trips over to the mainland to buy groceries and cat food, pay bills, to peruse the windows of the estate agencies – anything to keep busy. One afternoon, she went back to Bamburgh and sat in the exact same spot where she had sat with him, wondering why she lived her life always trying to recreate things.

There was a man on the beach with his son. She watched the little boy run full throttle to the water and then stop short before it touched him. Sometimes, she missed being a mother so deeply that she had to just fold in on herself and let the anguish of the lost opportunity roll over her. Maybe a baby would have made her more settled, more content, given her less time on her hands to think about herself. *I want that man to be Eddy, and that little boy to be our child*, she thought, in rampant desperation, recognising the drama of it – how it had all suddenly stepped up. Her common sense was telling her to get a grip; she had a different life to this alternate one she suddenly thought she wanted, and it would be best that she went back to London and got on with living it.

By day four she was going insane. She rang Mark and listened to his voice. There had been a family gathering with all his nephews. The youngsters were tiresome in their mischief. Their friends, the

Bradbury-Coombs, had done the dastardly thing of popping in unexpectedly when Mark was in the middle of his dinner. His meal was entirely ruined. He thought they'd never leave. Timothy Bradbury-Coombs drank nearly all his Scotch. Mark told her how dire the weather was, and how the Tube workers might be going on strike again.

She could have been talking to an occasional friend or a second cousin. If anything, it left her feeling guilty that she failed to miss him or to hugely long to see him. 'Do you think you would mind if I stayed on here a bit? There's still so much to do . . .'

There was a pause. Then, 'Do? What, for instance?'

'Well, painting. And I was thinking about the floors—'

'Floors?'

The lie lay in her conscience like a tumour. She had never deceived Mark, other than to tell him the shop had lost his dry-cleaning, to avoid confessing she'd forgotten to have Tessie send it in.

'I thought you were just freshening the place up, Ev. Not rebuilding it from the ground up.' There was a petulant note in his voice.

'I thought we said I'd stay here for as long as needed.' She was feeding him a lie that he would recognise as a manipulation.

'You said you would extend your ticket if you had to – yes. But I honestly didn't think you'd have to.' Mark had a way of appealing to her higher conscience for the right thing to prevail. When she didn't answer, he asked, 'Well, how much longer do you think you need?'

She heard the emptiness. The abandoned puppy. Despite his age and his accomplishments, there was a part of Mark that had stayed a little boy. He missed her like a child would miss his mother.

'Perhaps another week.'

'A week?' His disappointment was palpable. It should have mattered, yet all she could think about was the need to buy herself more time. Her heart pounded as she waited for his answer.

'Well, do as you will,' he said.

She tried not to let out her relief until she had hung up. For a brief second, she felt she'd signed a lease on freedom.

Then she did something that she knew crossed a line.

His street was a long row of pre-war terraces. She peered at numbers until she found his. It had fresh paintwork and a mint-green door. Out front by the gate were a child's pink bike and a pair of tiny pink plimsolls. Evelyn was driving her mother's old car. She parked it two houses away on the opposite side. After sitting there for about ten minutes, she got out and crossed the street, focussing on the clip of her heels to try to ignore the wild pounding of her heart.

She gave three tentative raps. She hadn't fully decided what she'd say if his wife came to the door. She tried to remember that, as far as Laura knew, she was just Mrs Coates' daughter. No one was going to read her face and know any different.

She could hear music from a radio indoors. Suddenly, she got cold feet. She was just on the point of turning around and sneaking away when the door opened and Eddy appeared.

'Evelyn?' Shock and mild annoyance registered all over his face. She heard a voice say, 'Who is it, Edward?'

'It's nothing,' he shot back, stepping outside and letting the door close part way. 'What are you doing here?' he asked, in a rushed whisper.

She flooded with shame. 'I came to see when you are coming back to finish painting. We still have a job to do.' She didn't really know what she was saying. It mortified her to act like she had a right to him. 'You didn't finish,' she said, almost curtly.

She could see the alarm in his eyes. 'I can't. I can't be there. Can't see you, be so close to you, and not be able to, to . . .'

The woman in the house said, 'Edward?'

'I can't handle this, Evelyn. I might look like I can, but it's too much for me.'

She nodded, and backed away while his eyes held on to hers. Then she turned around and almost broke into a run.

The last thing she remembered was hearing the door close a little too firmly. Like someone shutting out a potential intruder and trying not to give the impression they had felt threatened.

The following day, she went back to the paint shop. The woman behind the counter observed her with too much interest. Evelyn bought some supplies and hurried out.

Back at the car, she was trying to balance her purchases on one arm and open the boot with her free hand when she heard him say, 'Hello Evelyn.' It was as though her ribs collapsed with the weight of her relief.

'Can I help with those?' He was behind her. His manner was perfunctory. He didn't meet her eyes. Without waiting for her reply, he took the cans of paint from her, and her keys. 'Here.' He opened the boot and put the cans in. 'You shouldn't be doing this.' She thought he sounded mildly impatient.

She didn't know why he would have stopped to speak to her if he was going to be like this. 'I really don't need your help.' She tried to wrestle the third can off him, which was mildly absurd. He finally stopped struggling and let her take it, then held up both of his hands in surrender. 'You need some more white for the ceiling. We had run out.' Before she could speak, he had walked off, and she thought he was leaving, but he went into the shop. When he came out, carrying another can, he seemed more relaxed; it was as though she might have imagined his earlier hostility. It fanned her flame for him in a way she hadn't been prepared for. It no longer mattered that he hadn't come earlier. It mattered that he was here now.

'You were just passing?'

'I followed you.'

'Followed me? I thought you'd never want to see me again!'

'Well, maybe not on my doorstep. But I did want to see you again. Desperately. You're all I can think about. I was telling my friend Stanley I have this so bad it's ruling me like I never thought I could be ruled.' He moved in to perhaps kiss her neck and stopped himself. 'I tell myself I can't see you, I mustn't see you, but I can't stay away from you.'

'I thought you hated me now.'

He searched her face, like a man torn between loathing and enjoying this trial-and-error, hit-and-miss process of getting to know a woman. 'Hated? If anything, I thought you would hate me after how I behaved . . . Evelyn, maybe if I hadn't been married all these years I'd have had a bit more practice – a better grasp of boundaries and when to cross them. But then you showed up at my door. That was the biggest adrenaline rush I've had in this lifetime.'

She loved his confession.

'I need to kiss you, to have you in my arms. You can't run away from me again. We only have one life. We can't mess this up again.'

'But it's wrong.' She jumped into the car without really thinking, and slammed the door. What was she doing? Her hands clutched the wheel. She was light-headed. She put the car into reverse while he just stood there, clearly confused. She pulled out of the parking spot a little too abruptly. The car bucked. She stalled the engine, started it and tried to do it all over again, this time without the 'getaway driver' sound effects.

Then, through the rear-view mirror she saw him walk toward his van. She could feel the throbbing bass line of her heartbeat. He climbed into his vehicle. A moment or two later, he was following her.

Her hands sweated so much that she couldn't grip the steering wheel properly. She drove across the causeway to the island with a daredevil quality loose in her. He followed close behind. She wound down her window and let the salt breeze dry the perspiration on the back of her neck. When she arrived on the island, she drove the short distance to her street, the car bump-bumping over the uneven road. His was the only vehicle behind hers now. Her stomach flipped like a dolphin.

As she walked up her path, her legs were like puppy legs, not quite going the way she wanted them to.

She successfully unlocked the door on her first attempt. He was so close behind her that she could feel his body heat. Then they were inside her kitchen. She stood in the middle of the floor, and felt his hands on her hips, his breath a warm draught on her neck. 'Is it anything other than inevitable, Evelyn?' he asked. 'Because if it is, then tell me now and we won't do this.'

But before she could answer, he spun her around and kissed her. It wasn't very smooth. He dove in so quickly that he misaimed and got her nose. They both moved, and there was another collision of faces. But then . . . 'Third time lucky,' he whispered. Then he was kissing her smile.

It went from tender to hot in 1.67 seconds. Instantaneous acceleration. Exactly as she remembered. His hand at the back of her skull supported her head. The feel of his mouth – another man's kiss – was stunning, intoxicating.

Eddy's kiss.

His weight rocked her slightly off her feet. She reached up on her tiptoes to slide her arms around his neck, losing herself in the momentum of their passion, in the taste of him, in the feel of a different man's body. Someone taller, broader, harder, more into her and in touch with her than Mark, on what felt like every possible level.

Eddy's body.

She said his name. He said hers. They laughed. They had surprised themselves and each other. His gaze burrowed into her, touching chords of longing. She held on to him, clutching whatever part of him she could clutch, lost in the smell of his skin, his clothes, his body heat, the strength of him, his keen desire for her.

'Evelyn,' he said, after he'd carried her into her old bedroom. He picked open the fiddly buttons of her blouse and laid his hand on her rapidly beating heart. He looked moved, almost sad.

'What?'

He gazed at her, appreciating her, like someone who was being given something he thought he didn't deserve. 'Nothing,' he whispered. 'I'm just overwhelmed.'

She entwined her fingers with his.

He made love to her in a way that she had never known, gently unwrapping her from her remaining undergarments, then bearing down on her with the sort of manly, territorial claim that she'd experienced only in some outlying fantasy world. Once or twice, the image of Mark tried to force an entry, but she pushed it away. While she was here with Eddy on Holy Island, this was another life she was leading.

This was what it was supposed to be like, she thought, after. She had been right in sensing something was missing. This was missing. They fitted like teeth on a zip.

'You have an incredible heart-shaped face,' he told her, stroking her jaw like you would a kitten's. He'd said it before. The only description of herself that would ever matter. She was so moved to be feeling this intensity only now, at the ripe old age of forty, that tears rolled into her hair.

'I wonder what my mother would think if she saw us lying here,' she said, a long time later, after he had held her so closely that when she moved away from him slightly, her skin was saturated with their sweat.

'I hope she'd think it was the way it had to be . . .' he said, appearing moved by his own comment. 'I think we'd make a good plot of a movie. Small-town girl marries rich man in the big city, then she falls for her old life and her old love: the poor man with the bad singing voice, whom she once stood up.' He kissed her intermittently between speaking, like you might punctuate a long sentence with commas.

'It's a nice story. But it's a fairy tale, isn't it?' She only meant it lightly. She didn't want reality to rain down on them. Right now, she would do anything in her power to keep it at bay.

'I'm actually the reverse of a fairy tale, aren't I? Anyway, you've had the fairy tale already.' He rolled on to his back, and stared contemplatively at the ceiling, slightly melancholy; she could feel the shift in his thinking – reality was pressing in despite their desire to exist only in a bubble. He looked at her, intently. 'If I were a wealthy man, I'd love to give you everything you deserve, Evelyn. But I could really only provide you with a very simple life. Nothing like what you're used to. It would be naive to promise you love as a substitute for all that.'

She didn't need to ask herself if she was in love with him. It would have been a wasted exercise. She'd been in love with him from that very first day. Knowing it, as she knew it now, brought her mistake pressing either side of her head with monster-like hands – the mistake of having ever let him go. 'Love is never a substitute, Eddy. Everything else is a substitute for love.'

He stroked her face again. She thought vaguely of the life she was used to, and only how utterly detached she felt from it, now that she was experiencing something greater than the sum of all her life's parts. She touched his shoulder. Too much talking was going to shatter the fragile perfection of it, like blowing too near a dandelion clock. 'Let's not get too ahead of ourselves, though. Can we keep it light?'

'I feel like I'm in a rush because we have such little time.'

She told him that she had extended her ticket for another week.

'What?' he said, sitting up. 'Another week? Why didn't you tell me?'

Relief flooded his face suddenly. He kissed her before she could answer. Then he sighed and fell back on to the pillow again. 'But then this week will come and go, and then we're back here again, in this position again, aren't we?'

She leant over him, and looked seriously into his eyes, the ends of her long, dark hair pooling on his chest. 'We live for today – literally. Every minute we have together is a bonus we never expected. We take it, and we savour it, and we don't overthink it. We don't think, full stop.'

She popped another kiss on his mouth, kissed him all over his cheeks, his forehead. 'Can we do that?'

'We can try,' he smiled.

They deliberately stopped talking. They lay there, instead, just enjoying the composition of themselves, perhaps both of them trying to deny what it was all adding up to. Then she said – so much for not thinking – 'How can we have got in so deep, Eddy?' They had been born into the same world, but had found themselves in vastly different ones. They ought to have nothing in common. She ought not to feel right with him, but she did. 'You were just a man at a wedding.'

'I don't know how, Evelyn. But I was in deep the first second I saw you, and I'm going to selfishly and impractically want you in my arms like this until my dying day. That's just the reality of it.'

Something occurred to her, in that moment. She had a sense of possibility – a sense that some of the best days of her life hadn't happened yet. She smiled, because it was a lovely prospect.

FOURTEEN

Alice

'What's the prospect of you ever agreeing with me?' Justin is lying on his side, his head propped on an upturned hand, looking down at me. 'You're so contrary.'

'All I said was, it was a completely pointless film!' I grin at him because he's looking at me as though I'm an idiot. 'It had no ending. It just, well, it just petered out . . . It was a total waste of two hours of my life!'

'It did have an ending. You were supposed to supply it, using your im-ag-in-ation. You know, if you have one.'

I pick up a pillow and bash him over the head.

He grabs it off me, throws it across the bedroom, pulls me on to his chest by my upper arms and kisses me. 'Argumentative Alice,' he whispers. He flips me on to my back. I chuckle and knot my ankles around his waist. We have made love twice before that unbelievably banal, waste-of-life film – before and after our takeaway curry.

'Condom?' I say.

He looks at me, and stops. 'Gosh! We've run out.'

I push at his shoulders. 'What? How?'

'Excuse me, I'm always astonished by my own prowess, but even I didn't think we'd be doing it three times.'

'No glove. No love,' I practically sing.

He gives me a horrified look. 'God, you didn't seriously say that, did you?'

I beam. 'No.' I look across my shoulder. 'It was her.' I pull a face at the imaginary joy-killer. 'Shut up, you!'

'You're a nutter.' He pulls me to him again, to continue where we left off.

Afterward, we are back to the 'side position, propped up on elbow, looking at one another' thing, and I say, 'Doesn't it worry you that we didn't use anything?' It brings back memories of Colin. How – and this really is between me, my memory and the four walls – I used to try to convince him not to use protection. There was a time when I'd actually imagined that if I'd got pregnant, the very nature of learning you're about to be a father would have convinced him that he wanted to be one. I really was that deluded.

'Not really,' Justin says. 'I'm fine if you don't want to use birth control. I mean, I would understand.'

'Hang on . . . You want me to be the mother of your children? Out of wedlock?'

'Leave my Catholic values out of this, thank you!' He appears to be contemplating his proper response a second or two longer than you'd think would be necessary, given that it was a fairly basic question. Then he says, 'Well, obviously I assume we're going to, you know, have some sort of future together.'

'As in, get married?'

'That . . . Yes. But I'm just saying, as you get older, you think about these things more seriously. A woman's biological clock. Or at least, a woman you care about.'

'You think I'm approaching my sell-by date.'

He kisses me quickly and smiles – caught out. I go to bring another pillow down on his head.

'I'm not being insulting!' He pretends to hide behind his hands. 'Or maybe I am . . . In which case, I'm sorry; that was not my intent. I just mean that, well, obviously you want to have a kid when you know you're likely to have a healthy baby, right?'

I scowl at him. 'But there's never any guarantee of that.'

'No. But your chances of a lot of things increase with waiting, Alice. And, don't get me wrong, I'm thinking about myself in this, too. I'm thirty-eight. I also have a clock, in a way. I don't want to be a sixty-year-old with a teenager, or be worrying about paying for their education when I'm seventy. And, like I say, I just have a feeling we're going somewhere.'

'Why do we have to be going somewhere?' I'm not sure why I'm asking this. It is a lot like tempting fate. Perhaps it's because I'd always wanted a future from my relationships, and I'd never got one, so I'm operating with reverse psychology.

'Don't we?' He frowns.

I can tell this question has wrong-footed him slightly.

'Because if we're not, then you should say.' He sits up. He isn't chilled out any more. I have spoilt something. Again. 'I think it's important for honesty here, Alice. I certainly wouldn't want to be wasting your time, and, frankly, I don't want my own wasted, either.' He's become way too serious, and I wish I'd never said it. Why do I have to sabotage everything? It's so damned annoying. 'Time isn't really on our side quite as much as we always like to think.'

'Considering my womb is nearly collecting its pension.'

'Precisely.' He pretend-flinches, no doubt expecting me to attack him with a pillow again. I love his good-natured ability to change shadow to light.

'Justin. Can I ask you something? Do you ever know how to answer simple, harmless questions without always making a big, heavy deal of everything?'

He scowls again. 'What have I made a big heavy deal of? Fuck, Alice! You asked me if it bothered me that we didn't use birth control, and I said no!'

'You're such a weirdo.'

'Then we balance each other out. Because you're so perfect. Obviously.'

I beam another smile. 'Is right!'

We hold eyes, and I mentally say the things I will never say to him. With each passing day, Justin is turning out to be less and less like any man I've known, when it comes to his perspective on life, his maturity, and the fact that he genuinely seems to care about things that don't just directly impact himself. He never appears confused, like all the others – when it comes to what he wants and, more importantly, about whether he wants me. He seems so certain of us that I do not trust it. I will eat, sleep, wake up, and the fact that Justin is there beside me, happy to be with me, still feels like something sent to mess with me.

I owe him my seriousness, though, as it is a serious subject. 'I do want children, Justin – just to finish this point. Very much. But I would never rush into something to make it happen. I tend to be the kind of person who accepts things for what they are. Everything happens for a reason. So if it never happens, then some things are just not meant to be. I'll be at peace with my life, whether or not kids are a part of it.'

A lovely warm expression lights his eyes; I can't stop looking at them. 'I love that you have that perspective on things.' He takes hold of my hand, momentarily mesmerised by the sight of my fingers in his. 'It's just important for me that you know that I'm not going to string you along. I'm not the kind of person who would do that to someone. I didn't do it to Lisa, and I'd certainly not do it to you.'

Lisa. Justin rarely speaks of his ex-girlfriend. I am still not crystal clear on why they broke up. So when her name suddenly comes up again, it resonates with me perhaps more than it should.

I go on looking at him. He wants marriage and a baby. He's a fair person – he truly cares about me, perhaps on the same level as he cares about himself, because he doesn't want to string me along, any more than he wants to be strung along himself. How did I find this fabulous man? And yet am I ready for all that he is? Can I be the lawyer's wife, and mother of his children? Can I cope with his structure? With the intense, serious, sorted-out person he is – who, in many ways, is the very opposite of me? And then it dawns on me: What am I thinking? Of course I can cope! It's everything I've always wanted. Love. Stability. Family. A decent man. And I love him. Let's not forget that.

He gets up. He crosses the room and gazes out of the window into the spotted nightlights of Newcastle. 'I know we've not known each other forever, and I hope you don't think this is all moving too fast, but I feel something. It's just a sense of optimism every time I look at you. I felt it from day one.'

I am with him on this. I'd have called it rightness. Overwhelming, incontestable rightness and belonging. Yet coming out of his mouth, optimism feels bigger. I stare at his back, his broad, bare shoulders, suddenly remembering what he said about the ill health in his family. I say a silent prayer, even though I am not the praying type: *Please God, don't let anything happen to him, like it did to his dad.*

He turns around, meets my eyes and smiles. The qualities that make Justin different from any man I've known are the things that make me love him and yet are also the things that make me worry. He isn't emotionally one-dimensional. He doesn't seem to roll with the punches. There is a soft, gentle, thinking side to him that makes me wonder how strong he would be when push comes to shove. Though he would hate that I thought this.

'So . . . are we in love?' I ask him. I think of him just mentioning Lisa and wish he'd never said that name.

'Are you in love?' he asks.

Not how the answer was meant to go. 'Well . . .' I try to sound light. 'I've always had this policy of not being the one to say it first.'

It isn't true. Normally, I am the first one to say it: sometimes the only one. And the crazy thing is, sometimes I'd said it when I hadn't even felt it, which makes me wonder why I had this need to declare bogus feelings just to get them to state where they stood. Why did I want to know if they loved me first, before deciding whether it was mutual? It felt more than a little messed up.

'I'm not prepared to settle for anything less than in love, Justin. I sold myself short in my other relationships. And I don't know if that was because, at heart, I'm a bit like my mother – I tend to fall for unreliable men – or if I just have questionable self-esteem. But I'm determined not to do that again. I just don't need to be with someone so badly that I'll take whatever terms they offer me.'

I sense he's listening to me with every fibre of his being. He watches me for a long time, processing my words, processing me – or so it feels. I don't know what he's going to say, but somewhere far inside of me I almost want to say, *Don't*, anyway.

'Alice.' He's so damned grave. 'The one thing I can say is you deserve someone who is so completely sure that you're the one thing in his life he could never stand to lose.' He pauses. He's going to say, *But you're right. I'm not him.* Only instead he looks distantly across the room and his face floods with something more indelible than sadness; I can't say what it is, but I almost can't look. 'You know, all my life I've wanted to be like my father. The kind of man he was. The kind of husband, dad . . . My father loved my mother so much. They seem to draw energy and purpose from one another, and the spark that existed between them, well, you couldn't not see it. Even I saw it, and I was just a kid. And yet look how fast my mother remarried after he died, which made me wonder all over again . . . Had it all just been an illusion?' He looks back at me. 'Were they both acting a role, and doing it so damned convincingly because their values had made them believe they had to? Then I wondered, do you ever really know someone? Is there really only one person for us in this world? Or is that all a bit of a myth of evolution that we are sold to somehow make us commit, produce offspring and feel inadequate if we screw it all up? Could you probably love, and live with, anyone if you put your mind to it?'

'What's this got to do with us, Justin?'

He sighs, frustrated. He does this occasionally. As though the weight of his complicated thought process has to be lifted and repositioned once in a while just to make it bearable. 'Alice, you're a truly good person, and in many ways we have so much in common – our values, our outlook, the things we like to do . . . When I'm with you, I'm really not bothered about being around anybody else. I don't really care where we go, or what we do, so long as we do it together.' He comes and sits on the end of the bed, runs a hand over my cheek and twirls a strand of my hair around his index finger. 'I feel so at peace with you that way. You make me extremely happy. I look forward to getting to see you every day, and I know that, more than anything, I want to make you happy and do what's right by you.' His hand slides to the back of my head, cupping it. I can feel the pleasant press of his warm fingers. 'So yes, I believe I'm in love with you.'

I don't think I'll ever forget the way he looks at me. It's up there with the way he looked at me in that bar, that first day.

'So, what about Lisa? Were you in love with her?' When I see his face, I say, 'It's important for me to know. To have a picture.'

I can almost see his brain ticking through the right way to reply. 'I'm sure I must have thought I was, yes,' he says, after a short spell. 'There was a lot to love about her. But when it came down to it, it didn't go the distance.'

He has said a version of this before: about it not going the distance. But, undoubtedly, it had gone *some* distance. They had met at Oxford.

She was reading Law, too. She even found a job up North to be with him. They had lived together for two years, so I assume he must have been considering marrying her because he'd once said he'd never live with someone if he had no intention of a future. Justin is modern in so many ways, yet very old-fashioned in others.

'And Jemma?'

'Jemima!'

I always deliberately misname her.

'That was just a physical thing. It's a shame there wasn't more, but there wasn't. Not on my part, anyway.'

A physical thing that had gone on a long time. And she was very beautiful – enormously tall, and slim and dark-haired – because we had bumped into her once in Eldon Square. But I don't really care to think about that.

He looks at me forthrightly. 'If we can forget about ex-girlfriends . . . I suppose I'm just saying I think there comes a time in life where if everything that you have with someone feels good, feels right, and they are good, good in their heart and soul, and you want the same things, then you have to go with it. You have to decide you're going to make it work.'

'So that's what you're doing with me? Making it work?'

Way too much honesty! Justin has never disappointed me before. But I am disappointed now.

'Now you're going to try to twist it.'

'No.'

'You are. You're trying to hear what you want to have heard. To twist it. Because you've got issues with yourself. Maybe with what others have done to you, but you have to get over that.' He seems genuinely frustrated by me. 'What I'm saying – even though you've read it the wrong way – doesn't diminish what this is, what we have. We're not teenagers. I'm just trying to take a mature stance, that's all.'

'You could have left it at the bit about *So yes, I believe I am in love with you.* I'd have been fine with that.' I try to sound light again. He is right: I do try to find blemishes. Maybe because the quiet voice inside me would think that if my own father didn't think I was worth sticking around for, then why would any man? But I hate that strain in myself. I hate anyone even knowing it exists.

He draws my face in, until it's barely an inch from his own. 'Let me repeat. I want you to know it in no uncertain terms. I am in love with you, Alice.' He kisses me, slow and long. 'Are you happy now?'

I'm tired of this conversation. 'Happy enough.'

FIFTEEN

Evelyn

Holy Island. 1983

'I'm leaving Laura.'

They were standing in Evelyn's kitchen. It was almost the end of their week. A week of him working with her on the house as he sang along to the radio, and her smiling inwardly, listening to him; of Evelyn cooking for him, them eating in the garden, and kissing under the plum tree. Of their jaunts to various little villages along the coast, where they would wander in and out of tea rooms, or buy fish and chips in cartons that they would then sit and eat at the end of the pier, feeding the odd seagull with the scraps of batter – careful not to look too cosy in case they were seen and aroused suspicion. But the last few days had been heavily weighted with the threat of it all ending. It had muted all joy and all conversation. Now she could barely meet his eyes without the tears springing.

Evelyn was wearing one of her mother's dressing gowns. They had made love. He had dressed again in his gardening clothes. He had clung to her like he knew he was going to lose her, and even though she was busying herself by making tea, she was still aware of the bleak absence of his body. The ghostly pencil-line around where his love had just been.

'Eddy, you can't possibly leave Laura! This is insane!' She quickly abandoned the idea of making tea.

He searched her face, slightly stunned by her reaction, but she refused to look at him. 'Evelyn, I can't speak for you, or for how you feel, but I, for one, am not going back to the way things were. I'd rather be alone for the rest of my life than plod on with her after this.'

A flurry of panic went through her. At the idea of going back to Mark she felt only the blankness of impossibility. But, strangely, that didn't mean she wanted to feel this way. She recognised they had crossed a bridge to somewhere that neither of them was truly prepared to find themselves.

'You can't do it on my account. I won't let you break up your family for me!'

'But I love you. I've never felt like this over anyone. Only you, Evelyn.'

She floundered, thinking, *No! I have to downplay this! We can't do anything rash!* 'Eddy, you practically married your first sweetheart! You don't know if you could feel this way over someone else. You haven't had enough women.'

'*You* were my first sweetheart. Or, you should have been.'

'We don't know that we'd have worked.'

He looked at her in disbelief and frustration. 'Why are you saying this?' She had hurt him. 'Do you honestly believe – after the time we have just spent together; after everything we have continued to mean to one another – that we wouldn't work, Evelyn? Do you?' He was searching her face, but she refused to meet his eyes.

When she wouldn't answer, he said, 'You can believe what you want, but I'm certain there's a reason we had to meet again after all these years. And these last few days have proven this to be right. Tell me you don't believe that this was fate?'

'Even if all that's true, Eddy, you have a family. A child. You belong to someone else. As do I.'

'But we can change that! We have a chance! Evelyn, I want to do all the things with you that I should have been doing with you from the minute we met. I want to shop with you, go to the beach with you, fill up petrol with you, watch telly with you, plan holidays with you . . . I want to be able to be seen with you in public, without looking over my shoulder. I want to walk down the damned street with you, holding your hand. I want this *affair* word stricken from my mind. It's beneath us. I don't want to be ashamed. I only want to be proud of everything that exists between us.' He was right in referencing how covert they'd felt they needed to be. How many times, when they were doing errands around town, had she wanted to stop and spontaneously kiss him? But she'd had to check herself. Despite them trying on the idea of being an item, it had been so depressingly tempered by the fact that they were both married to someone else. And, if anything, he had hated that more than her, and she hadn't known that would be possible.

He held his head between both of his hands – this gesture of despair or silent panic she had seen before. After a moment, he looked up again. 'I want you to be my wife. I want to see the outline of your body there in bed. And I want to see that outline of you change over the years, Evelyn. I want to be with you when I'm old and know that maybe it didn't work out quite the way it should have, but at least I got forty good years with you – if I'm lucky enough to get that.' He paused, his eyes buzzing around her face. 'I want a life with you, and there's no reason why we shouldn't have that in this day and age. We're not living in our parents' era.'

She wanted to protest as strenuously as he'd declared his love, but his speech had robbed her lungs of air.

'I'm going to tell her tonight. And then I'm moving out.'

She jumped up from the chair. 'No! You can't be serious! Where would you even go?'

This broke his stride slightly. 'Well . . . anywhere. I'll get a flat. Or I'll live with you.'

She sat down beside him again, aware that a part of her was involuntarily withdrawing. 'Eddy, you're not being rational.' She had seen him as a man with values, with a strong moral code. Someone much like herself. Yes, they were doing a deceitful thing, but they weren't actually hurting anyone. But this – this reckless desire to dump all his responsibilities for love – *this* would hurt others. And the fact that he wasn't paying heed to that – it made her think less of him.

He gripped her shoulders and forced her to look at him. 'Just tell him you're not going back. You can get your stuff shipped up here. People do it all the time. It's not impossible.'

She opened her mouth to say something, something to drill some sense into him, but it died in her. He gently shook her. 'It really just comes down to this, Evelyn: do you love me and want to be with me? Because I believe you do.'

Tears built up. She felt the need to lie, but she couldn't leave here having lied to him about something this big. 'I do love you, yes. There is just a rightness when I'm with you, a sense of belonging.' Now she'd said it, she felt elated, as though saying it was all that was needed to give it the ghost of a chance. And yet there was a concrete weight of impossibility in her heart. 'In a way, I fully understand what I always suspected. I couldn't go on that date with you because I knew I'd fall in love – if I hadn't already. I was torn then, and I didn't want to be torn, I wasn't ready for that. But I'm not sure I'm ready for it now, either.'

She could see he was floored by her pragmatism and lack of faith. 'And you're wrong in what you say,' she added. 'You said it really just comes down to whether I love you and want to be with you. But it doesn't just come down to that! What would you say to your daughter?'

He looked genuinely mystified. 'Well, I'd tell her the truth. One day. When she was old enough to understand.'

'I mean now. What would you tell her now?' She knew she was putting him under fire and he wasn't used to it. 'You see, you haven't thought it through.'

'I don't believe I really need to think that part through! I'm leaving Laura, not April. I would never do anything to harm my little girl. I love her for all the world, and that's never going to change. I'm not going anywhere. I'm just going to be with you.'

'You would break her heart. Are you ready to do that? You're her father. You're supposed to set the values for her. You're not setting the values for April if you walk away.'

'One day she'll understand,' he repeated.

'But she'd always know you didn't put her first. You put you first.'

There. That was the crux of it. She wanted him to be better than that.

He held her eyes. She could almost see him searching to contradict her, but the truth was pushing back at him, harder. 'I don't think that staying with her mother for all the wrong reasons is teaching April anything, is it?' His voice had mellowed with doubt. 'She's not going to be better off being raised by parents who are just tolerating each other, knowing that they should never have been a couple. I should never have got back together with her all those years ago, after you . . .'

'Eddy! There was no *me*. It was one day at a wedding. One quite fabulous day that took us completely off guard, yes. But a day. That's all.'

It hurt her to say it, because it felt untrue, but she had to make him believe it. She had to somehow make him see sense. They weren't living in a bubble. Their perfect week together was perfect only because they had managed to keep reality at bay. But so many people's happiness was hanging in the balance.

He didn't seem to hear her. 'Anyway, I think you're being remarkably cavalier. It's easy to say all that, but no five-year-old would ever choose to have her parents split up just because of a concept she couldn't understand anyway.'

He wiped a hand over his mouth. It was clear that he could fight his corner, but Evelyn was the much stronger opponent. The tension came down a few notches. 'Do you have a beer?' he asked. She hesitated, then got him one from the fridge. 'You know what?' he said when he'd taken a big gulp. 'I think it's you who wouldn't be able to do it. You're using my situation as your excuse.'

She sat down again, exhausted from all this intensity. 'I don't have a child, Eddy, no. But I have a husband and I love him, even if it's more about loyalty and affection than passion. It's still love. I made a commitment to him. Everything can't all be about my happiness, can it? That's not how it works when you marry. Mark has never done anything bad to me. I can't just walk away.'

'Why not?'

His persistent naivety bothered her. She was starting to see it as a weakness.

'It'll break him.' She doubted that, of course. Mark would survive. But he would be massively changed. Besides, oddly, in all of her fantasising over the last week that she could live a life with Eddy, she had never once considered the prospect of ending a life with Mark. It was suddenly way too much to have to take on board.

He downed the rest of his beer. 'People don't break that easily, Evelyn. That's a myth people invent when they want to imply everybody else is as weak as they are. Are you going to live your life making excuses, rather than facing up to the fact that you want to be your own person?'

Had he hit on the essence of it? Perhaps she should never have married anyone. Perhaps she would have been better off being free to make her own choices, to forge new paths to new destinations, even if they were the wrong ones. She wasn't necessarily going to do any of it. But maybe she just needed to know she could.

'So what about me, Evelyn? If you're convinced that people can be broken, if you go back to him, you break me.'

The difference between the two situations was so obvious and irrefutable that she couldn't stop herself from saying it. 'Yes, but we've been a married couple for nearly twenty years. I've barely known you – properly known you – for five minutes.'

He bore the weight of the put-down quietly. She could see hope fading in his expression. 'So he wins because he won in the first place? He got you first?' He was defeated: a boxer losing consciousness in the ring.

'It's not about someone winning me. It's about me not wanting to live my life knowing that I did a wrong thing. I wish I could be different, but I can't.'

He was staring at his empty beer bottle. They didn't speak for a while. 'Then where do we go from here?' he finally asked, quietly, as though he feared the answer.

'Well,' she stared at him, her eyes burning with tears. 'I think we go nowhere.'

SIXTEEN

Alice

I had almost forgotten I'd ever rung Rick. I was so wrapped up in thinking about my conversation with Evelyn, over tea. Her telling me about her perfect week with Eddy. His being ready to leave his wife for her. The story just keeps echoing in me . . . Now that I see Rick's number on my call display, though, I have to wonder what's taken him so long. Has he lain low to work out what to say? Maybe he was never going to call back, but Dawn bullied him into it. Has he conferred with Justin?

When I pick up and say, 'Hello, Rick', I sound like I'm walking a tightrope two hundred metres above ground.

'Alice!' he says, brightly. 'I'm so very sorry I'm only just ringing you back. Dawn's mother had a stroke five days ago. It's pretty bad, and we're running backward and forward to Cheltenham General . . . What with that, and working and taking care of the kids, it's been all systems go, and I haven't had a chance.'

Relief makes me audibly sigh. I tell him I'm very sorry to hear about Dawn's mother. We exchange small talk. Then I say, 'I'm sure you can appreciate this is a very difficult conversation for me to be having, but I need you to tell me where he is, please.'

I can feel his hesitation, his puzzlement. Then he says, 'Who?'

I'm puzzled too, now. 'Justin.'

Another pause; somehow, I don't think he's acting. 'Well, what do you mean, where is he?' he says.

I try to stay composed. Threads of my sanity are knotting themselves and I'm trying to unravel them, otherwise I'm not helping myself. They were friends from their Oxford days. They had shared the same house, studied together, raised hell together, were both Blues for rowing. I can't imagine there's anything Justin won't have shared with his best friend. I explain what happened briefly and neutrally.

He makes a couple of astonished noises, then says, 'You're kidding!'

It truly hadn't occurred to me that he might not know.

I tell him about the short message exchange, about my chat with his secretary. 'It's been nine days. Nine days and I am none the wiser.'

'I don't know what to say. Alice . . . My God.' Then, after a hesitation, he says, 'You believe me, don't you?'

'Yes,' I tell him, after quick thought.

'I knew you'd both be back by now, but I haven't had a chance to ring him, what with everything that's been going on.'

'I would really like you to tell me what you were both talking about when you stood outside in the rain at our wedding.' I'm trembling. Hearing the words come out of my mouth somehow doesn't make the situation any more real.

'Alice, I . . .'

'Please don't tell me it's nothing, Rick. I know you were talking about something. I'd really appreciate you being honest with me.' I have the sense that perhaps Dawn has walked into the room. Of something being whispered. 'Has he met someone else?' I ask. 'Is that it? Has there been some sort of affair?'

He lets out a huge sigh. 'God, Alice! Look . . . No. It's not like that. And I don't know why he took off and left you. You're going to have to ask him . . .'

'But I can't ask him because he's not talking to me and he's not here.'

'I know. And I'm sorry.'

'But?' I sense one coming.

A whisper in the background. It's a second or two before he replies.

'But I do have some idea what it's about. I'm just not comfortable being the one to tell you.'

'Is he there?' It just dawns on me. 'Is he with you?'

'What?' he says, more in exclamation. 'No. Of course not. I'm just . . .'

Conferring with my wife? Because she also knows something you don't.

'Look, it's not my place. It's got to come from him,' he says. Then, surprisingly, after a moment or two, he adds, 'You know what he's like . . .'

And I think, *Do I?*

'When things get on top of him, he tends to retreat. To think. It's just his way. Perhaps that's all he's doing now.'

I remember Justin telling me about how, when he heard his dad had died, he ran away. He was only missing a few hours – he'd been hiding in a barn – but his mother had rung the police.

'Is he ill?' I ask.

'Ill? My God. No, Alice. He's definitely not ill.'

'The men in his family all have health problems.'

'He's not ill, Alice. Okay? I'm sorry.'

I feel this conversation is about to burst into flames. I don't mean to hang up on him; it just happens. It occurs to me to ring back and say, *Please tell Dawn I hope her mother will be well.* But the moment passes.

SEVENTEEN

'The girls in this painting are more glamorous than the girls in the others.' Martin is pointing to Edward Hopper's *Chop Suey*: two sophisticated ladies sitting opposite one another at a small table in a restaurant. Something about the artist's intent focus on the silence between them reminds me of tea with Evelyn, when she began to tell me her story, and, weirdly, of Justin and Rick talking in the rain.

Evelyn isn't here today. Michael said she hasn't been well. I remember how she seemed so changed that day, after she had finished describing her week together with Eddy. In a way, it has changed my thought process – made me ask myself some questions. Now I have been comparing Eddy's love for Evelyn to Justin's love for me, and finding it lacking. 'He loved me so much that he could think of nothing except being with me,' Evelyn had said. 'He wanted to leave his marriage. He wanted me to leave mine. He loved me to the point where he had lost all reason.' Her face had clouded. I'd thought she had been about to cry. I had felt so incredibly bleak, a quiet voice asking, *Why didn't Justin love me like that?*

'What happened?' I asked her.

She pulled out her pretty handkerchief again. 'I told him it was impossible. He had a family, and I had a husband who was my family . . .' A half-finished piece of carrot cake sat on her plate, and she stared at it.

'And that's where it ended?' I wanted to know so much more. She had managed to buy herself one week. But is that all it ever was?

Her hesitation held me riveted. 'No. But that's all I think I can manage to tell you today,' she eventually said.

She looked desperately tired and wrung out suddenly. When I peeked at my watch, I saw that we'd been sitting there for two hours. No wonder she had seemed to fade into the pattern on the chair. Listening to her story had been like watching an engrossing film where you can barely bring yourself to press pause to take a toilet break.

'I hope Evelyn is all right?' I say to Michael now. 'Perhaps you can give me her phone number so I can check on her later?' What happened after that week? Had she returned home? I'm concluding she must have. I am fascinated by how much I want to know.

'Of course,' he says. 'I am sure she'd love that.'

We stand in companionable silence, and eavesdrop on a conversation that Martin and Ronnie are having about the hats worn by the two women in the painting. Martin is telling Ronnie they are called cloche hats, which is amazing and absolutely right.

'Where are Martin's teeth?' I ask Michael, just noticing they are missing.

'Good question.' He shrugs in that languid way of his. 'Teeth can be a bit of a shared commodity at Sunrise . . . Whenever a set goes missing, they have a way of showing up in someone else's mouth. In Martin's case, whichever nurse identifies them first gets the prize of not having to bathe him for a week. He hates the tub.'

I gasp, then chuckle. 'Oh no!' There's something oddly magnetic about Michael's genuine, down-to-earth charm. I'm only really sensing the full force of it now. I can't imagine him ever becoming angry or letting anything get to him. I bet he loves dogs and has no desire to go bar-hopping in Ibiza.

'They just look more glamorous because the colours in the picture are bright,' Ronnie says.

'They're not really even talking. Maybe they're jealous of each other. Maybe it's to do with the hats.' Martin doesn't sound quite so authoritative without his teeth. I smile.

'You're right about the colours, Ronnie.' Michael winks at me again. 'But I don't think the women dislike each other. They're just having a serious conversation. One they have to break up with long pauses.'

He never patronises his patients, I notice. He never oversimplifies things or implies they can't understand. I've caught myself on the verge of doing it, and stopped myself, following Michael's influence.

'Apparently, a journalist who met the artist said Hopper was hopeless at small talk,' I tell them. 'He was supposed to be famous for his monumental silences. But like the spaces in his paintings, the emptiness was never really empty. It was weighted down with things that were best silently concluded rather than said.' Michael smiles when I finish, and holds my eyes. It's vaguely possible that he's flirting with me, which is pleasantly flattering, and slightly bewildering to this new bride.

The men become bored with *Chop Suey*. They're looking at Christina now. I wonder if they remember her from their intense previous visit.

'This one isn't happy, because she's crawling on the grass and looks sad,' Martin says.

'But we can't see her face to know if she's sad,' Michael says. 'All we can see is that she's looking up at a house.'

'You don't always have to see somebody's face to know they're sad,' Martin adds, looking at me a mite too closely, as though I'm giving something away. Or perhaps that's just my imagination. 'Sometimes, you can just tell from how they are.' His voice has a tender quality that touches me.

'If we can't see her face, we might think she's beautiful. If we saw it and it's ugly, we wouldn't care about her. The artist knows how we think.'

'I think we can't see her face because Christina could be any one of us,' Michael adds. 'I think this is what the artist intended. She longs for something she can't have again, and we've all done that in life.'

Gosh! I think. He's quite insightful about art. I like how he brings a bit of a personal interpretation that speaks of his own lurking disappointments.

'That's crap!' Martin fires back. 'It's because she's ugly. In all my life, I have known this to be true. Nobody's interested in ugly people. I've been ugly all my life, and it got me nowhere, but I've known some very beautiful people who were successful.'

This makes me chuckle.

'Well!' Michael titters, too. 'That's a very intriguing theory about ugly people you've got there, Martin. You should copyright that. You could make millions.'

'I tell you, ugly people and sad people. Nobody wants to be around them. Ugly women never marry rich men. Christina's not ugly, but she's sad. Maybe that's why she's ended up all alone.'

'It's because she's so alone in all that dull-coloured landscape,' Ronnie chimes in. 'The only thing there is the house that she can't go back to. You know what? I think she's lonely. I think she wants a man.'

'That's what I was just saying, dumbo,' Martin says. 'She's alone and she's not very pretty, and she can't get a fellow.'

I have to cover my smile. This is proving to be quite an entertaining day. I notice, though, that Eddy just sits quietly on the bench. He's wearing the same bright-red shirt he wore on the first visit. He's so thin, even with the help of a thick shirt tucked into his jeans; it's hard to imagine him the way Evelyn described him that day she first saw him in her garden. And yet I can easily picture them riding together in his truck on that first outing, him driving them through charming coastal villages, their picnic at the beach, their afternoons spent up in her bedroom, his declaring the certainty with which he loved her . . . her telling him – what were her words? *We go nowhere.*

I stare at the back of his fine-shaped head, and suddenly I recognise something about myself. The vivid way she described him has made me fall for him a little myself.

Perhaps we've undergone some telepathic thought transference, because Eddy turns and looks at me. He smiles. Something about the expression is self-aware. A connection flickers briefly between us and then is gone. I go and sit down beside him.

'What do you think, Eddy?' I nod to Christina. I can't help looking at his wonderfully expressive hands: the long, tapered fingers, the hands of a working man who had an unexpected artistic side. Did he, I wonder? I will have to ask Evelyn. 'This was Christina's home that she loved so dearly. Do you think Christina was wrong to leave?'

It's not as though I believe that oblique overtures about the past will get me anywhere. I just keep thinking of how he'd spoken last time, and Evelyn's belief that it could happen again.

He doesn't seem to register my question. At one point, though, his eyes comb over my face like he might be recognising me from his last visit. I'm on the cusp of saying something to perhaps bridge the connection, but by the time I can think of what, the moment is lost. 'Not chatty today, Eddy?' I gently squeeze his hand. 'I get my quiet days, too. We're a lot alike, you and I . . .' At the sight of our hands together, I inexplicably choke up.

We fitted like teeth on a zip . . . she'd said. How I loved that. Could I claim the same about Justin and me? And, if not, is that why he might have someone else?

'I'll not pester you, if you'd rather I leave you alone.' Uncertainty cleaves a huge hole in me.

'What would you call this painting if you had to name it, Ronnie?' Michael asks.

Martin beats Ronnie to an answer. 'I would call it *The Sound of Silence.*'

'That's a great title, Martin. Why would you call it that?'

'Because there are no dogs, no tractors, no cars. It's very quiet there.'

'What would you call it, Eddy?' I try.

And, without a beat of hesitation, Eddy says, 'I would call it *Regrets.*'

'Why would you call it *Regrets*, Eddy?' I glance excitedly at Michael, who gives me a short, pleased nod.

'Because she's yearning for something she's let go.'

My spirits are capering around like a bird. 'I agree, Eddy. She's incredibly torn, isn't she?'

'Yes, she's torn, and I don't want her to be,' Eddy says. 'I want her to choose.'

'What do you want her to choose?' I ask, but he doesn't answer.

'I don't like it.' Martin is covering his eyes with his hands. 'She's on the outside looking in at something she wants. She's in exile.'

Michael speaks quietly in my ear. 'Heck, since we've moved on from talking about ugly people, it's all taking a very negative turn.'

'Well, I think you guys are all barking up the wrong tree,' Ronnie pipes up. 'I think the painting is very hopeful.'

'Why's it hopeful, Ronnie?' Michael asks.

'Because she looks like she's going to get to where she wants to go.'

When I get back to my office, I ring Evelyn. She answers the phone, slightly breathless.

'Oh my gosh! What's wrong?' I fill with alarm.

'Nothing!' she says, and I can hear the sound of a smile in her voice. 'I wasn't feeling myself this morning. I thought it best that Michael go alone . . . But I'm fine now. I've just been dragging some boxes out of storage. It's winded me. Phew!'

I try to picture her in her world, in her flat she bought – the one Michael called swanky. 'Well, you should take care. Can't you get someone to do that for you? Michael?'

'My manservant, you mean? I am sure he would love that.'

I laugh. I tell her about the development in the gallery with Eddy. 'He called the painting *Regrets*. He said Christina is yearning for something she's let go . . . I thought the regrets word was interesting. I don't think anyone could really look at that painting and conclude that Christina has regrets. I've never even heard that interpretation before. So I wonder if this is a sign that Christina is triggering something on a deeper level for Eddy. Something, maybe, about you?'

The line goes quiet at first. Then she says, 'I doubt it somehow. We are probably just trying too hard to look for something.'

I don't really know Evelyn, but I do know that she's not normally this pessimistic. 'I realise it's possible we're hoping for something that might never happen. But it felt encouraging to me. I sensed he was bringing something of himself to the moment – that he wasn't just talking about a girl on the grass with a house in the background.'

'That's very sweet,' Evelyn says. 'And perhaps you are right. Someone once told me that there's no harm in believing something that makes you happy, so maybe I will believe that. Thanks to you.'

She still doesn't sound convinced, though.

After a beat she says, 'Anyway, how are you?'

'Me? Oh!' I don't know why the question takes me aback. 'I'm okay, I suppose.' Even I can hear the fallen note of my voice.

'If there's anything you would like to tell me, you always can,' she says.

'I've never been great at talking about myself.'

'Neither have I. But look how well I manage it!'

I chuckle. 'I loved your story, Evelyn. Or at least the part you've told me so far . . . You took me to your house, your garden. I saw your romance with Eddy as clearly as if it had been my own. But I'm not good with words the way you are. It's harder for me to express myself . . .'

'Well, it's easier to talk about things that happened a very long time ago. You have distance in your favour.'

'Does time heal?' I am not sure where the question comes from. 'Don't they always say time heals all wounds? I just wonder if I've at least got that to look forward to.'

The line goes silent again, except for the small, soft rushes of her breathing. I sense this question has distressed her. 'I don't think it does. Not really. It just makes the pain less uppermost.'

'I appreciate your honesty,' I tell her. But I don't like it. It terrifies me. Will all conversations I have with anyone, from this point on, somehow circle back to Justin? Will I really carry this around for the rest of my life – not an open wound but a permanent scar?

I suddenly remember that first day in the gallery. When she talked about wrong choices and consequences. 'Well, to cite another cliché, don't they say regret what you didn't do, not what you did?'

'Hmm . . . I particularly don't like that one.'

I feel like saying, *What if you'd never known a person could love you like he loved you? Then you would be exactly like me.*

'Are you able to tell me what happened next? After you told him you weren't going to let him leave his wife for you – I'm curious to know where this goes.'

She is silent again, and I can tell she is lost to the pull of the memory. 'You don't have to,' I add. 'Not if it's going to be upsetting.'

'I was torn,' she says. 'Eddy was right. Alice, I was wavering so very badly. I'd told him we both must get on with our lives, but I had absolutely no idea how I was going to walk away.' Her breathing softly rushes again. 'There was only one thing to do. I realised I had to see them – his family. They had to become real to me, because in my moments when I was vacillating, they were becoming bleary, and I was being able to convince myself . . .'

'That they didn't really exist,' I finish for her.

'Yes,' she says. 'So I drove to the community hall where he'd said his daughter took dance classes. I waited around, sitting slumped in the seat of my car with a silly hat on. I must have looked ridiculous, like a female Columbo . . . I recognised the little girl from the photographs Eddy had shown me. She was wearing a pink leotard and white footless tights. She had long, light-brown hair, and she bounded out of the car and ran ahead of her mother, over to some other children who were standing outside the main door with their mothers. I couldn't believe I was staring at Eddy's child.' Her voice sounds warm and wistful suddenly, and this touches me. 'She was such a cute thing. I was quite enthralled by the sight of her, and of course I felt awful! I couldn't believe I was nearly responsible for taking her father away from her. She was so young and innocent! I felt this incredible urge to protect her. The force of it stunned me.'

'What did his wife look like?' I ask her.

'She was attractive. Confident. Friendly. She stood and chatted animatedly to the other mothers. I'd expected someone more downtrodden.'

'Why was that?'

'I don't know. The silly notions we have . . . Perhaps if I had seen someone who had clearly let herself go, I might have thought she deserved having her husband fall for someone else – which might have made me feel better about it. But as it was, it all just felt sad.'

'Why did you feel sad for a stranger, Evelyn? You didn't even know her. She might have been a horrible person, a nightmare to live with . . .'

'Because I was sleeping with her husband. She was just a woman living her life, working part-time, taking her child to dance class, and she was standing there completely unaware that her husband wanted to leave her for me.'

'But it's life, Evelyn. It happens all the time.' As soon as I say this, I realise I'm not entirely convinced of it. Would I feel this pragmatic if I learnt that Justin had left me for some other woman? I highly doubt it.

'Well, it did what I'd needed it to do. Once I saw them, it repositioned the way I thought of Eddy. It gave him a lesser foothold in that place inside me where I saw him as mine.' She sounds terribly moved suddenly, as though she were reliving this in real time, and the pain is absolutely back to being uppermost. 'I realised that in order to break up a family, I had to create a false truth: that taking another woman's husband is okay, especially if perhaps you have succeeded where she has failed: in showing him that you need him more.'

'So you left and went back to London?'

'Yes. Sneakily. I didn't have the courage to face him. I just left a note pinned to the back door.'

'And that was the end of it?'

'If I find what I'm looking for in these boxes, they'll be able to answer that for you.'

I hear her rustling around again.

I don't know if she's being deliberately evasive, or just eager to get back to what she was doing. 'Hmm . . .' I say, smiling to myself. 'You have a way of drawing out a story, Evelyn.'

EIGHTEEN

I am grating Parmesan for my pasta – forcing myself to make some proper food for a change, if anything just to reclaim some version of a normal routine – distantly thinking of Evelyn spying on Eddy's wife, like Columbo, when the phone rings.

It's Sally.

I wipe my hands on a tea-towel, and pick up. 'Hi,' I say. 'I feel bad I haven't rung you back!' She's left about three messages.

'I've been so worried.'

'I know. Sorry,' I tell her. I realise that whatever little grievance I had against her, it's over now. 'I don't know. I just haven't felt much like talking.'

I stuff the phone between my chin and shoulder and reach for the bag of macaroni, but it splits as I pull it open and pasta scatters on to the bench and floor. I stare at it and sigh.

'How are you?' she asks. 'I mean, really. How are you doing?'

I squat to start clearing all this up, but my legs are too weak, and I wobble and have to put out a hand for balance. 'I'm not good, to be honest. I'm not very good at all.' I'd actually thought I was a little better earlier in the gallery, but coming home always reverses my mood.

'It's not so bad when I'm around people,' I tell her. 'Then I don't think about it.'

I suppose I know something's coming because I realise that her first words weren't, *Have you heard from him?*

'Alice . . . I have to tell you something,' she says. Then, as my heart pounds suddenly, she says, 'I saw him today.'

My head swims. I go to stand up but see stars.

'What do you mean, you saw him?'

'In town. I was coming out of the shoe-repair shop. He was in a car. A silver BMW . . . Alice, he was with someone.'

Justin doesn't drive a silver BMW. I am confused. The sauce is splattering, jumping out of the pan. I should move it off the hob, or turn down the heat, but my brain isn't instructing my hands. I back up, as though a threat is coming at me, crunching macaroni under my feet. 'What do you mean, someone?' I make contact with the counter, which stops me, and my legs almost give way.

'A woman,' she says, after a moment. 'He was with a woman.'

My blood is making a weird whooshing sound in my ears. It's like hearing the sea through a shell.

Justin. With a woman.

Everyone's sake.

'Are you still there?' Sally asks.

'Yes.' I swallow a gummy thickness that won't go down.

'Sorry. I hate telling you, but I had to. I mean, you have a right to know.'

I need to clear my throat. 'But . . . you said you *think* you saw him?'

'It was him, Alice. It was definitely Justin.'

He was with a woman. The words just keep coming back to me. Yet suddenly there's a partial clearing in the frenzy of my head, a light shining through. 'Sorry, Sally, I'm not sure . . . It could have been anybody, right? A client . . .' Justin is always out with clients. 'Someone he works with.' My mouth has gone dry. My top lip is curling and sticking under my top front teeth.

'But you said he wasn't at work. You said he was taking time off, didn't you?' Her voice brims with pity.

Did I? 'No,' I say, trying to think. 'Louisa said he was working from home. He can't just take time off work . . .'

I can feel speculation trying to flourish in the gap that follows – on both our parts. 'I'm sorry,' she says, eventually. 'I don't think it was a client, Al. I mean, I know it wasn't.'

My heart hammers – does she know something? Adrenaline and annoyance push it past where it feels healthy to go. 'But you don't know that for a fact. I'm not sure you can really say that . . .'

'No. But . . .'

'But what?' Her obvious reluctance to just spit it out sends ungodly terror through me.

'There was just something about them. They just looked . . . I don't know, together.'

Together. The word comes back, and back, and back to me. I frown. I can't relax my eyebrows. I can't rearrange my face.

'Sorry,' she says, when I've gone quiet. 'I know it must be so very hard to hear. I'm just reporting what I saw.'

'I'm not sure that's true, Sally. I think you're reporting what you believe you saw. There's a difference.' Part of me is thinking, if the situation were reversed, would I be so quick to notify Sally of this when I had no real proof of anything? Then the other part of me wonders why I am being so critical of her again.

'Anyway,' I go on, 'how was he going to meet some woman? We were always together. Either that, or he was working. And he'd never mess around with anyone at work – he hated that kind of thing. And if he had met someone else, then why marry me? It doesn't make sense.'

'I don't know,' she says, eventually.

His text said, Discovered something before wedding. 'He's not having an affair. Honestly, Sally, I just know he isn't. Don't ask me how I know, but I do. Whatever it is . . . Well, it's something else.' The confidence in my words convinces me of them.

'Okay,' she says. 'I believe you.'

But then the tiny betraying voice of doubt speaks so quietly that I barely hear it. 'Go on, then,' I say. 'You might as well tell me. What did she look like?'

NINETEEN

Evelyn

London. 1983

> Dear Eddy,
> I couldn't bear to say goodbye. I thought it wise I return to London immediately. It's best you forget me.
> Evelyn

Mark had been called into a meeting, so his driver was waiting for her at Heathrow. She sat in the back seat of the Bentley feeling disconnected from herself, like a passenger in her own life, watching the outskirts of grey London slide past her.

High Street Kensington looked the same. Yet walking into her three-bedroom flat in the small garden square just behind the high street was a bit like having an out-of-body experience. The daily routines of her life were there in abeyance like a lost memory that was returning in fragments. The place was suspiciously tidy. None of Evelyn's perfumed cardigans hung over the chair backs. There were no platform shoes in the hallway. No errant hairpins on the dining table. In fact, not a single piece of evidence on the bathroom counter that she lived here. It was as though someone had moved her out.

And that was how she felt from then on: emotionally relocated. Over the years, when coming home from visits up North, she had often experienced a strange limbo, unsure which life she was leaning toward reattaching herself to. When she had returned from her mother's funeral it had been the heightened sense of her own mortality that had troubled her: the reality finally setting in about where she stood in the grand scheme of her own identity. She was someone's wife, no one's mother, and no longer anyone's child. Without Mark, she would be without bearings, navigating her way around nothing. But now all her thoughts were of Eddy.

For the next three weeks, she drifted flatly between the events that defined her life. But nothing was quite the same. She tried to maintain her twice-weekly jazz dance classes in the sprung-floor studio in Covent Garden. Afterward, she would usually sip a cappuccino in the fresh air, listening to a Peruvian pipe band playing beside the central arcade, occasionally striking up a pleasant conversation with a stranger. But now she tended to sit in a corner and avoid people. On Wednesdays, she normally lunched with friends, but found herself drumming up excuses to avoid going. On Fridays, she clothes-shopped because there was a numbing anonymity among the racks of the season's latest fashions. Afternoons would normally entail a leisurely walk through Hyde Park with Harry, their cocker spaniel, then a trip to Harrods Food Halls to pick up dinner if they weren't dining out. But now she napped a lot in the afternoons. She convinced herself she was just tired, or run down, but secretly she knew it was because of Eddy. She missed him as though he had been the left ventricle of her heart.

It rained a lot that summer. She had written virtually nothing, just tied up a few loose ends on a couple of magazine commissions. Mark, who had known someone high up at the exciting new women's magazine *Cosmopolitan*, had originally got her a job there as an assistant.

Since its inception, the magazine had taken Britain by storm with its frank and entertaining acknowledgement of the fact that women were not just mothers and accessories for men. They enjoyed sex, they had dreams of transcending the typing pool and they were no longer happy to plod on with unsatisfying marriages.

The magazine's concept had unleashed something in Evelyn. She had presented one or two story ideas almost daily to the editor. They were good and current. As Evelyn pointed out to her editor over wine in a smoke-filled pub, in April 1975 everyone had been singing along to Tammy Wynette's 'Stand By Your Man', which had ascended the British pop chart. But by July, they had moved on to 'D-I-V-O-R-C-E'. Her editor had lapped it up. So, rather swiftly, Evelyn's job changed. She no longer answered phones and filed copy. She was given proper assignments, and invited to editorial meetings. These often took place over a boozy lunch down some buzzing side street near the magazine's offices. She lived for those lunches. Plus, she made friends of her own – *real people*, as she described them to Mark: those with whom she had something in common.

She would trot out of there on such a mission, armed with her story and her direction for the week. But after a couple of years, her career had started to become inconvenient. Mark had wanted them to take off on spontaneous trips and weekends. Her job was hindering his freedom. So, reluctantly, she had gone freelance. But the irony struck her. A woman had just been made leader of the Conservative Party, the nation had just passed the Sex Discrimination Act, and yet Evelyn Westland's ambitions were being curtailed because her job was getting in the way of her husband's good time.

Now, though, she was less motivated to find ideas for features, and was drawn to the fancy she'd long had of writing a novel. Sitting at her desk with pen and paper at hand, the idea of what the story would be about would hover but never fully land. Every time she tried to ask herself, *What do people want to read?* all she kept seeing was Eddy's face.

Once in a while, she popped into the magazine's office to meet with her editor. It was on such a day, about a month after her return from Holy Island, that one of the secretaries said there was a letter for her.

When she saw the postmark, everything seemed to stand still, except for the pounding of her heart.

How had he found her?

She took the letter to a crowded Italian coffee shop near Tottenham Court Road Tube station. The place hissed with gleaming machines that turned milk to foam. Its two tall windows either side of the door were steamed up, so you couldn't read the backward inscription of the name on the glass: *Mario's*.

Dear Evelyn,

His writing was neat and cursive. He'd even written the date in full, with the year – so very precise – which charmed her.

> I hope you will forgive me writing to you like this. I remembered the name of your magazine, and I enquired in a bookshop and found the address.
>
> Finding your note and knowing that you had left without saying goodbye devastated me more than I can ever tell you. But I know you did it because you thought it was what I needed, to shake some sense into me, and you were probably right.
>
> I should never have asked you to leave your marriage and your life for me. It was all too much, too fast, not to mention mad. I'd have had to be a very special man to compete with what you already have, and I suppose I'm realistic enough to know I am not that man. Expecting you to give up everything

for someone who has nothing by comparison was insanity, and I regret dreaming for a moment.

So why am I writing? I suppose because something has gone from my life now, but, for the time it takes me to pen this, I feel the thread of a connection again. Just the thought that you might be sat somewhere in secret reading my words cheers me up and brings me closer to you. I thought that after a month had passed I would start, in some small way, to get over you. But the opposite has happened. I am more certain than ever of my feelings for you. You are so ingrained in me now, Evelyn, that even if I never see you again I will always relive our time together, and fantasise that it didn't have to end. I will be haunted by *What if. . . ?* I keep playing you over and over in my mind – from that very moment I was in your mother's garden and I turned around and saw you coming down the path, looking like a fashion model, then everything that passed between us after that. And then back to twenty years ago – our meeting that perhaps affected me in ways that it didn't quite affect you. Sometimes, I think I must have dreamed the happiness I knew so briefly because of you.

I know that until the day I die I will never forget you.

In hindsight, it might have been best for my sanity if we had never met at that wedding – if I had never been there, or if you had been with a boyfriend, and I wouldn't have tried to stretch beyond my reach. But I did meet you. I just have to stop reading meaning into why.

I hope you have returned to your life and are happy now that you have got something out of your system. And if I have been in any way responsible for that, then it was worthwhile in the end.

No, I lie. What I hope is that you will come home.

Eddy

She was astonished by how beautifully he put words together. As the espresso machine hissed in the background, and someone's kid stood trailing his index finger through the condensation on the glass, she held in her hand the pressed pink fuchsia bell that had fallen out of the notepaper.

TWENTY

Evelyn drifted through the weekend as though she were furnished with light.

The routine was essentially the same as ever. She and Mark went to Buckinghamshire on Friday night, to their five-bedroom Georgian mansion that was only twenty miles outside London, set in eight acres of pasture and paddock. Normally, as soon as they arrived, Mark would become fossilised into sedentary, country life. They would walk the dogs: two basset hounds and a black Labrador – and Harry, the cocker spaniel, who lived with them in London. They would lunch together, and, in the afternoon, Mark would read the *Financial Times* in an armchair. Sometimes, Evelyn would bake an apple pie. On the land adjacent to the house, there was a converted coach house where the couple lived who tended to the horses and the dogs when she and Mark were up in town during the week. Evelyn liked the Kimberleys, and would pay a visit, taking over a little of what she had baked. When she was overcome with restless energy, she would take Thunder, her horse, out for a canter across the meadow; as his feet pounded the earth, the vibration set her free.

On occasion, she recognised that the house lacked the rumblings of children. Their marriage had needed to grow new life. The worst of it was that the Harley Street doctors had told them that they both were capable of producing a baby, just not with each other. She had wanted to say, *Is that the most scientific explanation you can come up with?* But Mark hadn't questioned its nonsensicality, and he wouldn't have thought it was her place to challenge an eminent doctor. She had often wondered, though, if he was secretly afraid of finding out that the problem might lie with him. It sat there silently between them, this ghost of some other, more fulfilled life that they each might have secretly felt they were owed. And so they kept dogs and horses, filling the blanks with lots of living things to convince them that no blanks existed: ignoring the truth that perhaps they should have adopted a baby years ago. Once she had turned forty, it seemed too late. They knew this because they had had the conversation for all of five minutes.

One day, the previous weekend, she had come across *Lady Chatterley's Lover* on a shelf in their vast library. She'd read it when she first moved to London. D. H. Lawrence's publisher had been acquitted in an obscenity trial at the Old Bailey a couple of years earlier. She had struggled to finish the novel then. But this time, she'd found herself reading it with new eyes.

Now she knew exactly how Constance Chatterley must have felt. In fact, by the time she had finished the novel, she was convinced she was Constance Chatterley. Only Constance hadn't loved her gardener, not nearly in the same way, so it was quite different. She had hidden the book in a special place, between two of her favourite poetry books, to make it easy to find again.

But this particular Saturday, Evelyn couldn't read or bake or ride because she couldn't settle all the thoughts that were running riot. There was no room she could wander into where she could stay for more than a couple of minutes, no chair she could sit on, no task she could complete. Possibilities were rushing at her. Every cell of her body was alive with him again. He was full, and real and he was back! She could barely keep the feeling inside of her. Eddy's voice, Eddy's eyes, his laugh, his touch, his kiss – his letter had brought him so far to the fore again that she imagined Mark would be able to actually see him when he looked her in the eyes. So, for that reason, she tried to keep her distance. But when they were together, in the evening, in front of the telly, she found herself observing him out of the corner of her eye. Since returning from her week with Eddy, she had done this often – studied Mark without him knowing – slowly pulsing with guilt at how she had betrayed him. But this time was different. This time, it was the disquieting variety of guilt that came with knowing it wasn't over.

On Sunday evening, they sat at opposite ends of the patio table overlooking the orchard that hummed and smelt of a rainy summer. They were eating Mrs Kimberley's cottage pie when Evelyn said, 'I hired a painter when I was back up home.'

'Oh yes.' Mark didn't look up from his food.

'Eddy, he's called. Would you believe it, but it turns out that years ago I was supposed to go on a date with him, but I never turned up.' She didn't know why she had said that. She had just wanted to say his name.

Mark prodded peas with his fork. 'Really? Well, that's odd.'

She stared at the top of his head, aware of an aching void of displacement and loss. 'Well, it's not exactly odd. It's just a coincidence. One of those "small world" things.'

Mark pierced his last pea.

'He actually used to help my mother in the garden. He's very nice. And a very pleasant-looking man, too.' She struggled to be casual, but was like china, cracking.

Mark looked up from his food. There was a beat of hesitation, where she thought, *He knows!* Then he said, 'Do we have any more of this? It's very good.'

She wanted to say, *I'm talking about adultery I've committed with a man I'm in love with, and you're more interested in a pie!* But, of course, she didn't. Getting angry at Mark to somehow assuage her guilt about Eddy was a strategy that even she couldn't approve of.

Even if she had said, *He came every day. We spent hours together talking, doing errands, and we even went to the beach together . . .* Mark would never be threatened by someone who had what he'd have labelled as a menial job. Besides, Mark was not the type to mistrust his wife. That would have been a character flaw and a personal failure he'd not have wanted to contend with – on her part, and on his own, for marrying her.

When they went to bed, she was relieved that he didn't want to make love.

They usually did in the country.

Back in London, Mark walked around their bed in his black socks and white shirt-tails, throwing a tantrum because he'd misplaced a cufflink. The contrast between her husband and her lover astounded Evelyn all over again. It was as though both men were standing at the fork of two long roads. Eddy was thinking of just hopping on his bike and flying off down there at lightning speed, and Mark was trying to decide if he should pack an umbrella.

'I don't know why you can't just come tonight. You have to eat dinner,' he said.

'I've told you already. I have a headache. And, besides, you know I'm not really needed.' Out of the corner of her eye, she watched him vent his anger by screwing up one of her face towels that had happened to find itself on top of his dresser, and throwing it on to the bed.

She knew that his bad mood was more to do with his inability to control her. It was the one contention in their marriage. 'It's your Northern-ness,' he'd say, implying that still, after all these years of living in London, Evelyn had failed to conform in the ways he saw as mattering. Once, when she had complained about how hard it was to make proper friends in London, he had suggested she take elocution lessons.

'I can't see how my accent can be the problem! Unless it's a problem for you.' She had glared at him. 'Is it?'

He had frowned as though she were a tiresome child. 'Of course it's not. But you're the one always complaining you don't fit in.'

'I thought you loved how I spoke? I thought it was part of what attracted you to me?'

'I do love how you speak, darling. Just not always what you say.'

He had been teasing her. But since then, she'd been determined to keep her accent. In fact, she decided she was going to work hard to re-introduce any ugly Northern terms she might have once tried to stamp out, just to annoy him further. But she didn't keep it up.

He was now fastening the cufflink that he'd found. 'What do you mean, you're not really needed? *I* need you. Doesn't that count? It's a bloody dinner. No one's asking you to change political allegiance or solve world poverty.'

Mark had a gentlemanliness that made swear words sound respectable. Something that had attracted her to him years ago. But recently, she had started to wish he would fume once in a while.

'If it's just a dinner, it shouldn't be a big deal then, should it?'

'Exactly. So why is it?'

'Oh Mark . . .' She thought she might burst if he didn't leave her alone to her thoughts of Eddy. 'I'm under the weather. I'm not in the mood to make polite conversation with another wife whom I don't even know . . .' She wanted to say, *I just don't think I can do it one more time, and I just don't see why I have to.* But that would have sounded selfish and spoilt, because it was selfish and spoilt. Generally, she played the dutiful wife, and sometimes she caught herself realising it wasn't even an act. Yet she often wondered why it couldn't have been her business dinner, with Mark trying to talk to some husband who didn't want to be there. The old Evelyn would have gone to make Mark happy, simply because she loved him and he asked very little of her. But getting the letter from Eddy had given her new power.

She pretended to browse through a magazine, hoping this would be the end of it. As she moved her eyes over glossy pages of type, she was seeing herself riding in Eddy's van, wishing he had driven their lives in a circle, back to when they had first met, so she could have her choice all over again.

When Mark was dressed, he turned and looked at her stretched out on the bed, with affection. He kissed her forehead. 'Have it your way. It would be nice if you're still up when I get home, though. I feel I haven't properly seen you or talked to you in ages.'

'But we spent the entire weekend together.'

'Yes. But you didn't seem there.'

Dear Eddy, she wrote, with delight, when she was certain Mark had gone and wasn't coming back. She had been surprised to see that Eddy had supplied the address of his friend Stanley. How uncharacteristically furtive of him!

> I was astonished to get your letter. I have not been able to get you out of my mind. I'm sorry I left so abruptly. It was cruel of me. But it was the only way I knew I would leave. If you had held me in your arms again, and said, *Don't go*, I would not have gone. All the reasons why I had to would not have mattered.
>
> I have spent hours analysing my feelings for you – whether I am genuinely in love, or motivated by a need for some colour in an otherwise monochrome existence. But now I see it as it simply is. I have everything I should want in my life, and yet there is something I want that seems to negate everything else.

And, for a brief time, I had it with you. I keep coming back to that day our eyes met in the church, and that sense I had, almost immediately, that you were going to be central to something. Strangely enough, I believe my mother knew. I am sure she hoped that somehow, with a little help, we would find a second chance.

Thinking of us is all that keeps me happy these days. I wonder how long this spell I'm under will last, or if I'm destined to think of you forever.

I wonder if you will go on tending to the garden until the end of the growing season? I know we had this conversation, but I am enclosing money for the next few months. I really don't know what my plans are any more. My resolve to sell the place has somehow weakened. I don't know what our letters – if this is the start of a correspondence – will mean. But I am going to take it for what it is: a welcome addition to my rather confused life.

By the way, you were wrong about something. You said you understood that it would take a very special man to get me to leave my marriage, and you didn't think you could possibly be him. Well, sitting here writing this, I couldn't envision leaving my marriage for anyone who wasn't you.

Evelyn

Was it too heavy? She suspected that she would end up regretting having encouraged him. But she had already pushed it through the postbox. It was gone now.

TWENTY-ONE

There were no more afternoon naps, and no more depression. His letters came quickly. He talked about his love for her, his dreams, his daily routine and how much brighter the world appeared through his eyes now that he was looking at everything around him but seeing only her. She hurried to post her replies. She told him how she was throwing herself madly into life with new gusto. How she'd had her hair done like *Dynasty*'s Linda Evans, how she'd shopped for clothes that she imagined he would like her in. How she'd gone to the opera and sat through *Madama Butterfly* without shedding one tear because she'd been fantasising about the life they might have together. By the time the opera was over, she'd seen it in all its full and glorious detail: Eddy conducting a successful landscape business to rich clients in London; Eddy and her dining with her friends on Fridays, whiling away their summer Sundays under trees in Hyde Park. She told him how she'd sold another article to the magazine, and had even begun her book, drumming up a rough outline from copious notes she had made over the last few months. She told him she would call herself Joanna Smart, if it ever got published. So that Mark would never know. She always signed off with, *Your Constance Chatterley*.

Then the letter came that changed everything.

My Constance Chatterley,
Your last letter was one I read over and over. I read all your letters multiple times – I can hear your voice in them and it makes me so happy. But this one was different. What you said has made me do a great deal of soul searching. The joy your letters give me, the joy I have from knowing you are still in my life, has changed my life. I'm not much of a writer. I spell as badly as I sing, and get clumsy and tongue-tied whenever I sit down with a pen. Yet you make me want to write better letters. You make me want to push myself to be a better man. Maybe if I'd moved away from here when I was younger, or tried harder in school, I would have amounted to something that would have made me worthy of you. If I could do it all over again, I would make that my mission. I always think of that knot I had in my stomach when I talked to you the first time in the garden – the same one I had when I thought we were going to go out, twenty years ago.

But I can't do this any more.

Being back there every second week in your mother's garden is too agonising for me. I think of you constantly, and I see you everywhere I look. I keep hoping that one day I'll glance up and you'll be there again, and you'll have come home, come back to me. Sometimes, I even find myself driving past the house looking for you, even though I know it's insane. But I realise I'm selling myself the same dream I sold myself briefly many years ago, and at some point I have to stop. You describe your life so beautifully, but that is your life – I was reminded of that in your last letter. Your life is there. It's not here. And, let's face it, I am never going to be a landscaper to rich people, dining out with your friends on weekends, which you tell me is how you would most like to see our story together play out. Evelyn, I will never stop wanting you. A part of me dies to think that Stanley won't have any more letters to give me, and that you'll find someone else to take care of the garden in my place, and then in time I will just be a distant memory. I will never let the passage of time allow me to forget you, or to love you any less. But I have to exercise whatever willpower I can manage to let you get on with your life, and somehow try to get on with mine.

It seems impossible to me that I may never see you again for as long as I live. But we can't go on like this forever, can we? So I am making this very hard decision for both of us.

Goodbye, Evelyn. I love you more than I have ever been able to adequately say. But loving someone isn't enough, is it? I realise that now.

PS. Nat King Cole's 'Unforgettable' was just on the radio. Every time I hear it, I will think of us sitting in the sunshine in your garden, talking about our dreams. It's up there with one of the best days of my life. Seems that nearly all of them have contained you.

A gasp, combined with a sob, came out of her so forcefully that she almost choked.

'No!'

She was sitting in the same coffee house. She must have said it out loud because people at the next table looked at her in shock.

The response tumbled out of her so eagerly that she could barely hold the pen.

> No, Eddy! I cannot let you do this. I wish I'd never written what I did. I suppose it was my unfortunate way of trying to impress upon you how much I think about you, how much I seem to exist only for you. You have taken me too literally. You living in London, being a part of my life here, is not how I see us at all – not really! I think I just thought that because it makes my being here more palatable to think of you with me. It doesn't mean that I want to stay.
>
> Please reconsider! I lost you once, through a very bad decision I made. I can't lose you again because I have somehow managed to say the wrong thing. Please write back quickly and tell me you didn't mean it, and that we can go on. I can't bear it if you are gone from me . . .

She only had to wait an agonising two days. But she knew what he was going to say even before she read it.

> I can't. I can't go on like this. It's killing me, and it's not fair to others. I want my fantasies to be of the woman I've got, not the woman I don't have. Or at least that's how it should be, shouldn't it? Somehow, I have to find a way to make that happen. But for now, given I can't have you, then my head has got to be free of you. Please try to understand. X

She had never, ever, even come close to experiencing the level of devastation that his letter brought. Perhaps it had to happen. Or she would never have known how badly she needed to say this.

I will leave him, she wrote.

TWENTY-TWO

Alice

Folding Justin's things and putting them in suitcases and bin liners is like emptying a house after a death. I try doing it with the radio on, but the voices grate on my nerves. I try silence, and can't bear that, either. I just keep seeing a composite of sharp, pretty features, and longish dark hair.

I vowed two days ago that if one more email or text I send goes unanswered, or if I phone him one more time and he doesn't pick up, then this is it; I can't go on like this any more. And yet when it's come down to it, I am strung out with doubt and uncertainty. If I tell him to come get his stuff, then I'm being the one to make it final. I'm never going to know if he would have come back eventually, after he'd taken whatever time he needed. And I don't know if my even thinking he deserves all this time is making me a considerate person or the biggest fool I know.

I manage to fill two suitcases and two bin liners. I look up at the empty wardrobe, staring at all the empty hangers – except for one that still has his khaki Burberry jacket hanging on it. I was with him on a business trip to London when he bought it. He'd treated me to a lovely indigo Prada dress, which had felt astonishingly extravagant; I didn't wear designer clothes. Even though I earned decently, I was rarely generous with myself. My mother hardly ever bought herself new clothes, or cared to look all that nice, so perhaps it was learnt behaviour. I remember thinking how easily he ripped through money. The fine hotel, the two-Michelin-starred restaurant. Seeing the jacket now, though, a memory comes to me.

It had been a few days before the wedding. I'd walked in on him in the kitchen while he was on his phone. He was wearing the jacket with his dark jeans and a white dress shirt. He looked scrubbed up, like he was off out. Normally, I'd have said, *Where are we going?*, but he got off the phone so quickly, and scribbled on a piece of paper. He placed it in his right pocket, then smiled, seeming not himself. I hadn't thought much of it. Looking back, of course, it was the kind of covert reaction that might have signified something, if you had been looking for it. But as it was, I just remembered thinking, *I wonder who he was talking to that he practically hung up on?*

I stare at the jacket now, at the deep, rectangular flap pocket. My heart gives a series of small skips. It won't still be there. Of this I'm certain. Yet when I slide my hand in . . .

It's a folded square. I don't remember seeing him fold it. I open it out.

On it, he's written:

25 Woodlands Ave. 2 p.m. 19th.

I read it again, taking it in strides: the address, the time, the date.

Who had he visited at 2 p.m. on the day before our wedding?

I click on to the computer and type the address into Google.

TWENTY-THREE

The Rightmove website describes it as *An opportunity to own a charmingly renovated, four-bedroom, Edwardian townhouse, complete with private, professionally landscaped garden*, though the property sold six months ago for nearly three hundred and fifty thousand pounds. I flick through the pictures, looking at the white fitted kitchen with the dark oak flooring, the picturesque bay windows and high ceilings, the master bedroom and bathroom – obviously whoever lives in there now would have put their own stamp on things. The estate agent would know, but I'm not sure how to make the phone call.

I recognise the street as I turn down it, from the Street View option on the website. The area is close to schools and a park, and is walking distance into town. I pull up a few doors down from number twenty-five, and switch off the engine. The house with the white front door. The door that presumably Justin knocked on. I sit there for a while. As with most terraces, there is little actual sign that anyone is home. Blinds are dipped at the windows. The gardens out front are too small for children to play in. There's a white van parked immediately outside – a worker's van – but as there's only street parking, the van could be anyone's.

I was wavering before I got here. But I'm not wavering now. I vow I'm not leaving here until I learn something. I have no actual plan of how I'm going to achieve this, but the pledge is made.

But still I sit here. Staring at a house Justin visited the day before our wedding – a house he never told me about – is more of a daunting situation than I even thought. I am pinned to this seat, pressed into the back of it as though by the terrifying proximity of a ghost.

Do it, I hear the voice inside me say. *Bloody go and knock on the door.*

I get out of the car and hear it slam behind me in the Sunday-morning silence. Funny, though: I've got a fit of the braves. The *clack-clack* of my feet on the cobbled road, on to the path. The groan of the low gate. My feet walking where Justin's walked.

I pause, hand raised to knock. Then: one, two, three. I stare at the wood and try to talk my heart rate down.

Nothing.

Four, five, six. Louder.

I am certain I hear movement.

A fussing with a latch?

The door opens.

I am face to face with a man. He looks at me, not particularly friendly. I'm aware of a grubby-white, sleeveless T-shirt, fat belly and arms tanned as far as the elbows.

'Hello.' I manage to find my voice. 'I'm Alice. I believe you might know my husband.'

'I don't know anybody, love,' he says, quickly, and good-naturedly. 'I'm just doing a job here.' He nods back inside, and wipes oily fingers across a sweaty forehead.

Of course. The white van.

'They had a burst radiator. Somebody put new ones everywhere except the bedrooms.' He shakes his head, as though he despairs of people. 'False economy every time.'

I stare into his pale-blue eyes, at the sty or little cyst on his lower lid. 'Who? I mean, do you know who lives here? Their name?'

It's hard to say whether he's a bit suspicious now, or if he just doesn't want to be bothered. Either way, all he says is, 'Look, I've no idea who they are. They found me in the phone book. Left me a spare key.' He coughs, a sharp and violent outburst that ends in him wheezing up a small storm. 'Always seem to get the emergency jobs when I'm off to the caravan with the wife.'

I'm dying to say, *Who left you a key, and where are they? And why would they leave a key with a total stranger?* But none of it will form.

He goes on looking at me. 'I'm sorry for bothering you,' I tell him. After a moment or two of registering my defeat, I turn and start walking down the path.

Then I hear him say, 'MacFarlane. You said you wanted a name. That's who lives here. Justin MacFarlane and his wife.'

TWENTY-FOUR

When I answer the knock on the door, Sally is standing there holding up a bottle of wine in each hand. My jaw drops. She pushes out her hip, and I see two more bottles peeking out of the top of her messenger bag.

'I didn't want us to run out.'

'You really didn't need to come,' I tell her as I watch her walk past me and set the wine down on the bench. I know she tends to be a home bird when she isn't running around after her daughters. Sometimes, I find it embarrassing that we are always gathering to sort out my relationship problems.

She turns and meets my eyes, her own brimming with kindliness and understanding. 'Er . . . you ring me and say, *Justin's got another wife*, and you don't think I'm going to come over?'

Insane as it is, I smile.

We sit at the small pine dining table. I tell her the whole thing in detail. Right down to the patch of sweat on the plumber's shirt. 'I'm sure it's not his wife,' she says, once I've told her everything I can possibly think of. 'I can't believe that in a million years.' The first bottle of wine went down so fast that I've opened the second. I told her we should let it breathe and she said, 'I think it's us who need to be able to breathe, not the wine.'

She is sitting in her rolled-up jeans, barefoot, with one leg lying across the opposite knee. I can see the hard skin on her heels.

'But how can you be so sure, when you and John think he's unknowable?' I can't resist it.

She gives me that look – slightly disappointed in me – and scoops her hair up between both hands, as though she's putting it in a ponytail, before letting it fall free again: something she does when she's thinking. 'He isn't a bigamist. On that I'd bet my life.'

'Would you really, though?' I realise I'm drinking without really tasting the wine, and I need to pace myself.

'My life savings then.'

We look at one another, doubt ticking away between us. I can't stop playing back how surreal it was to hear him say *Justin MacFarlane and his wife*.

'I don't believe it, either,' I tell her. 'Or, rather, I simply cannot bring myself to see how it could be true, but bizarre stuff like this happens, doesn't it? I mean, you never imagine it would happen to you, but maybe I am going to be one of those people . . .'

She is watching me when I come back from staring into space. 'Al, he was a plumber they got out of the phone book. Why Justin was calling him, I don't know, but I definitely wouldn't put two and two together and come up with a bigamist.'

'No,' I say, not sure I'm any more comforted or convinced. 'Maybe you are right.'

We talk for so long – going over the past, looking for clues – that it turns dark, and we don't bother to switch on a light. 'Would you have him back?' she asks me when there is quite possibly no more we can say on this topic. 'I mean, obviously if there is some acceptable explanation for this.'

I think about it. 'Well, here's another question. In my shoes, would you?'

'No,' she says. She taps a fingernail on her wine glass a few times, and I listen to it *ping-ping*. 'It's got nothing to do with forgiving, even if you could forgive him. I think, for me, he'd be too much of an emotional wild card now. I don't want someone whose reaction is to just disappear without accountability. I would never be able to come home without wondering if he was going to be there, and I couldn't live my life like that.'

'Like you can with John,' I say, after contemplating this for a while. 'John is always going to be there, isn't he?' I feel bad again for having had uncharitable thoughts about him; at least he's reliable.

'Well, obviously, yes.'

I wait for her to say more, as I sense there is more – she seems suddenly downcast – but she just looks away.

A long time later, after we've relocated to the rug with our backs against the sofa, I say, 'What am I going to do, Sal? Be honest with me.'

'I think there's only one thing you can do,' she says. 'But only you know if you can.'

The beach is deserted except for the occasional dog walker and diehard hiker. I am panting from my attempt at a run – sweat, rain and hair product trickle down my cheeks, into my mouth. A pain shoots up my hamstrings because I didn't warm up properly. My head pounds bluntly from lack of sleep and the fact that Sally and I got through three bottles of wine last night and woke up this morning like two cats, sleeping head to head in the middle of my sitting room floor.

I feel like I'm swimming from relentlessly going over the same story, and from booze; Sally told me I was mad to do anything other than call in sick to work, and sleep it off. Instead of continuing along the beach, I turn toward the parking area, deciding to call it quits. The rain is coming down hard. I try to walk fast, listening to the rhythm of it threshing my Gore-Tex jacket. The battleship-grey tide steadily beats the shoreline, and one or two seagulls sit cowering on the sand.

I am drenched and shivering when I push the car into gear, even though it's far from cold. I am disorientated, blank in my head. But I realise I'm not going home, like I thought. Instead, I load the satnav and find the address from yesterday.

Turn left, then follow the road for two miles . . .

I try to listen to music, waiting for the next instructions. Anything to bring my heart rate down, and stop the belting of blood between my ears. There is a traffic jam once I get back on to the main road – an accident, by the looks of things. I don't know how to divert and take an alternative route. I remember the banana in my handbag, dig for it, rip the peel back and push it into my mouth as I tremble. I stuff it down in a few seconds flat, gulp the bottled water and make a sharp turn right.

At the next junction, turn left.

Turning down the street, I see there are fewer cars than yesterday. Of course. A work day.

Louisa's voice. *Justin is working from home . . .*

I trot down the path quickly this time. Bang on the door. Someone is bound to be in there. I bang, and bang, and bang, and bang until my knuckles sting.

The neighbour's door opens. The sleepy head of a tall young man looks out. He squints into the daylight, clearly not properly seeing me. 'Can I help you?' An accent. The strong *h*.

'Who lives here?' I ask him, without any mind to my attitude or manners. 'Do you know them? What are their names?'

He musses his curly brown hair, and pulls a bit of a pained, bewildered face. 'Name?' he repeats, as though he's never heard that word before.

'Of the man and woman who live here? Your neighbours.'

'Man?' He shrugs, shakes his head. 'No man.'

He bends down, and I watch what he's doing, noticing the long, thin, darkly hairy legs, and the emerald-green bed shorts. He removes something – a sticky note – that has attached itself to his foot.

'What do you mean, there's no man?' I ask, when he stands up. 'Isn't there a man who lives here? A couple?'

'Maybe.' He shrugs again, looking slightly amused, as though he thinks we are playing some sort of strange game. 'I'm sorry. I don't know. Sorry . . .' Then he goes in and closes his door.

I knock a couple more times, but there is nothing. No sign of life. When I am back in my car, I reach into my pocket for my phone. Sally was right. I packed his bags for a reason. There is no point in them just sitting in the middle of the floor.

I have packed your stuff up. Please come get it this week. Or it goes to charity.

To my surprise, less than two minutes later, he replies.

Friday, 7 p.m.

TWENTY-FIVE

Evelyn

London. 1983

Her mother had left her some money. Plus, she had her income from journalism. She didn't need to take anything from Mark. Evelyn wrote down on paper her net worth divided by the number of years she might live to get a rough idea of what they'd have to exist on, excluding anything Eddy might earn. She calculated that if they lived frugally, there would be enough to see them through the rest of their lives.

Eddy didn't earn much, but they didn't need much. And besides, what was expensive was her lifestyle, not necessarily life itself. She had never been attracted to Mark purely for the money. His parents' stately home certainly hadn't made him more appealing, only less self-made. She hadn't gone to London to meet a prince, become a princess and live in a castle, much as Eddy might joke.

The flat would be the hardest material thing to leave. Admittedly, she was fond of it. While the bricks and mortar of it cost a disproportionate fortune, they were really paying for its proximity to Kensington Palace Gardens; to shops and cafés, flower stands, theatres and the parks of

London's West End. She had decorated it with great care, surrounding herself with the paintings, ornaments, cabinets and rugs that would give her timeless pleasure.

The dogs. The horses. She would miss them, but she would get a dog back home. Maybe once she became closer to April, the little girl could help her choose a pet. She had thought a lot about April and the kind of stepmother she would be. She would never disrespect Laura, or try to be another parent. At most, she hoped that she could be a positive role model, and one day they might be friends.

In one of his letters, Eddy had left her his phone number. He had made a note of the best time she could ring him, when his wife would not be there. She watched the clock, then took a large chance and dialled. He answered on the second ring.

His happiness sounded so heartfelt, like something specially prized that no one but she could have given him.

'I've been thinking, you have to do it first,' she told him. 'You have the most to lose, by far. So before I turn Mark's world upside down, I need to know that you are as able as you seem to think you are of looking your wife and daughter in the eyes and telling them that you're leaving them for me.'

'You still doubt me, don't you?' She could hear his frustration.

'I don't doubt that you want to do it, Eddy. I just don't know if you're as steely as you'd like to think you are.'

'You know what? I think you should do it first. After all, it's really you whose life is going to change the most. Of the two of us, you're the one I'm most worried will have second thoughts.'

'I won't have second thoughts, Eddy. I promise. I'm not going to say I'll do it if I know I can't.' She recognised the magnitude of the commitment, but it didn't faze her, because that's how certain she was. Eddy was right. It was the eighties now. Couples split up. Families survived. There was no need for a child to get hurt. Neither of them would watch it happen. 'I suppose we both have to take a leap of faith and trust each other,' she said.

After some back-and-forth discussion, they agreed that she would leave Mark and fly back North before Christmas, then Eddy would break the news to Laura in the early new year. If Evelyn waited until January, she was worried her nerve might fail.

She dreaded to think how the meaning of Mark's life would soft-focus when she left him. They knew a few divorced men who had lived it up like twenty-year-olds, enjoying the sexual advantage that their money brought them with younger women who would never have been interested in them years ago. It might have been a novelty at first. But eventually they craved the stability of a wife to come home to again – someone to see to it that their socks got washed, and that they remembered to visit their mothers. She couldn't really see Mark applying Grecian 2000 and partying at Annabel's, even though she didn't doubt he could attract a much younger piece of eye candy. His ability to be part-lover, part-father and part-infant would be a comforting fit for a certain childlike siren character. Still, though, it was strange to be picturing his future knowing she wouldn't be in it.

When they had come to the end of their conversation, Eddy surprised her by saying, 'Thank you.'

'For what?'

'For doing this. For me. I'll never forget you left your good life for me, and I promise you, Evelyn, that even though I can't give you much materially, I will give you all the love anyone can give someone. Every day of my life, my happiness will only exist if I know I'm making you happy. If I look at you and see the genuineness of it in your face.'

She thought that was the loveliest thing anyone had ever said to her.

She and Mark were one of a handful of couples dining on Saturday night in the small ivy-walled Italian restaurant, just off the High Street.

Oddly, Mark looked up from his *osso buco* and asked her, 'Do you think you're ever going to put your mother's house up for sale?'

She knew he was just making conversation, but it was timely, anyway. They weren't waiting for the money. In Mark's eyes, her family home was worthless. That wasn't unkind on his part, just the way he valued things.

She met his eyes, trying to keep the regret out of her own. 'Actually, I'm thinking of keeping it.'

He frowned. 'Keeping it? Why?'

'To rent it out and have some income.'

'Whatever for? Why would you want to have tenants in a property that you can't oversee because you're four hundred miles away?'

She couldn't bear his eyes. She looked down at her virtually untouched *fettuccine Alfredo*. 'Maybe because it's my family home. It's all I have left of my heritage. I don't want to let it go.'

He was disapprovingly silent.

'Maybe it's a silly idea,' she said after a while. *Tell him*, a part of her was trying to egg herself on. But she couldn't tell him in the middle of a restaurant. It was funny, but, until now, the idea of telling him had still borne an unreal, rather distant quality.

'I think it is a silly idea. I think you need to sell it and put that place behind you, once and for all.'

That place.

'You really don't have to speak of my home like that.' She was surer of her decision to leave than ever before now, even though she knew it was just anger.

He studied her as she sat there ramrod still, refusing to meet his eyes. Then he sighed. 'Well, look, for God's sake, if you need to go back again – for closure – if that's what it takes to finally let go, then do it. I'm not going to stand in your way; surely you know that.'

He was unwittingly giving her the 'out' she needed, and yet it felt so wrong to take advantage of his naivety.

Can I tell him I'm going back for a visit and then leave him a letter? Or should I tell him when I get there that I'm not coming back? Just like Eddy said . . . Then another flaw in this plan dawned on her. *Abandon him three weeks before Christmas! Why had I even thought of that? What kind of a person would be so cruel?*

Suddenly, the logistics of leaving him bore down on her, her conscience crushing her until she could barely breathe.

Mark sighed and went back to his food. It didn't help that he was giving her latitude. Although, if she was being unkind, Evelyn would have argued that in giving her options, Mark would never have expected she'd choose the one that he would have least approved of. Then he added, 'If you do go, though, I'll miss you terribly. You know that, don't you?'

His words battered her. She could feel her thumb and index finger gripping her fork too tightly, tears trying to well up. He was rarely effusive with his affection. It was odd that he had chosen to be so now.

A few days later, after wrestling with all this, she walked into his study. He glanced up from his desk, looking happy to see her. 'Mark, I've decided I do need to go back up North. Like you said. For closure. Just this one last time. And before Christmas.' Her heart beat erratically. She was so unused to lying that she was convinced the truth must be telexing itself across her forehead for him to read.

Perhaps he need never know about Eddy. This thought suddenly landed on her. She could just say that she missed Lindisfarne too much, so she was going back there for good.

Her plan still kept changing, practically by the minute.

'Do it then. If you must. Go.'

She could tell he was being gracious. 'I don't know why it can't wait until the new year . . . But if it can't, it can't. I just hope this time when you come home, Evelyn, you'll have settled matters, this thing, whatever it is, and I hope you'll be more at peace with yourself.' He had finished that sentence carefully. She wondered why.

'Why am I not at peace with myself?' she asked, quietly and without provocation. She was genuinely curious to know what he thought, given that he knew her better than anyone.

He pondered his answer, perhaps sensitive to the possible effect of it. 'I don't know. But you never are, are you? It's not normal, Evelyn. But it's the way you are. It doesn't mean I love you any less, though.'

She stood there with her head bowed. She didn't want him to see her tears.

They were tears of joy, tears of sadness, maybe tears of confusion. She didn't know what they were tears of.

It was only when Mark had said she could go that Evelyn was unable to actually see it happening. Even though, up until that moment, it was all she'd been able to see. It was too good to be true. Eddy would lose his nerve. She would take ill, or get hit by a car. Something would come along to sabotage it.

It only became real and possible again once she had stepped out of the small travel agency on the busy Brompton Road holding her ticket.

Then Evelyn made her first mistake. She agreed to lunch at the Royal Academy with Serena Bailey, an editor friend from her early *Cosmopolitan* days, who had left the business when she'd given birth to her third son. Serena was the closest friend Evelyn had made in London, a wise, serious girl, who also had it in her to be disarmingly frank and fun. Evelyn had noticed something about herself: she could be on a high one minute, then, the next, plummet and doubt herself all over again. But today she was almost running away with her own elation. Still, though, she vowed to say nothing about Eddy.

And then there was wine. Then there was so much cosy chatter, and since her mother died, Evelyn hadn't had a proper heart to heart with another female, and she missed it. Sometimes she caught herself wondering how she would ever exist without it. By going home, would she ever have a friend apart from Eddy again? Nearly everyone she'd known, she had lost touch with.

'I've met someone,' she said. Evelyn wasn't the type to blurt out her business to people. There were friends you could never tell. Serena was one you could.

A forkful of tangy lemon flan was on its way to Serena's mouth, but it never got there.

Evelyn tried not to concentrate on her expression. 'A man from home. Someone I used to know,' she said.

The fork was returned to Serena's plate, set down, as though she was reluctantly finished with food altogether now. 'You mean you're having an affair?'

Evelyn searched Serena's face for some evidence of reciprocated glee, but Serena watched her flatly: without judgement, but without joy.

Evelyn's confidence slipped. 'It's . . .' She talked to the flan on Serena's plate. 'That's not what I'd call it. An affair.'

Why did I tell her? She thought about Eddy saying how he no longer wanted to feel shame. She hadn't properly felt it until this minute. 'It's not like that at all, in fact. It's someone who touched my life a long time ago. Someone who should have stayed in my life, if I hadn't been so wilful. Someone I love.'

Serena made a doubting, sceptical face that was both friendly and slightly horrified. 'Love?'

Evelyn gave her a brief account of the situation, recognising that, as soon as the story set sail, it was shipwrecked, as was she along with it. What had possessed her to betray Mark, Eddy and herself? Not that Serena even really knew Mark. But still . . . She had found that when it came to the telling of secrets, one person tells one person, then it's a runaway train. Serena's eyes didn't light up. Not once. It wasn't the reaction Evelyn had expected.

'I'm sorry,' Evelyn eventually said, when she could no longer look at Serena's disappointed face. 'I should never have told you. It's not fair. It somehow makes you invested in my choices and my mistakes, and that's wrong.' She didn't know if she had told Serena because she was bursting to talk about him, or because she knew she'd have to tell someone eventually, so this was her test run.

'But you're seriously considering leaving Mark for this Eddy? Your husband, for this man you hardly know?'

'I know enough.' Evelyn's tone had steeled, slightly. 'I know more about him than I knew about Mark when I married him.' The difference was, she'd always felt she'd known Eddy, and she hadn't experienced that with Mark from the moment they had met.

But a little voice was saying, *Go on . . . What do you really know about him, compared to Mark?* When you cast aside bias, the truth was that if she had to list everything, beyond his upbringing, his dashed dreams and the fact that he was smitten with her, it would probably be a short list.

'Have you thought of the life you'd be giving up? Once reality sets in and you're back there, counting your pennies . . . Are you still planning on freelancing for the magazine? How would that even work when you're so far away?'

Evelyn heard the blood pounding in her temples. Had she respected Serena's opinion less, she might not have felt so discombobulated.

'I can get a job in Newcastle.'

'Doing what?'

'Writing. Or anything. Or nothing. I can support myself. I have savings. I have a house.'

Serena looked almost pitying. 'Evelyn, don't take this the wrong way. It's truly not my business, but haven't you ever thought that he was just an infatuation? Every married woman wants to think she lights some other man's fire, but that's all it is: a kind of flattery we seek when our husbands start taking us for granted. In this case, you have a bit of a history with him. He was your unfinished business, perhaps. Maybe you were meant to have a little dalliance with him, a nice memory to carry you through life. But maybe you should leave it at that. Cut it off while it's still a good memory. Accept you've been caught up in the nostalgia of it, but nostalgia, by definition, is a testimony of the past. It's a memorial to things gone, Evelyn. And you can't get back what's gone, simply because you're not meant to.'

She reached across the table and squeezed the top of Evelyn's hand, which was lying, rather dead, on the table. Evelyn couldn't move. She could only replay Serena's words and try to stop her tears.

'Perhaps you just need to be sensible and forget him, and remember how much you love Mark.'

Evelyn heard her gentle voice distantly. She stared at Serena's slim hand lying there on top of hers. She told herself the conversation didn't matter. But she knew that it did. That it would.

Three days before her flight up North, Evelyn set about composing her letter to Mark. He would read it after she had left. It was cowardly. But it was the only way she could it. She knew that if she saw the look on his face she wouldn't go, and she didn't want to run that risk. She had made a promise to Eddy now.

She tried to continue with a normal routine. But she was quietly saying goodbye. On the route she normally walked with Harry, she would absorb every detail of the park – trees, narrow walkways, horses on the bridle path – taking photographs in her mind. She stroked Harry extra fondly, and told him how she didn't want him to fret for her, and then she cuddled him and wept into his soft fur. She lunched with friends, convincing herself that she would be in touch with them again. But she knew she wouldn't. She would never be able to face their judgement, and they would judge her; she knew them well.

But she was convinced she was making the right choice. Or, if she wasn't, the choice was made already.

On the day of Evelyn's flight, December 17, the IRA set off a car bomb outside Harrods.

As the news broke, Evelyn was adding her last items to her suitcase: only her more practical clothes and footwear, plus the odd book, or photograph of her horse and the dogs bundled up in a nightdress. No sequined dresses from Harvey Nichols. No crystal perfume decanters. None of her Cartier jewellery, only her favourite inexpensive Murano glass earrings that Mark had brought her back from Italy; she treasured those.

She was in their bedroom with the radio on.

She heard the news bulletin without listening to it. A phone call to the Samaritans. An explosion. Christmas shoppers. Fear of an attack on Oxford Street. London on a high state of alert. Extensive damage.

Harrods. Mark had gone Christmas shopping. She had watched him retrieve his Harrods charge card from his desk drawer.

She tried to take a full breath, but it was trapped, like a bird that had flown into someone's house and was panicking to get out. She tried to move, but her legs were lead.

There had been a bomb at Harrods. Mark was at Harrods.

There was a slackening sensation in her lower abdomen. She managed to pick up the phone. From the end of the bed, she rang the operator and asked for the store's phone number. The muscles of her face quivered like a rabbit's. She couldn't get through when she dialled. She turned on the TV in the bedroom, and stood rooted there as she saw the full horror unfolding in Knightsbridge. Black smoke. Rubble. Smashed glass. Ambulances. Army vehicles. The walking wounded. Half-naked mannequins projecting like dead bodies out of the store's windows. She searched every face in the crowd for Mark's, imagining seeing him wheeled out on a stretcher. All this, while she was packing to leave him for another man.

It was her fault. She had somehow brought on this catastrophe. Losing Mark was going to be her punishment. She was a co-conspirator with the IRA.

Threads of her sanity started to come apart. Then she felt the warm trickle. It took her a moment to realise that she had wet herself. Before she could even think about changing her clothes, she bolted for the door and ran out on to Kensington High Street. It was damp and mild out, business as usual in the many boutiques, cafés and stores; the endless stream of people coming out of the building that housed the Tube station. Almost imperceptible waves of chaos were fanning out from Knightsbridge; the traffic was unusually gridlocked, more so than in rush hour. Then a taxi driver whom she'd flagged down told her, 'There's been a bomb at Harrods. You'd be wasting your money, love.'

'My husband is there shopping,' she pleaded. 'I have to find him!' She knew he was thinking, *Just my luck!* He quickly glanced her over, then, with a sigh and a headshake, waved for her to climb in. He struck out of the glut of cars, and rattled up a back street. She watched out of the window as they passed Queen's Gate, taking the longer route to avoid the brunt of congestion along Kensington Road. Filling in before her eyes were the edited highlights of their life together, dating back to the flowers and the invitation to dinner. When she could handle the stops and starts no longer, she dove out and started running.

She realised a little too late that she hadn't paid. She heard the driver call out, 'Come back, you bloody woman . . .'

She could see far down the street that Knightsbridge was cordoned off. She was sure she could smell death. She ran toward Beauchamp Place, where she regularly lunched with her friends, ran until the balls of her feet smarted and breathing hurt. Outside Harrods was mayhem. Police, panicked people, camera crews, ambulances, more panicked people, people on foot, people in cars, people on stretchers – she couldn't look, and yet she looked, and searched and couldn't see him. She asked an officer how bad it was. But she was just one panicked woman in a crowd of panicked people. As hard as she pushed to get closer – 'How many hurt?' – she was propelled back, authority figures growing stern, hands gripping her and telling her she couldn't be allowed closer; there might be another attack.

Another attack.

He's dead, she thought. While he was probably out buying her Christmas present, he had lost his life. Somehow, none of this would have happened if she had just been happy with him.

She stood in the middle of the push and shove of things, as police attempted to evacuate the whole area, inhaling the smell of blood and black smoke, wanting to vomit. She'd give anything for him to be alive. Anything. She would forget Eddy. She would stay. She'd be the wife Mark wanted her to be. She would never look back. She was freezing cold, and wet on her lower half.

She heard some American tourists talking about the bomb going off in Hans Crescent, about a mangled police car. Distantly, more sirens.

And then she saw him.

It seemed impossible, given the number of people. It was as though she had summoned him up and he had appeared on cue – maybe because, in the strange way that things fall, he had just heard her silent pledge that she wouldn't leave him if he did. He was walking down Beauchamp Place, toward Knightsbridge, where she was standing like a lost puppy. He saw her a moment or two after she saw him. He was carrying a small green-and-gold Harrods bag. He didn't seem hugely surprised – as though she made a habit of standing in the middle of Knightsbridge looking fraught.

He smiled.

She saw him, briefly, through the eyes of the young girl she had been when she had met him. As the intelligent, kind man she had looked up to, and loved. Who wasn't her ideal. Who was flawed. But neither was she a perfect human being.

'Evelyn,' he said, as she walked toward him. He had the slackened posture of someone who'd had a drink, or three.

He held out his arms. She was numb when he circled her. He pressed his warm cheek lightly to hers. 'What a thing!' he said. 'What a thing to happen!'

She could have cried at the tender feel of his cheek against hers. His skin was hot. He always burned up when he had been drinking.

'You're all right,' she said, and looked up at him. 'Thank God you're all right. I had an awful premonition that you were going to be one of them . . . I was so worried!'

He kissed the centre of her forehead. 'You shouldn't have been, silly. I knew exactly what I wanted to buy, and was in and out of there in a few minutes. I went to San Lorenzo for something to eat.' He hugged her tightly, the kind of embrace he hadn't given her in so many years. She could feel every beat of his love for her in that hug. Even if he never said the words *I love you* again, she knew he did, that he always had and he always would.

When he let her go, he looked curiously at her face. 'What's wrong?' He squeezed the thin tops of her arms. 'And where's your coat?' He immediately took off his, and placed it around her shoulders. 'Come on. Chin up. We're safe. Life goes on. I would suggest we go home and have a drink. But don't you have a flight to hurry off for?'

'What flight?' she said, her voice catching.

TWENTY-SIX

Alice

On Friday at 5:30 p.m., I have no choice but to go out for dinner with Victoria and a few of the girls from marketing. The fact that it's Victoria's birthday had completely skipped my mind. I'd popped out in my lunch hour and grabbed a card and a bookshop gift voucher. When she told me that she'd picked the same bar where I was first introduced to Justin's friends, it seemed like one more reason why I should have just said I couldn't go.

As is the way of these things, we don't end up ordering right away because some of Vic's friends are late and she wants to wait. My eye is constantly on my watch, and by 6:10, our main courses haven't even arrived, and I am almost eating my own nerves. I have to get out of here. But how? The music is loud. The girls are chattering and looking at me, but I'm sure they can see I'm not here. I am searching for the waitress. Where is the bloody food? I'm lip-reading rather than listening. The smile is dying on my face. Someone is making a toast. Everyone is raising their glasses. I raise mine. All I can think is, *I will be seeing Justin in less than an hour. In less than an hour, I will know.*

And then it happens. That thing where you're looking at someone and not actually seeing them, but they think you are. A man. He is standing with a group of men. He raises his glass to me, mimicking me, perhaps. Suddenly, it's surreal.

I have been looking at him because he is Justin. Or, rather, everything about this is something that has happened before. Me. Him – he is similarly attractive, similarly dressed, around the same age. The friends, in their suits and ties. They are standing in the exact location, nearer to the door than the restaurant. I stare at this man, wondering if I am hallucinating, if someone has spiked my wine. It hauls me back to that night. I had said I'd be there for 6 p.m. There I am: I can see myself, trotting down the street in stilettos, uncharacteristically late; Justin is a stickler for people being on time. I'm about to meet a few of his better friends. I don't want to be late. I should have just jumped in a taxi, but the fare would have been embarrassingly small. I am apprehensive. I want this to go well. I am almost there, unpicking the buttons of my trench. I'm hot now. I don't want to look harried, I want to look fresh and in control. My hand is on the door handle. I take a deep breath, give it a push.

He must have been watching for me. I see him right away and I witness the expression that alights on his face when he sees me, before he can stop it – as though time is a split second ahead of itself. That wonderful look that says far more than any of his muddled words about loving and being in love. Justin loves me. I know it now. It's there for anyone to see. His friend, who has his back to me, turns. Clearly, he must want to see exactly what, or who, has captivated Justin. And it's me.

Justin and I smile.

I am smiling now, captivated by my memory. The man across the room thinks I'm smiling at him. He waves over. He has just said something to a friend, and they're both looking at me with a certain animal interest. The very way Justin has *never* looked at me. It brings me back to my senses. I get up sharply, catching the table and sloshing drinks. I need to get out of here, but I'm travelling in the wrong direction. As I pass them, this guy who reminded me of Justin makes a grab for my arm, but misses. It isn't a particularly sophisticated gesture – something, again, that Justin would never have done. 'Oi! Where are you going?' he calls after me. His mates laugh.

This is the terrible, desperately painful thing about the moment – I want to go back. I want to rewind us to that look, when I knew he loved me irrefutably, when there was no doubt. If only I could be coming out of the toilets and seeing Justin there, not those other fellows. And we could write a different outcome, one that is still winding and ambiguous, but that definitely doesn't end up here. But instead I am in the here and now, about to return to my flat and find out at what point in intoning he would never leave me, Justin had already left.

My heart is racing. I cover my mouth, trembling and silently gasping at the same time, mentally talking away the urge to throw up: that drink on an empty stomach. I hear the muted thump of music and bursts of squeals and laughter. I pull up Sally's number on my phone.

'Where are you?'

I tell her.

'I thought he was coming at seven?'

'I can't face him. I can't look at him, Sal! I can't do it! I can't hear what his reasons are!'

'Al! You've got no choice!' She sounds as panicked as I am. 'Get it over with! It's already gone on far longer than it should have. You'll be okay,' she says, her voice softening. 'You will get past this. Sometimes, you just have to face what you fear the most. It's shitty, but it's life.'

I listen to her words, letting them calm me down. Then she says, 'What do you fear most, Al?'

I perch on the sill by the open window just to be near fresh air. I think about what it is, what it really is, while I try to breathe. 'Well, finding out, obviously. But it's also that moment when I realise he really and truly is gone. That there's no going back. How I'm going to feel.'

'I can promise you it's not going to be as bad as you think it is.'

'You're the last one who would know that.' There was no one but John.

'True. But deep down, you know this yourself.'

I look out of the window, which may not have been washed in years, on to Pilgrim Street below, and hear the voices of street life, a rustle of church bells. She's right. It is only Justin, not a hangman and spectators. And how bad can it be when I've already imagined the worst? 'Thanks,' I tell her.

'Go!' she says. 'And remember, Alice, if this is the worst thing that ever happens to you in your life, you'll look back on it and be thankful for that. I promise.'

'I'll try.'

I go back into the dining room, thrust forty pounds at Victoria's friend for my share of the bill, and run.

It's 7:25 when the taxi pulls up at my building. All my instincts say he's been and gone. I pelt up two flights of stairs. When I reach the door, I stop and try to catch my breath.

I can barely get the key in. *Please God don't let him have been and gone.*

When I go in, I see that his things are still there, exactly where I left them, in the middle of the floor. I gaze at them in baffled relief.

He hasn't been.

He isn't coming.

This is some sick game.

The flat is deadly quiet; not even the molecules in the air move, I think. I pluck at the strap of my bag, and let it drop off my shoulder, to the floor.

And then I'm aware of a presence.

Justin is sitting on the sofa, carefully watching me.

TWENTY-SEVEN

He's wearing a high-collared, pea-green shirt, open at the neck, and a new gunmetal-grey suit. He has one arm extended along the back of the couch, legs wide apart, like a sitting statue, the kind you see in the gardens of Parisian stately homes.

I sink into the nearest chair. 'Justin.'

Despite wanting to hate him, when I look into his face right here and now, I just want to go back to the way it was. I'd give anything.

'I thought you'd been and gone. That I'd missed you . . .' I've never seen such shadows under his eyes. Such rapid weight loss, especially in his face. He looks like he hasn't slept for days.

He's ill. I knew it all along.

'Been and gone? Good heavens. No. Why would you think that?'

He's still wearing the ring I slid on to his finger just over two weeks ago, which gives me a crazy sense of hope. And yet I see the distance in his eyes.

He studies the hand I've placed over my stomach. 'Are you okay?'

I nod, then quickly say, 'No, Justin. How can I possibly be okay?' I'm just trying to process all the mixed messages I'm getting. He continues to stare at me, but I could be a stranger he's mildly concerned about. Someone who slipped in the shopping centre.

'What about you? Is there something wrong with your health?'

He shakes his head, seeming surprised. 'No. Of course not. I told you, I'm fine.' Then after a moment or two, he says, 'I'm sorry. I don't know why I just took off. I just . . .' His misery, his conflict, is written all over his face; it's palpable. 'I'm sorry, I wish I could, but I can't really explain it to you.'

Our eyes lock and stay locked, for all the things that neither of us can say. Then tears spill down his face.

This stuns me. I have never seen him cry. Justin usually only displays his feelings once he's reflected on them, packaged them and positioned them. He is staring at a fixed point in space, just letting tears roll as though he can't even feel them.

After what seems like a very long time of my watching him like this, he rests his head on the back of the sofa. The shadows either side of his nose look more like bruises. I literally cannot get over how ghastly he appears. I stare at his prominent Adam's apple and feel a frustrated surge of pity. 'Why would you be so deliberately unkind, Justin? Who marries someone when he's got doubts, and then changes his mind a few days later and just walks out? What kind of person does that? And what was I? Blind, and stupid, and so into myself and my own happiness that I managed to miss the fact that my own fiancé didn't want to marry me?'

He raises his head and looks at me now. 'I didn't have doubts, Alice. I loved you, and that still hasn't changed. But other things have.'

'What?' I practically shoot up from the chair. 'Just tell me, for God's sake! I know you've got someone else. I've virtually seen it with my own eyes.' My throat prickles. I have never shouted at anyone like this before. 'I know. But I don't know why.'

He continues to look at me, calmly. Calm but distant. It strikes me that we were closer when we first met than we are now, as husband and wife. I can't rush to him and have him hold me, to have him ease and reassure me. It's illogical, almost. The emotional stop sign is right there. I can see it. He can, too, given he's the one who put it up.

I swipe tears with the back of my hand.

'It's not like that. Not at all what you're thinking.' He sighs, shakily, and I honestly can't tell which of us is finding this more traumatic. I know it's coming. I am listening and pushing it away with all my might. But I can't look away. 'What I should have told you, Alice, is that I have a son. His name is Dylan. He's three months old.'

I am falling in slow motion from a twenty-storey building and have just hit the ground. There should be profound pain, but I'm just too busy thinking how I could possibly have fallen from such a great height and still be alive.

'You have a son?' Oddly, despite my shock, a small part of me is thinking, *Is that it?*

'With Lisa.'

'Lisa.' I repeat the name of his ex-girlfriend. It echoes, trying to form significance, but it can't quite get there.

'It happened right before I met you. Literally, a few days. I ran into her at the courthouse. We went for dinner, probably because neither of us had anything better to do. I hadn't seen her in a very long time. She ended up back at mine. It was just that one time. But I suppose it's enough, isn't it?' He shakes his head as though still unable to fully fathom it. 'I didn't use a condom. I wasn't thinking. We never used them because she was always on the pill. I suppose I was falling back on old practices.'

He has a son, but he hasn't cheated. With his ex. The one he hadn't loved enough to marry. It was before we met. 'I don't understand. You've got a baby with Lisa. Okay, well . . . that's one thing. But how does that affect us?'

'I only found out the day before our wedding. She hadn't intended to tell me – perhaps never, actually. I don't really know.' He frowns. 'That's a whole other story I can't get into. She didn't want me coming back to her for the wrong reasons.'

I can't take some woman's motivations on board right now. 'You went to see them? To her house?'

He frowns. 'Yes. How do you know?'

'I found the note in your pocket. The one you wrote that day when I walked in on you, and you were on the phone.'

He thinks for a moment. 'Ah.'

'I've driven to the house, Justin. I talked to your plumber. I know you're living with her.'

I remember him once briefly saying that Lisa wanted a baby, and that getting her pregnant wasn't something he was going to take lightly. I'd filled in the blanks: Justin didn't feel secure enough about their relationship to commit to having a child. That was why he had ended it. It had made me feel good: clearly, he loved me more. 'I bet she wanted you back. Sex one time, then ending up pregnant . . . How do you even know he's yours? Maybe she's tricked you.'

'He's mine, Alice. And she didn't trick me.'

'But she wasn't going to tell you, then miraculously she ends up telling you the day before our wedding?' He was set up. How can he not see it? All my protective instincts rise to the surface. *She will not win.*

'Alice . . . That's not why Lisa told me, to dissuade me from marrying you. Far from it. She told me because she'd just found out that our child was born with a heart defect. Dylan suffers from a very serious condition called hypertrophic cardiomyopathy.' His eyes brim with tears again. 'Basically . . . it's one of the heart conditions that's commonly referred to as sudden death syndrome.'

I hear him, but the words fail to register. Sudden death . . . Heart condition. Baby. *Justin and his family with heart problems. The men who died young. His own father.*

I stare at him in disbelief. 'Your baby has a heart problem?'

He pinches the bridge of his nose. 'Quite a significant one, actually. Lisa only found out the week we were getting married. She needed to see me because the doctors needed to know my full family medical history. They said that talking to me could influence the course of his disease.'

'But . . .' It's like a puzzle with a missing piece. 'Why didn't you just say so? Why wouldn't you tell me there and then?'

'Because it was a day before our wedding! Everything was planned. You were so happy. *I* was happy. And then I get this news. I didn't even know I had a child, let alone a very ill child, and they wanted to know all these details from me, about my health, my family's health – things I could barely remember. It was crazy. I couldn't think straight. I didn't know where the hell I was . . .' I can't take my eyes off him, off his turmoil. 'I thought, okay, we're only going away for a week. As soon as we get back, I'll deal with it, and that's when I'll tell you. I'll deal with it then.'

'But we could have postponed the wedding, if you'd needed to!' I can't really picture the late-stage logistics of this, but I'm sure it would have been possible.

'Maybe. But at the time I thought I had it sorted.'

'How did Lisa find out about his condition?' I don't know which question to ask first. There are so many. I don't even know why I want to know. I just want a picture.

'A few things. His feeding. His breathing. The feel of his chest, apparently, when she touched it. It was like his heart was trying to jump out of his body because he was working so hard to breathe.' He puts his head in his hands.

He's thinking it's all his fault.

I shake my head, dazed. Dazed and disbelieving. 'So what does this mean, Justin?'

'Well, at this stage we don't really know. He's just had surgery, and he's still technically in recovery. There are a few possible outcomes. He could lead some version of a limited normal life. Or it could lead to progressive heart failure, and he may require a transplant. Or, of course, worse. It's still too early to say.'

'He's just had surgery?'

'Yes. That's the thing. That's what I found out while we were away. Lisa rang to tell me that Dylan had taken a serious turn for the worse. They needed to perform open-heart surgery, basically' – he wipes at tears – 'to save his life. And there was I, thousands of miles away on my honeymoon, sitting drinking wine on a balcony. And I'd only ever seen him once for about half an hour.' He shakes his head. He is clearly still very much reliving it.

The phone call at 4 a.m. UK time! I knew it wasn't from his office. 'Well, it's starting to make sense. But I still don't know why you couldn't have told me there and then. You could have explained and we could have flown back together.'

He looks at his feet. 'I don't know. I was only thinking that I needed to be there. Maybe there was something I could do. I . . . like I say, I can't explain it. I just needed to leave. To be on my own. To have a chance to think.'

He's being honest. No one could possibly lie and put themselves into this state if it wasn't genuine.

'But you must have known what you were going to do, Justin. Your note said you couldn't do this any more. You must have already decided you were leaving me for them.'

He looks through me, surprised, as though this is an entirely new take on the situation. 'I don't know if I'd really decided that. It wasn't that calculated. I was sitting there on the beach trying to act normal, and all I could think was I've put him here. This is because of me. Because of my bad gene pool. Because I carelessly got someone pregnant, Dylan will probably never know a normal life. And there I was marrying you – how could I have a child with you, now that I knew I was passing on all these problems? I could never risk this happening again. But then that's unfairly depriving you . . .' He looks at me, imploringly. 'Alice, you could have a life with someone else. A family – one you can't have with me now.' His speech seems to wind him. 'Do you see what I mean? This was all going round in my head.'

It's going round in mine, too. 'But that's insane, Justin! If you and I never have kids, I'm fine with that. Especially if it's because of medical reasons. I wouldn't consider it a deprivation at all! We could adopt.' I stare at him, and he's watching me, listening and contemplating. I can tell he's on a precipice, suspended between two choices; he might be persuaded my way if only I touch the right chord of his vulnerability.

'Your baby's condition wasn't your doing, Justin. If everybody decided not to have children because of family health conditions, there'd be only a quarter of the population . . . It was just the luck of the draw. I'm sure Dylan could have just as easily been born perfectly fine. So you mustn't think like that.'

'But I do think like that,' he says. And I know nothing I can say will change him.

I remember feeling so upset when he told me that, as a little boy, he couldn't understand how his dad could have died so suddenly. His dad was a doctor. He saved lives for a living. Justin couldn't understand how no one could save his.

He sits back against the cushion, extending his long legs, interlacing his fingers behind his head. I watch him as he stares and blinks at the ceiling.

'Come home. We can make it work. I'd love your son, because he was an innocent little boy and because he was yours. Don't you see, Dylan could have two families – one with his mum and one with us? He'd have three people who loved him. Can't you look at that as a positive? If we adopted, he could even have siblings.'

I have never seen him appear more conflicted. He puts his head in his hands again.

'I can't. I'm sorry.'

'But why can't you?'

I already know the answer.

He looks at me now. 'Because I want to be a proper father to him. I suppose for the rest of his life, whatever quality he's got, I want to be there fully for him. I want him to know what it's like to have a real family who love him. He deserves that. I don't want Lisa marrying someone else and some other bloke raising my kid. Others mightn't see that as a problem, but I do. I'm sorry.'

Echoes of everything he's ever said about his unpleasant life with his stepfather come back to me. How he said there's nothing worse than constantly trying to impress someone, trying to win them over to liking you, when you never can. Impossibly, it was as if everything he's ever told me about his childhood was said to validate his decision now.

'But you never wanted a child with Lisa.'

'But I had one, didn't I?' Then he adds, 'I'm sorry. It's just something I have to do.'

It's surreal. I can't believe my ears. 'So what about her, then?' I say after a while. 'Do you love her? I mean . . . you've moved in with her.'

'I've been staying there for practical reasons. We're not sharing a room. Trust me, sex is the very last thing on my mind. But do I love her? Well, I suppose, in some ways I still have feelings for her, because that's the kind of person I am. I don't get involved with people lightly. I don't switch it on and off when it's convenient. I've known her for a very long time. We had some good times and we had some less good times. She moved up North to be with me. And now by some crazy turn of fate she's the mother of my son and she's going through hell with this. I was never untrue to you about my feelings, Alice. Never. But life isn't simple and cut and dried.'

It blows me over. It all does. I want to fight, but I have lost already. 'So you think that because you've got a baby together, that you can be happy with her?'

He throws up his hands. 'You know, Alice, I am thinking first and foremost of my son. Two weeks ago, he might have died. At the moment, he's an unknown quantity. We're just watching and waiting and praying. But as for love, well, you can love people in different ways, on different levels, and, in any case, those ways evolve over time, no matter how you start out. I once told you that I'm not unrealistic about how these things work. I'm not some starry-eyed teenager. And neither is Lisa.'

I can't bear the words *love* and *Lisa* being uttered practically in the same sentence.

'Sometimes, you get your life flung at you, and you have to get on with it and make the best of it. I have to try to make the best of it. For my son.'

We sit in silence for a while. I try to grapple with it all. Then he says, 'Do you have something I can drink? A beer? Anything.'

'Sure.' I go to the fridge and pull out a beer. I am caught in that hellish place of disowning him and still caring about him: disowning him because I think he's wrong, and frustrated that I can't change his mind. I open the beer and hand it to him. Our fingers meet as he takes it. 'Did you eat?'

'Not since lunch.'

'Do you want me to make you a sandwich?'

'No. Thanks.' He looks perplexedly at the printing on the can, and passes it between his hands as if it's a foreign object. 'I'm sorry. I can't imagine what it's like for you hearing all this. I am not proud of the way I handled this, and how you've been hurt in the process. You must believe that.'

I don't know what to say, what response I can possibly make. 'So what are you going to do, Justin? How do things proceed from here?'

He looks right at me, quite calm now. Calm, but distant again. 'Well, I'm going to do what I have to do. I'm going to release you of me. I am sure you'll meet someone else, and one day you'll have a family with this person. And I'm sure in time you'll realise this was for the best.'

'But I don't want to be released of you.' Tears roll down my face. I fly my hand up, but can't stop them.

'I know. But you have to let me do what I think is right.'

I study him, wordlessly. There's nothing more either of us can say.

TWENTY-EIGHT

Evelyn

London. 1983

'What is it, Ev?'

Evelyn was lying on the sofa like an alabaster sculpture, with her head turned away from him. She was staring vacantly at the fire.

'Look at you. You're so pale.' He hovered over her, stymied by the sense of his own helplessness. 'You've got me very concerned. What is wrong?'

Mark always worried about his wife. Someone had once told him that happiness is something you feel only when you've given up focussing on its absence. But Mark wasn't sure Evelyn could ever be happy. Mark was convinced that Evelyn was depressed and it had come to some sort of head.

She looked at him, without really seeing him.

'What is the matter? Please tell me. You've not been the same since yesterday, since the bomb.' They had shared that pinprick of time, when she had suddenly caught sight of him, and he had caught sight of her, and his heart had somehow taken flight. Her face had been full of love for him in a way that he didn't think he'd seen before. Her eyes had glistened with tears. And it was then that he had realised how lost he would be if he were ever to be without her.

And yet, as he stood here, he could almost see her brain composing words. Words that would hurt him. He hoped she wouldn't speak them. He feared something, and yet he couldn't pinpoint exactly what it was.

He sat down in the leather chair opposite the fireplace, unable to take his eyes off her. Christmas was coming. He just wanted Evelyn happy for Christmas. She usually loved this time of the year – and he had always loved the pleasure she had taken in decorating their tree and ordering all their festive treats; she was like a child. 'What's got you looking like this, Evelyn? Tell me. You can tell me anything, you know that.' He said it, but it wasn't true. Then a horrible thought occurred to him: what if she is ill?

She slowly swung her legs around so that she could sit up properly. It seemed to take her a moment or two to orientate herself. She was ill. He was sure of it. She was going to give him horrible news. Suddenly, he saw his life unfolding without her. But that was the thing. It didn't unfold. It stopped. He couldn't see a future without Evelyn.

'There's something I never told you,' she finally said. 'Something you're not going to want to hear . . .'

She was dying. He would always remember: *Evelyn told me the terrible news right before Christmas.* He could already see the funeral: the cathedral, all his friends. Nineteen eighty-four. His first year as a widower. All these tomorrows rushed at him, blinding him like he had just stepped into a blizzard.

'I met a man when I was back home,' she said. 'My mother's gardener. Someone I knew years ago. We had an affair.'

He was sure he could actually feel the blood leaving his body. If he had been standing, his legs might have given out. His first thought was that he had misheard. His second was relief that she wasn't dying. His wife had slept with a gardener? Was that what she'd just said?

Maybe he wasn't hearing straight.

But he knew he was hearing straight.

And then it came to him. 'I knew,' he said, gazing at the floor. The pattern on the rug blurred, its sharp colours mingling through the glaze of his tears. Harry was lying on the rug between them, warming himself in front of the fire without a care in the world, just like Mark wanted to be. Happily married to a happy wife at Christmas, without a care in the world. 'What I mean is,' he said when he could speak again, 'I suppose I suspected.'

Had he? Well, perhaps not exactly that. But he'd always suspected that he would never be able to keep her; his time to lose her would come. Her spirited independence had attracted him to her years ago, and he would never have wanted to change anything about her, but he had hoped that, over time, she would have become slightly more stable. She had a good life – he'd tried to give her everything he could – and yet she seemed to long for the past more than she enjoyed the present, and he'd always known he could never give her that. He plucked absently at the edges of the dark-green throw that was strewn over the arm of the chair. He had a habit of fiddling with things when he got nervous. A habit from his boyhood. He used to have a slight stammer, too. But he had conquered that because people mocked him and he hated being mocked.

'So wait a minute. Am I to conclude you were going to go back and see him, this gardener' – he could barely say the word – 'yesterday?' Hadn't she mentioned hiring someone to paint the house? He hadn't really been listening, unsure about how a story about her mother's gardener could possibly be of interest to him. But why hadn't he listened? Evelyn never made idle conversation.

'Yes,' she answered, like a witness under oath.

'I knew,' he said again, with more surprise than animosity. He had known something was wrong as they had walked back home. Once she had got over the relief – at least, he'd thought until now that it was relief – of seeing him alive, she had seemed like a ghost of herself.

'Does anyone else know about this?' he asked. He would process it better if it was contained. But women could never keep anything secret. She'd probably told everyone at her dance class, half of Covent Garden and all the wives in their circle.

'No,' she said, and he all but wilted with relief. Then he felt guilty that this should even matter.

He sat there trying to read the situation. Adultery happened. That said, it was usually the husbands committing it. It seemed entirely different when it was a wife. *His* wife. He still couldn't believe it. He felt hurt more than betrayed. Just hurt. And sad. Normally, he'd have switched on the Christmas tree lights by now. The unlit tree felt symbolic. Her betrayal of him suddenly tore at his heart.

'So what does this mean?' he asked her, somewhat disgruntled that she appeared to have the upper hand, and he was having to almost implore her to tell him where they stood. But he dreaded her answer. He genuinely didn't know where this was all leading. It was hard for him to imagine her wanting to be with someone other than him. Not because he had a vastly high opinion of himself, just that he, himself, had never felt any need to be unfaithful, so it was hard to get his head around why she had. Though, he could have been unfaithful, he was sure, if he had wanted to be. It was what people of his class regularly did. But the difference was that he would have been discreet. And he certainly wouldn't have stooped as low as to do it with the hired help.

He was sure there must have been someone she'd have told.

'Are you in love with him?'

What a question. But it had to be asked. 'I assume you must be, if you're telling me this. Is that why you've been sitting here moping like this, Evelyn? Because you're married to me, but you're in love with a gardener from home?'

His wife had chosen to scrape the bottom of the barrel on some mission to make herself less depressed. He thought this uncharitable thought, but recognised he was only thinking it because his pride instructed him to.

Her eyes remained fixed on him, but she wasn't seeing him again. He thought that was his answer, right there. He studied her, oddly fascinated to be staring into the daydreaming eyes of his wife while she was in the throes of pining for another man.

And he was right. Evelyn was gone. She had returned to her house, to Eddy's warm arms. To their day at the beach. Their walks, their talks, their lovemaking. To the way he had sang to her years ago. To his sad gaze at the Mayfair Ballroom. Every time that song had come on the radio, she'd had to switch it off. Long John Baldry. 'Let the Heartaches Begin'. Two or three lines in, and she was ready to crumple.

Mark's voice sounded far away. In her peripheral vision, she could see the colourful oil painting of a summer garden that hung above their mantelpiece. They had bought it from a small Cork Street gallery. She could see the antique wall sconces from Sotheby's, and a bronze figurine on the pedestal table by the armchair that they had found at a flea market in Venice. The things they had chosen together, which might not seem important, yet they furnished their life and told of their history. She could see Mark in the foreground, sharpening again before her eyes.

He had just asked her if she was in love with her gardener.

'Yes,' she said. 'Or at least, I thought I was, yes.' In that instant, she felt so numb that she didn't know any more.

The word *yes* faded as Mark heard it, as he tried to un-hear it. Faded, then came back again. He continued to look at her. He ought to be thinking of her as a stranger now, a pariah. He ought to hate her, or at the very least be furious. And yet, for some odd reason, he couldn't. He saw this clearly for what it was: a symptom of this perpetual ridiculous homesick business in her. He saw it this way, simply because that was the best of all the possible explanations.

'What do you want to do then?' He hadn't dragged her kicking and screaming from that abysmal Holy Island, with the wretched tide that you were always planning your life around. If she hadn't wanted to be here, she should have left. If she didn't want to be here now, she should go. He wanted to say all this; he would have loved to say all this, but he didn't dare. He didn't like the way she was looking at him.

She heard his question. Her eyes swooped over his well-worn Burberry blazer, his maroon tie with the greasy stain on it that he must have acquired over lunch. Mark always missed his mouth when he ate, or managed to dangle his tie-end in his soup. Her gaze landed at his feet. His shoes were a bit of a disaster, too. He could afford plenty of expensive new ones, yet he always wore the same clapped-out pair that Tessie polished every day. Mark was shabby chic. She had seen that expression in *Cosmo* and thought, *Yes, that fits him*. She felt strangely detached from all of his quirks, though. She was looking at him as though he were a stranger, assessing him. Someone might have just introduced them at a dinner party. The face appeared suddenly years older, the skin pale and slack. His sparse, greying hair formed a halo of frizz around the top of his head. His eyes were bloodshot, and his shoulders sagged like a ragdoll's. There was something intensely grandfatherly about him. But something that made her still love him, nonetheless.

Mark wasn't at all happy at the way she was looking at him. He got up and went to fill his Scotch glass, just because she was making him feel twitchy. As he did, he caught sight of himself in the mirror. His reflection made him take pause. He was a vibrant, upright, attractive man in his prime. An affair with a gardener! What on earth had she been thinking?

He brought his drink back to the chair and sat down again. Harry went and nudged off a bauble from the bottom branch of the tree.

It struck Mark that he needed to be angrier. He had felt the rise of genuine pique a moment or two ago. But it had burned out like a log fire that starts off promisingly and then you don't quite know what suddenly happened to it. 'I'm presuming you want to leave me and go and be with him, your gardener,' he said, after he realised that she hadn't answered his question about what she wanted to do.

He drained the glass in one go. But he wasn't as calm as he might have looked. He sounded so rational, like a mediator in a debate. But he wasn't rational, either. Public school had taught him how to do the complete opposite of what his emotions were instructing. This whole thing was mad enough that she might actually do it. He didn't want to lose her. He loved her profoundly. Right now, it didn't matter massively that she might not love him back. She was looking at him in that strange way again.

She watched him polish off his drink. She could have said, *I want to leave you and be with Eddy, if he'll still have me.* The letter she had tried to write this morning – to explain why she hadn't shown up as promised – was in the drawer of her writing bureau upstairs. She hadn't managed to compose it. She had made her choice, and yet she hadn't committed it to paper. On one level, it was urgent that she sent an explanation to him; it was only fair. And on the other . . .

I could leave now. I could just get up and go.

Despite fading in and out of emotional blankness at times, she really had no doubts about her love for Eddy, even though she might have gently fudged it with Mark, just to be kind. But deep down, she knew that she didn't want to walk away from her husband, either – this man who was looking at her in a way that he had perhaps never looked at her before. As much as these paintings and vases, and chairs and rugs all belonged here, so did she. And Mark belonged here, too: he with her, and she with him. This was their life, and she couldn't really imagine it not being her life any more. Everything about London suited the person she had been happy enough to become. And, as much as she had questioned the happiness of that person at times, and as much as she thought she could leave it all, she really couldn't see herself walking away from Mark and the life they had made together. She just kept picturing him buying her Christmas gift in Harrods, and how he might have died doing it. There were different kinds of love. One didn't invalidate the other.

She thought, distantly, of Serena's sage advice about nostalgia, and how people would talk about her. Mark would be a laughing stock, and she worried more about that than what they would say about her. Then, inevitably, he would find someone. But he wouldn't really want to replace her. He'd be doing it out of necessity, because Mark needed order in his life, and order meant a wife. And in a way – knowing her messed-up self as she did – she would envy that woman he had chosen to try to love as much as he once loved her.

'I don't know what I am going to do. I'm only telling you all this for one reason, Mark. Because I've done wrong, and it's too big a thing to keep from you. I'm not a good enough actress.'

'Well, frankly, I would have appreciated you trying to be.' His last defence was a small attack.

She found this ironic. Sometimes, she felt that Mark only ever wanted to know the part of her that it suited him to know. He would cheerfully bury his head in the sand as to the rest. And that was one of the infuriating things about him. But it was part of their marriage's psyche. She couldn't hate him for it.

'I take responsibility for what I did. I never, ever, intended to be unfaithful, and I regret it in ways I could never begin to articulate. But you should know that my affair was a symptom of us, of how we are together as a couple, of what we've become. I have never fitted your mould. You married a human being, not a talking ornament. I wasn't going to be placed where you decided to place me, and polished once in a while. I am a person.'

It was sounding way more accusatory than she really intended, but she needed to be fully honest if they were to go on. 'Mark, what I'm struggling to say is that I had independent dreams and desires of my own that shouldn't have had to step in line with yours. If you hadn't expected me to have them, you should have chosen one of those stuffed blouses that your other posh friends married. It was only natural that I would evolve from that naive girl you walked down the aisle with. But you have changed, too. Let's not forget that. We evolved differently, and sometimes the differences are just too great for me. Plus, we should have tried harder to have children. It would have made us the family we haven't quite managed to be without them.'

He had absolutely no idea what to say to that. Talking ornament! She was a person! And now she wanted children? She'd hardly made a massive fuss about them before. When she acted like this – became all complex and rambling – it was completely over his head. There were a great number of pretty, airhead secretaries whom he could have married, who would have given him less grief, and a great many times he wished he'd picked one.

Well, not a great many times. But perhaps right now.

There was a tiny coil of gold tinsel on the carpet that Harry must have carried from the tree. He stared at it and said a silent prayer. *Please don't let her ever leave me.*

He had turned very still. Harry came over and nudged his hands.

'I'll leave if you want me to,' she said. 'If you'd done this, I don't know if I could have stayed with you. So I'll completely understand if that's what you wish me to do.'

He played this back to himself. It seemed that the decision was his. He didn't know if this was genuine on her part, or a strategy. He suspected it was genuine, because she looked too indifferent to have a strategy.

'You want me to tell you to leave, so that you can go to him and feel easy in your conscience. That's what I'm guessing.'

'I'm not going to him. He has a wife and a daughter. If I go, I split up his family, and the one who would suffer most would be his child.'

He was slightly relieved to hear about this child. In fact, thank heavens there was a child! Evelyn did have a conscience. It was one of the things he'd always admired about her. 'I've known for a very long time that you weren't happy, Evelyn.' He stroked the dog's ears, and once again tried to picture life without her and felt intensely sad – sadder than he'd ever imagined. 'I think you have mastered a way of being happy with your unhappiness, if that makes any sense. And I have just come to accept that this is how you are. And I've still loved you, despite it.'

She stared at him while he said this. It seemed he only ever told her he loved her when perhaps he sensed he was losing her. She felt he was coming back to her, and she to him. This evolution of theirs touched her soul. *All this, to end where we started – or to start where we almost ended.*

'But I will say this. If you love him more, and he makes you happier than you think is in you to be with me, then you should be with him. I won't stand in your way.' What was he saying? 'Or . . . if you feel you can forget about him and go on, then I shall forget about him and go on, too.' He stopped talking to the dog's ears and met Evelyn's eyes. If choices were a set of scales, he certainly hoped he had weighted this one in his favour. 'But I'm not going to try to win you back. I've been on similarly futile missions like that with you in the past. Trying to win a part of you that isn't even available to be won.' But he knew that if she stayed, he would never stop trying to show her that it had been the right choice.

I want to live two lives, she thought. *One with Eddy that's taken afresh without a history of disappointment. And this one, with nothing more to learn, and all its comfortable headway already made. I love two men, and I'll probably end up with neither of them, the way I am behaving.*

'As I've said, I don't want to leave. Unless you want me to go.'

They were being exceptionally polite and considerate. One of them ought to have turned it less civilised – and she might have craved that in the past: a rational discussion that would have progressed to the level of fighting baboons. But now she was glad of it.

Mark sat back in the chair and crossed his legs at the knee. His stomach let out a jungle-like growl that even made Harry pep up from the trance he was in from having his ears tickled.

It was 7 p.m. Usually, they would be eating dinner, then watching his favourite television programmes, which she didn't care for: *This Is Your Life*, *Benny Hill*, and *Sale of the Century*.

She knew this was what he'd be thinking – about their routine. Once again, it awakened the soft spot she had for his foibles.

'I don't want you to go,' he said. 'For purely selfish reasons that have nothing to do with how you feel about me.'

She loved the sad truth of it. She loved him for the guilelessness of what he had said. It struck her again that no one knew her like he did, and his knowing her so fully added a vital dimension to her life. Eddy only knew the side of her that she gave him, the one that flourished in his presence. Even though Mark wasn't romantic, wasn't perceptive or overly sensitive to her emotions, it worked; their weaknesses and strengths struck a balance that constituted a marriage. Its currency wasn't how hard their hearts throbbed for one another. It was the small daily revelations and reaffirmations of their quirky, entangled personalities.

'Then I'll stay,' she said.

He really hadn't thought for a minute that she would love this gardener person enough to want to leave her marriage for him.

But he was very – very – relieved to find that he had been right.

TWENTY-NINE

Alice

I'm just stepping out of my office to go and fill my water glass when I come across Michael standing there, almost loitering, by my door. We practically knock noses.

'Ah! Michael!' My flatness, the unflinching absoluteness of my misery, lifts slightly. 'We didn't have a meeting today, did we?' I glance around for Evelyn.

'No,' he says. 'I'm just popping in.' He looks slightly shifty, and ruffles his hair. 'I came by two days ago as well, but they said you were taking a few days off.'

'I had a tummy bug,' I lie.

'How are you today, then?' His concern touches me.

I am usually so good at putting on a smile. 'I'm . . . coping,' I tell him. I'm sure he must think I'm a little mad.

He looks at me kindly and says, 'Well, I hope you feel better very quickly.'

He's dressed more smartly today, in a black T-shirt and a loose, light-grey jacket. He's had his hair cut, and must have finally found a stylist who knows how to work with crazy curls. 'How is Evelyn doing?' I ask. Then I realise: he's popped in twice looking for me. 'I hope she's well?'

His limpid brown eyes latch on to mine again. 'She's fine. She's been clearing out some things in her flat. She wanted me to give you something.'

He holds out a bulky brown envelope.

'What is it?'

'Letters, I think.' He studies me closely. I know I have dark shadows under my eyes, and that I'm extraordinarily pale. It's as though he notices this. 'She told me to say these were what she was looking for the day you talked on the phone.' He shrugs. 'If that makes sense.'

'Really?' I take the parcel from him. 'How intriguing. Letters, huh?'

'We could find out who they're from if you open them.'

I chuckle. '*We*? They're meant for me!'

'My mother brought me up to share.'

'I bet you've read them already!'

'No!' His eyes smile into mine. 'I must admit that on the way over here I was tempted to take a peek, but deep at heart, I'm really not that kind of low-life human being. You know, haven't got a life yourself, so you steal somebody else's?'

'Ha!'

Still smirking, I slip a hand inside the package and pull out a stack of white, letter-sized envelopes tied with string. The top one bears Evelyn's name and a London address – the address of a magazine. They're definitely old: well handled, but clearly cherished, too. When I look up, Michael is observing my face, as though he actually couldn't care less what's in the package.

I skim through them. The ones that are addressed with a more cursive writing – Evelyn's presumably – are to a man named Stanley. 'Thanks for these,' I tell him. 'You can't imagine how touching it is to me that she'd do this . . .'

'If you want to know the truth, I think Evelyn is a little starved of female company. I mean, she sees a lot of women in the home, but most of them don't even know their own name, let alone hers. She's probably bonded with you because you're the first *compos mentis* female who has paid her any attention in a very long time. And you're kind, and she can tell.'

'How do you know I'm kind?'

'Aren't you?'

I put on my best growly face.

'Okay, then she knows you're not kind, but she doesn't care. She's desperate. She's going to foist her business on you, anyway. Because you're there.'

I laugh.

'Of course, if you ever get the burning compulsion to share what's in them, I'm your man. In fact, maybe I'll give you my contact details and my national insurance number before I leave. Just to make sure you can find me.' He thrusts his hands into his trouser pockets, looks over his shoulders, sassily, and whistles, as though he really is looking for his ID in his pocket.

'Ha! Thoughtful of you! Trust me, if I get the calling to blurt out Evelyn's personal business, you'll be the first person I'll ring.'

He winks at me.

As I'm arriving home, oddly cheered up, I receive a text from Justin that sinks me all over again.

> Deposited ££ into your account. What you spent on wedding + my share of rent for next 6mths until lease is up.

Ten minutes later, another comes in.

> I hope that one day you will be able to forgive me.

I deposit my pack of Marks & Spencer's Food Hall Scottish salmon on the counter, no longer feeling like eating it. I check my bank statement online. The money is there; he's right. I hadn't even thought about the flat, or where I'm going to live next. But this text suddenly puts it on the agenda. For some reason, I think of all the houses Justin and I visited – ones we thought we might see ourselves buying after we moved out of here – how exciting it had felt. None we had fallen in love with, though. Perhaps it had been a sign. I can't stop staring at the money. It's a bit like being paid off.

Snap out of it, I can almost hear my mother saying. On this note, I pour myself a glass of wine, and shove the salmon under the grill. Sally texts to ask if I fancy a night out, and my first instinct is to say no, but I type, You're on, instead. I eat my meal, sitting at the breakfast bar, with some pre-washed rocket I shake out of a bag. It's surprisingly edible. After, I top up my glass and take the letters over to the window chair. Since Justin's visit, I haven't been able to sit in my normal chair and stare at the sofa where he sat, looking so distraught. I move around it, glancing at it, like it's alive.

I start with the first letter – they have been arranged in date order. The one from Eddy begins:

> I hope you will forgive me writing to you like this. I remembered the name of your magazine, and I enquired in a bookshop and found the address.

I read Evelyn's reply, and the letters that follow. Several of them. Eddy talking about his dreams, his routine, his visits to tend to her mother's garden, his seeing her there every time, in his mind's eye. Evelyn describing her London life, signing herself as *Your Constance Chatterley.* What is it about the ability of letters to elucidate so much more than just words? I can feel Eddy's impatience, his frustration, his suspense, his relief, his grace and gratitude. Somehow, in their handwriting, I see

Evelyn and Eddy so vibrantly on those pages; I can almost hear their voices as though I have travelled back in time.

I get to that shocking one where Eddy says he can't go on like this any more. Then Evelyn's, saying she's leaving Mark.

The next letters contain their plan. I practically ingest them. The correspondence ends here.

As does my breath. I am seized by *What next?* But no. I have missed one. Perhaps in my re-reading of them I have reorganised them in the process. This one I haven't seen yet. On the envelope, Eddy has written *Return to Sender*.

> Dear Eddy,
> I've made a terrible mistake. I can't do it, for everyone's sake. I am so sorry.

I read it once, twice. I tingle with an eerie déjà vu.

> I thought I could go through with it. I meant it when I promised you; I meant it with my whole heart. But when it came down to it, I just found myself in an impossible position. It takes a brave person to radically change their life, and someone else's, and I suppose that person isn't me.
>
> I wish I had stayed all those years ago, then there would never have been a Mark to hurt. You would never have had a family to leave. And while I am a firm believer that we have to seize the day, and it's never too late to follow our hearts and do what we must do, I do believe it is too late for us. We have loved others – perhaps in different ways to how we love one another – but who is to say that one kind of love is worth more than another? That our love devalues another? Love finds its own level where it can exist most true to itself.

But I need to be true to myself, too. Even though I am distraught right now, and thoroughly and utterly broken-hearted, my decision to stay with Mark sits more comfortably on my conscience, as does knowing that if you do end up leaving your marriage one day, it will not be because of me.

All I know is that we have to make the most of the life we've made for ourselves, and try to focus on all the ways we are happy, rather than unhappy, with it. You have a wife who loves you, and a treasured child you never thought you would have, and I am married to a kind man who has given me a good life, and because of that I feel protective toward him; I can't cause him pain. We have both been blessed in ways we have underappreciated. We should cherish what we shared, and carry it quietly and close, always. But if you can't do that, then it's best that you forget about me.

I do love you. I always will. But when it comes down to it, I can't change who I am. I can't break Mark's heart, and I can't live my life knowing I broke up your family.

I hope you will eventually forgive me.

Yours, in my memory and in my heart, always,

Evelyn

Through a veil of tears, I hurry back over words, over sentences, full of anguish for both of them. Evelyn didn't do it. I just picture the older Eddy in his red shirt. Eddy talking about wanting Christina to choose. Eddy all those years ago, who would have been waiting for her, thinking she had chosen him, only to learn she had chosen someone else.

I go into the bathroom and fill the tub. I top up my wine glass, and light a group of three candles Justin and I always used to light when we bathed together. I strip off my clothes, and gingerly lower myself into the water. And as I sink deeper until I'm almost fully submerged, I play their story over, drawing out my favourite parts, and thinking about them. The sentiment, and the eerie familiarity of Evelyn's words about the ways in which we love, send a chill down my spine. Hadn't Justin said something similar?

I stare at the white-tiled wall. My feet propped against it. The nail polish I put on for Hawaii. *No*, I think. From the first time I heard about Evelyn and Eddy's story, I realised Justin and I didn't love one another as deeply and as definitely as that. Though I'm not sure many people do.

After I've lain there until the water has turned cool, a thought suddenly comes to me. So if she didn't leave Mark, why is she here now? What terrible wrong did she allude to that day in the gallery? I should have things to worry about that are closer to home, but I am not going to rest until I know.

I look at my watch sitting on top of the toilet lid. Ten p.m. Too late to call her?

THIRTY

Evelyn's is a ground-floor, period apartment in a former terraced house just a short walk from the Metro stop and shops. Its communal entrance serves all three units, with its black-and-white chequerboard floors, gilt mirrors and a vase of white lilies on a small reception table.

I sit in her lounge as she runs water in the kitchen for the flowers I brought her. 'I thought this might be nicer than talking on the phone,' she said when she let me in. The room is spacious, with high ceilings, decorative coving and sash windows. White carpets, white walls and minimal furniture make a stunning focal point of an ornate, brown-marble fireplace that has a beautiful oil painting of a garden above it.

'I've never had it on,' Evelyn says, coming back into the room carrying a tray of tea and biscuits, and catching me running a hand over the stonework. 'I rarely feel the cold! And real fires look lovely, but they're so messy to clean.'

'I want to know the rest of your story, Evelyn,' I say, once she's poured tea.

Evelyn holds the teapot still and studies me like I'm under a microscope. 'But first . . . you,' she says.

'Me?'

'You're not yourself. I'd like you to tell me why. In fact, I insist.'

Distantly, I hear the rumble of a train pulling into the station. I reach for a biscuit, noting the slight tremble of my hand. Something about that sound always haunts me. Trains are either arriving or they're leaving. Lately, I can't get the sight of Justin leaving out of my mind. I can't imagine this emptiness is ever going to go. Whenever I arrive at the door to my flat, all I see is Justin turning and looking over his shoulder, meeting my eyes that last time, right after he'd moved the last of his bags out into the hallway. The face of *there will never be any going back*.

And so, I tell Evelyn. I tell her in so much detail that the tea turns cold. In a way, it's easier than talking to Sally; Evelyn has never met Justin, and she brings a certain objectivity that pares everything down to its simplest form. She makes a fresh pot, and by the time I go to drink this new cup, the sun has moved around to the west and is illuminating a different patch of floor.

I don't think anyone has ever listened to me so thoroughly before. She seems to absorb my story with the complete cessation of thought.

'What do you think I should do?' I ask her. I catch myself realising that I actually love hearing what Evelyn thinks.

'Do? There's nothing for you to do. It's done, Alice. You might not understand him or agree with his choice, but it doesn't alter the fact that it's his to make. It's his own code he has to live by. He even said it to you: that he wants you to let him do what he thinks is right. So you have to have the grace to let him go, and to live with his choices. Don't be a clinger. Don't make it hard for him. Don't behave in a way you'll later regret. You can't fight to keep him, because you won't win.'

Her advice comes at me like a gentle hail of bullets. 'I know that,' I say, realising I didn't actually know anything for sure until now. 'I just don't know how to let him go. That's the part I am grappling with.'

'You have to keep reminding yourself that it's the right thing. That in four months' time you will have reached a slightly higher level of acceptance. Then in four more, the pain won't be nearly as sharp as it is today . . .'

'I can't decide if I should feel angry at him!' I throw up my hands. 'Should I? Would you?'

'If you even have to ask me that, then you're not angry. Not really.' She studies me with eyes full of understanding. 'From what you've told me of him, he did a hurtful thing, but he didn't do it to intentionally hurt you. I think he's probably a good man at heart, even though, of course, he could have perhaps handled it differently. But we could all handle things differently.'

'I know I should be thinking about his little boy, but I just keep thinking about her. She loved him. She lost him. She got him back.'

'I doubt it's anywhere near as simple as that. But don't envy her. Envy is the most futile of emotions. Sometimes, you are envying an idea you have about someone, but you're actually envying fiction.'

I think about this. Yes, the grey area between what we know and what we think we know. I think of how quickly I assumed that Justin was living in that house, happily ensconced in bigamy.

'I wonder, though, if the baby dies – I mean, I really, really hope he doesn't die; that would be absolutely awful – but if he does, will they still stay together? Is the baby the glue, and if the baby isn't there, is he going to regret leaving me? Will it fall apart? Or will he somehow discover that he and Lisa had been right for each other from day one – more so than we were?' I don't necessarily believe it. I just want someone to tell me I'm wrong.

'Who knows and who cares?' Evelyn gives me a look that says, *Come on! Way too much over-analysing!* 'You mustn't wonder, Alice. Personally, from what you've said, I'd entirely believe him. He's only thinking about his son right now. It's guilt that's driving him. Guilt and responsibility. And I, of all people, know what it's like to drag around guilt.'

I have so many more questions. There is so much more I want to say. I'm a curious cross between burned out and fired up. 'Guilt that you didn't go to him when you said you would? Can we stop talking about me for a moment? I need to hear somebody else's happy ending. Please.'

Evelyn cocks her head, and seems to contemplate this. She stands up. 'I think perhaps we should take a short walk to the shops. Perhaps our legs need to be stretched before the next instalment of the mammoth talking session. What do you think?'

We take a pleasant stroll in the sunshine. At the corner shop, Evelyn buys a pint of milk.

'You told him you couldn't leave Mark for him,' I say as we begin walking back. 'That must have been so very hard.' Was it hard for Justin? I would love to know how long he wrestled with his dilemma.

'I told him it might be best he forget me – and he did. And now I'd give anything for him to remember me! Isn't that ironic?' She is slightly breathless, from emotion rather than exercise.

I stare at our feet – my blue-and-white Converse, and Evelyn's neat little tan loafers; we are walking in perfect step. I watch our rhythm for a while. Evelyn tells me about the bomb, and how her doubts had suddenly crystallised in that moment. 'He sent the letter back to me, along with all the others. His way of telling me that he was rather disgusted at me, I suppose.'

'But it was your right to change your mind, Evelyn!'

She stops walking and looks at me. 'But because of my actions, I ruined a man's life!' There are bubbles of tears in her eyes.

'But . . . I don't understand. How did you ruin his life? You just told him you weren't leaving Mark for him.'

Evelyn goes to the wall, and perches on it, even though there isn't much room due to an overgrown hedge. 'I don't know how well you remember the dates of the letters . . . I was supposed to move back there in December. The plan was that in the early new year he was going to tell his wife. But he jumped the gun. He told her while I was still in London, and then I didn't leave Mark, and his wife booted him out.'

'Oh. Oh my . . .' I try to visualise this. I can imagine Eddy attempting to undo the damage he had done, and can see how that might not have worked.

'It's hard to live in a small town and be under the scrutiny of people who have nothing to do but interest themselves in your drama. His wife felt she'd been made a huge fool of. Everyone was talking. There was all kinds of tittle-tattle flying about . . . Maybe some women would have thought that Eddy should have been the one hanging his head, but I suppose everybody has their threshold for how much humiliation they can stand.' She looks at me. 'She must have just wanted to get as far away from there as possible. Which I can understand. She took their child away. She obviously wanted to inflict the ultimate punishment.'

'That's insane! How could she get away with doing that? He had rights!'

'Alice, this was thirty years ago. Things were different then. And you have to remember you're dealing with a Northern, small-town mentality. Back then, the women held a lot of power in these matters. If Eddy's wife wanted to play hardball, there was precious little he could do. He didn't have money to hire solicitors and fight his case . . .'

Something isn't right here. 'How do you know all this? About how it all played out?'

'Eddy's friend, Stanley. He was a very good friend to Eddy, and, in a way, to me.'

'Ah! Stanley! Of the letters!'

Evelyn nods. 'I could hardly write to him at home. So I wrote to Stanley's address, and he passed them on to Eddy.' Her face darkens again. A hedge presses up against her bare arms, and I see small scratch marks on her pale skin. 'He was so impulsive! Stanley said he wanted to prove to me that he could really go through with it, because I'd had my doubts. But I thought we'd settled all that! I didn't ask him to prove anything to me!'

I feel bad she's so upset in the middle of the street. It's truly incredible that this was thirty years ago and she's as overwrought as if it had just happened yesterday.

'But Evelyn, he was a forty-five-year-old man. It was his job not to screw things up for himself, not yours.'

'I know. But I knew he was impulsive. I should have been more careful with my promises. You can't mess with someone's heart, make pledges and then just walk away and claim no responsibility for the fallout. If I had never let it get that far, none of it would have happened. My friend Serena was right. I should have walked away after the affair and let it stay a nice memory.' She looks at me, candidly. 'Those are the best memories, you know. Memories of things that end when they should. Always remember that.'

I think about this. Not sure how this will impact my memories of Justin down the road, but Evelyn's distress stops me from dwelling on it for too long.

'So that's why no one ever visits him? Because, really, he has no family now? He only has you?'

Evelyn nods. 'He only has me.' Tears roll down her face. She determinedly pushes them away. Someone walks past with an off-lead Lab; the dog trots over to her, and she places a hand on its head. The owner smiles. When they pass, Evelyn says, 'Oh, I felt such pressure! It was awful. I phoned him shortly after I sent the letter telling him I couldn't go through with it. I just wanted to hear his voice. I wanted to hear that he wasn't as devastated as I knew he was going to be, if that makes sense. But he was very short with me. He said never to phone him at that number again. He didn't say that his wife had already made him leave – that he only happened to be there because he'd gone back to get some of his things. Stanley told me all this, but I had to press him.'

She gives a tiny whimper, like a small animal. It cuts my heart. 'I felt this weight of what I'd promised. I remember, after the bomb, thinking, *But I have to leave him! I have to honour my end of the deal, but I love Mark, too. Mark loves me and needs me! I can't go!*'

Her head has a slight tremor. I sit on the wall beside her and squeeze the top of her hand. 'Evelyn, I understand you need to get this off your chest, but you have to let it go. It's in the past. We have to make peace with our past, don't we?'

I say it, but will I be thinking about Justin thirty years from now? Distraught with the memory of what he did? No, I vow. No matter what, I will not be like Evelyn.

Evelyn upturns her tiny hand so that her palm meets mine. The last woman I held hands with was my mother in the final hours of her life. I'd felt so desperate for us to somehow make our disagreements water under the bridge, in that short span of time, to make up for a lifetime of distance. I feel the firm press of her fingers.

'I suppose I should have felt flattered that he was ready to leave his family for me. But, in a way, it made me think less of him. Deep down, I didn't want him to be the kind of man who would put me ahead of his responsibilities. It struck me as a character flaw.'

She looks at me when I must appear momentarily lost for words at that. 'Shall we walk again?' She gets up. 'I'd like to go home.' We walk the rest of the way in companionable quiet.

'I am a bit confused, though . . .' I say when we are back in her sitting room. 'When did you come back?' There is a small photograph of a man on a walnut-coloured occasional table by the bay window. I noticed it earlier. I couldn't quite make out who it was. My eyes fasten on it again. I wonder if it's a young Eddy.

'I don't think I can face another cup of tea,' Evelyn says. 'How about a whisky?' She walks over to a small drinks cabinet. 'Or maybe a sherry, at this hour, is more civilised?'

I laugh. 'I think I'd like the whisky, if that's fine by you.'

Evelyn reaches for the crystal decanter. I am fascinated by her classic furniture and taste, the air of good breeding that hangs around her, even as she does something as rudimentary as pour us both a drink, placing in each glass one perfect-sized ice cube. 'I came back four years ago, after Mark died. He had pancreatic cancer. It was very sudden. He was only seventy-one.' She hands me a glass. 'We weren't the kind of couple who went around declaring our feelings, you know. Mark wasn't a true romantic, whereas Eddy had it in his soul. I never knew if Mark had any idea how much I loved him. If he thought I'd stayed with him only because I'd felt it was the safer of two options.' She looks fondly over to the bay window, and I realise that the man in the photograph is, of course, Mark. 'So I stood over his grave and I told him how much he'd meant to me. Everything I could never say to his face.'

This threatens to break my heart. 'Did you ever sell your Holy Island house?'

Evelyn smiles. 'Not right away. It was rented out. Always nice tenants. They took good care of the place. I moved back in for a time. With some savings, I was able to afford to take Eddy out of the home run by social services and put him in Sunrise. It was mainly the gardens that attracted me to it. I knew they would give him pleasure. I visited as often as I could. But the journey to and from the island was too much, so I decided to sell the house and buy this place, so that I can walk to Sunrise.' She pulls a joyless smile. 'He'll never know I came back to be close to him. Nor will he ever know that I lived with one man, whom I loved dearly with my whole heart, yet I thought of Eddy every day from the last day I saw him. How messed up is that for a life?'

'You don't know what he knows, Evelyn.' It was depressing, though. To be such a capable, vibrant person with so many passions, then have the entire story of your life go missing from your mind.

Evelyn doesn't answer. She just stares at the cube of ice in her drink, and chinks it against her glass. 'I once read that very often we assume when we get to a certain point in our life that it's all over. We're done for. But so long as one person remembers you, it's not over.'

'So the visits to the gallery, Christina . . . You're doing it because you want him to know it's not over?'

Evelyn gives me an enigmatic look, then smiles.

THIRTY-ONE

Mark

London. March 1984

When the letter came, Evelyn was in hospital. She had a cyst on her ovary that they discovered was cancerous. The doctors removed her womb, to be on the safe side. The stay in hospital was protracted because she had lost a lot of blood. While she was there, the magazine forwarded the limited contents of her postbox to her home address, along with flowers and a note saying, *As you don't drop in for messages like you used to, we thought we should send this letter on to your home.*

Mark received the delivery. He took the flowers into the hospital for her, of course. Evelyn loved flowers, and filled their home with fresh ones weekly. But the letter, well, that was a different matter. He hadn't opened it. He wouldn't do that, not even when it was addressed to someone who had once betrayed his trust. But he had seen the postmark. It was easy to guess who it was from. She was recovering from major abdominal surgery. They had begun to put all this behind them. Giving it to her now just didn't seem like the helpful thing to do.

THIRTY-TWO

Alice

A couple of days later, we arrive at the entrance to Sunrise. Evelyn was right about it being a pleasant place. I've only once been in a care home, when my stepfather's mother was admitted to one, but it hadn't smelt as nice as this one. A receptionist greets us, and Evelyn enters our names in a guest book. 'Is Michael in?' I ask the girl.

'He just went for lunch. Probably be back in an hour,' she says. And then, to Evelyn, 'He's in the garden. Lawn day.' She takes the flowers that Evelyn brought, says, 'Oh gosh, aren't these lovely?' and gives her a fond smile.

Evelyn leads the way down a narrow hall that exits through a glass conservatory, where three or four elderly men sit around a small, antique table playing a board game. They look up and greet her as she passes, their curiosity quickly turning to me. Evelyn nudges me. 'Careful. You'll be setting off heart palpitations all round. And, in here, that's a frightening prospect.'

We find a seat on a wooden bench overlooking a large, well-manicured lawn, with flowerbeds, and two parallel oak trees, like goalposts, either side. It's extremely private and pretty, and the air is spiked with the scent of flowers and a salty sea breeze. The gardener is riding his lawnmower, and, sitting beside him, his frame towering over the gardener's, is Eddy. The man waves when he sees Evelyn.

'Look at him! He's so happy!' The sight of him makes me smile.

'This is what he loves most, just being out there with the gardener.'

We sit quietly for a while, just watching him, listening to some squalling birds having a fight at a feeder on a nearby tree.

'How are you feeling?' Evelyn asks.

'I still don't know. I'm in a daze, in some ways. I suppose work is keeping me busy, and when I get home I'm tired and I sit down and start thinking about it, but my mind just goes blank again. Then, the other day, I came across a small cream photo album with a little red lotus motif on it – Justin brought it back for me from a business trip to Florence. I flicked through the empty plastic sleeves and thought, *God, not a single picture in it!* Not that there probably should have been; we'd hardly had time to set about filling it, and who actually develops film these days, anyway? Nonetheless, it says something, doesn't it?'

I glance at her – at her little pink ear with its tiny diamond bezel set in gold.

She catches me studying her. 'Can you honestly say that, in your heart and soul, you believe you were meant to be with Justin? And that you feel that way, even after all this?'

It's a direct question, which takes me aback at first. 'Well, considering everything I've heard of your love for Eddy, and his for you, I can probably say that, no, not in the same way. I may have thought it earlier. Though I distrusted it – I distrusted his certainness. Perhaps because he was ready for everything too quickly. Marriage, children . . .'

At the thought of children, something new occurs to me: if his baby had been born perfectly normal, would he have still left me for them?

'At the time, because I've always been romantic deep down, it all felt like it was the real thing. But then Justin isn't a romantic. He's a pragmatist. So you see' – I look at her again – 'I can't make proper sense of it.'

With the beating of the sun on my face and the stillness of the garden, with only the drone of the lawnmower advancing then subsiding, I feel oddly peaceful with this intimate conversation. I could never have said all this to my mother, who lacked a certain emotional objectivity when it came to the topic of men. 'I don't believe many people have the kind of certainty that was between you and Eddy,' I say. 'I once got so annoyed at Justin when he couldn't just say, yes, he was in love with me. But, in a way, now I see his point. But then how do you know when someone is The One? Is it because you know all the others definitely weren't?' I laugh a little. 'Maybe being in love is one part circumstance, another part faith and the other part imagination.' I meet Evelyn's interested eyes. 'Yet you knew Eddy was The One.'

'I think what fully brought it home to me was when I saw him quite by chance in the Ballroom five years later. He probably should have long since forgotten me by then. But when I saw how his face was so flooded with what might have been . . . I will never forget that overwhelming, profound regret I suddenly had. How much I wanted to run to him, yet there I was standing across the room with Mark! It was a very bleak feeling for a young married woman to be having. I would not wish that on anyone.'

'I wish I'd known Eddy. In some ways, he reminds me of Justin, even though they're very different.'

'My guess is that Justin was quite a serious fellow? Not lots of fun?'

'He's not a joker or a person who likes to be the centre of attention. Though he's definitely got a sense of humour. But he isn't one of these people who freewheels through life. He tends to take all the wrongs of the world on board and act like it's his obligation to fix them, and that can be tiring at times. Sometimes, even when he was supposedly having fun, I sensed he was play-acting, maybe because he wanted to appear that way, but he knew he wasn't that way.' I shrug. 'He'd probably be really offended if he knew I thought that.'

'Well, maybe you need someone a bit more happy-go-lucky next time.'

I close my eyes to the sun again. 'Urgh! I don't want to think about next times.'

We sit for a while, then take a stroll. 'Are they ever coming back?' I ask of Eddy and the gardener, whom we can no longer spot.

'Sometimes, he takes longer when he knows Eddy's really enjoying it.'

'That's sweet.' It's charming how everyone likes Eddy so much. 'I've been thinking that I need to see Lisa,' I say, out of the blue. I glance at Evelyn, sideways. 'You know? Like how you wanted to see Eddy's wife?'

'Why?' Evelyn asks. 'What are your real reasons for that?'

I think for a moment. 'I suppose I just feel there's this need to look at her and have her look at me – for us both to somehow confront what's happened. Maybe because they're all off there in their own corner, and then there's me, over here. He wasn't just a passing boyfriend. He was my husband! And I just feel like there needs to be a conversation . . . Is that entirely bonkers?'

'Not entirely. But I'm not sure a conversation would be very productive, or would end well. I think if you want to see her, it should be for closure, to help you move on. To sort of see them and make them real. Remember, that's why I did it – to help me walk away. Though there's no guarantee it will help, not when it comes to the erratic tug of our emotions. I thought I'd walked away when I went back to London after our week together. But when Eddy's letter came, all that went out of the window.'

We stand and contemplate one another. The sun suddenly beams its brilliance on us, and we are caught in a moment that Edward Hopper would have rendered in vibrant simplicity and colour. After a weighted pause, I say, 'What a life we lead! Well, some of us, anyway!' I think of Sally and how uncomplicated her love life is, with its long-time marriage that I used to think must be tediously dull. Perhaps I am a little envious of her, after all.

'You know what I realised a very long time ago?' Evelyn says.

'I love hearing all the things you've realised, Evelyn!'

'Anyone who judges us secretly envies us. Anyone who thinks they've done it all better than we have is lying to the one person we should never, ever, lie to – themselves.' She smiles. 'To finish what we were saying about Lisa, though, if you do go to see her, just remember why you're doing it. Not out of hurt and anger or a self-pity trip. Not to get him back, but to let him go.'

'Crazily, I still think he's going to change his mind and come back. That he wrote that note in a state of shock, and that he's still in shock, but that it will pass and his love for me will float back up to the top of his priorities. I just have this hunch that when I am least expecting it, he'll phone or send a text and want to see me . . .'

'You should set you sights on someone else now, Alice. On someone like . . .' She stops, then says, 'Michael!'

For a moment, I think Evelyn's telling me to set my sights on Michael, then I realise she's said his name because he's walked through the door.

'Oh!' I laugh, and put a hand over my mouth. He gives me a very suspicious look indeed.

'Wow. I've never seen anyone so happy to see me, except my uncle's dog.'

I beam at him. 'Your timing was impeccable. But you'll never know why.'

'Alice is just relieved to see a male who isn't on oxygen,' Evelyn says, and gives him a small, tight hug.

Michael gazes across the lawn. 'Are they still out there? Do we need a search party?'

'I hope your lawn man doesn't charge by the hour,' I tell him.

Michael's eyes smile. 'Okay, girls, let's go put the kettle on.'

Much later, as we walk back to Evelyn's flat, where my car is parked, I catch myself in a state of reflection about our afternoon. 'Michael's nice, isn't he?'

'And he's not taken. At least, not that I know of.'

'Nice and single? Hmm . . . Sounds like two good reasons to steer clear!'

We arrive back at the door to her flat. 'I've had a wonderful day, seeing you again,' Evelyn says, and she kisses me.

'Likewise.' *More than you can know.*

She scrutinises my face. Then she places a tiny little warm finger under my chin, and lifts it. 'Why so glum suddenly?'

She's amazingly perceptive. 'Oh! I don't know . . . Because I'm going back to that lonely flat? I suppose, I have my moments where I think, *How am I ever going to put this behind me?* But funnily enough, as I say it, I hear a voice inside me telling me that I will. Is it Sally's? Evelyn's? *No,* I think. It's mine. Rhetorical. Almost progress.

'You will, Alice.' Evelyn grasps my upper arms. 'You have lost something, but you will find something – possibly even someone – in his place. I promise.'

'We're not talking about Michael again, are we?'

Evelyn smiles. 'Well, not all love has to be grandly romantic love. You just think that because you're still so young.'

'I'm not that young. At least, not to me!'

She opens her bag, and takes something out. 'I wanted to give you this earlier,' she says. She's holding another small envelope. She looks quite solemn.

'Another letter?' This one is a manila envelope. Yellow and sturdy.

'Not quite. It's something that was sent to me. By someone who cared. Take it. Don't open it now, though. Wait until you are alone and feeling a tiny bit brighter.'

I take it, wondering what on earth it can be. 'Aren't you going to give me a hint?'

Evelyn says, 'I think I already did.'

THIRTY-THREE

Monday is a bank holiday. I manage to sleep for a staggering fourteen hours, and I actually dream that I went to see Lisa. I wake up horribly disturbed and more confused than before because in the dream she's nice and I really like her. In the early afternoon, after I've made myself bacon and eggs, I venture out for a run.

The beach isn't as busy as I'd imagined, considering the weather is good. I run the path, but can't get into my usual groove. When I concentrate on the pounding of my heart, I find myself thinking about Dylan's heart. In fact, so many things have led me to think about Dylan's heart. After I left Evelyn's, I went straight home and googled his condition. I read until my head hurt, digesting all the medical terminology, comparing this clinic's findings to some other's. It all sounded as bad as Justin had said. Then I ended up googling *dementia* and *Alzheimer's*, and reading some of the stuff Michael had emailed me, which I'd almost forgotten about. Somehow, I finished off an entire bottle of wine, and recognised that I'm going to have to take a look at my drinking.

I run out of steam, come to a stop, bend over and pant like a stressed dog. I am hanging there, panting, when I hear a car horn.

When I glance up, there's a red Datsun. A clapped-out relic from the eighties. Someone dark-haired at the wheel. I'm trying to see who they're tooting at, then . . .

'Michael!'

He rolls down the passenger window, all smiles. 'Hi.'

'What a freakishly random coincidence!' I tell him.

'Freakishly random? Or it might just be a plain, old-fashioned coincidence.' He looks me over in my running gear. 'Did you know that Evelyn's very concerned about you?'

'Is this déjà vu?' I ask him.

He smiles. 'It does have a degree of familiarity.'

My foot aches and I'm holding it up by my ankle, twirling to ease the short, sharp pain. I stop the movement, and stand there on one leg, like a pelican. 'So you've followed me to the beach to tell me that?'

'The beach and Evelyn's concern aren't related, I promise. I often come here. It's my thinking place. I find I can't think anywhere where I can put a TV on to distract me from the purpose.'

I smile. 'Do you run as well?'

'If I need the toilet. Or if I've a prospective date on the horizon. Otherwise, I usually sit just here and eat ice cream. Often one in each hand.'

'No ice cream today then?' He looks like he's caught the sun, and it makes him appear more Mediterranean than British.

'First, I have to stare at the sea and contemplate life. At that point, it's usually ice cream or suicide.'

'So we might have something in common!' I chuckle. I really don't know when the last time was that someone made me laugh. 'So why is Evelyn concerned about me this time?'

'Well, I'm not supposed to say.'

'Why not?'

'Because I'm not supposed to know the thing that you wouldn't want me to know.'

'And what thing is that?' Then I gasp. 'She told you? About my personal life?'

'Not about your entire personal life. Just the highlights.' When he sees my face, he says, 'Hey. I don't invite it. It just comes to me.'

She is trying to set us up! The little devil! *You will meet someone in his place . . .*

A playful twinkle appears in his big brown eyes. I like his eyes. They're the best part of his face. 'I thought you were joking before, Michael, but I think maybe you *do* need to get a life!' I feel a little betrayed. Evelyn!

'I've been trying for thirty-one years. I'm sure it'll happen some day. But until then, other people's lives are constant fodder for my entertainment.'

I start walking – limping. He throws the car into gear, and crawls alongside me. 'All she said was you were going through a stressful time because of a broken relationship. We could share an ice cream and contemplate a joint suicide pact?'

'You mean an ice cream each, or one between us?'

'That depends on who's paying.'

I wag my finger. 'I'm doing this for Evelyn. Just so we're clear. You can report back to her that you followed me to the beach and I haven't killed myself yet, so she needn't worry.'

'I didn't follow you to the beach. Though I might next time. Now that I know you come here.' He reaches over and unlocks the passenger door. 'Hop in,' he nods to my foot. 'And I don't mean literally.'

He buys us cornets from a van, and we eat them on a bench overlooking the sea and the few families who are scattered on the sand, trying to pretend it's hotter than it really is. 'Remember when you wanted to know what was in the letters?' I say.

'It's run between me and my wits every day.'

I playfully bat his arm. 'Anyway . . .' I tell him the gist of Evelyn and Eddy's story. 'So essentially, she loved two men. She had to choose. She didn't choose Eddy. He only found this out after he'd already left his wife for her. Then his life was wrecked.'

Michael's a great listener. He only breaks eye contact when he has to lick his ice cream before it leaks down his sleeve. 'I don't think Evelyn's ever going to know if he forgave her. He's never going to know that she came back for him. Life is so unfair sometimes.'

'Of course, she tells it a little differently.'

My hand freezes with the cornet midway to my mouth. 'What do you mean, she tells it differently? You know all this already?'

He beams a smile.

'So I've sat here for half an hour telling you something you already know?'

'More like forty-five minutes.'

'Why didn't you stop me?'

'I'm quirky like that. Besides' – he captures my eyes again – 'I enjoy listening to you.'

I shove the end of the cornet in my mouth. 'Ha!' I say, with my mouth full. 'You're a strange guy.'

'Tell me another story.' He puts his hands behind his head. His elbow fleetingly makes contact with my hair. 'But this time, feel free to pick one I haven't heard before.'

'Oh, I think I'm done with stories for one day! Why don't you tell me one? But a happy one. Or if not happy, then scandalous.'

He seems to think. 'Okay. Well, this might qualify. Especially if you have a thing for the pathologically ridiculous . . . The truth is, I don't always come here to sit in my car and eat ice cream. I came here today for a tryst in a hotel with a friend.' He indicates toward town with a flick of his head.

'A tryst?' I gasp. 'Wait a minute . . . I thought you said you didn't have a life?'

'Well, once in a while I get so much life that it makes up for the other 96 per cent of the time when I have none. You see, I've become close – I suppose you'd call it – to my best friend's wife.' He sees the alarm on my face. 'I know. You're shocked. Don't be. It's not *that* morally reprehensible. I'm a good Catholic boy, and Alex is no longer my best friend. In fact, we don't even speak any more. We fell out a long time ago, over me judging his life.'

'This story is definitely not what I was expecting!'

'Given I know all about your life, I thought it only fair you know all about mine. To even things out.' He rumples his hair, as though he's just been doing a spot of interplanetary travel and has landed here unexpectedly while en route to Jupiter.

I laugh, despite myself. 'Go on then . . . I think I'd better brace myself.'

'Okay, so, Janette – Alex's wife – found out about one of his affairs – well, not really one of his affairs, more like *all* of his affairs – and she left him, and, of course, it was my shoulder she cried on. So I was forced to take sides. I took the side of fair.'

'And you slept with her.'

'No.' He looks surprised. 'I kissed her. Today was supposed to be about us sleeping together. Her idea to take it further. But I didn't want to.' He glances at me again and does a double-take at my expression. 'I know. You've absolutely never, in real life, or even on television, heard a man say he didn't want to sleep with a woman who was offering it.'

'You're right. I haven't.'

'Well, to be honest, it is a bit different. Aside from feeling biologically messed up, you feel a bit of a cad when you turn a woman down, don't you?'

'I wouldn't know.'

'Men are supposed to never turn down sex. And what kind of nut would say no to an afternoon of passion with a beautiful woman who's got the hots for him?' He looks right at me. 'Apparently, I would.'

'So why did you?' He has an appealing twelve o'clock shadow. I can imagine someone sinking into a nice, long, slow kiss with him. 'Too close to home?'

'No. I mean, that's not ideal. But I'm not in love with her. Even though I don't really know why. Besides, it doesn't help when I'm convinced she's just looking to replace Alex with the first loyal lapdog of a man that comes along.' He gazes into the distance, in contemplation. 'Put it this way, when I'm old and suffering from dementia, I have a feeling it won't be Janette dragging me to art galleries to help me remember our love story.'

'Ah! That's incredibly sweet!' I tell him. In fact, I'm so disarmed by his sentiment that, for a moment or two, I am utterly smitten with him.

'So I told her I was sorry, I'd made a mistake. It wasn't what I wanted.'

'Ouch! That must have stung!'

'She told me she's going to go back to Alex. I think the comment was designed to get at me. Apparently, women do these warped things.'

'So what did you say to that?' I find myself hanging on every word of his story.

'Well, she's an adult, it's her choice. But it's a messed-up choice.' He pulls a resigned smile. 'It's amazing really; I don't know how it happens, but emotional basket cases love me for some reason.'

I chortle. 'So there are others?'

'My rejects formed their own self-help group. I think membership is in its hundreds, and growing. I tend to stay away from women with abusive ex-husbands, women who abuse their ex-husbands, women who cut themselves, women who order salads, anyone who has had any form of plastic surgery and anyone who refers to themselves as a friend of my sisters.'

'Sisters?'

'I have four of them. My mother is from Newcastle and my dad's a randy Italian.'

I gasp. 'Oh my! So you must really understand women if you've four sisters!'

'Not really. When you have to try to understand all of them every day of your life, it becomes the most confusing thing that's ever happened to you, so you set yourself other goals.'

We walk slowly for a while, continuing to chat about all kinds of deep and then completely trivial things. He's easy to talk to. I can't help comparing it to that first date with Justin, where he grilled me about everything from children to my real father, and I'd been so certain I was failing all his tests.

Michael and I talk about art. About Evelyn and Eddy again. 'You said you weren't in love with your friend's wife.' I've been dying to come back to this. 'Do you believe there's such a thing as being in love, Michael? Or is it a state of mind we all want to invent? A bit like God. If he doesn't exist, we have to create him.'

He looks at me as though I've just said that Hitler was a really sweet man. 'Of course it exists! What kind of nutty question is that?'

'Explain it for me. Like I'm an idiot.'

'Well, I can't, can I? It defies words. You just know when you're in love. A bit like you know when you're hungry or tired. It's primal. It's formless. But it's very real.'

We return to his car because he offers to drive me home. 'What made you want to become a nurse?' I ask. 'Let me guess. Was it your slavish devotion to cleanliness?' I pick up a fetid white sports sock that's hanging out of the pocket of the car door and dangle it at him.

The gears groan loudly as he shifts them. 'Well, I could say I had the calling from an early age to help the dying or demented, but it's really nothing as noble as that. I was going out with a girl who'd just become a nurse. She got a lot of job satisfaction, she was decently paid and she said British-trained nurses were in demand all over the world. So I saw an opportunity for money and travel.' He throws up his left hand. 'That's why I now drive this great car and I'm still living in Newcastle.'

The car gives an unexpected spontaneous lurch, and I chuckle. 'But you do get job satisfaction.'

'Yeah. The old folks, you know . . .' He switches on the radio, but the sound quality is deplorable. 'They really only come to us when their families can no longer cope – when somebody's given up on them ever being any better than they are. So the way I see it is, I might well be the only person in the world who carries any hope for them. I feel honoured, in a way. I get to be the last one to believe in them.'

'That's so touching.' I look at his bulky hand resting on the gear stick. He says some of the sweetest things! 'It's lovely that you see it like that. Most men – well, their minds wouldn't work that way.'

'I'm not really a fully evolved man.' He switches channels, and leaves it on a static-y Nina Simone singing 'Don't Let Me Be Misunderstood'. 'Remember, I grew up with four sisters. I have a large girly side, apparently.'

I feel so close to him. It's like I've known him forever instead of just a few weeks. 'So do you really think a person can forget everything, Michael? I mean, you must have thought about it quite a bit. Surely, if you've loved someone very much, some small memory of them must stay with you? Even if you can't connect the person your eyes see to the person who is there dimly in your heart?'

I'd give anything for Eddy to remember Evelyn. Even if it was just for a minute. I shake my head, dismayed, already fearing the answer.

'I don't know, Alice.' His kind eyes scan my face. 'I gave you all that stuff to read . . . I wish I knew. I've read a lot of conflicting things. Some of it I want to believe, and other stuff I'm afraid to believe. So I've sort of made my own belief out of it. I'd like to think that our memories, where they concern love, anyway, are stored forever in a special vault that can never be touched by anything bad. Even if we can't completely associate them with the person or thing we see before us. We know we are loved, and that we have loved, and we take that with us to our grave.'

Why do all these utterances always lead me to thoughts of Justin? And then I remember what Evelyn once said. About how we place ourselves in the context of meaningful things: the family we have loved, and the people we have loved, and without that we are nothing. We have no context. And that's what I feel like now. Like I have no context.

I cannot push the feeling away. For the rest of the journey, I can't drag conversation out of myself; I speak only when he wants directions.

Somehow, given that he now has a small window on to my life, I sense he knows why.

THIRTY-FOUR

I am either going to be brave, and do this, or I must put the entire idea out of my mind for good. But even with the exercise of giving myself these two options, I know which it's going to be.

I park across the street, fifty metres back from the front gate – pretty much where I parked those other times. Twenty minutes, then I'm leaving. Knowing my luck, I'll raise the suspicions of a zealot of the neighbourhood watch committee – they'll be saying, *There goes that weird woman who was asking the plumber and the man next door about who lives here* . . . I pretend to mess about on my phone and look businesslike and purposeful. Behind my sunglasses, I manage to turn my head one way while looking the other, though it's painful.

The thought that Lisa is probably inside that house with Justin's child is something I can hardly comprehend; Justin's baby, Justin's future, right behind that red front door.

I stare at the house until my eyes burn. I am still not sure what I expect to see. Justin coming home? Lisa running out for groceries with the baby? Perhaps nothing. Justin might be working late. He could be at the gym. Or perhaps he doesn't do that now that he has an ill son to hurry home for.

Am I going to knock on the door again? Now that I'm actually sitting here, I know that Evelyn was right. What would we even say? I am just readying myself to leave when I see movement at the window. My stomach lifts and drops. I can see the outline of a woman. She's standing in profile. She appears to be chatting on the phone. I realise that if I can see her, she can possibly see me. Does she even know what I look like? Do I ever cross her mind? Is she capable of feeling pity or even a note of guilt toward me? Would she think, *God, that's poor, long-faced Alice! Justin's actual wife of a few days.* Then would she fly into a panic and ring him? Would Justin phone the police, worrying there was going to be some sort of standoff? I realise this is just my overactive imagination at work, but nonetheless, no, I'm definitely not going to knock on the door.

It could be that I'm staring so intently I'm seeing movements that aren't even there. I blink, look away to refocus and look again. She's gone.

Come back! I say, under my breath. But nobody comes to the window again. I suddenly realise my fingers are clenched in my lap and my back is saturated. I wouldn't make a very good private eye.

I sit here until 6:30 – already ten minutes longer than planned – thinking, *Come on, let something happen, give me a bit more than this!* Because now I don't know why I'm fixated on seeing her, but I am.

I'm just about to give up when, oh, look at this . . . The woman has returned to the window, this time with the baby. I'm given only the briefest glimpse before they disappear again. But then, miraculously, a few seconds later, the front door opens.

Right there, standing on the doorstep, as though deliberately presenting themselves for my benefit, is Lisa, with Justin's little boy.

Seeing them is more unsettling than I anticipated. Lisa isn't what I imagined, though I had no reason to imagine anything, given he said so little about her. She's average height and sporty thin. She is wearing tight, pale jeans and a loose-fitting, flesh-toned T-shirt. Curtains of ebony hair hang past her shoulders from a severe, 1970s-style centre parting, like a young Ali MacGraw. When Sally had said the woman she saw with Justin in the car was pretty with long dark hair, his other girlfriend had sprung to mind: Jemima – the one we crossed paths with in town. Lisa holds Dylan preciously, as he gazes somewhat flaccidly over her right shoulder. He's a large baby – though it's possible he's bloated from medication. Yes, that's what it must be. I can't stop the sting of my tears.

It happens all too quickly. I'm so focussed on the baby and Lisa that I barely register the arrival of a car. I'm only conscious of someone walking up the path when I realise that Lisa is walking down it. She has come out to greet someone.

Justin.

My breath catches. I cannot take my eyes off him. Justin always walks tall, like a very confident person, yet nothing about it is put on. He's just naturally rather graceful for a man. He's wearing his mid-grey suit and a mauve shirt open two buttons at the neck, his tie dangling out of a pocket – his purple Gucci one; last time I'd seen it, I'd packed it in the suitcase. To any passing observer it's a Kodak moment. Dad comes home from work and is greeted at the door by Mum and big bouncing baby. Baby is passed through the air, from Mum, to Dad's waiting arms. Dad lifts baby high; baby is suspended there above Dad's head. Dad pulls him close and plants a kiss on him. I'm certain I can hear the smack of that kiss from the car.

I am transfixed. It's like rewinding to the time before I knew him, when I had just caught sight of him in the bar, waving to catch the barman's attention. In that split second of my objectivity, as he lifts his son gently into the air, I recognise him for exactly what it seems he now is: an attractive family man who belongs to someone else.

I should go. Must go.

I can't. I can't rally myself to leave.

I just want to sit here and watch them until the end of time.

The baby's colour isn't good. I see that quite clearly now. He's pale and he's definitely bloated. But he looks happy. Or is that my imagination?

He looked happy the second he saw his dad.

I watch Justin say something to Lisa, and then I watch them walk back to the house. Then Lisa looks across the street, though not at me. Oddly, though, it's a look of melancholic finality, or something else I can't pinpoint. Or perhaps I just think it is. Then she follows them inside. The door closes.

I did notice one thing, though. Justin didn't kiss her. I'm not sure if he even touched her; I don't think he did. His focus was all on his little boy.

THIRTY-FIVE

I'd forgotten about the envelope. Evelyn had said open it when you're alone and feeling a little brighter, though I'm not sure I can claim to be that. I think I've observed a pattern. The worse I feel about my own life, the more I seek escape in Evelyn's.

I sit cross-legged on my bed, the last of the evening sun streaming in through the bare window. I'm the woman in Hopper's *Morning Sun*. After a moment or two of enjoying the warmth and the peace, I open the envelope.

It's not a letter. Intriguingly, it's an old newspaper cutting dated March 18, 1984. It has been folded into quarters. The fold lines are fragile, so I take care when opening it out.

My eyes go straight to the headline: *Newcastle Man in Coma after Bar Brawl.*

On the left-hand side of the page is a photograph, maybe two square inches in size: a face I instantly recognise.

And then I see the name.

THIRTY-SIX

'Eddy is my father.'

I only have to look at Evelyn for the tears to roll down my face.

She nods, and tries to say something, but is at a loss for words. Instead, she steps aside to let me in. I walk into her living room and drop into the nearest chair. Since reading the article, I've been suspended in a state of shock – like jumping from an airplane and hovering sixty feet above earth, bracing yourself to land, but puzzled as to why you're not moving.

I still haven't landed.

'He's my dad,' I say, as though repeating it might make it more real.

'Yes.' Evelyn finally speaks. 'He is.'

It takes me a while to compose myself, to be able to get all this out. 'I wondered why you went into such detail . . .' I try to swallow the blockage of emotion in my throat. 'I thought maybe it was just the writer in you. You more than painted a picture of him, Evelyn. You took me there. You made me know him. I felt I was you. I felt I knew him like I was you.' I frown. 'That was all deliberate.'

She mops tears with her knuckles, and nods. A silver bracelet slides down her arm. On it is a single charm of a tiny woman wearing a top hat and sitting on a silver horse. I stare at it, and at the pale-blue veins against her papery pink skin. I can't reconcile the Evelyn I thought I knew with the person whose actions broke up my parents' marriage and cost me a father. They could almost be two different people. Or perhaps I'm the one who has changed. I don't know who I am any more.

'I wanted you to know about him; as much as I could tell you, anyway. I wanted you to know the truth – that he didn't abandon you. Events didn't happen the way you were possibly told – or not told. I realise there is probably a lot you weren't told.'

She meets my eyes, and I glimpse the tender yet determined streak that I'd observed from day one.

'He would have wanted you to know that. More than anything in the world, he would have hated you living the rest of your life believing he ran off with some woman and didn't give a damn about you because he didn't love you.'

I listen, but am reaching ahead. 'In all your conversations you never mentioned his daughter's name, or his wife's, for that matter. That must have been quite a feat! I'm not sure how I didn't twig.'

Or had I perhaps had an idea? When I saw Eddy that first day in the gallery, I'd likened his good looks to those of the matinee idols I grew up watching. But could I have possibly remembered him? Did one's memory even stretch that far back?

I just keep revisiting that moment when I read Eddy's full name. The complete slap of impossibility and disbelief.

'I haven't really thought of myself as April Alice Fairchild in years.'

'You hated the name April. Your father told me. It was one of the first things he ever said about you, actually. No one you knew was called April, you see. You were only five years old, and yet you knew your own mind enough to know you wanted to be called a popular name.'

She speaks about me as though she was there, witnessing my childhood. Then I think, *But in a way she was.* At the reference to my father in this context, though, a feeling of pleasure tries to surface, amidst the confusion. 'I did hate my name. It was a little too Doris Day . . . Some silly kids in my class used to call me March or November . . . When I went to Uni I started going by Alice – my grandmother's name. I felt I suited it better. It was just way more me.'

'I know. I saw the roll call of honours graduates. I saw you in your graduation gown.' A note of pride appears on her face. 'The alumni magazine listed that you'd taken a position here in Newcastle. That's how I knew.'

'I don't understand. Were you keeping track of me?' This, too, is only dawning on me now. 'You must have been! I mean, how did you orchestrate it all?'

'There wasn't much to orchestrate. I think I must have had a little help from forces beyond our control. Forces of right.' She briefly looks up at the ceiling. 'I kept in touch with Stanley, as you know, simply because I couldn't sever the link to Eddy entirely. I knew that your mother had moved away. I knew about the terrible thing that happened in the bar . . . Stanley was aware how much I blamed myself.'

She appears to wilt. I've seen this before – where something she's thinking seems to bring her to her knees. 'Stanley died last year. He was eighty-four. He was a good man. He was a fine friend.'

After a moment, she regains her train of thought. 'As for other details . . . it was quite easy for me to find things out. I was a journalist, remember? Even if you had worked in Timbuktu, I'd have found you and told you what I felt you needed to know. But, as it was, it ended up being a lot easier than that. The exhibition was just a perfect opportunity that presented itself – pure fluke. When I saw the picture of *Christina's World* in the newspaper, it brought back so many memories of my own yearnings for Holy Island and my home. I just thought that if there was anything that could get through to Eddy, turn on a light in his mind, perhaps that image of Christina could . . . And there, at the heart of it, was you.'

I find myself once again in a rush to talk and a rush to listen. 'I don't know what to comment on first, Evelyn! My head is spinning! I feel so terrible because I just assumed my father was a shyster. Because my mother led me to believe that.'

'If it hadn't been for me, you'd have grown up with him in your life, and you'd have known what a good man he was. And Eddy wouldn't have ended up with a brain injury and then dementia!' She cups her mouth for a second or two in a soundless gasp.

I suddenly think of the burden of guilt. And, of course, this makes me think of Justin; Justin and his guilt about his gene pool. I feel so desperately sad.

'I can't imagine what it's like for you to learn all this, or how I would react if I were you, Alice. Or what you must think of me. I hope you don't feel manipulated. I wasn't trying to get close to you to somehow make it easier to drop this on you. I felt a genuine bond with you, and I still do.'

'I don't know, Evelyn.' I honestly don't know how I feel toward Evelyn right now. 'I think the magnitude of it all is hitting me in waves. I suppose I'm just taking it all in and waiting for the next thing to hit.'

'The one thing I have always wondered,' she ventures, 'the thing I couldn't possibly have guessed at – did you come back up here to work because you knew you were from here originally? I've always wondered what you knew about your roots.'

For a moment, I almost forget what I knew. 'It's all a bit confusing, really. I have no memories of having lived anywhere other than Stockport. My mother had a North East accent, and my gran used to come to visit us, but we never came up here, oddly – though I'm not sure if it was odd to me at the time; it was just what we did. I think we may have gone once, to Whitley Bay – which was where my gran lived.' Memories have been trying to refresh themselves before my eyes. 'She would mostly come to us, and we'd go on beach holidays – sometimes with Alan; mostly without. We'd go to Wales and Cornwall; my mum loved it there.'

Saying it now, it did seem odd indeed. But there was a lot that I hadn't questioned because my mother never gave me room to. 'Moving up here for work was pure coincidence. After Uni, I applied to public galleries all across the country. Newcastle was the only one to offer me a job.' I narrow my eyes. 'You didn't have a hand in that, did you?'

'Good heavens!' She places a hand on her heart. 'Now you're giving me a little too much credit!'

For the first time, I smile.

'It's weird, but you know when you were telling me about how Eddy was supposed to wait until after Christmas to tell his wife, but he jumped the gun? Well, I remember that shitty Christmas! I remember suddenly being palmed off to go stay with Gran, then when I came home, my dad wasn't there. I remember it was Christmas morning, and I wanted to open my presents, but not without him. I kept asking my mother, and she finally said I had to just do it because he wasn't coming home.' I frown. I can see her. 'She was very . . . changed. Distant. Somewhat indifferent to me. I opened my presents and I remember thinking no one cared that my Christmas was spoilt.'

'I'm so sorry, Alice,' Evelyn says.

'I think he might have come to my house in Stockport once, too. I can't be sure . . .'

I had taken the bus home from school with my friend, Trish. I must have been about eight years old. Right as I walked into the house, I heard Alan's voice, and my mother's, and that of a stranger. A man.

They stopped talking as I came in. They were in what my mother called *the posh room*, the one that rarely got used, except when I practised piano. There was a tall, dark-haired man sitting near the piano stool. All he could do was look at me for what felt like a very long time, then he said, 'Hello, April.'

'*This is your stepfather's friend*, my mother said. I can't recall what she said his name was.'

This friend shook my hand. No one had ever shaken my hand before. I remember saying, 'Can I go play now?'

He stayed for dinner. My mother seemed springy and tense. I remember thinking my stepfather and his friend didn't talk very much – for friends. He did ask me lots of questions, though. About school, my friends, my subjects, my piano. He was very interested in the fact that I could play. At one point, my foot caught his foot under the table, and I pulled both of mine back, determined to keep them out of the way. I didn't eat much of my dinner, and I thought I would die if anyone suggested I play the piano, but thankfully no one did.

I daydreamed about him after. But I was like that. All my report cards from school said the same thing. *Alice never pays attention. Alice is always in a world of her own.* Somehow, I made it grandly romantic – the stranger who had watched me as though we had shared something my mother and father were unaware of.

'Will Dad's friend be coming back?' I remember the nervous glee in my voice. He was possibly my first crush. My mother was washing dishes. She stopped washing for a moment. 'Why do you ask?' she said, flatly.

I can remember the tiniest detail of a bluebottle hitting the window, as though it, too, felt the weight of my mother's disapproval and was dying to get out.

'No reason,' I said.

I tell Evelyn all this, and say, 'I wish there was a way I could know if it was him for sure!'

'I don't know if it was him,' Evelyn says. 'Stanley never said anything about him having gone there. I would have thought he'd have told me if he had.'

'It probably wasn't him. I'm probably just grasping at straws.' I try not to feel too downcast. 'How did it happen? The fight? Have you any idea?'

Evelyn's face takes on that look of haunted melancholy again. 'Well, according to Stanley, your father started going out a lot after your mother and you left. I think he was drinking a bit more than usual. He was in the bar. I think he knew the two men. One of them must have said something to him about it – you know, there's the whole Northern male's moral code when it comes to people messing around with their wives – anyway, Eddy threw the first punch. And he wasn't like that. So whatever they said must have been something awful to provoke him.' Evelyn places a hand over her mouth, momentarily silencing herself. 'People think that in real life they can punch and kick each other like they do in the movies and nothing bad happens. People fall down, but then they get up and walk away. They never end up with a brain injury' in movies . . .'

The words *brain injury* make me flinch.

'He was in hospital for five months. He was in a very, very bad state. I only learnt this after – Stanley knew that if I'd known it at the time, I'd have upended my life all over again. He made a surprisingly amazing recovery, considering the extent of his injury. But he was never the same. He lost his driving licence, which impacted his job, of course. He suffered off and on with seizures and headaches.'

The man who had come to dinner looked healthy. It clearly hadn't been him.

'It was just such a terrible twist of fate. Whatever he'd done, he didn't deserve getting his head kicked in. He didn't deserve ending up like this . . .' Evelyn breaks off and looks at me with alarm. 'Are you all right?'

'I think I just need air.'

Downstairs, in the garden, a fine mist of rain falls on my face, reminding me of my wedding day. I take a few long breaths, letting the cool gusts of wind blow the ghosts away.

A few minutes later, Evelyn comes out.

'Did my mother know about his head injury?'

'I don't know.' We stand shoulder to shoulder, staring out at nothing.

'I caught her reading something from a newspaper once, and she was crying at the kitchen table. She put it away when I came in, and bucked up. Maybe my gran sent it to her.' It's incredible how all this stuff has come back to me.

'It could have been anything.' Evelyn looks at me.

'If she knew he was suffering, and still she kept me away from him . . . Isn't that heinous? Maybe I would have helped him get better faster . . . Motivated him to want to live.'

'But he did live. And I'm sure you motivated him, whether you were there or not.'

I gently touch her arm.

'I'm just scrambling to put this all together, and wondering why I can't remember him. It really bothers me. How can I have no real memory of my own father?'

'You were five years old. You probably hardly saw him. He was always working. When he came home, you'd probably already be asleep.'

'I don't even know how I felt when she took me away. I think I was just puzzled in general about why we had to move. I think I remember missing him and wondering why he wasn't there, but then I must have just got used to him not being there, mustn't I?' I rub at the fug in my head. Once again, I am filling in so many blanks with assumptions. 'I remember being sad a lot, and sort of cast adrift, and somehow that feeling never entirely left me.' An old boyfriend once hinted at it – that I couldn't be entirely happy for very long.

'Children just want to feel safe. If your mum was there and was telling you everything was going to be fine, you'd have probably just trusted that, and got on with living your little life.'

'So you think his dementia is connected to what happened to his head?' I think of what Michael said. I wonder if he knows I'm Eddy's daughter? He's aware of my last name. Then I think, *Of course he does.* Oddly, this doesn't bother me the way it might have before. I seem to have accepted a lot of things remarkably fast.

Evelyn meets my gaze. 'I'm almost certain his dementia was triggered by the attack. And none of it would have happened if it hadn't been for me. He must have looked back on everything that went wrong for him – losing his marriage and losing you, and then his accident – and rued the day he ever met me.'

In that moment, I feel Evelyn's pain as profoundly as if it were my own. Maybe some people could be angry with her. I am not one of them. I gently grip her spindly upper arms. 'You don't know it for a fact, Evelyn. Look at Ronnie and Martin, and so many others at Sunrise – they never had a head injury, yet they've all fallen victim to the same fate. You're not responsible for what happened to him.'

'Moderate to severe traumatic brain injury does predispose people to dementia, actually. I do know that for a fact, Alice. By the time I'd moved back here, Eddy was only seventy-one, and he was already too far gone to know me. There is not a doubt in my mind that his early dementia was caused by his head injury.'

I hate that she has this perception. 'Evelyn, he was in the wrong place at the wrong time. Maybe if alcohol was involved, he couldn't turn a deaf ear when he should have. The fight could have happened for any reason. You don't know what they said to him. It wasn't your fault, and I can't imagine he blamed you for one minute – not for anything.'

Evelyn surprises me by kissing the pads of her own fingers, then pressing them on to my lips. 'Thank you for saying that. It means a lot that you're trying to make me feel better. That you care enough.' Tears roll down her face. 'I just wish I could have got to tell him how sorry I was.'

I cite what Michael said – his touching words about our memory when it concerns love. Rain clings to Evelyn's hair like an intricate, bejewelled hairnet. There is something beautiful about it. 'I'm sure there's a part of him that knows you feel guilty and that you've done your best for him – and for me. He might not be able to communicate it. But deep inside of him somewhere, he knows.'

'Do you believe that?' Her face is vulnerable, like a child's. For a moment, Evelyn is no longer the one with all the wisdom. I am. I find it a disarming switching of roles.

'I believe that wholeheartedly. Eddy knows.'

THIRTY-SEVEN

I am eating a smoked salmon wrap at the Theatre Royal café when I get a text from Justin.

Need to see U. 6 p.m. BB?

Bookshop Bar. One of our regulars.

I knew it. He's cleared his head and seen sense. He wants to come back.

I stare at the words like I'm trying to crack a code. Trying to decide how I feel about this. What I will say. It takes me ages to work out how to reply. Then I simply type,

OK.

He's seated at our regular table by the window. I spot him from across the road. The naturalness of this makes my heart somersault. He's wearing one of his best suits. He has his head down, and is fiddling with his BlackBerry. How many times have I seen him like this? He was always there first – the ever-punctual Justin. How many times have I knocked on the window, and he has looked up, already smiling, knowing it was me?

When it's safe, I hurry across the road, unable to pull my eyes from him. We can do it. If that's why he's here. We can go back and make it work . . .

He must sense my eyes, because he looks up. We are separated only by the window. He smiles. But the smile is different: distant. For a second or two my feet slow down and I think, *Oh my gosh! I can't go in!*

Walking here, I'd had it sorted. We'd take the baby at weekends – give Lisa a chance to find another man. We'd buy that house we'd been planning to buy, the one we had never quite found. Dylan would have his own room, of course, and a special set of clothes that he'd keep at ours. There'd be another room for when we adopted – maybe a little boy from Syria or somewhere; a child who would make Dylan realise how lucky he was. Maybe Dylan would even help us find him when he got a bit older.

Justin looks at me again, as if to say, *Why are you just standing there?* So I walk to the entrance and go in, flooded with hope and dread. The bar is packed. I squeeze past bodies. A few men glance me over – how many times has this happened, too? I arrive at his table. He stands, kisses me cautiously on the cheek. As I pull out the chair, I have to catch my breath at the familiarity of it. It's as though there never was a baby. Lisa is long in the past. It's just us, meeting after work on a Friday, something I've looked forward to all day.

When we are seated, almost touching knees, he looks expectant, and I feel a confusing flurry of possibility again.

'So . . . ?' I say.

His gaze settles on my throat, on the small silver Tiffany starfish pendant he bought me for my birthday. I'd put it on this morning and hadn't thought to take it off when I'd got his text.

'How are you?' he asks. He sounds like he genuinely needs to hear.

I don't know what to say. I don't want to talk about how I am. 'If you lose any more weight you'll disappear,' I say, instead.

He holds my eyes. 'Regular meals are a bit of a thing of the past.'

I am saved from adding anything by the arrival of the waitress. We order two apple martinis, as normal.

'Can we have a bowl of spiced nuts?' Justin asks the girl.

Our routine. The martinis – two of them each – would always be followed by dinner. 'Why am I here?' I ask. It might be direct, but I need putting out of my misery.

He sits back, and crosses his arms. His head tips back slightly. He sighs. Sally would have said he was being dramatic. I can't help but think, *For God's sake, just be settled in your choice, now that you've made it – if you've made it!*

Seeing him still looking like this – like he's in emotional traction – I regret taking any pleasure in him not kissing Lisa. Life's too precious for me to live it like my mother.

'I really wanted to see you, Alice. I miss you, naturally, and I think of you so much, and I'm trying so hard to keep it all together . . .'

Sally would say, *He's playing the victim, when it's you who is the victim!* But in a way we are all victims.

'Will you ever be able to forgive me?' he asks. I'm sure this isn't what he's come here to say. 'I know it's insane for me to even hope that you ever could. I just can't stand knowing how much I've hurt you.'

So I should forgive you to make *you* feel better? Or *myself*? 'I'm not sure it's something that requires forgiveness, Justin. It's, well, it is what it is. That's all.' I hate that expression. But this one time it's appropriate. Surprisingly, I feel no animosity toward him. I feel nothing. I stare out of the window at the rush-hour traffic sliding to a stop at the light.

'I suppose, maybe I understand you, if that makes you feel any better. I understand why you did it. I mean, I think I do.'

He wipes a hand across his face. He looks as though he's woken up from a long nap and hasn't managed to pull himself together. Is he back to work now? Is he still sleeping in Lisa's spare room? I remember what Evelyn said. *You mustn't care.*

The waitress brings the drinks. She asks if we're planning to order dinner, and Justin answers with a pretty straight-out *no*.

'What's been going on, then, in your life, lately?' he asks when the girl leaves. The *no* is still echoing. He doesn't even sound like himself. This isn't something he says.

I imagine telling him about Evelyn, the gallery visits, the discovery of my real father: he would love this. It's so odd to think he doesn't already know about such a significant change in my life. The reality that I can't really say any of this hits home with full force. We have passed the stage of sharing life's dramas, great or small. I don't want to do anything that will re-attach myself to him, now that I'm feeling a modicum of distance. So I tell him a bit about work, but it's too strange to try to talk to him the way I always used to. Even casual conversation is a sore reminder for us.

'How is Dylan?' I ask.

I'd hoped he might look positive for a second, but instead he says, 'He came through his surgery fairly well. But we still don't know. He has another hospital appointment next week.'

If he knew I'd seen them . . . 'Well, I will definitely keep my fingers crossed.'

'Alice,' he says quickly, so I know the real reason I am here is coming. 'I wanted to tell you face to face. I'm looking into getting an annulment.'

He lets the word sit there for a moment, scrutinising me for my reaction. 'This way, we don't have to wait a year before we can divorce. If we both agree to it, it can take between six and eight months. But the grounds aren't always straightforward, so I'm having to seek advice from a family lawyer to see if we qualify.'

Because I am so motionless, he says, 'Are you following?'

I stare at him, blankly, then say, 'Yes. I mean, I'm not sure. No – I don't really understand. Why the rush?' Because he wants to marry Lisa soon, to make it all neat and official?

'There's not a rush on my part. But I thought, perhaps . . . I thought you might want to be free sooner so you can . . .'

'Run out and bag someone else?' I almost laugh.

'That's not exactly what I was thinking. No.' He looks almost annoyed and slightly hurt. 'I was meaning . . . I don't know. Just that maybe you wouldn't want it hanging over you. The reminder.'

'And an annulment is going to make it cheerfully go away, is it?'

I take a sip of my drink, and stare at the nuts we haven't touched. The word keeps writing itself across my vision. I can't meet his eyes, even though I know he is waiting for me to. When we quarrelled in the past – though it was never over anything much – and I refused to look at him, he would tilt my chin with his index finger until I did. It was his way of finding out if I was really upset with him, because he said he could read just about everything in my eyes. I never really was, of course. I imagine him doing this now – and him smiling, and us acknowledging that we are fine again: that all this was nothing. But, of course, it doesn't happen.

'Isn't an annulment a Catholic thing? So that you can marry again in a Catholic church?' It's snarky, but I can't resist it. 'I think your mother once talked of someone getting one . . .'

'It's not that kind of annulment. Not to do with the Church. It's simply a declaration by a court that the marriage was not legally valid, or has become legally invalid.'

Not legally valid.

I only ever want one wife.

The words become bold and underlined in my brain. How impersonal we are. The way he's talking, it's as though I'm a solicitor he's consulting. I can't drag my gaze away from a fixed spot on the table.

It's perhaps the cruellest thing anyone has ever said to me, and the fact that it's Justin saying it makes it agonising on a whole other level.

'I thought it would be better . . . Sorry. If you prefer it, we can wait for a divorce. It won't be complicated. It's not as though we own property together, or have children.'

I look up now.

'Sorry,' he says again. 'I'm not doing too well here, am I?'

I'm not even sure I believe him, and I have always believed him. Maybe Lisa put him up to it. I stare at his upper body. The wide shoulders. The blue-grey shirt, open at the neck, with the red tie yanked midway down his chest. He'd do that the moment he stepped out of his office. I once asked him about it, and he said, 'Do you ever feel like work has got both hands around your neck and is strangling you?' I'd smiled. I'd never felt like that.

'Do what you have to do, Justin.' I say it quietly, flatly. 'Whatever you want, I won't stand in your way. You're the lawyer. You just let me know what you need from me.'

'Are you sure?'

I nod.

'Thanks. I'm . . . I suppose I'm grateful for that.'

And I suppose he's finished now.

I stare out of the window, calmly picturing us divorced, or annulled. It actually doesn't seem so huge. Mainly because I don't feel married. Maybe he was thinking of me, not himself, when he thought of an annulment – to give him the benefit of the doubt. As if this isn't ironic enough, tomorrow will be Saturday, a full month since our wedding day. The fact that we are initiating ending our marriage a month after we confirmed it is nothing to do with me, as I once – or a million times – feared. It's a product of Justin's complex moral character. His burden, not mine.

My mind skips forward to Christmas. If we do get this annulment, all this will be over for us. I'll spend Christmas with my father and

Evelyn, and Justin will be with the son he only recently learnt he had. This puts it into perspective.

'Are you planning on marrying her?'

He looks at me, uncomprehendingly. 'Marrying? God, Alice, I'm not thinking about that. At least, certainly not at the moment. All I can focus on is my son, and what we might be able to do to help him.'

'I'm sorry,' I say, wishing I could retract the question. I am sorry for everything. Even for the things I had nothing to do with.

He gazes out on to the street. Not a part of him moves. I study his handsome profile, imprinting it in my memory, thinking that this could well be one of the last times I ever see him.

He'll marry Lisa at his first opportunity. They have a child. His Catholic values will see to it that he does the right thing.

But it doesn't really matter. I think I realised that this afternoon. I think I knew then that even if he had wanted to come back to me, I wouldn't take him back. And even if he asks to come back tomorrow, or in four years' time, my answer will be the same. Sally was right. Justin is a good man, but he's an emotional wild card. He has morphed into something else altogether, and it doesn't matter if the old Justin I once loved could ever return; I don't think I want either of them any more.

I look down the length of the bar with its long mirror and its wall of shiny booze bottles. There is some relief in my epiphany. I lost a husband and gained a father. And somewhere along the way, I made new friends. Evelyn said that perhaps I need someone less buttoned-down. If I am ever to meet another man I want him to be more like Michael. Uncomplicated and easy-going. Even if he carries sweaty sports socks in the pocket of his car door.

I look at Justin and, for the first time, I see the possibility that everything is going to be okay.

The few sips of alcohol have hit my empty stomach hard. 'Shall we go?' I say.

He frowns, looking momentarily confused by my haste. I suddenly correct what I concluded earlier. This will definitely be the very last time I see him, outside of, perhaps, a courtroom. And by the collision of messed-up emotions that register on his face, I can tell he's thinking the same thing, too.

I pull off the platinum wedding ring – it's already left a small impression in my skin, even though it's spent such a short time on my finger. I place it on the table by his martini glass.

'Justin.' I watch him stare, uncomprehendingly, at the ring. 'I wish your little boy all the luck, and all the good health, in the world. I wish him the best life anyone could have.'

And then, when I feel I can say more without choking, I add:

'And you.'

THIRTY-EIGHT

There are cards with cuddly bears, butterflies, balloons and gothic fairies. Cards with cakes, cupcakes and my age in gold or silver foil. Cards for a *Special Daughter*. Gradually, the themes become more grown up with the passing of time. Always, he's written the same thing. *For April, my daughter, who I think of every day. With all my love.*

Out of each one falls a ten-pound note.

I sit cross-legged on Evelyn's floor. We are going through her 'treasure trove' of a storage box, as I call it.

'I found them among his things when we were moving him into Sunrise. I saw that they were all addressed to your home in Stockport, and they'd all been returned.'

There are cards right up until I turned nineteen, then we moved. Or at least, my mother and Alan moved as I was off to Uni by then. 'I still can't get my head around how any person could hate someone so much that they wouldn't even let him send a birthday card to his only daughter,' I say to Evelyn. My eyes are blinded with tears. Since learning that Eddy is my father, all I can picture is a tall, lean man sitting alone on a bench in the middle of an art gallery, a man who wears a shirt the colour of bright tomatoes, and how different that is from picturing nobody at all.

'You just have to remember she loved you, otherwise you will go insane.'

'It's not enough.' I stare at the card that has *Look who's turning 8* on the front, along with a package wrapped in a pink bow. 'I wonder how he felt when he was posting it, knowing that in a few days it would be sent back.'

'However he felt, he didn't give up.'

'No.' I smile sadly. 'You know you mentioned going to my ballet school to get a look at my mother and me . . . ? Well, the other day I remembered those lessons! I think my father took me once. I can vaguely picture him sitting quite out of place amongst all the mums, and I kept turning around to watch him while I was supposed to be dancing. I remember the teacher trying to coax me to pay attention . . . It's so vivid – not his face, but more a feeling.' I look off into the distance. 'I felt proud.'

Now, every day, memories are unlocking themselves like tiny, almost tangible miracles. All I do is grasp at them like snowflakes before they melt. 'Then I was on the swings at the park, and he was pushing me higher and higher, and I was a tiny bit panic-stricken, yet thinking, *My dad won't let any harm come to me . . .*' I almost can't continue. 'Again, I can't really picture him; I just have a sense of him being there. A sense I've always had, I think.' Frustration beats me down. 'It's so little! Two or three damned memories. It's all I have of him.'

'Your father loved you,' Evelyn says, gathering the cards into a neat stack. 'That is what you have of him. Like a lot of men, he was impulsive. He never saw it in terms of having to lose you in order to gain me. He foolishly saw himself as having everything. Once in a while, we all have that fantasy.'

'I don't know why she kept him from me, Evelyn!' There is no getting over this. 'Even if she did it for the right reasons, it amounts to dishonesty, doesn't it? She let me go on believing something bad about him. She never gave me enough information so I could make up my own mind.'

A flash of rage and hate suddenly comes to me, but just as quickly, it dies back. It isn't hatred; it's just a profound sense of betrayal. When I was small, that was one thing. But when I got older, I had a right to the truth!

'I'd be so curious when she said things like, *You're just like him!* The way she said it: *him*. The venom! It was so odd being told you had something in common with someone you didn't have the first clue about.'

'I can't really imagine,' Evelyn says.

'I confronted her when I was about fourteen, and she flew into a rage. All I was ever led to believe – he was a shit who left us for somebody else.'

'I'm so sorry, Alice.'

I think of what Justin said on our first date. 'I should have tried to find him. I must admit my own wrongdoing in all this. I was an adult. I didn't need their permission. I should have gone looking for him so I could make up my own mind. Instead, I spent all that wasted energy on crappy relationships that were going nowhere, without realising my father was actually out there, so close by. I was too wrapped up in my own life . . . Then my mother got sick and had treatment, then the cancer came back in her liver, and then shortly after she died, my stepfather died. I was just so caught up . . . Running down to Stockport between working full-time . . .' I recognise the inadequacy of my excuses.

'I suppose I just kept thinking they must be right about him. In all these years, he never once tried to find me. I always thought there must be something he could have done to be in my life. I wanted him to move mountains to find me. I was his little girl!'

'But now you know he did try.'

'He was my blood, Evelyn.' As Justin had so keenly reminded me. 'He was part of me, and yet I never knew which part of me was like him, did I? Because I never got the chance to know. He'd done something wrong, yes. But he paid, didn't he? His punishment was to never see me grow up.'

'Alice, people are complicated beings. You will never truly know your mother's side of things. I personally have never fully grasped why I am the way I am. Why I could never be happy. Why what I had wasn't enough.'

I curl on her floor in a foetal ball, and she rests a hand on my hip. Just the sound of Evelyn's voice is like cool ointment on a wound. 'I think part of the reason I didn't want to find him was in case it proved what I'd already thought – that he really didn't care. I think it was plain fear. The fear of finding out for sure that I wasn't worthy of being loved by my own blood parent.'

Justin had once hinted at this being at the root of my insecurity. I'd been horrified to think that my self-doubt was so transparent.

'It's a big thing to do. It's something you have to be ready for. You can't be pressured into it,' Evelyn says. 'Don't focus on what you did or didn't do. Just focus on what you can do now.'

'Hmm . . . You're a great one to give that advice, Evelyn!'

'But I learnt from my mistakes, Alice! All that matters is what I've done about things, not that I let them nearly destroy me in the process. And you will do it all so differently.'

I swiped at tears. 'I'm tired, Evelyn. I lost a husband and gained a father in such a minuscule time frame. It says something positive about life. But it's taking some adjusting to, nonetheless.'

'I think we should both try to get some rest. It's been an emotional time.'

'That's the understatement of the century, isn't it?'

She smiles. 'You're welcome to stay here tonight. The guest room is always made up.'

'Thank you, Evelyn. I would like to stay the night. And thank you for something else.'

'For what?'

'For loving him the way you did. You're an amazingly good woman. If it weren't for you, I'd have assumed he was out there somewhere, maybe remarried, with another family – maybe another daughter whom he loved in my place. I'd never have known he was a lonely old man with dementia who would never remember me – not because he didn't want to, but because he couldn't help it. And the truth isn't pretty, but it's important. More important than what we choose to believe, and the reasons we choose to believe it.'

We are both too choked up to speak. People were wrong. Love wasn't about never having to say you're sorry. Love was forgiving. 'I'm so pleased it was you that he loved.' I take her hands in mine. 'That he was lucky enough to have you love him. No matter how it turned out.'

'And I'm so very pleased that he has a daughter as fine as you,' she says.

THIRTY-NINE

'I want to go somewhere loud and crazy and fun!' I say to Sally as we trot down the Quayside's cobbled path from the restaurant, looking for a bar to have a nightcap.

'Okay.' She hiccups from dinner. She's a little drunk. It's amazing how keen she is to go out at night now suddenly. Or perhaps she's just being a good friend.

We go into the one bar that has people spilling out on to the road. 'Just to finish what we were saying,' Sally says, as we order a drink. 'Maybe your mother sent you your father, given you lost her and you lost Alan. You know . . . if the dead can affect the lives of the living. Maybe she sent him because she knew you'd lost Justin and you needed a silver lining.'

'Maybe,' I say, rather than brush it off. I suppose it costs nothing to think positively about the situation, but far more to think negatively. Evelyn would no doubt approve.

'Anyway, on another topic . . . I meant to tell you, there's a nurse. A male nurse. At the care home . . .' I'm only saying this because I'm drunk. 'I quite like him.'

Sally looks blown over by a feather. 'Oh my God! Alice has got a new man already!' She raises a brandy glass. 'I wouldn't have thought that even *you* could manage that so fast.'

'I've not managed anything! I'm not interested in him! Not like that! I just . . . I like him.'

She grins. 'I think those are two of the same thing! But go on . . . What's he like? Describe.'

It's just mindless conversation. 'Hmm . . . He's kind of, well, Italian. Or, half Italian—'

'Which half?'

'His father.'

'Thank God.'

'He looks a bit like a young Mark Ruffalo—'

Sally's eyebrows shoot up. 'So he's one of the sexiest men on earth?'

'That might be a stretch,' I chuckle. 'But he's got nice eyes. Big, kind, brown and soulful.' I can see them right now. 'And he's funny, in a dry kind of way. He's not particularly tidy. He's got loads of sisters. A warm personality. I love the tender way he treats Eddy, and he seems a little in love with Evelyn, which is cute.' I sigh.

'You're crazy about him and you don't yet know it!'

'Oh! I knew I shouldn't have said anything! You've got the wrong idea. Completely.'

'There's nothing wrong with having someone else lined up. He sounds charming.'

'He's four years younger than me. He is charming. And he's not lined up.'

'Uh-oh.' Sally makes a thumbs-down gesture. 'A toy boy!'

I know when I'm being teased. I take a sip of her drink, mainly because I've finished my own. 'If anything is to happen, it won't be for a very long time. I know you think I bounce back fast, but this time's different. My heart is still very confused. But it gets a tiny bit less confused every day. I suppose the good thing is, despite what I said about being back with Justin and making it work with his baby, I'm not sure I'm cut out for that, to be honest – even if it were an option. To be with a man while his ex hovers on the periphery of our lives . . . And even on the topic of children, I do want to have one of my own – if I can. When I said it didn't matter and we could adopt, I think I lied. I mean, I think it was just desperation talking.'

I draw breath. This is new insight into myself. I'm gaining it as I speak.

'And all this is to say . . . ?'

'That I'm not unhappy with my life.' I plonk her empty glass down.

Sally studies me, and her face suddenly changes. 'I *am* unhappy with my life.'

I stare at her, unmoving. 'Say again?'

'I said, I am unhappy with my life. Very unhappy with it, actually.' She looks down into her lap, briefly, before giving me a pleasureless smile. 'Or, I should say, with aspects of my life. But this particular aspect happens to be a big one. In fact, I think we need another drink.' She lands the barman's attention and orders us another round.

'What aspect are we talking about, exactly?'

'Exactly? John.'

'John?' I was sure she was going to say work. The anti-social hours. The endless client dramas. It's a regular lament.

'I'm going through a phase. For a while now.'

A crowd of punters arrives at the bar, so we have to crush up. 'What kind of phase?'

'A "have we run our course?" phase. I thought it would pass if I never mentioned it. I thought that mentioning it would somehow make it self-fulfilling. But it happened again right before your wedding. I got that horrible feeling that your life with Justin was just beginning, and mine with John was somehow over.'

'What?' I could not be more astonished. 'But you never said!'

'Naturally, I didn't want to say anything ugly and pessimistic about marriage to an upcoming bride. Then, after your honeymoon, well, Justin disappearing tended to eclipse the fact that my marriage has lost its sparkle.' Sally looks across the room, disconsolate again, for a second or two. 'I feel I've known him for so many years, Alice. And that's because, well, I have. It's been practically all of my adult life! He's the only man I've ever slept with, and I love him with my whole heart, but I love him like I'd love my brother. And I don't want to have sex with my brother. I don't even want to kiss my brother. Frankly, I don't want my brother curled up on the sofa with me watching telly every night. To be honest, I just want rid of my brother. That's all.'

I have never heard her speak like this. I can barely keep disbelief off my face.

'But how can I have known you all this time and not heard this before?'

'Because I've felt bad about even thinking it. I suppose I haven't wanted to be the person I'm finding out I am – if that makes sense. I've longed to be satisfied with a warm, true love with my first boyfriend that lasts forever. But it's not real. At least, not for me. Our marriage is a smokescreen. It has been for a long time.'

'But you have your precious girls . . .'

'Of course. And we've had some very happy years. John is a truly lovely man, and I wish we could be one of those couples who reach their golden anniversary knowing they never wanted anything different. But I think, if we're all being honest, many of us probably recognise that our relationships have a lifespan. Some of us push through that because we're afraid of the alternative. But I'm not actually sure if I'm afraid. I think there might be someone else out there.'

'You're talking like it's over.' Of all my married friends, Sally and John are the ones I'd be least likely to imagine splitting up.

'I think it probably is. It's over in here.' She prods her chest.

'God! Does he know? Does he feel the same?'

'Yes, I imagine he does. He's not an idiot. Every night, when we sit there watching telly, I'm sure it's going through his head too: that we're in a dying relationship. But neither of us is going to be the first to say it. Because once it's voiced, something will have to be done about it. And maybe we're only just starting to see that the time might be nearly upon us. I think we've tried to make it work for the girls, but they're nearly grown up now. We can't use them as our excuse much longer. Alice, we're nearly empty-nesters, and we're both only in our thirties! It's mad! I look at my daughters and I envy them, because I just wish I had that same, fresh, looking-forward feeling – like life is all ahead of me, rather than behind me.'

'But you're always so physical with each other!' I remember Justin saying that couples who were forever molesting each other in public usually were the ones in crisis. I had thought that was very cynical.

'It was an act,' she says. 'Probably for each other, rather than for other people, though.'

We sip our new drinks, with this thing out there now: Sally's secret sadness.

'I think I just want to be given my freedom. I want to go out and flirt and not feel bad about it. I want to imagine what sex might be like with someone I find attractive, and maybe even get to experience it. I think I want to feel like I'm with someone I'm not stuck with. If that makes sense.'

I'm reminded of what Eddy told Evelyn about my mother. How he loved her, but how we change. 'Do you suppose anybody is happy with their life, Sally? I mean, really and truly happy with everything?'

She runs a finger around the base of her brandy glass. 'Of course. Millions. We just don't know any of them.'

FORTY

'How is that orange tasting, Eddy?' Michael hands him the last segment.

'It's very juicy,' Eddy says, enthusiastically. 'But – ooh! – it tingles in my jaw.' He touches near his ear.

Evelyn and I smile. We've come into the conservatory to enjoy the sun and the view of the garden. It's the first time I've realised that we have the same aquiline nose. I have his skin, too; we both tan easily. I am lean through my hips, with long legs, like my dad.

This is why he looked familiar. On seeing him, I was seeing myself.

'Good morning, Julian,' Evelyn says to an elderly man who walks slowly past us, dragging an oxygen tank.

'He always likes his game of golf,' Eddy says, following Julian with his gaze. Michael has just removed the towel he'd tucked down Eddy's shirt before he started eating.

'Eddy thinks Julian's oxygen tank is for his golf clubs,' Michael tells me, under his breath.

I smile into the palm of my hand.

'I usually read him stories from the newspaper,' Evelyn says to me. 'World events, you know. He likes to stay informed, don't you, Eddy?'

Eddy is looking at me, and doesn't seem to hear.

'Do you want to go for a ride?' The gardener passes us on his ride-on, and waves.

'On the bus across the lawn?' Eddy perks up.

Michael beams another smile at me. Then he says, 'Eddy, do you recognise Alice from somewhere?' Because Eddy keeps on looking at me.

'No,' he says, seeming sadly puzzled. 'I don't think so. I'm sorry. I'm not good with faces. But she is very pretty.'

'That's fine, Eddy,' I tell him. 'There's no reason for you to know who I am.'

His face brightens suddenly. 'Is she your daughter?' he says to Michael.

I can't help but squeal with laughter.

'You certainly know how to pay a guy a compliment!' Michael pulls a horrified face and passes the paper cup to Evelyn. It's Evelyn's job to make sure Eddy takes his pills along with some water.

'Why do I have to keep taking these?' he asks.

'We all have to take these when we reach a certain age, Eddy,' she explains. 'They'll make you feel the best you can be.'

'I don't think that's going to be very good,' he says.

'I've already taken all of mine,' Michael pats the top pocket of his nurse's blue tunic. 'They clearly haven't given me a fountain of youth.'

We chuckle again.

'You must be having a positive effect on him,' he whispers to me as Evelyn feeds him his pills. 'This is the most talkative we've seen him in a very long time.' His breath creates a pleasantly warm draught on my neck.

'Would you like to read him some articles, Alice?' Evelyn asks.

Michael winks at me. 'I'm off to do my rounds.' He wheels his medication trolley toward the door. 'Stop by the office before you leave to say bye-bye.' Then he adds, 'My child.'

I chortle again.

'I try to choose cheerful stories,' Evelyn says when he's gone. 'Sometimes, I do the crossword puzzle. Once or twice, he's even helped me find words.' Pride crosses her face, briefly. 'If you want to sit and read to him, I might pop back home. I've a few chores. I could come back in an hour?' She's already standing up.

'Thanks. Take the time you need.'

Evelyn kisses Eddy's cheek. 'Sometimes, he falls asleep. So don't be surprised if he doesn't last long. When I come back, we can take him to water the plants, if you like. He loves doing that, don't you, Eddy?' Devotion fills Evelyn's eyes, and a part of me can't look, because it touches me so deeply.

'Yes,' Eddy says, automatically, blankly.

Once Evelyn has left, we sit there. The first time I've been alone with him in thirty years. But with everyone gone now, Eddy doesn't seem to realise I have stayed. I comb the newspaper. It's not easy to find a cheerful story, but eventually I come across a cute one about a child and his Dartmoor pony. I read it slowly, looking up once in a while to see if he's still awake. And he is. His eyes are glued to my face the entire time.

By the time I've read a couple of other stories, Eddy's chin has dropped to his chest. I can watch him without him knowing, which is perfect. The thick, steel-grey hair, recently cut, parted to the left. The noble head, perfectly aligned with the spine – immaculate posture, even still. The shallow rise and fall of his chest and the gentle rumble of his breathing. I sit like this for what feels like ages, picturing him pushing me on the swings, watching me in my dance class, reading Evelyn's last letter telling him to forget about her.

His left hand is curled by his leg. I stare at it for a while, then slip my fingers between his index finger and thumb. My heart is pounding. I'm surprised he can't feel the vibration of it, transmitted through our veins. I am fascinated by the sight of us holding hands, seeing myself as a little girl dragging him into the park toward the swings, while he says, *Hold on! I can't run as fast as you!* A memory? Or do I just wish it were?

Evelyn comes back an hour or so later. I have lost track of time. She sees us holding hands, and smiles. Eddy is still sleeping. 'We should leave him now. I thought I'd take you across the street for a late breakfast. And Michael wants to come, too.'

'Michael?'

'He said it's his parental obligation to supervise.'

I laugh. 'Oh dear! This joke will never end!'

I pick up my bag and cast my dad a final glance. When I pop a kiss on his cheek, he smells of the orange he ate earlier.

FORTY-ONE

There are three more of these visits in short succession. Usually he sleeps. He's not as communicative as before, though; I feel we have regressed.

One day, Michael wheels in an old-fashioned stereo and the home's donation of old records. We select some songs from Eddy and Evelyn's era, and play them for him. He loves the music! He rests his head back, and his facial expressions seem to ebb and flow along with the tune. Then, when Michael downloads The Ronettes' 'Be My Baby' on to his iPod – the song Eddy had hammed it up to, to Evelyn, at the wedding where they met – it's fascinating. Eddy raises his head. He leans in close to the iPod docking station. You can almost see him listening, intently, as though each lyric were a brain-teaser, slowly peeling away layers of a mystery that he's set on getting to the heart of.

'He remembers how you met!' I whisper to Evelyn.

'Either that, or he's never seen an iPod before.' She smiles.

I wonder if we are giving up hope.

But then something amazing happens a few days later. There are only four of us at the gallery this time. Martin tripped and broke his foot five days ago. Ronnie refused to change out of his pyjamas. Eddy walks right up to *Christina's World* and stares at it.

'Do you remember a special house, Eddy? Is that what you see when you look at *Christina's World*?' I ask him. Now, I feel a whole new debt to that painting. A new unanticipated reverence; it was Christina who brought us all together, after all.

Miraculously, Eddy says, 'Yes.'

'What do you remember, Eddy?' Michael pushes gently.

Eddy's eyes are still fixed on the painting. He is standing with his thumbs and forefingers tucked in his jeans pockets. Today, unlike other days, he stands taller and impregnable, the posture of the young Eddy. His response is so completely certain of itself. I can't quite fathom the change.

'I remember there was a house,' he says. 'And I remember there was a girl.'

Evelyn turns as still as a statue. I think we all do.

'Whose house was it, Eddy?' Michael asks. 'Do you recall?'

'It was Evelyn's house,' Eddy says, without a beat of hesitation.

'Do you mean this Evelyn, here?' Michael asks.

Eddy follows the direction of Michael's finger. 'This Evelyn,' he repeats. But it seems rather parrot fashion; there's an empty look in his eyes that makes my heart sink. Evelyn and I squeeze hands tightly. I don't know who is giving comfort to whom.

'Can you tell us anything about Evelyn's house, Eddy?' Michael clearly isn't discouraged.

'It didn't look like that, did it?' Evelyn prompts. But I can hear the false note of faith in her voice. 'It had flowers. Lots of flowers, didn't it, Eddy?'

'Fuchsia!' he says, almost instantaneously, and Evelyn places both hands over her nose and mouth, and slightly sways.

'Fuchsia were one of her favourite flowers,' he says. The slight cataract dullness to his gaze disappears. His eyes suddenly became luminous, like freshly polished glass.

'Whose favourite flowers, Eddy?' Michael asks.

And as fast as he asks it, Eddy says, 'Evelyn's.'

I stare at him in amazement. For the first time, the two Eddys I have known – Eddy from the stories, and the elderly Eddy who stands here – are exactly the same person to me. Time has narrowed. The past has caught up. The man who pushed me on the swings is right here. He's never been anywhere else. I rest a hand between his shoulder blades, still intoxicated by the feel of his skin and bones under my fingertips.

I look at Evelyn; she still has her hands over part of her face. Tears are streaming either side of them.

'You were a gardener once, weren't you, Eddy?' Michael pats him on the back, his fingers briefly making contact with mine. 'That's why you enjoy weeding at Sunrise Villas, and you enjoy riding the lawnmower. And you know that looking at flowers makes you happy.'

Eddy searches Michael's eyes, then moves on to me. I have a sense that comprehension lies just beyond his grasp, clearly eluding him as he reaches for it. Then he looks back at the painting. 'I planted the flowers for someone. I planted them for Evelyn.' His tone is definite and sure of itself again. We are moving in and out of focus. In one smooth move, his eyes come to rest on Evelyn.

Then it's somehow miraculous. His face transforms again. He looks like he's seeing an almost-forgotten ghost from his past.

'Yes!' Evelyn says, her voice filled with a twitter of girlish joy that I haven't heard before. 'You did! You planted all kinds of flowers – jasmine, sweet peas, roses. And she loved them always, just as she loved you. And they still bloom there, to this day. Just like her love for you.'

I remember Evelyn saying that she'd insisted that the new owners didn't dig up the flowerbeds. They had apparently looked at her as though she were cute, endearing and a tiny bit mad. But they'd given her their word.

Eddy is studying Evelyn as though she were an intriguing riddle he's determined to solve. This curiosity lasts a moment or two, but then he frowns, his eyes returning to the painting. 'There are no flowers in

Christina's garden. If there had been, she could have sat out there and been happy.'

'But she was happy there!' Evelyn jumps in. I am fascinated by how she is speaking in the third person. Perhaps she is afraid of shattering the moment by making it too real and too much for him. 'She used to sit in her garden with people she loved – her mother and father at one time, and then someone else – a man who meant the world to her. A man she loved and thought of every day of her life.'

Evelyn looks at both Michael and me, as though for help. Her fingertips move from the centre of her chest, to her chin, then back again. By the intensity of her expression, I can tell she's more shaken up than perhaps she ever imagined this moment would make her.

'Do you remember that man, Eddy?' Michael gently asks.

Eddy gazes off into the near distance. It's as though his mind is a searchlight coasting over a black sea, looking for a lost ship.

'Do you recognise this house?' Evelyn seems to regain herself, and smartly digs in her bag. She shows him the picture she once showed me.

At first, he doesn't appear to realise that he's expected to look at it. Then, warily, he takes it from her. He stares at it long and hard, at the small stone cottage with the blue front door. At the young girl standing alone in the garden.

He doesn't say a word. But a smile of wondrous infatuation suddenly transforms his face.

FORTY-TWO

Today, I've brought them to the beach. It's mild and sunny. I have packed sandwiches, beer and a chocolate cake from my favourite German baker. Next week, I'm driving them to Holy Island, to see Evelyn's old house.

'Remember the treasure trove?' Evelyn says, saucily now that Eddy has nodded off. She reaches into a large leather bag, pulls something out and flips open a page of what's clearly a school scrapbook. Among the postage-stamp-sized portraits of the Class of 1955, she singles out one with the tap of her finger.

'You!' I cry.

The young Evelyn is wearing a modest, navy-blue dress with a crocheted cream collar. 'Well, look at you! Your long wavy hair. You look like a young Veronica Lake.'

Evelyn dips her chin, in that cutely coy way she saves for compliments. 'I was twelve years old when I had my first permanent wave. They doused your head in chemicals, stuck pin curls in you and then baked you to about two hundred degrees until you were nearly cremated.'

I chuckle.

'I found these, too. They were among his things.'

The photo shows four young women, in evening dress, holding cocktail glasses. The photographer has caught them right as they're bursting into laughter. Three of them are brash and busty. But it's the girl on the left who has a gentle candour in her eyes that says she's more interested in the photographer than the jokes. 'Look how stunning you were, Evelyn!' I say. She's wearing a sleeveless, black shift dress and a leopard-print pillbox hat perched at a jaunty angle. Her thick, dark hair has been flipped at the ends, and around her wrist is a single strand of pearls.

'It's from the wedding, right?'

Evelyn nods. 'Eddy took it. If only I could go back to that moment and feel that thrill again. I would give anything.'

'Oh my! This is amazing! You look so dignified and regal! No wonder he couldn't take his eyes off you, Evelyn. *I* can't take my eyes off you!'

'Oh! Silly!' She passes me another one – of a sports team – and taps a small face in the back row.

'Is that my dad?' A hand flies to my mouth.

'Yes. The date's on the back. He was thirteen.'

The same beaming smile. The same dark, thick hair. Seeing him as a boy unleashes quiet heartbreak.

'He wanted so badly to be a professional footballer, but he was needed at home, to earn the bacon.'

I brush away a stray tear. 'My mum destroyed everything with his face on it. Even their wedding photos.' Oddly, I think of Justin. I'm glad now that I didn't make life difficult for him by making it hard for him to leave. Not only have I kept my dignity, but I've proven to myself that I'm better than my mother.

I can't stop gazing at him. 'I never, ever, expected to see my dad as a teenager.' When I eventually pass the photo back to her, she kisses it, briefly, and smiles at it, coy and proud.

I wonder what his life had been like at home, what his mother and father were like. Because by moving me away, my mother had robbed me of grandparents, too. 'We have to show him the pictures when he wakes up!'

One of Michael's stash of articles said that even if we forget everything else, memories of our childhood linger like perennial ghosts, amorphous but never entirely stamped out. I take comfort and encouragement from this. In some ways, you can really only account for your life where your memories begin, and before that you exist somewhat at the behest of those who know you. A bit like dementia, only in reverse. The end of life and the beginning can be almost the same.

'I want you to have it,' Evelyn says. 'He would want you to.'

'I'll take good care of it.' I smile. 'Now I have a photo of my dad! This makes me happier than you could ever know.'

'And you'll take lots more.' She taps her temples and stares at a sleeping Eddy.

Back at the home, I open his window, and the room fills with the chirps of birds making a play for a feeder. Eddy stands right behind me looking out on to the gardens.

'I like this view,' I tell him. 'I could stare at it all day. It's so peaceful and green.'

'In winter, the birds have nothing to eat. I think they want to go home, but they don't know where home is,' he surprises me by saying.

'I think they quite like hanging out here in the summer,' I tell him.

Evelyn is refilling his water jug in his en suite bathroom. I pull the small photo from my bag.

He walks over to his armchair and sits. I crouch beside him. 'Do you recognise anyone in this picture?' I ask him, gently.

At first, he doesn't look, then when he does, he shakes his head.

'You might not know this, but one of these boys grew up to be my dad.' I gaze up at his face, pulsing with a restless optimism. 'Do you know which one was my father, Eddy?'

His eyes go blankly to the photo again.

I sink. I've been too fired up since what happened in the gallery. 'That's okay.' I squeeze his knee and try not to sound oppressively defeated. 'You know what? I think I'll tell you another time, when you're a little less tired.'

'How are your piano lessons?' he asks, without skipping a beat.

I am standing up. The shock of it makes me lose balance slightly. Evelyn has now come to the bathroom door, and I hear the catch of her breath. 'What did you just say?' I ask.

His eyes are fastened on mine, so brightly. 'You were taking piano lessons. You had your music all set out.' His voice has a note of triumph about it.

'Yes!' I put both hands either side of his face and kiss him swiftly on his brow. 'That's amazing! You're right! I was. You came to visit me. You stayed for dinner.'

'I know I did,' he says, seeming quite pleased with himself.

'You recognise April!' Evelyn comes over to us, breathless and sprightly like a bird.

'Of course,' he says, as though there is no possible reason why he shouldn't. 'You are my daughter.' He looks at me. Then, to Evelyn, he says, 'And you're my wife.'

FORTY-THREE

In the party room, a dozen or so elderly people, who have no idea that today is any different from yesterday, sit in chairs in a circle. Three nurses run plates of goodies to them from the buffet. 'Rhinestone Cowboy' has just switched to Wings' 'Listen To What The Man Said', and one of the nurses is unsuccessfully trying to coax a sing-along, with only one patient – Ronnie – joining in.

Today is Evelyn and Eddy's joint birthday celebration. She'd failed, until a few days ago, to tell me that their birthdays fall only one day apart.

Michael is sitting beside me and Eddy near the bay window. Suddenly, Martin walks over to us, as though on a mission. 'Wings was the group formed by Paul McCartney after the Beatles split up. But soon after that a terrible thing happened to Paul. He was shot by a mad man. Someone took his life and ended his talent.'

'You certainly know your music, Martin!' Michael winks at me. It clearly doesn't matter to him that, in Martin's mind, the wrong Beatle had died.

A short while after, I try to get Eddy to engage with me, but it's not promising. There have been no more glimmers of recognition. I have come to accept this. I will go on talking to him about the past, and tell him the remarkable story of how I came to know him. I will not give up on my father now that I've found him, no matter what state his mind might be in. He has remembered me once. He might do so again. I take enormous strength from Michael's belief that our memories, where love is concerned, are stored forever in a special vault. No one and nothing can touch them.

When I look up, Michael is slow dancing with Evelyn to Rita Coolidge's 'We're All Alone'.

He's wearing a fitted, white T-shirt that shows off his muscular upper body and firm upper arms. He appears to be concentrating very hard to avoid stepping on Evelyn's toes. From time to time, he joins in on the odd line of the song. Once in a while, his eyes meet mine. Just the presence of Michael in the room makes me smile.

'Your turn,' he says. I realise he's holding out a hand to me.

'Oh no!' I clasp my hands behind my back, quickly. 'I've got two left feet.'

'Well, I've two right ones, and we can't look any stranger than this lot.' He nods to a few of the nurses, who are good-sportedly dancing with each other.

I get up, and there's a funny feeling in my stomach. Can it be the butterflies? 'This one's for you, Evelyn,' Michael says, dragging me into the middle of the floor. It's Nat King Cole's 'Unforgettable'.

'Do you think all these nurses will wonder if I'm your girlfriend?' I ask, when I'm in his arms. We're almost the same height. But he's broad and his chest is hard, and I like the feeling of him against me. I'm aware of the intermittent press of his fingers in my back.

'Oh heck! I'm really hoping. But I'm sure they've already gathered I'm out of your league.'

'You really shouldn't say that about yourself. I mean, even though it's true, of course.'

'Actually, I shouldn't sell myself short. I'm the sex symbol of Sunrise Villas. This happens when you're the only male under the age of seventy.'

I chuckle, and his fingers give another somewhat communicative press.

'Look at Evelyn and Eddy,' I whisper, my lip catching the tip of his ear. Evelyn is gazing at the back of Eddy's hand as she tenderly strokes it. 'You know, I downloaded Long John Baldry's 'Let the Heartaches Begin', and she wouldn't even let me play it, because the memory hurts too much. Makes me feel so cheerless! No one will ever love me like that.'

'Me neither. It's a tragic waste of potential. We should drink to that some time.' He pulls me a little closer so my cheek can almost sense the warmth of his.

His hand tightens on mine. We dance like new drivers trying to master the three-point turn. 'Fancy exploring some other corner of the floor?' I tease.

'Let me work out how.'

'You're not really a bad dancer,' I tell him. 'You're horrendous!'

Suddenly, he sweeps me in a skilful arc, casting me free with a single hand, then catching me before I lose balance. It's like a lovely fading in and out of anaesthetic. Next, our feet seem to follow each other like sprightly lovebirds. 'You can dance! Why were you pretending you couldn't?'

'I wanted you to like me for the right reasons.'

'This is quite lovely, you know. It really is,' I say, when I'm done chuckling. And I'm not playing with him any more; I'm rather beguiled and serious.

Then we go to get the cake.

Michael sticks three candles into the cream.

'Three?' I slump over the counter watching him.

'One for Evelyn, one for Eddy and one for you.' He strikes a match, and holds my eyes before he lights the candles.

'Why am I getting a candle? It's not my birthday.'

'In a way, it feels like it should be. Something commemorative, anyway.'

'Aw!' I place a hand on my heart and feel happy tears come. 'I've never had anyone light a candle for me for such a nice reason.'

'You'll have to let me do it again then, sometime,' he says. And we smile.

We carry the cake in together.

'Three cheers for Eddy and Evelyn!' Michael pushes open the party room door, and we burst into 'Happy Birthday', along with the nurses. Very few of the patients seem to register the singing. It could well be the least jolly party on record. But Martin and Ronnie clap, and Evelyn is smiling.

'Is it my birthday?' Martin asks. 'How old am I?'

'It's Eddy's and Evelyn's,' Michael tells him.

'Is it?' Martin looks disappointed. 'How old are they?'

'How old do you think I am?' Evelyn asks.

He studies her, then quite definitely says, 'Fifteen.'

We laugh. 'Evelyn is seventy, and Eddy is seventy-five,' Michael says.

'I'm seventy-five?' Eddy repeats suddenly.

Evelyn takes hold of his hand. 'You are. We were born five years and one day apart. We met at a wedding. Then we met again, properly, many years later.' Evelyn winks at Michael. 'But I think that's where we'll leave this story for now.'

Eddy looks at her as though he's adding one more random clue to an ongoing mystery.

'I'd like to stay here tonight,' I tell Michael, as we eat cold pizza and drink a beer some hours later in the staff kitchen. 'If it's okay for me to sleep on the couch in his room.'

'You might regret it. He wanders a lot. You might not exactly sleep.'

'If he wanders, I'll wander with him. If that's all right.'

'Of course. And we do have a spare room here for guests. If you get tired, you can always go in there and rest properly. No one will bother you – or at least, we can hope. It'll be like a dry run for when you get old.' He smiles, still looking at me with so much affection. 'I'll unlock the door for you and leave the key on the inside.'

'Michael,' I rest a hand on his pleasantly muscular upper arm, recognising, as I do, that I actually just want to touch him. 'Why have you not been snatched up by some lucky young woman?'

'I don't know. Older ones seem to like me more.' His face fills with devilishness.

We walk to Eddy's room now. 'Tell me,' I say, because I have to ask this. 'Did you know all along that Eddy was my dad? I think you must have done. The names . . . Evelyn's stories.'

'Ah!' I see a tell-tale flicker of guilt in his expression. 'I can't really say. Remember I once told you I can keep a secret? But, say I didn't know, I'd know, anyway.' He smiles. 'You look like him.' He taps the end of my nose. 'The hooter's a dead giveaway.'

I laugh. 'My hooter! How can you call my lovely nose that?'

'Well, it's the high cheekbones, too . . .' He looks at me with a certain prolonged objectivity that makes me flush. 'It's obvious to anyone with eyes.'

'That might well be the best thing anyone has ever said to me, Michael,' I tell him, very quietly. 'It actually makes me happier than you could ever know.'

We stop at Eddy's door. Michael's bare arm accidentally grazes mine; the warm brush of his fine hairs is a lovely static charge. 'I'd like to make you happier than you've ever known,' he says. And he says it so quietly that I have to stare into his eyes for a sign that I've heard him correctly.

All the things I should say line up. I'm not ready. It's too early. How can I ever trust again? But he places one finger on my slightly parted mouth and presses there, his eyes busy telling me something. Michael isn't in a rush. Michael is modestly saying, *Fall for me in your own good time.*

I kiss his finger and smile.

FORTY-FOUR

Evelyn is one of the most enigmatic people I know. Every time I see her, she has a surprise for me.

'I found it!' She gives a joyful little skip. 'I've looked everywhere. I knew it had to be in one of these amazingly bountiful boxes somewhere.'

In the centre of Evelyn's lounge are about eight storage containers with their contents – everything from a corset to ancient-looking magazines – strewn all over the place.

'My gosh, it looks like you're having a jumble sale!' I laugh.

She hands me a book. It's a glossy paperback with a simple, intriguing cover of a dark-red Venetian blind pulled part way down a window. At the bottom, in embossed gold, are the words: *After You Left, A Novel, by Joanna Smart.*

'Who's Joanna Smart?' I ask, but immediately realise. 'Oh gosh! You are!'

'I was published in 1987 by one of Britain's most venerated publishing houses.'

'This is fabulous!' I turn the book over and scan the blurb.

They meet at a wedding. They know each other for only one day. But it's a day that changes the rest of their lives . . .

One magazine has called it, *A modern-day* Lady Chatterley's Lover. 'It's the story of you and my dad!'

Evelyn's eyes light up. 'Well, it didn't start off that way. I'm not really sure what it started off as. I think I always had the theme, I just needed the right story to hang it on. And when I met your dad again, I found my story. It was like it had always been there.'

I look at her tears and think, *God, is it really possible to cry for an entire lifetime over someone?* 'But the title? You were the one who left, not Eddy?'

'Yes. And yet you can never know how many times I've played over the vision of him walking away from my front door when he'd come to take me on our date. As I stood and peeked from behind those curtains . . .'

My brows pull together. I can't bear to picture it. I flick through the first couple of pages. 'Look! You dedicated it: *For Eddy*.'

I just want to disappear into a room and read. I quickly find the first page.

Northumberland. 1983

At first all she saw was the back of his head. He was on the other side of the vast laurel tree that divided two sections of the garden . . . I skip ahead. *He always came on Tuesdays, her mother had told her.*

'After he would leave, after we had made love and I was glowing from him, I would scramble to get it all on to paper. Everything I'd done and felt and said, all day. Everything he'd said . . . I was always good at shorthand. I knew that abysmal secretarial training would finally come in handy.' She smiles. 'I'd like you to have it, obviously. You didn't have the benefit of knowing him as a dad. So at least this way, you're going to know Eddy, the man – more of an account than I've even been able to give you.'

I clutch it to my heart. She watches me, and there's a vaguely self-satisfied expression on her face, and I love it. I am unspeakably grateful to her.

'I walked away from Eddy. Justin walked away from you. Neither of us did it because we'd stopped caring. You and your father both lost the person they loved to someone else. You have more in common than you might have thought.'

I think, *But I don't want to be like my father. I don't want to have loved and lost and never know love again.* Yet I know life is long, and there will be good things ahead. They already have a face.

'I'd like to read it to him, if you think it's a good idea.' As a child, I remember the curious tenderness of being read to. And now I think I'll enjoy being the one to tell the stories.

'I think it's a lovely idea.'

'Did you write any other novels, Evelyn?'

'No. And, of course, this one is out of print. That copy might well be the only one left on the planet.' She attempts a laugh. 'I was commissioned to write a second book, but somehow I couldn't pull it off. So I had to pay back some of my advance. I don't think the publisher was very pleased.'

'You could have written the flip side of events – what would have happened if you had chosen to be with Eddy and left Mark. Or, if you hadn't watched him leave that day. If you had gone on that first date.'

'I don't think I was altogether clever enough to invent stories. They had to come from some place of truth in me. Besides, I hate *what ifs*.'

I fan through the pages, enjoying their draught on my face. And then I see something curious.

'What's this?'

Lodged in between the pages is a small airmail envelope. On the front, in writing that I now easily recognise, is written *Evelyn Westland*, and the address of *Cosmopolitan* magazine.

Evelyn gets up from the floor, and squints. 'I have no idea. What is it? A letter?'

'It's addressed to you, Evelyn. It's unopened.'

She stares at it, slightly daunted. 'Good Lord! Open it. Read it to me.'

'I can't, Evelyn. I can't read your letter. It's personal.'

'Please! You've read all the others. I don't have any more secrets.' She manages a humourless laugh. 'One has definitely been more than enough.'

I slip my thumb under the tiny lip of the flap, which hasn't stuck properly. The folded page inside is flimsy, so lightweight that I could probably read the words straight through it, if I didn't want to drag out my suspense.

'It was written on March 10, 1984, Evelyn.' I start reading.

To My Love, Evelyn,

I wasn't going to send this, in case unearthing the not-so-distant past might upset you, but lately you have been on my mind even more so than usual, if that's possible, and I don't quite know why. I hope there's nothing wrong, and you are well. I hope that you have managed to put everything that happened behind you, without entirely forgetting me in the process.

I realised you might be left with the impression that I was disappointed in you, because I returned your letters. I don't really know why I did. A knee-jerk reaction, perhaps: another example of me not thinking straight. But it certainly wasn't because I was angry with you. I completely understand why you couldn't go through with it, and I can promise you that I bear no ill feelings toward you whatsoever. Not now. Not ever. I could never think badly of you, and I hope you believe that, or our love will have failed somehow. You once said it a long time ago – our timing has always been off. I would have been a very lucky man if I'd managed to get you to stay here for me when you were that young, beautiful, go-getter girl I knew for only one day. Our paths crossed again in a way that I promise you I will never forget, and even when we get our bleak moments, Evelyn, we have to remember to be glad of that. I, for one, will always remember the happiness I've felt just to know you and love you, and not for one minute would I have wanted to miss out on that.

Life hasn't been easy lately. I should have handled some things differently, and I will try to put it all right as best I can. But I suppose this is my long-winded and rather clumsy way of saying that I want you to know I have no regrets about us. You are part of the fabric of me. If you hadn't been in my life, I would have lost out on knowing so much of what I now know about myself, and about my capacity to love, and I will hold this belief until my dying day. My hope is that you feel the same – that you don't regret a thing that happened between us, or how it turned out, and you never will, no matter what happens down the road.

I'm sure it's unlikely we will ever meet again – though I personally will never say never, because that's just how I like to think. But, nonetheless, I will always love you, and knowing you've loved me will always brighten my days.

Yours, Eddy

'The date . . .' Evelyn looks at me. 'March 10. He wrote this eight days before he was beaten up.' Her face turns grey, in a way I've never seen before, not on any living person. 'He said he'd been thinking of me more so than usual, and he hoped there was nothing wrong. Well, it was impossible for him to know this, but I was quite sick.' She is clutching her fingers, and I can tell she's working herself into a small frenzy. 'I had to go in for surgery. The magazine must have forwarded the letter to my home.' She is looking at me with wide, riveted eyes. 'Obviously, Mark must have received it. He'd have seen the postmark and guessed who it was from.'

'But he didn't open it.'

'No. Mark would never read someone else's post.' Her face floods with tenderness when she speaks of her husband.

'But he didn't throw it out, either.'

She is off looking into space, clearly trying to piece together the more elusive bits of the puzzle. 'Of all the places he could have put it . . .'

'He put it where he knew you would find it, Evelyn. Because like you said many times, he was a good man. Do you think he knew that Joanna Smart was you?'

Evelyn gasps. 'Good heavens! I don't know! The book wasn't published then. I was finishing it while I was convalescing.' She's frowning. 'I suppose it's possible he knew. I never told him I'd written it because I didn't want to hurt him, or embarrass him. But he did have friends in high places. It's possible he knew someone at my publishing house.'

'Or maybe he'd just seen that the book was special to you somehow.'

'I kept it on my desk for a long time. It's possible he knew it was special to me.' The anguished look comes back. The one I will forever associate with Evelyn. 'Eddy said things hadn't been easy for him. That's because by the time he wrote this, he'd have split up with your mother. Everyone would have known . . .'

'But he was trying to say that, despite the enormous price he paid, you were still worth it.' I gently stroke her slender forearm.

'At that point he didn't even know that the worst was to come.'

'No. But he said that he regretted nothing, and neither should you. No matter what happens.' I grip her hand. 'Perhaps it was prophetic of him. You have to believe it. Personally, I do.'

Evelyn shakes her head. I can tell she recognises the time has come for her to stop tormenting herself, as have I: to put the past in the past and close a door. 'I always imagined he wished he'd never set eyes on me . . . I held on to that idea for years.'

'It's amazing what we assume, and how wrong we can be. I, for one, will never assume what I can't possibly know.'

'He said he was going to try to put things right, as best as he could.' Her eyes brim with wonderment and tears. 'But he never could. Circumstances didn't allow him to!'

'Maybe not. But you did. You put it right for him. You helped him do what he couldn't do himself. Isn't that the measure of true love?'

Evelyn's eyes go back to the letter. I watch her. I can't take my eyes from her. It's the face of that young, go-getter girl that Eddy talked about, reading her very first love letter.

When she looks up again, she is flushed.

'He forgave me,' she says.

I smile. 'Of course he did.'

FORTY-FIVE

Before She Left

Evelyn

Northumberland. 1963

They had just entered the church. Evelyn's eyes were still adjusting from the bright sunshine to the dim, dust-mote-filled interior. She had noticed him immediately. Noticed him in the way that a young, single woman is always subconsciously sifting through the gravel hoping to come across a diamond. It was second nature to look without necessarily expecting to find. So, on finding, her faculties had taken a short holiday.

She was aware of her friend Elizabeth prodding her. A young usher, who appeared overly keen on doing a good job, was waiting to escort them to their seats. It was a small gathering, at this point weighted to the bride's side. The robust scent of lilies still couldn't overpower the musty smell of church that always turned Evelyn a little morbid. She could see hats, some with more feathers than a peacock, others like colourful flying saucers. But who cared about hats? She was pleasantly thrown by something else she was seeing.

He was standing by the altar, almost with his back to her. He was tall and broad, with a thatch of dark, healthy hair and, from what she could see of him side-on, there was something disarming about his smile. He was standing with a shorter, stocky, ordinary-looking lad – presumably the groom, judging by the aura of tension around him. The usher led them to their row. The pianist was playing one of those classical tunes you often hear at weddings, only Evelyn couldn't say what it was called. Catching sight of him had stormed her senses. She was aware of the guests glancing up as they arrived, giving their outfits the eye. But every cell in her body was wired to the man up at the front. Once she'd sat down in their pew, she could observe him at leisure, while Elizabeth muttered in her ear.

A heart rush. A tingle of promise to the day. She hadn't really wanted to come, given that she had never met the bride, or her intended, and she knew no one except for her friend.

He was joking around with the groom. It was amazing what you could tell about someone's personality by just observing them. She found herself inwardly smiling when she sensed he was being funny, warmed by him, as though she'd known him for years. Then, he ran out of steam and solemnly bowed his head.

She had yet to see him face-on. It was becoming an exhilarating tease. Only when the pianist launched into 'Ave Maria' as the bride arrived did he finally turn around. Then everything faded into the background, except for his face. She watched him, slowly, if you could watch someone that way, acutely aware of trying to prolong her pleasure. So when he happened to look over, perhaps sensing someone's eyes on him, Evelyn had already contained her surprise.

He blushed, deep red, a colour that intensified the more he looked at her. Neither one could pull their eyes away, until Evelyn absolutely had to, because she was about to burst.

The ceremony passed. She heard low voices, the distant repeating of vows. At one point, right after he'd handed the groom the ring, he looked back at her and seemed to blush again.

'If I told you that every time I look at you, I think I'm going to bungle it before I even speak, would you decide I was undeserving of you?' he asked her a few hours later.

The first thing he ever said to her. This was after confetti on the church steps, after pink fizz by the tennis courts with a cluster of Elizabeth's friends – he'd gone off for photos with the wedding party. She looked him bluntly in the eyes, determined to deliver her reply without a smile. 'No. I'd decided that before you even spoke.'

She had played a deliberate game of cat and mouse with him – moving to chat with someone else the second she sensed he was coming to talk to her. Finally, she'd positioned herself alone, by a window. He had followed, on the button.

His smile gleamed. There was no end to the amusement in his eyes. 'Why are you looking at me like that?' she asked, burning with her awareness of how fanciable he was.

'Like what?'

'Like that!' She flew a finger to his face. 'You're making fun of me now.'

He placed a hand in his trouser pocket, leaning to say in her ear, 'Have you ever thought you might take yourself a bit too seriously?'

'Hmm . . . Strange thing to say to someone you don't even know! Why am I sensing that you and I don't have two minutes of normal conversation in us?' She was always more comfortable being sparky. She pretended to look around the room, bored.

He was observing her, sportily, yet warily. Like someone considering jumping off a cliff, but wondering if the water really was as deep as people said it was. 'Why is your glass empty, by the way? Ah! I know! *You're* the one they said was uptight about alcohol! Takes herself too seriously, is a bit high and mighty, stands in the corner, has no friends.

I remember. That's why you're giving me no choice but to come and rescue you from yourself. Because I'm gallant like that.'

She snuffled a small laugh.

The music was a tune no one seemed to like. The dance floor had emptied. Eddy hadn't yet serenaded her with 'Be My Baby'. The song he was supposed to be singing to the newlyweds until he changed his tack and tried to woo her with his terrible voice that really wasn't a terrible voice; it was mainly the episode that was terrible. This monumental embarrassment was to come later. As were so many things she had no idea about.

He got her another drink. 'For the lady.' He handed her a goblet of Babycham. 'And a brandy in it for good measure. To loosen you up.' He smiled. 'Go on, Evelyn. Live dangerously for once.'

She had a nettling old uncle who always used to say something like that. 'How do you know I don't live dangerously all the time?' she asked, taking a sip and finding it blow-your-head-off strong, but she was determined not to flinch. She'd have knocked back the entire glass to prove a point.

'I don't know. You're all a bit *Roman Holiday*, aren't you? A bit *Audrey*.' He was scrutinising her. She felt his eyes saw nothing but her.

Her jaw dropped open. She was aware of the girls beside them, watching them. She searched for a comeback, but it was too late.

She had noticed that, after the photographs, he had undone his top button and cast off his bow tie. She was sure he wasn't deliberately trying to look dashing and dreamy, but he was succeeding regardless. His shoulders were practically making contact with the walls. He was unfairly fit and handsome. She couldn't work out whether his skin was dark, or his shirt was ultra-white; it was hard to say in the frosted party lighting. But his eyes were piercing sapphires. It made him hard to look at – and hard not to look at. It was a challenge that was completely foreign to her. With most men, she ended up looking at them witheringly and walking by.

The music changed. Eddy snatched her hand. 'Okay, we're dancing.'

She practically coughed up bubbles. Before she could protest, he was hauling her on to the dance floor. She recognised the minimal, lullaby-like strum of Roy Orbison's acoustic guitar – 'In Dreams', a recent chart-topper – and barely managed to offload her glass on to a high-top table as she flew past it, powerfully conscious of his fingers clasped around her small hand.

'*Okay, we're dancing*?' she mocked. 'Is that *common* for, *Would you care to have this dance?*'

She was aware of the girls still watching them. It was ironic that she'd come to the wedding knowing only Elizabeth and had somehow managed to snag the best man.

'It's caveman for, *I have to have my arms around you or I'm going to go mad.*'

Roy started singing about closing his eyes and drifting into the magic night, and Eddy took her in his arms, and she chuckled. Despite wanting to maintain the stroppy act, she was failing with every try. In his arms, she was on air, weightless, gliding like a bird. Their feet fell into a spry rhythm that unfolded with the song's suspenseful, pervading tempo. Eddy's ad-libbed dance steps were a brave cross between a tango, a waltz and a foxtrot, but somehow, together, they worked the floor like two people who had spent a lifetime dancing together. 'Good heavens, you're such an exhibitionist!' she scolded when she sensed him laying it on a little for his female fan club.

'That must be why I want to kiss you.' His chest bore closer, his face moving in.

She gasped.

'Don't worry. I'm saving that for later.'

A tiny part of her had the nerve to be disappointed.

She was so aware of his hand on her mid-back, she could discern that most of the pressure came from his baby finger, and the next two. Was she really going to know what it would be like to kiss him, later?

They stopped ribbing each other now and just listened to Roy doing his thing. The lyrics were making her suddenly reflective. She concentrated on the juddering intensity of the tune, and the intoxicating nearness of her body to a man's: a man she found heart-stoppingly exciting. She allowed herself to dwell on it for a moment, to pay a sort of homage to it. Once in a while, he placed his cheek to hers, briefly, just lay it there before removing it. *Come back, cheek!* Her hand was perspiring in his; she was vaguely self-conscious about it. They stayed like this, close and quiet, letting Roy carry them away with their own private thoughts. She was turning melancholy and she didn't know why. He could be Gregory Peck. Or Laurence Olivier. Anthony Quinn or Henry Fonda. In his arms, she was Lois Maxwell or Julie Christie. Never had she been so aware of a man's physical presence, the feeling of her fingers curved over his semi-cupped hand. How could you be so affected by a hand? Roy was singing about waking from his dream and finding her gone, his voice becoming its characteristic falsetto; Evelyn was bereft now. Inexplicably. In exactly one week, she'd be gone – to a whole new life. She didn't intend to think of this; she supposed she was just silently taking stock of things.

I'm leaving, she thought, blank with the irony of it. *I have a job lined up, and a flat-share. This has always been my dream.*

Why am I leaving, again? Someone tell me . . .

Roy's words about how some things can only happen in dreams were almost too much. She tightened her grip on his hand, squeezing, and closing her eyes. Eddy responded by stroking the side of her finger with his thumb.

'You know, I think you might be warming to me.' His breath caressed her ear.

'Whatever gave you that false impression?'

The sound of his lovely laugh reverberated in her heart. Sometimes, it struck her how she was always aching for things not yet gone.

'You're too much of a challenge for me, Evelyn. What am I to do with you?' His hand made a short foray to the crest of her bottom – accidentally, by the swiftness with which he corrected it.

She knew what she wanted him to do with her.

She could smell the powdery scent of his aftershave, and detect his shoulder muscles shifting through his clothes. She wanted him to kiss her almost more than she wanted to see old age. There was a naturalness in the way they went together. It had been there from the first second. This was what made it sadder.

She'd leave, and somebody else would get him. The thought – the bare injustice of it – just sailed through her head, and it astonished her how much it upset her.

She met up with Elizabeth in the toilets.

'You lucky duck,' Elizabeth said.

'I'm not feeling lucky. In fact, unlucky would probably be the word.'

'What are you going to do?'

'Tell him I'm moving to London soon. Then go home with you, as planned.'

'I thought he had a girlfriend. I think he might have just broken up with her, maybe.' Elizabeth looked confused. Elizabeth was never far wrong.

If she had met him at any other time, she'd have brooded on this idea. As it was, she just thought, *Then this isn't to be taken too seriously. He's on the rebound. It would be doomed, anyway.*

'I'll see you home,' he told her, later, when they had stepped outside, after his mortifying song. They had sat on two peeling, white-painted, wooden chairs and talked – talked for hours – while she unconsciously denuded the chairs of paint.

She peered to see her watch. The music had ceased ages ago. Most of the guests, bar a few drunken stragglers, were long gone.

'I've only had two beers. I think you can trust me not to kill you.'

She trusted him, anyway. Next, they were bulleting across the causeway in his car. She wound the window down. Strands of her hair danced against her cheek. The sand was slowly weighting with pools of seawater. Very soon it would be unwise for him to cross back. The sun was just coming up, and she didn't want to let him go. Seals were singing on the sandbanks, puncturing the tonelessness of the morning. 'I'm missing you already and I haven't even said goodnight to you yet,' he said, and snuffled a small laugh.

She didn't answer, just processed the scope of what he'd said as she distantly listened to the language of larks rising on the morning air. He had taken hold of her hand.

'When can I see you again?' he asked, when they arrived at her door. He had got out of the car and come around to her side. 'I mean, I assume I'm going to get to take you out on a proper date?' He didn't even say it like it was a question.

She had a feeling that everything about her life was going to be decided if she answered *yes*. And it was a glorious feeling. She was open to the recklessness of it – was sailing with it as though this were a new and enchanted form of travel. And yet . . .

He was already kissing her.

They must have kissed for ten minutes. Or perhaps it was two. When he stopped, she was dizzy. She was even more certain, and even more confused. 'If you don't go now, you won't be going at all,' she warned. Soon, the sea would fold around the island, wrapping up the locals in their own little world for those isolating few hours, dispassionately curbing an element of your free will. This occurrence of Northumberland nature would always sink Evelyn into the doldrums because she didn't yet know the extent to which she was going to miss it.

'And that will be just perfectly fine by me.' He appeared in no hurry to go.

Looking out to the causeway, the increasing swell of grey seawater was now bathing the feet of a heron who was standing, blinking, in the sand.

'Hanging around one moment longer is a very bad idea,' she said, thinking, *Will I see him again, or won't I? Fate is going to have to decide.*

Still he didn't make any attempt to move. 'Friday at seven o'clock?' he asked. 'I'll come right here for you.' He glanced up at their house, seeming curious and charmed by the place where she lived.

She found herself nodding, wordlessly.

'I take it that's a *yes*, then,' he called after her, playfully.

She began walking to her front door. When she got there, she turned and looked at him again. He was getting back into his car. She watched him roll down the window.

'If I get stuck, will you come rescue me?'

'No!' She chuckled, and parroted his words from earlier. 'Go on, Eddy, live dangerously!'

He beamed a smile at her, then two seconds later he sped off. As she pushed open the door, she paused for the briefest of moments and listened to his engine burn a path through the silence.

ACKNOWLEDGMENTS

I was inspired to write *After You Left* after reading an extremely touching and fascinating article in the *New York Times* about how looking at art can have a positive effect on the brains of those suffering from Alzheimer's. Many museums actually offer private tours to groups of dementia patients, and the results have been so encouraging. People who are normally disorientated and uncommunicative have responded vividly to paintings and have been able to engage and express themselves in ways that surprise their loved ones, even if it's just for a short time. Given that it seems we all know or have loved someone with the disease, I thought this story might not just entertain readers, but perhaps bring a sense of hope and comfort. One of the paintings mentioned in the article was Andrew Wyeth's *Christina's World*. I had never heard of the painting, but I looked it up. From that moment on, I was intrigued. I wanted to know all about Christina, and found myself researching Wyeth and his subject, and from there the story about Evelyn was born. At the same time, my mother was moving from our home in Northern England to Canada to be near me, and we were saying goodbye to our family home in Sunderland. It was a very emotional time for me, and I suddenly knew exactly how Evelyn had felt all her life – torn between two places. I hope you enjoy reading it as much as I enjoyed writing it.

I would like to thank my brilliant agent, Lorella Belli, for her sound direction and endless enthusiasm, and for believing, as she did, in this novel. Huge gratitude also to my wonderful editor Sammia Hamer; I am most lucky to have you, and the Lake Union team on my side. Thanks to Victoria Pepe for your excellent suggestions to improve the novel. I am also grateful for my supportive family and friends, and everyone who has bought my novels in the past or recommended them to others. Last but not least, thanks to Tony for being the best husband I could have ever hoped for.

ABOUT THE AUTHOR

Carol Mason was born and grew up in the north-east of England. As a teenager she was crowned Britain's National Smile Princess and since became a model, diplomat-in-training, hotel receptionist and advertising copywriter. She currently lives in British Columbia, Canada, with her Canadian husband.